THE MAGICIAN

OF HOAD

THE MAGICIAN OF HOAD

MARGARET MAHY

MARGARET K. McELDERRY BOOKS
NEW YORK LONDON TORONTO SYDNEY

MARGARET K. McELDERRY BOOKS

An imprint of Simon & Schuster Children's Publishing Division

1230 Avenue of the Americas, New York, New York 10020

For information about special discounts for bulk purchases,
please contact Simon & Schuster Special Sales
at 1-866-506-1949 or business@simonandschuster.com.

The Simon & Schuster Speakers Bureau can bring authors
to your live event. For more information or to book an event
contact the Simon & Schuster Speakers Bureau at
1-866-248-3049 or visit our website at www.simonspeakers.com.

Book design by Debra Sfetsios

The text for this book is set in Goudy Old Style.

Manufactured in the United States of America

10 9 8 7 6 5 4 3 2 1

Library of Congress Cataloging-in-Publication Data

Mahy, Margaret.

The Magician of Hoad / Margaret Mahy.—1st ed.

p. cm.

Summary: A young farm boy who possesses mysterious powers
is chosen by the king to be the court's royal magician.

ISBN 978-1-4169-7807-7

ISBN 978-1-4169-9735-1 (eBook)

[1. Fantasy.] I. Title.

PZ7.M2773Mag 2009

[Fic]—dc22

2008023000

TO HARRY, BIDDY-BRIDGET, AND JULIA.
KEEP ON TURNING THOSE PAGES!

CONTENTS

Prologue   *xiii*

PART ONE: TRANSFORMING

Among the Lions   3
A Courtyard Full of Women   7
Cassio's Island   12
The Dissolving Window   17
On the Causeway   20
An Unfinished Smile   24
No Return   33
Kings and Fathers   38
Sons without a Father   44
Broken Glass   50
Dysart's Story   68
Made, Not Born   74
Naked on the Edge of the Sea   79
The Battlefield   94
Overlapping Dreams   96
The King, the Hero, and the Magician   101
On Being Protected   106
Into Diamond   115

PART TWO: THE RAT OF DIAMOND

A Man of Diamond   125
Refusing to Bend   138
Through a Hole in the Wall   144
A Ragged Shadow   155

PART THREE: CHOOSING THE CAGE

Celebrating a Wedding   171
Setting the Forest Free   186
Entertaining Visitors   193
True Kingdoms   226

PART FOUR: GONE

Challenging the Hero   239
Luce's Choice   246
Returning to Diamond   260
Revelation   264
A Vanishing   276

PART FIVE: THE MELTING

To the Islands   285
A Blow Falls   291

Hanging from the Wall   298
A Damaged Voice   306
"There's This Thing That Must Be Done First" 316
Melting   321

PART SIX: THE CHALLENGE

Saving Dysart   331
The One Man   338
Losing a Way   341
A Turning Key   354
The King Returns   362
A Key Turns Again   368
Quicker than Quick   374
In the Arena   382
Cayley's Story   389

PART SEVEN: INTO THE WORLD

Happy, but Not an Ending   399
Becoming the True Magician   406

THE MAGICIAN
OF HOAD

PROLOGUE

ONE FINE DAY, AS THE SUN ROSE, tranquil but implacable, five remarkably different lives began working their way toward one another. They had been such separate lives, it would have seemed impossible that they would ever lock together, but a Hero, a Magician, a farm boy, a noble girl, and a Prince were working their way to a meeting on the edge of a city of tents. That particular city, clapping and flapping in the wind, as if it were applauding itself, had become familiar to the Hero, the Magician, the Prince, and the noble girl, but it was quite alien to the farm boy, though when he finally won his way through to Tent City he found some aspect—some part—of himself already there, mysteriously waiting for him. That boy was about to be completed in a way he had never anticipated. A story has to begin somewhere. This story begins here.

PART ONE

TRANSFORMING

AMONG THE LIONS

Among the ruins, late cabbages, carrots, and turnips grew in straight lines, overlooked by five lions with scrolled manes and smiling faces. Earlier in the year these lions had worn wigs of green leaves and scarlet flowers, but now the bean stems were brittle, and the flowers were gone. All that remained were large, dry pods rattling with the seeds of next year's crop and a few tattered leaves.

It was autumn but the gardener was still working up and down between his remaining rows of plants, his bare back shining like copper in the autumn sunlight, his long black hair tied back with a plaited ribbon of flax. As he worked he whispered under his breath, smiling into the crumbling soil. His name was Heriot Tarbas and he was twelve years old.

As he worked he sang a little, then whispered again, happy at home on his farm, in his own place, among his own people. During the last three years the catastrophic headaches and the twisting fits that had marked his entire childhood had become much rarer. Of course the dreams hung on. He still dreamed that dream—the one in which he found himself sitting on the wide windowsill of an alien building, looking in at a boy several years older than he was and sending in an urgent message: "Know me! Know me. I'll protect you until then, but you have to recognize me when the time comes. Then it'll be your job to save me. I'll need you and you'll need me." That dream, along with other less defined ones, certainly hung on, but at least he was growing out of the old feeling that something ravenous was feeding on him and tearing him into two. Perhaps, in time, the dreams would fade and disappear and he would become an ordinary man like his brother and cousins, just as hairy and just as strong.

A farm cat stalked toward him, sniffing at the freshly turned earth, and Heriot scooped it up, scratching it under the chin and staring deeply into its yellowish eyes, and as he did, someone said his name inquiringly, so he grew immediately quiet, anxious that his private conversations with cats and gardens shouldn't be overheard.

His older sister, Baba, was looking over the wall behind him. Heriot looked back cautiously. Since she had grown up and been pulled in from the fields to work in the kitchen and dairy, she always seemed to be blaming him for something. But on this occasion at least, she was excited and cheerful.

Heriot had one particular eye—his left eye—that he called his puzzled eye. It didn't always see straight. Now he covered it with his left hand and stared back at his sister, knowing she had come into the garden to tell him something exciting.

"The Travelers have arrived," she announced. "Old Jen sent me to bring you in. But don't think you're getting out of work. You'll be given some other job, that's all."

She grinned and vanished. Heriot cleaned his spade and hoe, then set off down the path that led from the garden to the walled courtyard of his sprawling home. He and his mother, the family herb woman, had planted ferns around the outside of the courtyard wall to keep witches at bay, interspersing them with daisies, well-known sun signs, now working their way into a prodigal autumn flowering.

The house had been built within the walls of a ruined castle, but these days it seemed to have become part of the castle, growing naturally out of the stone shell, for any of the first rooms that were still intact were either lived in or used for storage. Beyond those original, uneven walls, built of huge blocks of stone, Heriot could glimpse a dairy and an old barn, alongside the roof of a new one. Then, beyond all those roofs and walls, broad fields sloped upward, patching the hillside until, toward the top, the hill shrugged itself casually out of the farm's control. From the very top of the hill the black rock Draevo, though eyeless, looked back at Heriot darkly, just as it had looked at him ever since he could remember.

Once or twice a year the Travelers would arrive in wagons painted all over with stiff, angular figures whose significances were forgotten, with star patterns, histories, and emblems, until it seemed that mere horses must find it impossibly heavy to pull so much art from one side of Hoad to the other. Looking at these designs, Heriot found himself believing that, beyond the farm, the world lost its reality.

Of course the farm was real—there was no doubt about that. Then beyond the farm lay other farms, mostly undivided by walls and hedges, and then a village, while on the other side of that line of hills was the sea and the dark shape of an island—Cassio's Island, connected to the mainland by an amazing causeway three leagues long. But after that there was nothing for Heriot but dim space and echoing, meaningless names. To the north lay Diamond, the King's city, and to the west lay Bucazaz, the inner plain where, years ago, his father had died in the King's wars. At this very moment, Heriot vaguely knew, leaders and generals, even the King and his three sons, had gathered together along with their enemies, the Dukes of the Dannorad, and were negotiating to end such wars forever.

Beyond Bucazaz lay Cordandeygo and Rous Barnet (the city among the mountains). These were all a part of the land of Hoad, and where Hoad ended, across the mountains or the sea, other lands took over . . . the Dannorad, Camp Hyot, the Islands. The countries were described in books and pinned down with those meaningless names. All Heriot could picture was a mist in which those names came and went, undulating like dreaming fish.

A COURTYARD FULL OF WOMEN

When he came through the gate, Heriot found the kitchen courtyard was full of women, but that did not surprise him. During the terrible wars vaguely called "history" in which Hoad and its neighbors, the Dannorad and Camp Hyot, had advanced, clashed with one another, and retreated bleeding, Heriot's family had lost most of its men. His cousin Nesbit, a survivor of the last battle, was the farm's oldest man at thirty. On this occasion, however, the courtyard was not altogether without other men. Heriot could see a very small male cousin, a baby in his mother's arms, and the Traveler men, along with a tomcat so sure of himself he had stayed behind to watch the visitors after other cats had fled. Strange and glittering in the sunlight, the Traveler men wore padded jackets and round hats made either of sheepskin or quilted silk, hung with enameled beads and tin charms, clothes more suitable to the mountains they had crossed two weeks earlier than to the plains. Around their strong throats hung chains, strung with mirrors the size of coins, beads of agate, carnelian, and tiny irregular fragments of lapis lazuli.

Great-Great-Aunt Jen stood among them, pointing and gesticulating. A cap with flaps coming down over her ears covered her gray hair, while her calm face, as round as a loaf of bread, brown and crusty, too, wore the expression of someone utterly accustomed to obedience.

"You'll be our guests tonight," she was telling the Travelers. "We'll kill and cut up a sheep, and we'll set up a fire in the big hall. I'll send for the men out in the hills. You're very welcome, I can tell you. It's good to have you back."

Heriot watched her with uneasy pride.

"There's no need for it," said one of the older Travelers. "No need for any special bother, that is. We've just come to see the tokens and the words, carrying on the custom, like."

"We always welcome the chance for a party," Great-Great-Aunt Jen replied, a little sternly, as if he had made light of her hospitality. Her dark, unexpectedly sad eyes fell on Heriot.

"You! Heriot!" she said to him. "Run and tell Nesbit and the others that the Travelers are here."

The Travelers' spokesman looked at Heriot with interest.

"He looks better these days," he said.

"He was never sickly . . . well, not exactly," Great-Great-Aunt Jen replied casually, though Heriot saw she became cautious as soon as his old trouble was mentioned. "He's getting over it, whatever it was. Off you go, Heriot. Quickly, now."

"Run fast!" said another Traveler. "I'd say it was going to rain."

"Heriot could help to bring wood in," cried Baba. "I'll run for the men. And he hasn't told the eggs yet."

"What do you mean, he hasn't told the eggs?" someone—a woman—asked from behind Heriot. "Told them what?"

"It's a gift he has," Great-Great-Aunt Jen replied, and once again Heriot saw on her broad face that familiar trace of—what was it—doubt, distaste? "He can tell which eggs will hatch cocks and which hens, and say how long ago they were laid."

"Oh, he's that way, is he?" said the speaker, as if she knew all about such talents. "He's one of those. I thought you farmers had lost the gift."

She stood in the gateway through which Heriot himself had entered a moment earlier . . . a young woman in the long, striped skirts and black short-sleeved smock, fastened down the front with buttons of bone, that all Traveler women wore. As they turned to look at her she came forward, walking freely in spite of her long skirts, while those skirts and the petticoats under them made a silky, sifting sound against her hidden legs.

"Azelma, our wise woman," said the Traveler leader proudly, jerking his thumb at her. "She's only a girl, but she has some of the old gift. She can see through walls, read closed books, and tell the future in patches. Even read minds. Of course she's too bold, you can see that, but they do say that those who carry the gift burn up with it."

"Heriot hasn't got any gift," Baba said. She hated to hear anyone else praised. "He's slow."

"I'm not slow," Heriot protested. "I'm on my way now."

"Not slow in that way . . . ," began Baba. Heriot could see her straining to be off and away, over the fields and up the hill. His head filled with images of long waves and a dark island. His sister was longing to see the sea.

"What's got into you, Baba?" Great-Great-Aunt Jen cried impatiently. "I've told you what you have to do. Now do it!"

"Great-Great-Aunt Jen . . . ," began Baba, but Nella, who was married to Radley, Heriot's older brother, tucked her arm under Baba's, shaking her head. Heriot found his own arm taken and looked up, startled, into Azelma's face.

"Here," she said, talking across him to Great-Great-Aunt Jen and shaking his shoulder slightly as she spoke. "Do you know what you've got here? Does anyone out in the world know about this one? This one can read thoughts."

"He's not reading anything from anyone," said Great-Great-Aunt Jen. "Off now! Off!" She clapped her hands in Heriot's direction, and edging out from under Azelma's hand, Heriot made for the gate.

"Well, talent or not, you've made a mistake this time," he heard his mother saying. "He's just an ordinary boy."

"Ordinary?" Baba's voice cut in. "He sees crooked and he has fits."

But the disputing voices died away as Heriot ran, leaving behind not only the courtyard, his family, the Travelers, and the disturbing Azelma, but that past self . . . the one who dreamed over and over again of sitting on the window ledge, looking between rich hangings at a bed with a twisted fur coverlet, and a boy with mouse-brown curls, staring back at him from odd-colored eyes . . . one blue and one green. He had stared back with fascination and fear, as if Heriot, that dreamer on the wide window ledge, were not another boy but some sort of monster, and sometimes his lips had moved, but Heriot, dreaming, had never been able to make out what he was saying. Sometimes the boy had pointed and seemed to yell. Sometimes he had hidden his face in his pillows and refused to look out at Heriot. But that was all over and done with. It had to be.

CASSIO'S ISLAND

Once clear of the farm buildings and pens, Heriot Tarbas skirted two wide fields, each with its own name, then crossed another diagonally, scrambling through well-known holes in hedges or hoisting himself over dry stone walls. The fields grew steeper as he climbed the hill, and he was out of breath as he climbed the last fence and reached the top at last, clapped his hand over his confused eye, and looked past his little finger to the view on the other side of the hill.

The whole world seemed to tilt. The stretch and sigh of the sea seemed to swell toward him, while the sound of his own hard breathing was briefly swallowed by the greater breath of breaking waves.

Dominating the horizon, dark with forests on its landward side, was an island . . . Cassio's Island, the home of the Hero of Hoad and Revenger of Senlac, one of the rulers of the people Heriot's family called "Secondcomers." There were towns and a castle and a whole busy life on Cassio's Island, but none of this could be seen from Heriot's hilltop. From there the island looked completely empty.

Still, it was not drifting; it was firmly tethered to the mainland. Many years ago the same people who had once lived in the ruins of the castle that now held Heriot's home had built the causeway . . . a road over which traders and messengers could bring goods and information from the King to the Hero and back again. And every now and then the Lords of the counties of Hoad, along with the King and his family and other Secondcomers, gathered on Cassio's Island to watch men fight to the death for the right to be Hero. Heriot had never set foot on the causeway. His only travels were to the nearest village with Radley or his cousin Wish, for Great-Great-Aunt Jen discouraged any of her family from wandering, and Heriot most of all.

"In many ways it's best not to be seen out in the world," she had told him over and over again in her calm, dry fashion. "Work hard, keep your head down, and don't let the Secondcomers catch sight of you . . . not even Lord Glass, though he's a kind man compared with a lot of them. Take it from me, the Lord's eye is the King's eye! So keep out of sight."

Just down the hillside Nesbit, Wish, and Heriot's brother, Radley, were carrying stones to block a big gap in the wall, washed out during the previous winter. Shouting and waving, Heriot admired Radley's wonderful shoulders and back, and the way the sea air had persuaded his shoulder-length hair into ringlets. If Heriot had a single ambition in the world, it was to look and live exactly like Radley, who was swinging rocks as easily as he swung his baby in the courtyard at home.

"Don't tell me!" he said as Heriot came up. "She wants us home! Is it because of the storm?" He nodded at a solid bank of cloud, which was moving toward them, gray at its leading edge but billowing blue-black on the horizon.

"She wants you home because the Travelers have arrived," Heriot said, watching Radley set the stone in place as precisely as if it were a chessman on a board.

"Which tribe?" asked Wish, but Heriot didn't know.

The three men stopped working, straightened up, and began to wander up the hill, joking and laughing with one another, but for some reason Heriot didn't want to go back to the farm. He hesitated, watching them climb, half expecting Radley at least to turn and call him to heel. But they went on and up, past Draevo and out of sight, talking all the time without noticing he wasn't tagging along behind.

Heriot turned toward the sea and the dark forests of Cassio's Island. He didn't want to see Azelma again or hear her suggest he was different from everyone else in his family. He didn't want to be forced into thinking of himself as anything but plain and mostly invisible.

Somewhere on Cassio's Island was a port where ships put in, and somewhere beyond the forests was a city that held the castle of the Hero—one of the two great spirits of Hoad—at present alive in the person of Carlyon of County Doro. Somewhere on that island lived a whole population of men and women who were loyal to the Hero first and the King second. This was not only allowed, it was an ancient rule.

"It keeps the King just a little humble," Great-Great-

Aunt Jen had once declared. "Once the Kings of Hoad used to be the Heroes as well, but it's too much glory for one man to have both Hero and King alive in him at the same time. Sometimes they're contrary spirits. They might tear him apart."

The causeway was still green, a quick arrow pointing out to the island. On a day like this, a fine day when usual events were yielding to strange ones, someone might walk along the causeway and step onto Cassio's Island and stand just for a little while in a place that was almost another country. It was not forbidden; it was just something no one in the Tarbas family had ever done . . . at least not as far as Heriot knew.

Two years earlier he had stood on that hilltop with his family, looking down on the causeway at glittering columns of men and women. According to the customs of Hoad, a young man called Carlyon had challenged the Hero, Link, and the King and his court were carrying him to combat in the Hero's Arena. To Heriot, looking down from above, the parade had seemed more than royal. It had seemed to him not a company of mere Kings and Princes, but one of sun bears, centaurs, and strange, stalking birds as beautiful and passing as dreams. Three days later they had returned, carrying Link's body in great splendor, leaving young Carlyon, Hero by conquest, to discover the island on his own and take possession of his hidden city. Heriot had believed the whole world was being paraded past the farm in a glittering thread so he could take note of it, but by now brambles and wild grasses were pushing in on either side of the narrow road, which on this particular day, at this particular time, was totally deserted.

And now, as he walked along the causeway, with his whole family left behind him on the other side of the hill, Heriot was seized with a lonely elation and began to run and leap and to fling up his arms, chanting under his breath, spinning wildly, shouting wordlessly. Feeling he could twist all the way to the island, he turned cartwheels, until he toppled over, laughing as he fell, only to sit up in the middle of the road, staring wildly around him.

Then he relaxed, laughed at himself yet again, and breathed deeply, taking conscious pleasure in the smell of salt and seaweed and in the lap and rattle of water in the rocks on either side. The thought that the sound went on and on like that (water on rock, rock on water), whether there was anyone to listen to it or not, gave him a sort of relief. *Free at last*, he thought, without having the least idea just what it was he had been freed from, and set off once more along the wild road . . . the central seam of the causeway.

Directly before him at the end of the road was a stone arch.

At first it seemed enormously far away, and insignificant compared with the wide expanses of sea and sky, but suddenly he found he could not look around it or over it anymore. Suddenly it had become the only thing the world had to show him.

A great fountain of seawater erupted beyond it, and then another and another. Heriot approached it warily. Increasingly the arch seemed to drain color and shape out of everything around it, even the water and the autumn air.

THE DISSOLVING WINDOW

And then, at last, he had reached it, was walking under it, then standing for a moment to read the inscribed names of the Heroes. Carlyon's name was there, freshly cut into the old rock. Heriot put a tentative hand out to touch the names, trying to imagine his own name carved among them. But the stone would not accept his name, even in imagination. He wasn't noble, and only men who were born to nobility were free to fight on Cassio's Island. Heriot moved out from under the arch to stand on the island itself.

Directly in front of him, the forest began. Looking into it, he felt uneasy—and this first uneasiness grew stronger. It could not be shaken off. On his right, the road skirted the edge of the wood for a little way, while on his left, the long, sinuous, swelling waves cast themselves onto the rocks over and over again. Fountains of spray, forcing their way through unseen blowholes, leaped into the air, while the whole island creaked and muttered and gurgled. Heriot could hear it, even though he was concentrating on something else.

The forest in front of him had a door. It hung on huge iron hinges between two columns of black stone. But there were no walls on either side, and it was a gate that seemed to demand walls.

"No wall!" Heriot mumbled. "Door but no wall! Hey, you! You couldn't keep a cat out! It'd just walk round you." But the door would not be mocked. Out of its stones and iron and its dense wood there reflected, like ancient stored heat, a terrible weariness, as if the gate might choose to fall on him, crushing him into the dirt, out of boredom and nothing more. Not only this; little by little he began to feel certain that someone was watching him.

Abruptly he was invaded by a single terrifying image. Somewhere behind his eyes a window of black glass sprang into existence. It seemed it had always been there, though he had only just become aware of it, and he suddenly believed that, for years and years, a hand had been rubbing, rubbing against the glass with a soft patience as the black barrier had grown thin and then thinner. In a minute it would finally dissolve under the pressure of the preoccupied hand. In another moment he would be able to look not only forward but backward, too—far backward—backward into himself, and he would see something terrifying, something that would change him forever.

This waking dream, almost a vision, came and went in a moment, but it frightened him so fiercely that he spun away from the gate and saw, in the long grass on his right, a flattened patch as if some animal, no larger than a dog, had been lying there. The grass blades were still moving, in the act of springing up again. Heriot understood that, only a moment earlier, something must have been curled up there, hiding itself from him. Only a moment earlier something must have been watching his approach and had chosen to disappear. He clapped a hand over his puzzled eye and stared at the space with the eye that saw straight. So he fled—fled from the gate without a wall and from the flattened patch of grass; fled away from the fringe of Cassio's Wood, out under the arch, and onto the causeway.

ON THE CAUSEWAY

Once again it seemed to stretch endlessly before him, dimmer and cooler than it had been, for a drift of cloud had sidled over the face of the sun. Its beauty was still there, but it no longer moved him. As he had walked toward the island, its great length had not mattered. Now the causeway seemed endless. He needed to get himself home again—he needed to be contained once more, surrounded by cheerful arrivals, happy endings.

But even the causeway wasn't endless. Panting and struggling and sprinkled with the first rain, he reached the place where he could climb away from it. He was just about to leap onto the slopes of his own farm when something happened that was beyond description. He stopped midstride, falling to his knees as if he had been clubbed down. Deep inside his head that black barrier was finally dissolving. Something from the other side rushed out and ran through him like a contradiction of everything homely. Something looked directly out into the world for the first time, using Heriot's eyes. And for some reason the most frightening thing was that this intruding force was not a stranger but a wild part of himself . . . a part of himself he had never suspected but immediately recognized. At some time in the past something had happened to him, had violated him over and over again; something had fed on him. Somehow, back then, during the time of his fits and headaches, perhaps, he had been torn in two, and now, suddenly he was confronted with that other—that torn-away self. But now, though it was part of him, this rag of self was a stranger, settling back into him without fusing into him, becoming an occupant.

The landscape in front of him, the whole hillside, broke into a shifting mosaic of colored crystals, skewed madly, and contracted, before swelling back into a recognizable form, while Heriot, filled with a terror so extreme it was like pain, toppled sideways onto the edge of the path and lay there, whining through clenched teeth, clutching the grass stems. He was worked on by such vertigo that, even with the whole earth bearing up under him, he still believed he was falling. Inside his head something demanded recognition. He gasped. Inside his head that new, separate self breathed in too . . . a gigantic first breath.

In the outside world Heriot gasped again. "It's all right!" he muttered. "It will be all right. Take another breath. Last a bit longer. It will end." This was what he had learned to say to himself during the violent cramps, fits, and headaches of his early childhood . . . those times when he felt that something was stealing whole pieces of him . . . devouring him. "It will end," he repeated, though he couldn't hear his own voice. "It will end. It will be over."

Now, as if he were looking out of blackness through a far-off window, unnaturally clear, he saw the boy of his dreams, not in bed this time but standing on a great confused plain, dressed in rich strange clothes, staring back at him.

"Help me," Heriot said, but the boy looked frightened and puzzled, then vanished as completely as if he had been blown out like a candle. In the silence that followed, he heard, coming in at him from somewhere, a deep, slow breathing, and made himself breathe in time with it. It was several minutes before he understood it was only the sound of the sea.

He opened his eyes and looked into a tuft of grass half an inch from his nose. Fear continued to subside. He began to move his hands and feet, to sit up, to stand, to run. For then, indeed, he did run. He scrambled wildly until he was back onto Tarbas land.

He had changed. Something new was stirring in him . . . a new nerve . . . a new appetite, anxious to be fed. However, he was too alarmed to try and make any real contact with this . . . this thing . . . this wild presence he had carried within himself unknowingly until it had swept in from the other side of the black barrier. He began climbing again and kept on climbing until he reached the spot where, only a little time ago, he had stood beside his brother and looked out over the sea to Cassio's Island.

Something moved on the road below. Heriot stared down, screwing up his face a little as wind blew in on him.

Someone was walking away from Cassio's Island. He stared, narrowing his eyes. A woman carrying something heavy—a woman carrying a child, who lay limply in her arms, while another child trailed behind her, getting left behind and running, every now and then, to catch up. But the woman seemed to take no notice of her follower. She stumped along, looking neither right nor left, up nor down, looking straight ahead as if the road might vanish if she took her eyes from it. The child behind her, on the other hand, was staring around all the time and suddenly came to a standstill. Looking up, it had seen Heriot standing on his hilltop, looking down. Knowing he was seen, Heriot waved rather incoherently, feeling himself become more wonderfully ordinary by making this ordinary human sign. The child stared up at him for a moment longer, then waved back, before turning and racing after the woman, who had walked on without once glancing over her shoulder at the child she was leaving behind.

There was a flash of lightning and a sound as if a tin sky were being beaten apart. Unable to distinguish any longer between inside events and outside ones, Heriot half believed he was responsible for the harsh sound, but it was only the storm sweeping in from the northeast. The bruised sky had taken on a luminous sheen, but directly overhead the sun still shone through a haze of finer cloud. Heriot turned and ran. He was going home with the storm growling at his heels.

But the day had not finished with him. Though Heriot believed that after what he had just gone through he couldn't be frightened any more, he was wrong. His strange ordeal on the causeway had prepared the way for yet more terror, and this time there would be witnesses.

AN UNFINISHED SMILE

Heriot had left the courtyard full of women but came home to find men drinking and gossiping as they watched the storm roll over the hills. Radley, Wish, and Nesbit, tall and bushy as trees, were planted in the center of the yard with a younger cousin, Carron, beside them, just as tall but narrower, more agile, and more wordy, too. There were about ten Travelers, both short and tall, and a neighbor or two. The courtyard was bathed in a wild light, the sun shining rebelliously through the first clouds, painting the western hills, which in turn reflected distant light from their jagged crests down into the courtyard. The men stood in an unnatural coppery glow that was flicked occasionally with whips of lightning.

As he slid through the gate, Heriot heard Carron holding forth in his quick, eager way to one of the Travelers. Heriot closed the gate behind him, then leaned against it, breathless with exhaustion and relief.

"They'd call that treason," he heard the Traveler saying to Carron in a startled voice. "Their present King may be a

Secondcomer, but we have to count them as men of Hoad by now, even if we were here first. And lucky for us if they do have a King to keep them in order."

Heriot could see Nesbit rolling his eyes at Wish, full of despair at Carron's dangerous arguments.

"If there's a King, the King should be one of the first people . . . one of us," argued Carron. "Not that we really need a King or a Hero. A long time ago even the Secondcomers—the Hoadara—used to choose their leaders. All the people got together and worked things out among themselves. Every man counted. It wasn't just one family with all the power."

Heriot stared. He blinked and shook his head, then stared again. Someone was standing behind Carron, someone he hadn't noticed when he first came through the gate; though now that he had seen this stranger, it seemed impossible to notice anyone else. He screwed up his face trying to focus on the man, who seemed painted with a darkness that had sunk into him, right to his bones. Cut, this man would bleed black. Even his face and hands were shadowed, which made his light eyes, fixed intently on Carron, particularly startling. And his hair was red—a crimson both dark and bright, braided and wound into a tight cap around his head.

Heriot, still unnoticed, moved a step or two closer, frowning and doubtfully biting his lower lip. There was something about the stranger's stillness that made his heart jolt unpleasantly. Even the most impassive faces have some sort of movement, but this face was entirely frozen. Light reflected oddly from the upward turn of an unpleasing smile . . . a smile begun but unconcluded, as unnatural as a diving gull arrested midair.

"Heriot!" shouted Radley, suddenly noticing him standing in the gateway. "Where did you get to? We could have done with an extra pair of hands."

As if the sound of Heriot's name had somehow released him, the frozen stranger's half-finished smile suddenly widened. He gracefully embraced Carron from behind by flinging one arm around his neck and at the same time drove a narrow blade into him. Heriot thought he felt the thin destruction of his own heart.

"And another thing . . . ," Carron said, turning to the Traveler on his left, apparently unconcerned by what had happened. At that moment Heriot began tasting blood. His own mouth was suddenly full of it. He gave a cry. The sound that ripped out of him was inhuman even to his own ears. Everyone in the courtyard started and spun round. Radley ran toward him, followed by Wish and Nesbit, while Carron, looking more curious than concerned, came behind them. As he advanced on Heriot, Carron's eyes darkened. Crimson curtains were being drawn across them. They filmed, then overflowed with tears of blood, which left trails on his cheeks and blotched the stones of the courtyard behind him. Heriot screamed again, backing away, but as Radley reached him, he turned, seized his brother, and buried his face against him so that he needn't see any more.

A great babble of voices blended into the single sound that was most familiar to him . . . the sound of family interest and argument. The kitchen door flew open, the footsteps and voices of women asking questions rang above the exclamations of the men.

Radley was shouting. "What's happened? Let's take a look."

But Heriot didn't want to look up and find himself staring into Carron's bleeding eyes. Something splashed on his hands, and he started and cried out as if the drops had burned him.

"It's rain, Heriot, nothing but rain!" Radley cried, shaking him slightly. "Stop it! There's nothing wrong."

"It's blood!" Heriot screamed.

"There's no blood here but yours," said Radley, so bewildered he sounded angry. "You've bitten your lip, I think. That's all."

"What's wrong? What's happened?" Joan was asking . . . Ashet was asking . . . Baba was asking . . . their voices coming in on top of one another.

"What's wrong?" asked Great-Great-Aunt Jen, and everyone heard *her* question.

"That's the sort of thing I was telling you about." Carron's voice sounded somewhere in the background. "They make out there's nothing to it, but he's always likely to flip."

"Let's get him inside!" shouted Nesbit. "Here comes the rain." And at that, the clouds seemed to split open and rain poured down, soaking them in seconds.

As Radley carried him toward the house, Heriot lifted his eyes at last and looked frantically over his brother's shoulder, through the veil of tumbling raindrops, at Carron, whose face, alight with interest, was quite unmarked by a single smear of blood. Big splashes of rain shone for a moment like silver coins pulled out of shape, and were blotted out almost immediately by the downpour. A door opened and closed. Then the kitchen embraced them all, its air thick with smells of cooking and another ancient smell—the smell of time, which no scrubbing or rubbing could totally clean away.

"Take him through into the big room," Great-Great-Aunt Jen was ordering, and he heard the familiar creak of a heavy door, a sound that had always made him think the house was asking a question over and over again.

Light dimmed. As Radley laid him on the long table that ran down the center of the room, Heriot found himself staring up into a series of interlocking arches carrying a ceiling that had once been painted to look like an evening sky.

"He was terrified," Radley was saying in a puzzled voice. "But there was nothing to be frightened of, was there?" There was a ragged chorus of agreement. Heads bending over Heriot turned and nodded.

"Here's his mother," said Great-Great-Aunt Jen, and Heriot's trembling grew less at the sound of her calm voice. "Maybe he started out trying to trick us, and tricked himself into this state. He must have known I'd be cross with him, vanishing for ages just when we're busy." But Heriot knew that if it was a trick, he was the tricked one, not the trickster.

"He's bitten his lip almost through," said Radley. "That's not acting."

"He's had one of his fits," Carron said. "He'll get over it. He always does."

Radley now became angry, something that almost never

happened. "He hasn't had one for three years, and when he did it was different from this, so just forget it, Carron!"

There was a burst of confused conversation as every other Tarbas in the room expressed an opinion, most agreeing with Carron but sympathizing with Radley. Heriot felt relieved at the thought that it might be his old trouble in a new form. But there had been no pain, only one inexplicable shock following sharply on another. His mother took his hand, but as she did so, another face showed up beside hers, vivid, amused, a little sympathetic, a little scornful. It was Azelma, pushing in through the family.

"He's had a vision," she said. "I told you! He's one of those."

And she peered at him, interested in his fear but untouched by it. This time the chorus was made up of Traveler voices, all agreeing with Azelma.

"Anna," said Great-Great-Aunt Jen to Heriot's mother. "What do you think?"

"Don't ask her, ask *him*! He's the only one who can tell you!" Azelma said. And she flashed a triumphant smile down at Heriot.

"Ask him!" repeated the voices. "Yes! Come on, Heriot! Pull yourself together. Why? What happened? What did you see?"

Heriot pushed himself up on his elbows and stared at Azelma.

"Come on! It's not an illness!" Azelma said impatiently. "More likely a talent!" Heriot spoke, but he hardly recognized his own voice, it was so roughened by the force of his earlier screaming.

"I saw a man in black standing right behind Carron," he said. "Face blacked out—hands, too. But his hair was red, and braided tight." Everyone waited critically for him to continue. "He was still as stone—and Carron was talking on and on. . . ."

"I'll bet!" muttered Radley.

"And then the redheaded one smiled and . . . and stabbed Carron, and Carron just—his eyes filled with blood, all his teeth were . . ." Heriot waved his hand. "When he smiled there was blood round every tooth but he kept on talking. . . ."

"He would, too!" Radley agreed.

There was an outburst of comment, as every Tarbas and every Traveler had something to say.

"Oh, come on! Don't you recognize what the boy's just told you?" Azelma's voice sounded above the others.

Great-Great-Aunt Jen came round from behind him to look directly into his face. When she spoke next it was in a voice he had never heard her use before. "All in black?" she asked him. "With braided hair?"

Heriot hesitated, touching his swelling lip gingerly with the back of his hand. "It was red, his hair," he said at last. "Not ginger! Red! Done up like a plaited cap. Dyed."

Great-Great-Aunt Jen stepped back from him as if he had tried to spit poison at her. "Yes," she said. "I've heard they dye it that color."

She turned to Heriot's mother. "Anna, your son appears to have seen one of the King's Assassins giving Carron what they call the King's Mercy. Mostly they have their faces painted white, but for assassinations they blacken up."

For once the family fell silent. They huddled together a little, while at the end of the table, the Travelers drew slightly apart from them. Great-Great-Aunt Jen went on.

"I've heard stories about those Assassins—Wellwishers, people call them, giving a good name to a wicked shape. It mightn't mean anything. Perhaps it's nothing but his old illness after all, but with the pain turned into a bad dream."

"Maybe Carron's talk brought it on," suggested Nesbit. "He's been sounding off about the King. Boys' talk! Silly stuff."

"Get Heriot to bed," said Great-Great-Aunt Jen. "Then we'll talk about it."

"Maybe he's jealous that I'm the one who's going to Diamond," shouted Carron, as Radley carried Heriot out of the room. "Maybe he's jealous because I'm moving on. Well, it'll take more than Heriot's babbling to frighten me."

"But how could he get a picture of a King's Assassin if he didn't even know they existed?" Azelma was asking.

Radley carried Heriot upstairs, his mother coming up behind them, to the narrow room Heriot had shared first with Radley until Radley married, and then with Carron, until Carron grew too important to share a room with a younger boy.

"It's probably a pinch of the old people in you somewhere," Radley told him, helping him take off his shirt. "It showed up in Ma's family from time to time. Didn't it?" He looked over at their mother.

"In the Tarbas family too!" she replied. "I've always suspected Wish had it."

"Wish?" Radley protested. "Not Wish! He's straight enough!"

"Maybe," she agreed. "After all, he's a farmer, and they don't make farmers—the ones who are taken that way. They beat themselves against the world, trying to get deeper and deeper into it. They don't settle."

Heriot was shocked. They were speaking together as if he couldn't hear them—as if he wasn't there.

"I *am* settled," he cried. "I'm settled here."

His mother started and looked down at him a little guiltily.

"Of course you are. I was just running on," she said.

★★★

In the end Heriot slept and dreamed riotous, unwieldy dreams that slid away from him as the rain roared all night on the roof above his head. By the time he woke, it was early morning, and watery sunlight was slanting onto the floor. In spite of the storm the Travelers had moved on, and the farm was just the farm, a map that seemed to be inscribed on a parchment, a parchment that just happened to match up with Heriot's skin.

no **RETURN**

Heriot wasn't really ill, in spite of the two waking nightmares that had come at him so quickly, one smashing in on top of the other. He lay in bed, feeling as consumed as cold ashes, trying to will himself into being his earlier self once more. The whole family knew about his vision of death and blood, but the moments on the causeway, the dissolving of that black window in his head and the feeling that some alternative self had crept out from behind it to work its way into him in some different way—all this he kept secret. He didn't want to add to the rumor of his own strangeness. And besides, he felt that if he didn't share the memory, it might somehow shrivel and die away. Deciding this, he felt suddenly hopeful, as if, by some wonderful chance, he might be allowed to live through recent days again and do everything right the second time round.

He watched the ceiling of his room lighten still further, then got up, dressed himself, and went downstairs, intending to enjoy everyday life as completely as he could . . . intending to take it in and use it to drive the strangeness out.

★ ★ ★

For Heriot there was to be no return to everyday life. His place in the world had been part of a compact that was now dissolved. He knew it at once when he stepped into the noisy kitchen, and an unaccustomed silence fell.

Heriot stared around at the women and children, at his great-great-aunt, his sister Baba, at Ashet (Nesbit's wife) with her twin daughters, at Radley's Nella holding her baby against her shoulder, and at Joan, Wish's wife, moving to stand between Heriot and her little son.

"You think I'd hurt him?" Heriot shouted.

"I know it's not your fault," she answered nervously, "but if you see anything bad, I don't want him to know about it." Heriot stared from one to the other.

"Well, come on, Heriot," said Ashet, who had always liked him. "Get yourself something to eat. There's a bit of porridge left and some buttermilk."

He sat in the homely kitchen. Masks of beasts and men carved on an ancient bit of wall looked out over his head, and below was a long inscription in a language so old that nobody could understand it anymore.

His family talked around him and over his head, but now Heriot was excluded when glances were exchanged, left outside of the magical flashing of eye to eye by which the family constantly kept in touch with itself. And later in the evening, when the Tarbas men came home and they all came together for dinner, there was a space around Heriot that no one seemed willing, or even able, to share with him.

Slowly, over the next few days of advances and retreats, he came to understand that he was no longer a simple, gardening brother. He had become someone through whom a prophetic beast might bleat or bray, making pronouncements of doom. At the kindest, he was now a presence with which even his family could no longer feel easy. Nesbit, Ashet, and Joan accepted him without complaint, as an injury they could not heal and must endure, protecting themselves by looking around him as often as they could. He began to imagine that, as he walked by, their flesh actually crept, and he tried to spare them by looking away. On the other hand, Wish began to single him out, but this only made him nervous, for Wish seemed nervous too, struggling to say something without knowing quite what it was he had to say. Even Radley's warmth was touched with sadness, as if he were mourning a brother whose place Heriot had unfairly taken.

The only person in his entire family who seemed at ease with him was Baba, who was quite happy to share her kitchen work, such as peeling old potatoes, skimming cream, and churning butter. Her teasing and complaining was one of the few familiar things that did not change, so, for a while, he welcomed it and kneeled beside her in the kitchen, helping her chop onions for the soup pot that constantly simmered on the back of the fire bed. Heriot did most of the chopping, and Baba did all the talking.

"Well, I think you're lucky," she told him. "You'll get away from here. They'll do something . . . put you to work in Diamond, perhaps, though they're not letting Carron go, not until he learns to talk a bit more carefully. But you—

you'll get clean away. Something's happened to you, but nothing will ever happen to me."

The despair in her voice astonished him.

"Everything in the world's going on out there," she cried, waving her hand at the kitchen door and the view of the hills beyond, "and I'm stuck here. It's not fair."

Heriot realized his difference had set Baba free to talk about her own differences, as if they must now share a view of the world. But Baba wanted desperately to leave the very place Heriot wanted to get back to.

After a while the kitchen and the dairy and her pacing dissatisfaction worried him too much, and he took to wandering in the fields, edged out but unwilling to move away from the farm that contained all the warmth, all the food, all the companionship he knew. He would get up in the morning, cut bread and cheese, and walk up onto hillsides where sheep grazed. There he would hide himself in a copse or under a hedge, staring intently down into the grass or out to the blue tracery of mountains barely distinguishable from the sky. His silences became longer and deeper and his visits to the house more furtive.

He took food up to his room, where his mother sometimes joined him. She talked very little, but she had always been cool. Besides, Heriot knew, without resentment, that Radley, her oldest and simplest child, had always been her favorite, while he would always be linked in her mind with the death of his father.

He took to plaiting his long, thick hair in fine braids, just as the old traveling men sometimes did. He'd always admired this ancient style, and after all, he had plenty of time these days. Out in the hills he sometimes pressed himself desperately against the earth's rough skin, trying to force it to acknowledge him as its true child, commanding it to feed ease back into him. He felt acknowledgment, but of a strange, dry kind somehow beyond comfort. There was to be no simple way back.

It was quite by accident that he was at home one gray day in early summer when Lord Glass, the King's Devisor, rode into the courtyard, searching for a Magician.

KINGS AND FATHERS

Late one afternoon, on the very day that Heriot
Tarbas felt the black window in his head dissolve
and the huge, possessing fragment of himself sweep
out and over him, Linnet of Hagen, her mother, her
nurse, her father's marshal, and a small guard of campaigners came riding out of a winding pass and onto the edge of
a high plain set around with mountains.

There, far in the distance, Linnet could make out the
southernmost boundary of Hoad trembling with cold, yet
bleeding fire out of its mountains, and between her party
and those distant fires lay a battlefield. Fourteen days earlier, the seven counties of Hoad, including her own county,
Hagen, had fought their eastern enemies, the Hosts of the
Dannorad, to a standstill, and now the noble families were
coming together to celebrate the victory and to witness the
beginning of what was already being called the King's Peace.
History was being made, and they were to be part of it.

Linnet and her party made their way along a track that
wound between mounds of broken wheels and weapons,

strips of shredded canvas, piles of dirt flung up to make temporary, frantic defenses . . . debris of the last battle. Among the trenches and mounds Linnet saw a drifting population of shabby men and women picking over fragments, searching for anything valuable that might have been left by the first wave of searchers, and she wondered, with a sort of captivated horror, just how it would feel to come unexpectedly on a little piece of someone . . . an eye staring up at the sky or a hand with a wedding ring on it.

As they rode toward the city of tents, another party came riding to meet them, bathed in the rich light of the late afternoon. Linnet made out a pointed helmet lined with blond fur, and a robe of golden velvet embroidered with roses set in delicate medallions of black. For the first time in her life, she was seeing the King of Hoad, and she thought the man beside him must be Carlyon, the Hero of Hoad. His handsome face sat squarely above a finely pleated, almost womanish, white silk shirt; a long white coat fell in swooping folds from his huge shoulders. It seemed that Linnet and her mother were to be greeted by both the King and the Hero, twin emblems of the land, both more myths than men. But Linnet looked eagerly past these legends, searching for her own father among the men who followed the King. His face, harsh yet smiling, made her forget all others, so that later, when she tried to recall the welcome, all she could remember was a glittering shape, golden but blurred, riding beside a shining white one. Later, she was to find herself half believing the King's clothes might ride and rule on their own, without anyone inside.

Then Linnet stared at two young men, neither of whom

looked back at her with any interest whatever. The handsome one, being the taller of the two, seemed as if he must also be the older, but he was so good-looking he had to be Prince Luce, which meant he was a year younger than the slighter, round-faced, fair brother beside him, Betony Hoad, the King's heir. Linnet knew she was considered a possible bride for Luce, so it was Luce she studied most intently, until her nurse, Lila, nudged her. She realized that, just when she most wanted to be regal, she had been gazing and gaping like a simple girl who had never seen such glory before.

"My oldest son . . . Prince Betony Hoad," the King was saying to her mother from somewhere under his helmet, gesturing with a pale hand, while the round-faced Prince smiled a curious, wincing smile, as if, by naming him, his father had struck him a blow. Linnet wondered about the third Prince, the mad one. Was he out among the tents somewhere? He was almost never seen; indeed, some stories said he ran on all fours, like a dog, and Linnet's father had told her, sounding slyly triumphant, that the Prince's madness was a sign of some sort of flaw in the King's power.

They had arrived in a city of tents and pavilions whose streets and landmarks were constantly changing. They passed through a series of shelters made of rags and sticks put up by poor camp followers, who included women and little children, and then through a whole market of booths for peddlers and money changers, burning torches and braziers flaring dangerously in the early evening. Temporary smithies . . . kitchens . . . painted wagons and herds of horses . . . everything enchanted Linnet as they rode into Tent City. The gypsies of Hoad, those mysterious Travelers (mostly called Orts in Diamond because they were the leftover scraps of a people who had lived in Hoad before the King's people took command of the land) stood braiding ribbons into the manes of the horses they had already sold. They looked up as the newcomers rode by but did not smile. The wind, lifting strands of rusty hair from Linnet's forehead, smelt of freshly bruised grass, but under this innocent smell there was a taint that made her wrinkle her nose a little, an edge of decay that came and went, so that, sometimes, she thought she must be imagining it.

Linnet had believed she would stay with her father and mother and attend all the King's parties, so she was furious when, after a few hurried hugs, kisses, and promises, she and Lila were led in another direction. Yet her disappointment was blotted out almost at once, for there were so many new and amazing things to be seen on the crowded, muddy tracks running between the tents. In spite of weariness Linnet wanted to laugh aloud, not because things were funny but because they were so surprising. *Tomorrow*, she thought still later, as she tumbled to sleep, *tomorrow I'll be part of it all. Tomorrow will be nothing but excitement and surprises.*

But next morning she found she was expected to study just as if she were at home, not with Luce, who was beyond study, but with the third Prince, the mad one. He was a whole two months younger than her, and though nobody was supposed to say so openly, everyone knew there was something wrong with him.

Carrying her quills and book, Linnet stumped crossly after Lila to a pavilion on the edge of the city of tents. Inside, with a small, folding frame set up in front of him to serve as a desk, sat Dysart, Prince of Hoad.

He had rough, wavy, mouse-colored hair that stood on end like a puppet's wig, a big nose, and a wide smile. His right eye was a light clear blue, while his left was hazel, so it was as if two different people were looking out of the same head. As she came into the tent, he caught her expression and burst into wild laughter. Later she was to think someone had stolen part of Dysart's life, and he filled the empty space by laughing, and that she had been able to tell this from the first moment she ever saw him.

His laughter died away as she stalked by him without another glance.

"You've brought only one book," he said curiously.

"It's all I need," Linnet replied, noticing with alarm, however, that he had a whole pile of books beside him, some of them wrapped in silk and velvet, as if they were treasures. Suddenly she didn't want the mad Prince to know her book was her only book, and though he continued to stare at her with undisguised interest, she refused to look back at him.

"People say you're fierce—they say you were born with teeth like needles," he said inquisitively. "Go on, show me. Smile!"

"And people say you're a fool," Linnet retorted. Then she was ashamed, partly because her words made her seem rough when she wanted to be graceful, and partly because she sounded unkind. But he answered in an unexpectedly patient voice, as if he were correcting a mistake he'd corrected many times before.

"Not a fool. Get it right: I'm mad," he said. "There's a difference between a foolish Prince and a mad one." Then he laughed again.

The wall of the tent beside him sucked in, then billowed out again, as if the very weave of the canvas were breathing. Dysart's careful pile of papers swarmed up into the air around his head. He grimaced and made an odd barking noise at nothing, while the papers drifted down around him.

SONS WITHOUT A FATHER

In the next few days Linnet studied the endless history of Hoad, but she was also part of ceremonial entertainments, standing beside her father, feeling his strong hand holding hers as the clowns and fools of Diamond performed their dances, or catching her breath as teams of campaigners, led by the warriors known as Dragons of Hoad, clashed with one another in mock battles. Linnet cheered for Luce, who rode with the Dragons, and hoped he noticed her out of the corner of his eye as she urged him on.

They were living in a city so mixed that Linnet might see, all within a few yards, ladies sitting in chairs of gilded leather or working men with heavy yokes over their shoulders carrying lavatory cans and buckets of kitchen refuse out beyond the boundary of Tent City. Linnet learned to tell the campaigners of County Glass in their green jackets from those of County Doro, who wore long leather coats with the fur turned in, and to recognize all the banners along with the Lords they represented . . . the seven Lords of the seven counties of Hoad: Argo, Dante, Glass, Isman, Doro, Bay, and her own county, ambivalent Hagen.

From the edge of the camp she could stare curiously across the battered plain to the other city . . . the camp of the Dannorad. The King and his older sons passed like mirages of gold and silver between the two cities, for in a great pavilion between the camps, men of both Hoad and the Dannorad, maps spread between them, were working in and out through the natural lace of valleys and spurs that knitted the lands together. As the victorious one, the King of Hoad could have demanded everything, but Lila declared (just as if she knew all the secrets of the golden pavilions), that the King wanted a peace that would *hold*— something stronger than the frail truces of the last two hundred years—and was prepared to be generous to former enemies, for generosity seemed as if it might forge a true reconciliation.

In the evening the two tent cities entertained each other with banquets and parties given by firelight, the King's parties being the grandest of all, and there the Dukes of the Dannorad and the Lords of Hoad sat together, talking and laughing as if they had not spent so much of their recent history trying to kill one another. Out from the shadows came clowns on stilts, jugglers, acrobats, fools, freaks, and fire-eaters. One of the King's bodyguards always stood behind him, ready to taste the King's wine or to guard his back.

"That's an Assassin," whispered Lila dramatically.

Linnet had heard of the Assassins, even in Hagen. They were the bogeymen of Hoad, faces masked in white paint like the faces of dangerous clowns. It was said they never died, that their heads held no brains, only a space in which a King might lodge an order, and that once the King had put a name in that space, nothing could save the man to whom the name belonged.

Prince Betony Hoad had a constant attendant of his own, Talgesi, not an Assassin but a young man of his own age who had once been his whipping boy and had taken all his beatings for him, for no nurse or tutor was allowed to beat the heir to Hoad while his mother was alive. Both Prince and servant wore the same expression. When one smiled, the other smiled. Occasionally Betony Hoad might murmur something aside to his companion, and they would look into each other's eyes as if they were the only real people in a world of ghosts.

Not all the fallen campaigners had been buried. The scent of their decay (the very scent that had greeted Linnet when she first rode onto the battlefield), carried in on the south wind, was part of every spectacle and public occasion. For all that, as the excitement and strangeness of Tent City worked their spell on Linnet, she found herself unexpectedly touched by another magic.

Partly because she didn't want to admit that Dysart might know more than she did, she began to read and to learn the rhyming histories of Hoad by heart. Reciting couplets she had learned the night before, she smiled across the tent at the third Prince, triumphant because she was just as clever as he was and could be part of the wide world whenever she wanted. Though she was Linnet of Hagen, a county that seemed closer to the sky than to the rivers, plains, and beaches of the rest of Hoad, she too could invoke the King and the Hero, those vast spirits made tangible in Dysart's father and the warrior Carlyon. The Hero was particularly glorious at present because single-handedly he had killed ten soldiers of the Dannorad, avenging the massacre of every single man, woman, and child in the remote Hoadish village of Senlac.

Without quite meaning to, Linnet became a Dysart watcher and saw how a mischievous wind, which no one else seemed to be able to feel, followed the Prince like a playful dog, fluttering his papers, tumbling the world a little whenever he walked by. The left side of his face didn't quite match up with the right. It was not just his differently colored eyes that gave him this unbalanced look; he had an odd smile in which the right side of his mouth curled up more than the left, yet when he wrote or turned pages he used his left hand. He was so lopsided, Linnet found it easy to understand why he was only brought out on occasions when royal children were traditionally displayed like banners. Yet, during their studies, whenever Dysart recited the tales of Hoad or talked about Diamond, the King's city, or quoted old aphorisms about the King and the Hero, he seemed to pull himself into a different shape and to become somehow . . . not handsome, exactly, but remarkable.

"What's so wonderful about Diamond, anyway?" Linnet asked him one afternoon. "It's not the only city in the world."

"It's the King's city," he answered, interrupting her just as she was about to talk about Hagen's Rous Barnet, her own city. "Diamond's the shape of the King."

"And your father just happens to be King," Linnet cried

derisively. "I suppose you think that makes you great too!"

Dysart stared down into the pages of his book as if he could see indecipherable words swimming like fish behind the lines of ordinary print. When he spoke again it was in an odd, uncertain voice—as if he were trying out a new idea as much on himself as on her.

"No," he said. "Kings have sons, but Princes don't have fathers."

"You can't have sons without fathers!" argued Linnet.

"But what if the King hates us all?" Dysart said doubtfully. "Betony says he does, because a long time ago, before my father's father and brothers died, before he ever dreamed he'd be King, he was married to a woman from the Second Ring of Diamond . . . she wasn't noble or rich, but he loved her. When he became King, he had to give her up because the Queen of Hoad has to be noble."

"Did your father have to be King, then?" Linnet asked. "If he loved the first one best? He could have stepped back."

Dysart was silent; then he gave a long sigh.

"More than anything, everyone wants to be King," he replied, "but you have to be next in line. My father was the next in line, whether he wanted to be or not, and when the time came, he . . ." Dysart paused. For once he didn't smile. "Anyhow, the time came, and being the chosen one, he *did* want it," he added. "I think when it came to him, he wanted it so badly that wanting altered him. He gave up his first life. He gave up being one man and turned into another. He turned into a King."

Earlier they had been given the task of writing a poem thirty syllables long, in the approved style. Dysart had written:

The man in the crown
Rides by. Moving beside him,
Stretching before,
His dark and breathless shadow
Engulfs the bright, breathing land.

Days became a week . . . three weeks . . . and Linnet grew bored with the city of tents, the distant, glittering King, and the cold wind with its taint of decay. She began to long for home. But perhaps everyone had grown weary. Lila told her one evening that, on the very next day, there was to be a break in the negotiations. Lords who lived close to the plain would get a chance to go back to their homes for a few days. Even the Hero was going to ride back to Cassio's Island. And though the King was staying on the battlefield, along with his sons, there were to be festivities. On the next day there was to be a picnic, and both she and Prince Dysart were to take part. Linnet was delighted. She was longing for something to happen: She was longing for changes.

BROKEN GLASS

Out on his farm in County Glass, Heriot Tarbas was sitting on his own in a corner, playing cards. He was draped in a thick woven rug with a hole for his head and slits for his hands. A chilly wind was blowing around the courtyard, but apart from any wind or weather, he was now in the habit of covering himself up as much as he could. The cats suddenly looked up, then flattened themselves to the ground and fled, but his little cousins clustered around, staring in amazement at the stranger who rode into the courtyard, staring at his long, green coat edged with fur and his boots, so soft and polished they looked as if they were made of silk rather than fine leather. He wore gloves, and the fingers of the gloves were crowded with rings. His face was far older than his short, bright chestnut curls might have suggested.

Heriot stared like everybody else at this shiny insect of a man, out of place yet utterly commanding in the Tarbas courtyard. His authority sat on him so naturally that every-thing around him immediately grew subservient, yet his voice, when he spoke to Joan, was gentle rather than commanding. Heriot couldn't hear all that was being said, though he gathered that Great-Great-Aunt Jen's presence was being demanded. What he could make out was an unfamiliar accent, much quicker and more clipped than the family voices, and more careful.

Joan hurried off. Lord Glass turned and looked around him. A breeze turned back the edge of his green coat to show a scarlet lining embroidered with gold. Heriot's mouth opened a little. He was bewildered to think that a man might ride with such a coat belted across when he could ride with it open, showing off that wonderful lining.

A progressive disturbance, beginning somewhere on the second floor of the house and rattling down the stairs, marked Great-Great-Aunt Jen's rapid descent into the courtyard. Out she came, hesitated, and then gave a stiff bow to Lord Glass, who immediately dismounted and turned toward her, holding out his hand.

"Jenny Tarbas," Heriot heard him say, and thought that "Jenny" was an unexpectedly sweet and yielding name for a woman as dauntless as his great-great-aunt Jen. She was taller than Lord Glass, but he acted as if he were the taller, easily accepting a square of bread and a glass of wine from Wish.

"Through this gift of bread," he was saying in a formal ritual, "obligation returns to your Lord and magnifies the King and the Hero who are boundless in the land."

Heriot knew Lord Glass was not just Lord of County Glass, but Castellan, Lord Palantine, the King's Devisor, and one of the Council of Ten (those of the General

Council who most closely advised Hoad the King, a man who had given up his own name and taken the name of the land when he first came to the throne, and who would not reclaim his given name until he died). Lord Glass was one of the Lords on that mysterious plain on the other side of the hills, where the King and the Hero, together with Lords and Dukes, were struggling to negotiate a peace of some kind with the Dannorad, that ancient enemy of Hoad. It was strange that he should be here and not there among the other Lords, where fortunes and futures were being settled. Heriot could tell Great-Great-Aunt Jen's anxious welcome was not simply because he was the rock upon which so much of their prosperity depended. Some other anxiety was involved. Her voice rose with a vague desperation, and for the first time in his life Heriot heard her say something that was almost a lie.

"What boy? The place is full of boys."

Lord Glass laughed and patted her arm. His next words were lost, but then a slight turn of his head brought his voice clearly to Heriot's ears. "And, Jenny, we're too old for these games, you and I. Word's got around. Even out here people enjoy gossip, and gossip flows. So just put the perplexing Heriot here before me, please. You might as well do it now as later."

Great-Great-Aunt Jen slowly turned and looked over at Heriot, sitting in his corner, the cards spread out in front of him in their four suits—Earth, Air, Fire, and Water. She crooked her finger at him, so he carelessly swept his cards together before he rose and, sliding them into his pocket, walked reluctantly across the courtyard. Great-Great-Aunt

Jen met him and took his hand, placing him directly before Lord Glass.

"This is my great-great-nephew Heriot Tarbas, my lord. He's a good boy, very dear to us all. I don't know what you've been told, but he'd never intend any harm to Hoad, the land, or the King. In many ways I don't think he believes they exist."

"Well, I am here to convince him they do," Lord Glass replied. "Hello, Heriot Tarbas . . . your fame has gone abroad in the most gratifying way."

From behind Lord Glass, Wish was making impatient signs to Heriot, so he made a clumsy, ducking movement that was his idea of a bow. "Now I'll come to the point at once, something that I almost never do. Someone tells me you have had a vision of a sort. Is this true?"

Heriot's thoughts began to run quickly but somehow coolly. He shot a look at Great-Great-Aunt Jen, then looked back to Lord Glass.

"I warn you I shall take silence for assent," said Lord Glass a little sharply. "Don't stand there looking stupid, because by now I know a lot about you. I know you're not stupid, and if you pretend to be, I will get cross, and we won't get on. Don't you think that would be a pity?"

"My lord, you're confusing him," Great-Great-Aunt Jen cried indignantly.

"Come now, Jenny, he's not so very confused," Lord Glass said. "I'll swear he knows exactly what I'm talking about. Heriot, I didn't come alone. Just look toward the gate there, and my companions will ride through." He raised his gloved hand by way of a signal. "First, on the bay horse, comes Dr. Feo, the Queen's astrologer and the master of the King's clocks. He is very wise and tutors noble children in Diamond. And behind him, look carefully, is that a face you know? Ah, I see it is."

The second rider, on a white horse, pushed his white hood back from his bloodred hair, and it was the Wellwisher, the Assassin of his vision. This time he was dressed entirely in white, his face painted and powdered white, but Heriot was in no doubt about whom he was seeing. The pale blue eyes with their dreadful emptiness, the straight nose under the dyed and braided glittering hair were part of his memory forever. He would always recognize the single nature of this creature, who seemed entirely without the many falterings self-doubt puts into the human heart.

"Oh, I'd definitely say you were recognized, wouldn't you, Cloud?" Lord Glass fluted cheerfully, lifting his eyes from Heriot's stricken face.

The long lips parted. "He recognized me," said Cloud in a very soft voice, little more than a whisper, touching the corner of his eye reflectively as though minutely adjusting his vision, and then falling silent again.

"It is the recognition, you see," said Lord Glass. "I understand your boy has not left the farm, and Cloud will swear, moreover, that they have never met, for he has never once been here. And yet apparently the boy described him in detail, and news of that description has seeped over to the old battlefield."

Great-Great-Aunt Jen looked around the circle of faces as Wish came up from the stable and stood behind the women and children.

"Someone has been talking of Heriot's illness," Great-Great-Aunt Jen said to him. "I hope it was no one in our family."

Lord Glass signaled to Dr. Feo and Cloud, dismounting as he did so. "People will do it, Jenny, they will do it," he said cheerfully.

"The boy's mother had better be sent for," said Great-Great-Aunt Jen in a resigned voice, and she gave Heriot's shoulder a reassuring pat. "Baba, get your mother, will you? Wish, it might be a good idea to call Radley in. Come, my lord. Will your companions come with you?"

"Oh, Feo will. I may need him, and somehow I think it would be hard to keep him out," Lord Glass replied. "He's such an enthusiast. Now, Cloud would prefer to stand here by the door, wouldn't you, Cloud? He's a very observing creature—and his presence always makes people *think*, you know, and to my mind that's always a good thing, particularly out here in the country where we can easily become so casual."

"Anna," Great-Great-Aunt Jen cried as Heriot's mother arrived from work in the still room, wide-eyed and anxious. "Don't worry, Anna. Nothing's wrong, but come to the big room with us. Baba—will you and Joan bring wine and cakes?"

Lord Glass, following Great-Great-Aunt Jen, marched through the house into the big room with a self-confidence Heriot resented. Lord Glass promptly seated himself at the head of the table, inviting Great-Great-Aunt Jen, with a courteous wave of the hand, to sit in one of her own best chairs, and pointing Dr. Feo to another. Lord Glass's smoky eyes flitted with curiosity over the glass lamps and the carved chests where curtains and blankets were kept folded in dried camphor and lavender. Baba and Joan carried in trays of glasses and goblets.

"Very nice, Jenny," Lord Glass said. "Oh, it warms my heart to see that you have fallen on good times. So well-deserved, too! And now, Heriot, you're not the first person we've met who is reputed to have had a vision. Feo here is quite an expert on visions, so I want you to tell him everything you can about yours, particularly what it felt like. And, in return, Feo may be able to help you understand what happened."

"Speak up, Heriot," said Great-Great-Aunt Jen. "There's nothing to be afraid of." But she was frightened herself, even as she said this, so it was not in her power to comfort him.

Dr. Feo was a slender, stooped man with a grimacing smile that curved his lips down rather than up. He had very long, well-kept hands. He smiled at Heriot now, folding these hands one over the other as he prepared to listen. Heriot, speaking into the space between Dr. Feo and Lord Glass, began telling the story of his courtyard vision. Born on a farm, he had often seen blood, for animals were always being killed and cut up for food, but as he recalled Carron's face and his lively lips spilling words and blood with equal passion, he stumbled and grew silent, putting his hand over his left eye, his puzzled one, to stare hard at Lord Glass for a moment before he dropped his hand and looked at the floor again.

"Well, Feo?" said Lord Glass. "Is this child a Magician of Hoad, or is this another wild goose chase?"

"How could he be a Magician of Hoad?" asked Heriot's mother. "The Magicians of Hoad are madmen . . . so empty of themselves that something else talks through them. That's what we hear of Izachel, the King's Magician."

Lord Glass saw Heriot glance at her and read something in his expression.

"A good point!" he agreed. "Izachel is a Magician, and like most Magicians, he gives mysterious and enlightening utterances . . . he reads the minds of other men and tells the King what he reads there . . . but at the same time he's an idiot in almost every ordinary way, a prophetic doll. Of course, having said that, there are at least two exceptions in our history. The *rational* Magicians of Hoad. And great blessings they have been to the Kings for whom they worked. Now it is possible, just possible, that Heriot might be a rational Magician. After all, he's one of your people, and you are like the Orts, the ones you call the Travelers. You are all descended directly from that ancient people, the Gethin, the ones who lived here hundreds of years ago . . . the ones waiting for us when we first landed here. Now I am a King's man, and I have to follow all possibilities, no matter how remote. Feo, you have studied the Magicians of Hoad, including Izachel, for years. I need your opinion."

Dr. Feo sat Heriot in front of him, took his wrist, laid cool fingers on his pulse, and began to question him about his vision. Had anything like this ever happened to him before? How did he feel afterward? Did the figure of Cloud appear quite solid or could he see through it? He stared with large, melancholy hazel eyes deep into

Heriot's own eyes, and then asked him to look into a crystal, to breathe some smoke from leaves burned in a bowl, and then to watch a silver pendulum swing backward and forward.

When the pendulum stopped, Dr. Feo turned to Lord Glass.

"There are some characteristics," he said cautiously. "There's certainly a discontinuity in the flow of his awareness . . . a jump of some kind, as if something else was pushing in on him. And he might not know it, but he watches the pendulum and me simultaneously. It's worth pursuing."

"Well, I can't read what you call awareness, but I can read faces," said Lord Glass. "Jenny, Dr. Feo is very excited at the prospect of working with your great-great-nephew."

Dr. Feo smiled politely and looked at Heriot with a benevolent expression, in which there was a hint of something that was not at all benevolent.

"What are you going to do about all this?" cried Heriot's mother.

Lord Glass gave her a smile that was all his own—sweet and yet without kindness.

"We're merely messengers, my dear," he said, "sent to convey Hoad's interest"—Lord Glass hesitated—"and Dr. Feo has just told us your boy is worthy of the King's interest. Apparently he is very promising."

"For what, my lord?" asked Heriot's mother, the very question Heriot was secretly asking too.

"Who can say, my dear? But do not take a somber view of things." Lord Glass waved his hand, and then, drawing off his gloves, he poured wine for himself and Dr. Feo, choosing to drink from the most elegant goblet. "Now be honest . . . er . . . Anna, is it? May I call you Anna? Ask yourself what there is here for anyone with his apparent talents. Country life is wholesome and charming in its way . . . but it is limited. Mind, I'm not criticizing, but I believe he will come to be grateful for the chance that takes him to Diamond."

"Well," said Great-Great-Aunt Jen, "you still owe us some explanation, my lord. Why take him? We're not under obligation. We're not at war."

"Come now, Jenny," Lord Glass said, holding his goblet up and looking at her over the top of it. "Think of El-El or Zazareel or, more recently, Izachel—think of the mysterious part Magicians have played in our lives over hundreds of years. A Magician is a treasure to a King, and any Magician automatically belongs to Hoad the King, so your boy will come to Diamond and make his fortune. Because of course, as you may have heard, even Magicians age, and Izachel is no longer reliable. Our King really needs a Magician, and your boy may very well do."

It was at that moment Heriot truly understood that he was going to be taken away from the Tarbas farm, from the kitchen courtyard and garden, and from the unfolding fields. It was then he truly understood that his own wishes would not be consulted. At that very moment Lord Glass said, "After all, it isn't for you to decide, is it, Jenny? Just suppose you were to beg me to leave him be, and just suppose I gave in, not that I would, for I'm not nearly as benevolent as I try to make myself appear, all that would happen would be that someone less talkative but very much more unpleasant would wait on you. You would suffer, the boy would suffer, and I would suffer too, for my hesitation. There is no decision to be made beyond Feo's, and his decision has been made."

Heriot looked up, his hands clenched together before him. "Don't I get asked?" he cried abruptly, and Lord Glass turned to him, surprised and shaking his head.

"My dear boy—certainly not!"

Heriot turned, not to his mother, but to his Great-Great-Aunt Jen.

"Don't let them take me," he cried.

"I have to," she answered.

"Why?" Heriot asked her, and felt something gathering thunderously in him. Once again a storm was on the way. Once again he thought he might be about to crack in two. "I don't want to go with that Cloud," he exclaimed furiously. "I'm frightened. Frightened sick!" He sounded angry rather than frightened, but all the same, within himself he was terrified. *Same old fear*, said a voice somewhere in his head. *Drive it out! Get rid of it!*

"Don't shout, Heriot," Great-Great-Aunt Jen was saying sternly. "Be brave. Face up to it. I can't help you."

"Do I have to help myself, then?" demanded Heriot.

Something moved behind his eyes as he turned to look at Lord Glass. Something that had made a private space for itself in his head looked out of him. But to use the talents of whatever it was that lay on the other side of the fracture, he had to acknowledge it.

"You're all changing me," he cried desperately. "You're making me change." He began to tremble . . . the glasses on the tray shuddered along with him, softly at first and then with an added clamor. The wine spiraled up the sides of the decanter, and the decanter itself danced and spun on its round foot, flashing sparkles of light across the walls and ceiling. The wine goblets spun and sang. The slender jug danced on its tray, the windows hummed, each one on a separate note but in disturbing harmony, rising higher and higher, until Heriot's teeth ached with the sound. Great-Great-Aunt Jen looked around wildly, his mother raised her head and stared at him incredulously, but both Dr. Feo and Lord Glass now seemed to recognize him beyond all doubt. The glasses chattered on in shrill voices, the goblet sang and signaled, the jug rang, the windows hummed higher and higher, until they were screaming, pitched on the very edge of possible hearing, and then suddenly everything in the room that was made out of glass burst into clear splinters. Heriot felt his eyes roll back in his head and his eyelids close over them, like curtains drawn over windows through which too much might be seen.

Dr. Feo caught him and held him tightly, even patting him, as if he were a good dog who had done well.

"Just see how radiant Feo looks," said Lord Glass in a voice that contrived to be shaken, querulous, and somehow entertained as well. "Now I would be very annoyed with anyone who treated my treasures like that, but Feo has it in his power to forgive all, though of course in this case, it is not his own property that has been harmed. Feo? You're pleased, are you?"

"Oh yes, my lord," said Feo, sounding excited. "I think the boy made powerful use of some despair. . . ." He coughed apologetically. "I would surmise that he wanted to strike at you, but he realized that if anything happened to you, his family might suffer, so he attacked, we might say, by association."

"Might we say that?" inquired Lord Glass, arching his brows.

"The glass!" said Dr. Feo eagerly. "Not another thing was touched, only the glass. I think it might be a play on your name, a sort of pun."

Lord Glass sighed deeply. "There are people who suggest that now that the wars are over, I no longer take risks on behalf of Hoad." He stood up. "We must go at once. There is no need to pack anything for the boy. Hoad will provide adequately—even generously."

"Sir," protested Anna angrily. "You took Heriot's father for your wars, and he never came back, and now you're taking Heriot. It's not funny to us."

"My dear," said Lord Glass, speaking now in a very different voice. "I have a superficial nature that can't gracefully abide some of the acts I am bound to perform. I joke about many things, including my own misfortunes. My father lost three sons in the King's wars, and I lost my eldest. But, like me, you have other boys coming on, and that's why I am the King's man, since after all our wars, he has turned powerfully toward peace and may well turn us all with him. His reign has brought many blessings, I think, and may bring more, no matter what you may feel at the moment."

"It's true," Great-Great-Aunt Jen said with a sigh. "We're bound to submit. Heriot's our sacrifice this time round."

"And a piece of good advice from one who knows: Keep your other boy away from Diamond. It seems more and more likely Heriot had a vision of a future possibility, so Diamond might not be altogether suitable for your Carron. Keep him at home or try some other city. Now, boy Heriot! We'll sleep at my house tonight and take you to the old battlefield tomorrow. Indeed, they are hammering a primitive peace together out there, and I am expected to strike in myself on the part of the King," Lord Glass said. "Say your good-byes rather quickly, my dear. And think of all this as an adventure—maybe the road to fortune."

Heriot looked deep into those smoky eyes for a moment, then let his quivering shoulders relax and gave a long sigh.

"If I must, I must," he said submissively. "May I take my cards with me? They're out in the courtyard." He held his breath.

"The cards." Lord Glass looked at Great-Great-Aunt Jen rather than Anna. She looked doubtful.

"It's an ancient set," she said. "We wouldn't get another like that. But all right. Be quick."

Heriot smiled a little, turned, and gave Lord Glass an appeasing glance.

"That's a good boy," said Lord Glass.

Heriot moved slowly to the door, expecting that at any moment someone would remember he had put the cards in his pocket, and he would be called back sternly.

However, as they began talking again behind him, he arrived safely in the kitchen.

"Heriot," said Baba. "What's happening? Are you to be taken?"

"Tell us!" cried Ashet. "Don't keep us waiting. Is your fortune made?"

Nella, with her baby in her arms, smiled at him.

"I'll tell you in a moment," Heriot replied, amazed at his own easy, natural voice. "Look, I'm to get something for them . . . something from outside." He came to the door of the kitchen, where Cloud was watching the little ones of the family running in circles and jumping over a tiny stick. Cloud smiled.

Shuddering inside his clothes at the sight of an Assassin overlooking the babies, Heriot walked calmly past, offering no explanation or excuse, then out through the courtyard gates. And then, at last, he allowed himself to run, to run as fast as he could into the old barn. Once there he climbed a ladder into a loft, piled with loose hay. He burrowed into and through, letting it fall behind him. For a moment he thought he might stick there and smother, but finally he won through.

On the other side of the piled hay there was a very small window directly under the peak of the roof. Turning to face back the way he had come, he sat on the sill, reaching out and then up, until his desperate fingers, groping up across the outside stone, encountered a familiar hold, a channel made to drain rainwater into a stone cistern.

As Heriot began wriggling up out of the window, angling himself and holding his breath as he did so, he heard voices questioning and feet beginning to pelt across the courtyard. As he pulled himself out onto the roof, feet began to shift the hay in the space below him. As he rolled down softly into the cleft between two ridges of stable roof, he heard Lord Glass's voice.

"Cloud, I am to blame. I saw him put those cards into his pocket. But we're wasting time. He will have made for the hills." The footsteps retreated.

Heriot had begun to breathe rather more easily when suddenly he heard Wish's voice. "He'd be too big to get through that window, wouldn't he?"

"Right!" said Radley from somewhere, and then added, "All this, it's some sort of mistake."

"Get away with you!" Wish answered. "He's something really wild. I've always known it. We fling them up from time to time, don't we? They're like a throwback to the old people, the Gethin. Still he's ours, not theirs. So we won't look too closely. Come on now, before they get suspicious."

Then Wish set off walking rapidly . . . treading heavily . . . as if the sound of his boots might be sending some sort of message up into the space above him.

Heriot lay still, listening to the search going on below. When night came down around him, stars pricked into life. Silence fell. Finally, in spite of the hard tiles and the cold, Heriot slept for a while, only to wake shivering, frowning, puzzling, and staring up into the night while the stars, wheeling above him, stared back without sympathy or even curiosity.

And at last . . . at long last . . . the first, faint transparency moved above the eastern horizon. Heriot had no choice. He must move on. Aching with cold, wet with night dews, he slid to the edge of the dairy roof, arriving at a corner cut back into rising ground, where he crouched for a moment, trying to wring life back into his fingers before lowering himself over the edge of the roof. His cold hands, not yet properly restored, let go before he was ready. He had only a small distance to fall, but it was hard to judge distance in the dark, and the impact drove his knee into his stomach, so that he rolled on the ground, winded. A dog began to bark, but there was no response from the silent house. Picking himself up, limping to begin with but recovering as he jogged, then racing away, Heriot made for the hills.

Over the last few weeks he had kept silent about his experiences on the causeway. They were part of his own secret nightmare, and anyhow, if they made no sense to him, how could they possibly make sense to anyone else? The subsequent vision in the courtyard had at least had a sort of story to it. But what sense would it make to say, "Something has altered inside me. That thing that used to feed off me, always tearing into me, has been driven out. It's changed—changed. Now it's living inside me, pulling me into another shape. I'm changing too. I'm becoming something different." Though the causeway had been the setting for such confusion and terror, Heriot nevertheless ran toward the sea, thinking of the series of long beaches stretching eastward to Diamond and of the many hiding places they offered. The wet ribbons of tidal shore, running for leagues to the left and right of the causeway, were like roads that might be traveled quickly, and the tide, being a reliable servant, would wipe out any tracks he left behind.

Beyond the tidal zone, hills of dry sand covered with yellow lupins gave way to deep woods filled with leafy rifts, caves, fallen trees, holes. Heriot imagined himself turning into a wild man of the seashore and living on berries, crabs, birds' eggs, and wild honey.

I'm out in the world, he thought. *I'm on my own. It's an adventure. It's just got to be an adventure.* And he ran on and on.

DYSART'S STORY

Meanwhile, out on the edge of that last battlefield, strange days were coming and going, like pages being flicked over. Flick! Flick! Flick! What? A week gone by. And then another. In the great tents in the center of the plain, the King with his Magician at his elbow, the Hero with his sword at his side, together with the Lords of Hoad, faced the Dukes of the Dannorad, slowly arguing their way, day after day, toward a peace of some kind. A lasting peace, perhaps. Everyone knew it was what the King was set on, but somehow, after all the years of advance and retreat, battle and bloodshed, the enthusiastic growth of twining hatreds, it did not seem possible.

Linnet had grown weary of it all. At first it had been new and exciting, but she quickly became bored with the city of tents and all its strange contradictions, tired of the mud, tired of days that seemed to go on and on without arriving anywhere. She even grew tired of the formal occasions when she and her mother were paraded before strangers, just as the King's three sons were being paraded. There they were, lined up like pieces in a game: strange Betony Hoad with his servant Talgesi; handsome Luce, who might someday be her husband; and sometimes even Dysart—the mad Prince—silent and closed tightly in on himself on these public occasions, almost as if he might betray himself by laughing aloud when everyone else was serious.

"They are close to agreement," Linnet's mother told her. "But it has been decided there should be a break of some kind so that people can stretch their thoughts and turn things over. Lord Glass has ridden off somewhere on some errand of the King's, and the Hero has gone back to Cassio's Island for a few days."

There was no great break for Linnet, however. She and Dysart were still obliged to study together. They sat with their books and papers around them, pretending to work but often arguing in a way they both enjoyed. Dr. Feo had ridden away with Lord Glass, and though they had other tutors, there were often times when they were left on their own. It was in one of these times that Linnet looked across at Dysart sitting in his chair, reading and twisting a finger in his hair as he did so, and asked him a question that had tormented her for some time.

"Why do they call you the mad Prince?" she asked.

He looked up as if he were thinking the question over, and when he turned to look at her, she could see that he was working himself up to give her a long answer.

"I don't think I am mad," he said at last. "But I think I was born to be haunted."

"Haunted?" Linnet sat back. "By ghosts?"

"I don't know," Dysart answered rather irritably. He

shrugged. "Could be ghosts, I suppose, although it goes back a long way, back before I knew there could be such things as ghosts." And then suddenly he began to talk, words pouring out of him as if they had been held in for a long time and were glad of release at last.

"I don't remember when it ever began. . . . I think I might have been about three or four years old the first time. I'd wake up in the darkness, all sweaty and strange. I felt as if I was being digested in some terrible gut . . . becoming meat of its meat, but still being myself inside that meat."

"You felt you'd been eaten?" Linnet exclaimed.

Dysart hesitated. "I suppose so. It was weird. I felt that what was happening to me was really happening to someone else, but I was caught up in it. I do know I was always terrified out of my wits, but even then I knew that no true man of Hoad gives in to fear. So I didn't give into it. I just clenched myself up into a fist." As he spoke, Dysart clenched his fists so tightly his knuckles whitened under the skin of his hands. "I held myself together against whatever the . . . well, the *invasion* was, no matter whose dream was coming down on me, until morning came."

"What was trying to invade you?" Linnet asked, glad to hear herself sounding skeptical.

"I don't know," said Dysart crossly. "I still don't know. I know what I felt, but none of it makes any sort of sense. I always thought—well, I was always utterly sure—that there was someone in the room with me . . . someone waiting for something. I don't mean Crespin, even though he was always there, snoring away in a bed at the foot of my own bed. It was someone else. Mind you, I wouldn't even try to see anything. I'd just screw myself up, elbows in, knees up, eyes pinched shut. Hour after hour. But once I felt the first light of day on the other side of my eyelids, I'd open my eyes just a chink and turn my head. And then I'd see him, sitting there silently on the sill of my window, face turned away, staring down into the city . . . just staring down as if he had all the time in the world to admire the view." Dysart looked across at Linnet and laughed, but not in the way he usually laughed. "My ghost!" he said, nodding to himself. "Well, more of a demon, maybe. I don't know."

He fell silent. Linnet stared back at him. For once she had nothing to say. He was telling a tall story, and yet at the same time she knew he was being serious. He was trusting her with his nightmare. Not only that, she found she was believing him.

"Go on," she told him. "Tell me the rest." For she knew there was more to tell.

And after a moment, Dysart did go on, telling her, yet telling himself at the same time, listening carefully to his own story. Perhaps it was the first time he had set it free in the outside air.

"I did try speaking to it sometimes, though not with words. I'd try to get its attention with squeaks and grunts . . . sounds that were sort of asking questions . . . that sort of thing. Sometimes Crespin would wake up and catch me acting in a strange way, and of course he told other people." Dysart shrugged. "Once I was seriously ill, and my ghost suddenly appeared in full daylight, sliding in between Crespin and the doctors, who didn't seem to see or hear as it spread its left-hand fingers across its own face"—Dysart spread his long left-hand fingers over his own face as he told her this—"as it laid the right hand on mine. Its fingernails were odd lengths, a funny thing to remember. Anyhow, when it touched me the fever slowly drained away. I felt as if I'd been saved. Well, I *had* been saved, but I don't know why."

Dysart shrugged and stopped again, looking at her half-defiantly, as if he were expecting some derisive comment or question. Linnet still had nothing to say.

"So, anyhow," said Dysart at last, "I'd wake and wait, like I told you, and sometimes if I was alone with it—no Crespin or anyone—I'd get impatient and scramble toward the window, yelling, 'Here I am!'" But I could never touch it. It would simply dissolve into air and shadow. So then I'd climb into the space where it had been and sit on that big sill and look out from my room up there at the top of Crow Tower, across the courtyards of Guard-on-the-Rock, and down into the city below. And I'd see what I suppose the ghost had been seeing . . . all that gilt and glass and wood and stone spread out like a parade. And somehow the sight of the city always drove my fear back into the place where it usually lived, tucked in, all cozy and calm, under my ribs. At times I wondered if the dissolving ghost might be the city itself, trying to get in touch with me."

"Didn't you ever tell anyone?" asked Linnet after a short silence.

Dysart shrugged again and gave an impatient sigh. "In the beginning I told them over and over again. But who would believe me? It sometimes seemed as if that demon was somehow my only true friend, watching me from that windowsill, giving me nightmares but rescuing me from a different sort of nightmare, something I could feel building out there, and always dissolving when I tried to look at it closely. Morning after morning I saw it soak away into the city out beyond my window, just like water soaking into sand. I did try to tell. I did try to tell Crespin, and Dr. Feo. And a few others they brought to look after me. But they didn't believe me. And anyhow, words collapsed when I tried to use them. They all became grunts and humming."

Dysart stood up and walked restlessly about the room. Linnet knew he had still more to tell her, and she waited in silence.

MADE, NOT BORN

At last Dysart burst out, "I've always felt I was made, not born . . . made accidentally. Betony . . . Luce . . . they feel like *intended* men. I feel like an afterthought. It took me a long time to accept that I was the only one who could see the ghost, but by then I'd become partly invisible myself. People began looking around me, and I wasn't so much mentioned as muttered about. Sideways muttering!

"Mind you, in the beginning they really did try, in spite of my grunting and crying and pointing at empty air. Because—let's face it—a mad son! Well, that's the sign of a great imperfection in any King's reign. They did their best with me, but none of it worked. If I was given any traditional task—as page boy, say, at one of my father's feasts—things always went wrong. Flagons rattled. Glasses fell over. Wine climbed up the inside of goblets and spilled over all those lips of silver and crystal. Something uninvited was always walking along beside me, pushing into my space and twisting the world around me. Invisibly twisting it! Still does!"

He laughed, shaking his head. "No wonder the whole court sighed and looked away tactfully as I stumbled on by, plates and glasses falling to the floor. Even you heard the gossip up there among your mountains. Almost the first words I heard from you were, 'They say you're a fool.'"

"But you asked me if I had pointed teeth," Linnet replied.

Dysart laughed again.

"Fair enough!" he said. "As for me, back then—well, I toughened up inside my haunted space and started making fun of the world around me. Because there's always plenty to laugh at, thank goodness. And, in the end, a sort of conceit took over. You've probably worked that out for yourself, and I didn't *want* to be believed. That demon came to be . . ." He hesitated, frowning, then said carefully, ". . . my inside certainty of my own special nature, if you know what I mean. It had something to tell me when the right time came, and when that right time comes I want whatever it says to be mine. Mine alone. I'm the one who's done all that suffering for it. And the really strange thing—stranger than all the rest of it—is that sitting on the windowsill, huddled in the space where the ghost had been, I used to feel that down below me, down in that twisting old city, the crown might grow straight out of the skull of the King, and Princes, being made of legends, not meat, would never be digested by darkness . . . not even for a moment.

Linnet listened, confused, but fascinated too. Dysart looked sideways at her.

"Sorry!" he said, and shook his head as if he were trying to shake away some thought that turned into confusion when he tried to put it into words. "So," he went on, "every now and then I crouched there in ghost space, feeling a sort of triumph as I spied on the city, high above everyone else, except for my father in the Tower of the Lion. But then, he was a sort of ghost himself . . . still is, really."

Dysart sighed and stared into space for a moment before going on briskly. "Anyhow, as I spied on Diamond, somehow I found I could feel it all . . . I mean *really* feel it all . . . everything . . . not just Diamond but out *beyond* Diamond . . . the whole land of Hoad—mountains and forests, salt pans, sand hills, herds of white deer in the woods and black horses on the plains . . . the lot. Long before our Hero, the great Carlyon"—Dysart sounded slightly sarcastic at the expense of the Hero—"long before he single-handedly avenged the massacre of Senlac, I knew as much about Senlac as if I had walked its street . . . and it only had one . . . it was all it ever needed . . . a village of about eighty people, with an ancient graveyard many times bigger than the whole village. Some crowd descended on them—probably Dannorad, though the Dannorad always denied it—and killed every one of them. And then the Hero swept in and killed the killers."

As he said all this, Dysart had begun pacing backward and forward, a flood of words bursting out of him. Linnet could tell that he had stopped thinking of her. Now he was talking only to himself, reminding himself of who he was, and telling a story he had told himself over and over again.

"Of course, the wars were still going on back then, but I swear that over in the Tower of the Lion I could feel my way into my father's dream of peace, which was growing stronger. In the beginning he hadn't thought he would ever be King—but war had killed his father and brothers, so when his turn came he grabbed the power of it and began striking back by declaring war on war itself. Sometimes I think his dream had something in common with my illness and that I caught it from him, though in another form." Dysart paused, standing sideways in the doorway, staring out into the city of tents. Then he swung around to face Linnet, and his voice became suddenly passionate.

"I've wanted to tell all this to someone who . . . well, all of a sudden, over the last few days I've really wanted to explain it to you. I don't want you to think I'm mad in the way everyone else does. Anyhow, in an odd sort of way I feel you just might believe in my ghost. And you might understand how it happened that, sitting in that haunted space, watching the city and dreaming of Hoad, I came to feel I had a magical life. All right . . . yes . . . perhaps I was the mad Prince, but secretly I thought I might be the *true* Prince . . . the one who finally becomes King, even though he has two older brothers with dreams of their own. But just thinking that sort of thing is close to treachery, isn't it?"

Silence came in on them. Then the sides of the tent panted in and out. The outside world was reminding them that it was still there.

"Do you still see your ghost?" Linnet asked at last.

"No," Dysart replied. "Well, not often. Not in the way I used to. But I feel it in the air around me at times. I feel it nudging at me . . . breathing in my ear. Feel it brushing against the thoughts in my head, and when it does that, it throws me off balance. The day we met, the day they first brought you into the scholar-tent, something happened to my ghost. I felt the shock of it. Remember?"

Linnet suddenly remembered the pages flying up around him as if they were being whirled around by a wind that no one else could feel. Dysart seemed to see her remembering, and he nodded slowly. "No wonder they think I'm mad," he said. "It's hard to tell the difference between being mad and being haunted."

NAKED ON THE EDGE OF THE SEA

A few hours before Dysart, Prince of Hoad, began telling his story to Linnet of Hagen, Heriot Tarbas began climbing a hill, hoping his ascent would be undetected. He climbed as quickly and quietly as he could, sliding through long grass, or dodging from bush to bush. When he reached the rock Draevo, he leaned against it for a little while, looking back down at the farm, feeling he might be seeing it for the last time.

At that time of day it was nothing but a series of black and gray masses, buildings, yards, orchard, and garden. Roosters crowed. The dew on certain angles of roof and wall was beginning to catch the light, and there was a suggestion of movement at one of the doors. It might simply have been Baba and Ashet setting out to bring the cows in, but Heriot wasn't prepared to wait to find out. He realized he must have left tracks in the wet grass . . . tracks that, if followed, would zigzag remorselessly to his retreating heels. So, turning, he plunged down toward the sea and didn't stop until he had put the first of many little headlands between him and the top of the hill.

By now the sun was well risen. The light, flooding in over the sea and across the sand, was strong and yet somehow a little shy as well, just as if the sun had to reintroduce itself to the land. (Remember me? Shall we dance?) The coastline stretched ahead, unwinding like thread from a spool—a series of looping bays, some of them little more than creases in the series of hard, rocky faces the land turned to the sea. "What shall I do?" he asked himself. And then, "Well, here I am and I'm going somewhere." And then, "Yes, but where am I going?" There was no answer to this question. He moved on steadily but in no great hurry now, for he imagined he had left the farm and the possibility of pursuit behind. All the same, he still walked above the tideline, first in the light, dry sand where he left no footprints, and then, after jumping from stone to stone down to the water's edge, along firm, wet sand, certain that the waves would wash out his traces almost at once.

He had walked for a long time and around several headlands when he came to an abrupt stop. Somewhere someone was frying food, and Heriot found he was starving. Going silently from one patch of lupins to another, he came quite suddenly on a tethered horse, a huge animal, all of seventeen hands, sniffing from time to time without great enthusiasm at the coarse sea grass. And there beyond it was a naked man, sitting on a black cloak that he had spread out on the dry sand, and cooking himself a morning meal. The man's back, half-turned toward Heriot, was as powerful as Radley's, but Radley would have had black wavy hair, the ends twisting into ringlets, falling down over copper-colored shoulders. This man had, instead, a wide, springing halo of red-gold hair, shedding drops that ran down his pale back in slow tears.

Beside him was a cloth set with a wineskin, a loaf of bread that looked very fresh, and thin slices of smoked beef, delicately veined with a little fat. There was also a sausage, which the man was cutting into rings, so that he could toast them on the end of a long stick. His clothes lay folded to one side of him. For all his nakedness and the campfire breakfast, Heriot knew he was not looking at a vagrant. The way the man's hair was trimmed, the pure whiteness of the cloth, the elegant way the beef was sliced, the warm blush of light along the blade held out to the fire, all suggested someone used to money and style. Yet what Lord could he be, alone on this remote shore, naked in the late autumn morning, cooking sausage with a knife that looked beautiful, ancient, and wicked?

A piece of driftwood crumbled. The man shifted, half turning his head. Heriot opened his mouth to speak, feeling his intention fly out ahead of his words. Then, before he actually spoke, he had an overwhelming answer. Unhappiness poured into him, unhappiness shot through with a terrible ferocity, accompanied by another feeling, a twin to misery, a feeling he could not name though it made him shrink back among the lupins. These feelings were accompanied by a huge irritation. The man was deeply unhappy about something and, at the same time, angry with himself for his own unhappiness. Somewhere along the line, he had done something terrible, and though he wasn't sorry he had done it, the memory of doing it was infuriating him.

These wild emotions were flowing directly from the naked giant before him, and though Heriot was receiving them, they belonged to that man alone. Heriot stepped back as silently as he could, but the man turned sharply, teeth slightly bared. Then, seeing Heriot, he paused and relaxed; he smiled; he even laughed a little at his own momentary shock. His red-gold eyebrows arched with astonishment, his long, thin-lipped mouth turned up at the corners in a curling smile that reminded Heriot of the smiles on the faces of the carved lions in his garden at home. That tide of savage feeling seemed to sink rapidly away into the rocks and sand, though it did not totally disappear.

"Don't look so frightened," the man said. "You're welcome, whoever you are. I could do with company. Sit down and have breakfast with me."

Heriot looked around doubtfully, not knowing whether to retreat or advance.

"It's a command," the man said, a different tone now creeping into his voice. Heriot slowly obeyed, baffled by some quality in this encounter. It was hard to think that anyone with such a warm, easy, amused voice could be the source of the menacing distress that had assailed him only a moment earlier.

"You're one of the Orts?" the man said after a moment. Heriot looked confused. "A Traveler? Yes?" the man added. Heriot's black plaits and olive skin had misled him.

"Half and half, I think," Heriot said cautiously. "Like,

I mostly don't travel. Well, I might be traveling right this minute, but only just."

"Oh!" said the man, as if he understood everything. "You're running away, then?" Heriot did not reply, and the man, nodding as if Heriot's silence was an answer, clapped a slice of beef between two bits of bread and passed the sandwich over to Heriot, who, even though he felt shy in the presence of a stranger both naked and noble, took it gratefully. The man looked at him closely, apparently puzzled.

"You're not a girl by any chance, are you?" he asked.

"No!" cried Heriot indignantly.

"Oh, do excuse me!" the man exclaimed, lifting his eyebrows in amusement at Heriot's vehemence. "You look so shy, and then your long hair made me wonder."

"Our lot like it long," Heriot explained.

"So your father wears his long too?" asked the man, grinning a little.

"I don't know about him," Heriot said doubtfully. "He was in the King's army, and died before I was born."

"I've placed you now," said the man in a more subdued voice. "You come from among those ruins over the hills back there, don't you? You're one of *that* family."

"Right!" Heriot agreed. "The Orts wander, but our lot, we stand still in the old place." He gratefully accepted a ring of sausage from the end of the knife.

At this moment the horse suddenly swung around, lifted its head, and put its ears forward. It nickered, and another horse, farther down the beach in the direction from which Heriot had come, neighed faintly but distinctly. Heriot scrambled rapidly to his feet, cramming the ring of sausage into his mouth as he did so.

"Someone chasing you?" asked the man sympathetically.

"Well, they could be," Heriot said. "Not that I've done anything wrong," he added hastily. "It's just I don't want to go to places where other people want me to go, that's all."

"Hide!" the man suggested. "No one will search too closely around me, I can promise you that."

Heriot gave him a grateful glance and wriggled back among the lupins as quickly as he could.

"Get yourself comfortable," the man advised. "I've had to hide a few times in my life, and it's important to start off by being as comfortable as possible."

"I know," Heriot said, thinking of his wretched night on the roof of the old barn. If he put his hands against the ground, the rhythmic approach of the strange horse could be felt like a heartbeat under his palms, but it still took a few minutes for it to arrive. And there was Lord Glass himself, curiously resplendent in his marvelous green coat, trotting toward them. Heriot's self-appointed protector, who had continued very calmly to make himself a sandwich of beef and bread, stared, started, and leaped to his feet with a shout of incredulous laughter.

"Dorian, Lord Glass!" he shouted. "You of all people! What are you doing out here on a deserted beach in the early morning?"

"This is County Glass, after all," Lord Glass replied, dismounting. "It is my county. What are you doing here, naked and solitary as the first man in the world? I thought you were taking advantage of the break to put your island in order. A change for you, my dear! No flash of steel! No splash of blood!"

"I wanted to be on my own," the man said. "I wanted to think things over. It looks as if the King might get that great peace he has worked for, but what happens to the Hero when there's no need for his heroism? After all, I'm not so old: nearly forty—that's still young. I've got a long way to go. Anyhow, I thought I'd come back to my own place and enjoy a little solitude."

"You wanted the war to go on?" Lord Glass asked as if he could not quite believe what he was hearing, but the man merely laughed.

"Can I offer you food? Drink? You'll have to drink from the bottle, mind you. And then you can tell me just why you of all people have appeared out of nowhere." His voice changed, growing suddenly eager. "The King hasn't had second thoughts about my suggestions, has he?"

"No," said Lord Glass. "The King never has second thoughts, my dear. And as for me, I'd love to sit, tipping the bottle and gossiping, but unfortunately, I'm too busy to be sociable. I was sent to escort a young man to Diamond. He's turned down a royal invitation, and you know just how pressing they can be. You've haven't seen a dark-haired boy, have you? I left Cloud following what might have been tracks in the sand back there, and cast on ahead myself."

The man ignored the question. "Cloud?" he exclaimed. He sounded thunderstruck. "This boy . . . do you want him alive or dead?"

"We were intended as his escort, not his huntsmen." Lord Glass sighed. "It's a long story, my dear."

"I haven't seen anyone," the man answered, "but if I do, I will look at him very carefully indeed. He must be a treasure."

"Well, if you do come across my runaway, you could bring him to the Tarbas farm over the hill. Largely unharmed, of course."

"Of course," the man agreed rather savagely. "By the way, what has this boy done to deserve such very distinguished attention?"

"He represents a possibility, nothing more," Lord Glass replied. "As you know, the King likes to collect curiosities of nature."

Through a cross-hatching of stems and a stipple of leaves beyond them, Heriot watched Lord Glass wheel his horse and ride back the way he had come. He wasn't sure why the naked man, so familiar with Lord Glass, so lordly in himself, had chosen to conceal a runaway.

"Stay where you are," the man murmured, as he, too, stared after Lord Glass. Then he began dressing rapidly, talking all the time in a low but sharpened voice. "I'll take you up in front of me and carry you farther down the shore if you like. Lord Glass is a true King's man, so I owe him a bad turn. You can edge out now . . . he's well around the next headland."

As Heriot scrambled out, his hair catching on dried stems of lupin, which were behaving as if they were trying to pull him back into hiding, his protector turned to face him, wearing a very different expression from the one he had worn earlier. "I take it you know who that was?"

Heriot said nothing. He watched the man knot a sash of brilliant color at his waist, then twist it to display its fringe.

After that he slid rings of turquoise and silver out from his pocket and then, one by one, onto his fingers. Naked and pale, he had been a casual companion. Dressed and colored in, he had suddenly become a master.

"Lord Glass is a great man in the land," the man said, straightening the rings, then holding out his hand in front of him as if he would be able to admire them better from a distance. "He's the King's Devisor, and his closest friend. If you've really done nothing wrong, he'd be good to you."

"I just want to be let alone," Heriot said.

The man laughed. "Too much to expect!" he replied. "After all, I wanted to be left alone too, and you broke in on me, disturbing my thoughts." His last words sounded brotherly. Heriot's heart warmed to this voice.

"Lucky I did, though," Heriot said cheerfully. "No fun having thoughts like those—all black and savage. It must be good to have a break from them." The man had been shaking the sand from his cloak, but for a fraction of a second he froze, smile fixed, eyes staring straight ahead. He recovered in the same moment, and as he slung the cloak around his shoulders, he said in an absent voice, "Thoughts like what?"

Heriot already knew he had made a mistake. "Just joking," he said apologetically. The man did not press him for any more answer than that.

And then, a moment later, they were cantering, even galloping along a stretch of hard sand, Heriot clinging on to the horse's mane, his rescuer's powerful arms on either side of him. He laughed aloud with relief and pleasure, and the man responded by laughing too. "Wonderful to go free!" he shouted.

"Run off like me, then," Heriot cried back.

"Ah, but I never run away!" the man replied. "Never!"

They slowed down to pick their way around one rocky headland, cantered again, then slowed a second time, as they confronted a narrow stretch of stones that ran between the sea and the severe cliffs that seemed to beetle out over Heriot and his companion. Perhaps a quarter of a league farther down the shore, Heriot could see that these cliffs dwindled abruptly to banks and were cut by an impatient stream, which split into a series of winding channels before reaching the sea.

At last the man spoke, pointing over Heriot's shoulder. "If you go up that stream, you'll come to a path. You can't miss it. It's quite easy to see. Just keep going until you get the aqueduct in your sights. The aqueduct marks the main road, and after a league or so, the road forks into two. The left-hand road is the one that leads to Diamond. And once you're in Diamond, you can lose yourself forever."

"Diamond?" Heriot exclaimed blankly. "I've run off so they won't be able take me there. Where does the right-hand road lead to, then?"

"It leads to the plain, but the plain's crowded at present. Probably will be for a few more weeks!" the man replied. "All right, then! Live in the woods if you can, but remember, it'll be winter soon. And for some reason I get the impression they'll be searching for you very carefully indeed."

And then he slipped his hand in under Heriot's hair to take the back of his neck in a gentle but disturbing grip. "Why do they want you so much?" he asked.

"Lord Glass is our Lord," Heriot replied glibly. "We're under obligation to him." His companion laughed; his grip on the back of Heriot's neck tightened slightly. Heriot felt himself being shaken a little.

"That's not a true answer," the man said. "Come on. Tell me. Why do they want you?"

"It's nothing I've done," Heriot said at last. "It's more what I am. What they say I am."

"And what do they say you are?" the man asked. Heriot shrugged, and the hand tightened still further. By now the grip was painful.

"They say I'm one of those Magicians," Heriot blurted out despairingly, and suddenly knew, beyond any doubt, that he must move on at once. He swung his right leg across the horse's neck and withers, slipping from under his companion's grip toward the ground, which seemed an enormous distance below him.

The man remained sitting on the horse, staring rigidly ahead.

"You read minds?" he asked in a noncommittal voice. "You read what was in my head back there, didn't you?"

He looked down at Heriot. His eyes were a clear, shallow green, like rock pools carrying the hint of a deeper sea. "My thoughts. You knew what I was thinking." He swung himself gracefully down from the horse to stand over Heriot. "Is that why you looked so alarmed?"

"I didn't try reading you," Heriot said. "I didn't mean to. What you were thinking back there, the feeling of it, just pushed in on me."

"Well, not everyone wants his thoughts to be read," the

man remarked. He held out his hand. Heriot hesitated, then, very cautiously, he took it. "So good-bye, Magician," said his companion. "Because I'm afraid I really must move you on. No sign of anyone coming after you?"

Involuntarily Heriot turned his head to look west, though the curve in the cliffs cut off almost any view of the way they had come. Something whispered slickly beside him, but even before that whisper reached his ears, he had received a warning. Later he remembered it as a furious jolt that somehow thrust him out of the man's grasp and into the margins of the sea. At the same time something burned him, or so he thought at first, as pain slid up his ribs and slanted into the flesh under his arm. His companion's hand snatched at him, but Heriot was already free, still spinning away . . . spinning with the shock of the original warning. Suddenly knee-deep in restless water, still actively retreating, he looked up once more into those pale green eyes. The horse snorted and backed. Its master, knife drawn, advanced another step or two as Heriot moved back, his hand clapped under his arm.

"You knew that was coming, didn't you?" the man said, sounding interested. "Otherwise it would be all over."

"But I've done nothing," Heriot cried.

"Sorry!" the man replied briefly. "It's not what you've done. It's what you are. You're just too risky," he added, as if this was an explanation that Heriot would naturally accept. The horse shifted uneasily as the man gathered himself to finish what he had begun.

Heriot shrieked with an unexpected hatred as much as with fear and found he had the capacity and even the will not merely to express pain but to impose it as well. The sound he made was so startling, the man stepped back from him. As the cry tore its way up from somewhere deep inside, Heriot's wild braids of hair stirred and lifted and lashed like serpents, and he felt himself transforming. Even the sea shrank from the dreadful sound he was making. The water surged away around his legs and left him standing on wet stones. On and on he screamed with no pause for breath, until the very earth winced and shivered, toppling Heriot onto his knees and flinging the man sideways.

Over Heriot's shriek came the cry of the horse and the thud of its stumbling hoofs. In front of him the man twisted gracefully over and onto his feet again, his rising somehow a continuous part of his fall. Then he made for Heriot, his face twisted with fury and repulsion. Heriot let himself tumble, rolling over and over, leaving a series of brief, bloody patches on the stones behind him. The man overtook him, grabbing at him and swinging the knife high—and at that moment something enormous struck both of them, tearing them apart once more. Emerging from confusion, Heriot found himself scrambling back into the shadow of the bee-tling cliff, while the freakish wave that he had somehow commanded rushed wildly back once more, then swept in toward them again. As his enemy, hampered now by soak-ing clothes, came forward, Heriot could see he had lost his knife. However, he was still implacable.

"I could strangle you with one hand," he said, which was true.

A single stone fell from somewhere above and smashed at his feet. The man lifted his eyes to the cliff under which

Heriot now crouched, and his expression changed. Shingle and dust began trickling lazily from somewhere overhead, but Heriot did not take his eyes from his enemy.

"We'd both be buried," the man said. There was a flicker of reluctant awe on his face.

"Not me," Heriot croaked, and believed this was true, although he could only guess at what the man might be seeing. He was certain he did not have a cry left in him, yet he clapped his hand over his left eye and took a breath, curling his lip back once more, feeling his face somehow alter, as he smiled a smile he knew he had never smiled before.

"Don't!" the man cried, stepping back, grimacing as he did so. "After all, you can't prove anything," he said, speaking to himself, but also as if Heriot would understand just what he was talking about. "And after all, *I* am the Hero. I'm beyond the law. I've never backed off from any man," he added contemptuously, glancing up at the cliff again. "But you, you're not a man. You're a sad little monster."

Then he spun on the wet stones and walked away, rounding the headland without once looking back, leaving Heriot lying on the stones behind him.

For an hour Heriot lay like this, his gaze so fixed, his breath so shallow, that anyone coming on him might have believed him dead. But then, suddenly, he sighed, sat up, and looked at his scarlet side and the dark patch on the ground. He stood; he walked out from beneath the cliff, turned, and looking up at it, saw its entire face cracked into a puzzle of fine lines, an incoherent version of the ancient inscription in the kitchen at home.

"Watch out!" said Heriot in a new, hoarse voice. "Watch

out, you! Watch out! I'm a sad little monster." Bleeding, exclaiming, warning his shadow, and threatening his recent murderous companion, he began wandering, caught up in a strange dream woven both of pain and the curious impression that the person feeling that pain was not a true person but a figure in a story that had never been told before.

He dragged himself through bushes, climbed a slope, and came back, at last, onto a definite road. Home, he thought, was somehow behind him, but he must not go there. Instead he wandered on, swaying and mumbling, until he came to a place where the road divided, the wider and better-kept part of it swinging to the right, the narrower and more uneven track turning left. "I'm not going to their city," he said aloud. "I'm going the other way, whatever way that is. I'm going there."

And he stepped onto the left-hand path, limping along, curving around two bends, after which he found he must stop, for everything hurt too much, and since it seemed he must have saved himself by now, he had an inner permission to lie down peacefully.

THE BATTLEFIELD

How long he lay there, seeping blood and dreaming, he could not tell, but a sound made him look up. At the same time he felt an advancing shadow suddenly moving across him, and then stopping. He looked up and saw that a cart had drawn up alongside him, and the man driving the cart was looking down at him with curiosity and concern.

"What's happened to you?" the man asked. Heriot felt it was a question he had been asking himself over and over again, and since he didn't really know the answer, he couldn't tell anyone else. All the same he sat up, wincing as he did, inventing a possible reply.

"I had a fall back there," he said, waving his hand vaguely. "I cut myself." His voice sounded strange and lost in his own ears. "I banged my head. Broke a rib, maybe."

"I'm on my way back to the plain," the man said. "I reckon there's room for you to lie in the back of the cart, but don't go bleeding on my trade goods."

Somehow Heriot scrambled into the back of the cart

and flopped down once more, filled with immediate relief, for he no longer had to think about direction or taking step after step. Moving onward and away was now the horse's task, not his. Unexpectedly he found the world spinning away from him, and filled with relief because someone else had taken over, he did indeed fall into a sort of sleep.

In this sleep he dreamed he was sitting on that high windowsill once more, but staring, now, into an empty room. The bed was there, straightened and somehow deserted. The fur coverlet was smoothed out for once. And that agile boy with the odd-colored eyes who had always been there, staring back at him as if he was somehow expecting Heriot to give him a message, was gone.

★ ★ ★

He woke with no real idea of how much time had passed. All he knew was that the cart had come to a standstill, and tilting his head sideways, he could see the man had gone too. The horse was hitched to a hitching hook in a stone wall and was feeding from a nose bag.

Heriot sat up slowly. Ahead of him stretched a great plain cupped by hills. It seemed as if he was on the edge of a shallow bowl of open space, but that space was seething with an energetic life. He was surrounded by tents, some of them so large they looked like castles of canvas. And there were people coming and going . . . men for the most part . . . soldiers, perhaps, Heriot thought vaguely, men with hair cut very short and swords at their sides. A few of them were as dark as he was, but many more of them were marked by a fair stubble and glanced indifferently at him out of blue eyes. He was in a world of strangers.

OVERLAPPING DREAMS

Heriot breathed deeply and felt the breath go into him like a thrusting spear. The blood on his shirt was stiffening as well as staining. Under his thin cover he could still feel a movement, as if tiny insects were running down his side, but he took no notice of this faint trickling. Above everything else, Heriot was consumed with raging thirst. He looked into the maze around him. Somewhere there must be a place where he could find something to drink.

Moving gently, as if he were a fragile bubble-man who might burst at any moment, Heriot edged himself up, then slid down from the cart, to stand, looking around vaguely before setting off, unaware of the curious glances he was attracting, unaware of just how strange and out of place he looked with his long braids of hair and bloodstained shirt, wandering through a city of tents that was preparing to celebrate a great and powerful declaration of peace.

He hadn't gone very far before he was challenged. His arm was seized, and he thought, at first, it must be by one of the soldiers. But as he turned, wincing, he found himself face-to-face with a young man—not much more than a boy, really—almost as ragged as Heriot knew himself to be. And there, behind this boy, was a group of other boys, all looking at him as if he were something to be eaten and enjoyed.

"You! Who are you?" the young man asked him. Heriot stared back, blinking.

"Go on! Who are you?" the youth asked him again, shaking him this time, looming over him.

Heriot gasped a little, pierced through and through by the pain in his side. His name, even in his own head, no longer made any sense. It was nothing but an echoing sound. "Who are you?" he had been asked. Well. Who was he?

"I . . . I don't know," he stammered at last. "I think I'm a dream man."

"A dream man?" his captor cried derisively. "Dream this, then!" And, saying this, he raised his left hand and struck Heriot a swinging blow on his right cheek. The other boys cheered. Heriot staggered in the savage grip.

"Why?" he yelped in protest. "Why? I've done nothing to you."

But in some vague way he understood that this gang had been skirmishing around, looking for something to torment, some stray dog perhaps, something that would suffer and die for their entertainment, and to them, bloodstained and alone as he was, he had become that stray dog, a dog that would never be missed.

The grip on his shoulder was twisting him to the ground, and suddenly they all closed in on him, striking and kicking, while beyond them, fair-haired soldiers marched by as if nothing was going on. He tried to connect himself to the power he knew to be lurking somewhere within him, but for some reason he couldn't touch it. Perhaps he had used it up, protecting himself from the knife of the naked stranger. He remained nothing but a tired boy being beaten by others.

Better to be killed by that other one, Heriot thought, swinging up his arms desperately, trying to protect his head. *Better that knife than being kicked to death. Quicker!*

But suddenly another voice was shouting, shouting imperiously as if it expected to be obeyed. "Leave him alone! You there! Leave him." And his attackers fell back, while, bruised and bleeding yet again but free from his enemies, Heriot, who had screwed his eyes tight, rolled over, then opened them again.

The first person he saw was a girl . . . a girl in rich clothes staring down at him, as shocked as if he were an animal being slaughtered in front of her. Then he looked at the person in the act of dropping onto his knees beside him, and found himself staring up into odd-colored eyes, one blue and one hazel, blinking under a mop of mouse-colored hair . . . someone Heriot recognized, even though they had never met before. And, as the boy stared down at him, Heriot saw his expression changing . . . saw him jerk back on his heels as if he, too, had been given a shock, looking so startled, his startlement was almost a form of fear.

"You!" the boy cried softly. "You! Hey! You're my ghost. My ghost." He looked over his shoulder at the girl standing behind him. "This is *him*! The one I told you about, the one who's been sitting on my windowsill all these years." Then he looked back at Heriot. "I'm the only one who's ever believed in you," he muttered.

Heriot took a breath. "Fair enough," he mumbled. "You must be the only one. I don't believe in myself either. Not right now."

The boy began to recover from that first shock.

"You can't be a ghost," he said. "Ghosts don't bleed. You'd better come with me and I'll take you to our doctors. We'll work it out later—that you-and-me of things, I mean. The dream business."

Slowly, slowly Heriot stood up. He was glad to have someone friendly to talk to. The sound of his own voice began to make the places around him real. He was also glad to be with someone slightly smaller than he was, someone who could be leaned on easily, though before he put his hand on the boy's shoulder, he looked rather doubtfully at those grand clothes.

"Likely I'll bleed on you," he said. "Most of the bleeding's over, but it keeps on starting up again. And that kicking will have set it off."

"Forget it," the boy said. "They'll clean any blood off me." He laughed. "It's what they're there for, to make me respectable." He laughed again, a curiously wild laugh, as if he were joking with something beyond reason.

"They won't make me respectable, not ever," Heriot mumbled, still panting a little.

Suddenly the boy, who was also his support, stopped. Heriot, head bent down, could feel that they were making way for others. Shadows moved across them. Horses' feet drew alongside, shifting and shuffling in the mud. Feelings of apprehension flooded Heriot, but they were not altogether his own feelings. Somehow he was feeling his companion's response to the world in front of them. Heriot looked up, expecting to see strangers, but to his astonishment, an astonishment immediately touched with a kind of weary despair, three of the four riders were known to him, two because he had met them before, and the other . . . Heriot let out a sound that was half a groan and half a growl.

THE KING, THE HERO, AND THE MAGICIAN

The foremost rider, the stranger, was a man in blue and gold wearing a golden helmet that was also a crown. Lining himself up neatly on the left hand of this crowned figure rode Lord Glass, while on his right was the magnificent man who only a few hours ago had tried to kill him, dressed in velvet and lace now, but not too grand for Heriot to recognize. And he could feel the man's inner shock, like some sort of echo of his own, as their eyes met. *How did he get here?* they were both asking themselves. But he dared not spend time staring back at his enemy. Instead he let his gaze slide on to the fourth rider . . . a white face looking out of the shadows of a black hood. As he met the eyes staring out of this white face, they blinked rapidly, and the face seemed to shrink away from him, deeper in under the hood, as if it were trying to hide in shadows.

And now, in spite of his pain and his tiredness, something ferocious happened to Heriot. He'd never met the hooded man, yet he knew him at once. He recognized the quality of the power this man gave off, and knew—beyond all doubt—that since he had been a small child, perhaps from his very birth, this man, this creature, had been aware of him, had somehow hovered over him, had somehow fed on him, feasting on the power that now seemed to be so much a part of him, and throwing him into huge disorder. At last he was confronting in a tangible form the consuming essence that had torn into him over and over again in his nightmares, triggering agonizing headaches and the violent, twisting fits that had so disfigured his early childhood. He was face-to-face with the predator who had torn him in two and who had forced some part of himself to hide behind a black window in a lost part of his head. But up on the hillside, with Cassio's Island on his right hand and his home on the left, that protecting division, that black glass, had dissolved. He might be confused. He might be troubled and exhausted, but standing there in the city of tents, he was almost a single man once more.

"Dysart! Who is your friend?" asked the crowned rider in a grave and formal voice.

"He's just—oh, someone I saved," the boy who had volunteered to be Heriot's crutch answered, with something almost impudent in his voice. "As you would know, Lord King, the edge of a battlefield is a great place for saving people."

"Those others tried to kick me to death," Heriot mumbled, "but this one saved me. Maybe that's why I've sat on his windowsill all those years—maybe I needed him to know me when the time came." The men on horseback stared down at them in silence. Their expressions didn't change, yet Heriot felt an odd startlement thrilling through them, as if he'd just answered a riddle they'd been asking themselves for years—a riddle they had all largely derided. "I knew him straight off," Heriot said, then paused. "But I only know one of you," he added, lying quickly, somehow knowing that lying was the safest thing to do just then. "I know Lord Glass."

Now Lord Glass opened his mouth, but the boy called Dysart raced in to speak first, glancing sideways at Heriot.

"You're in grand company," he said. "This is my father, the King of Hoad. And that's Carlyon the Hero of Hoad, and Izachel, the Magician of Hoad." He spoke the formal titles as if he were making fun of them.

There was no way of truly taking in everything he'd been told. For all that, Heriot felt himself straightening, and then, incredibly, he felt his battered face twisting into that ominous smile—that smile he had smiled only once before. He felt that smile fly out from him . . . and felt the riders receive it . . . each one in a different way, though momentarily, they all seemed to shrink from him.

"Some Hero!" Heriot said, directing his smile at Carlyon.

"Just for a moment my breath was quite taken away from me, but I can clarify things," Lord Glass said quickly. "Lord King, this is none other than Heriot Tarbas, the boy who—"

The crowned King turned sharply, interrupting him.

"What? The one who . . ."

"That very one, Lord King. Right at this moment he might look like a scrap left over from the battle, but I promise you, he has the power. Dr. Feo will confirm it. Heriot Tarbas, it seems you have had some adventures since I saw you last."

Still partly supported by Prince Dysart, Heriot continued to stare at Carlyon, Hero of Hoad. He dared not look at the Magician—that shadow of a creature—just a little beyond the King and the Hero.

"Too many adventures," he said at last. "Too many to tell about. I'm nothing but a secret man." He saw the Hero's tight expression alter and saw his hand, which had moved to hover over the hilt of a sword that hung at his side, move back just a little. "I climbed and fell," Heriot said. "Broke a rib, maybe."

He barely understood what he was saying or why he was saying it. It was partly because he feared that, even in that grand company, the Hero might strike him down. Yet, even as he lied, he felt the secret he shared with Carlyon suddenly twist and turn into a sort of power within him, for he knew something about the Hero of Hoad that no one else knew, and the knowledge was not to be carelessly spilled and wasted.

"I think perhaps I should take Heriot Tarbas to the doctors' tent," Lord Glass said. "After all, he's from my country. His family are my people."

"And I'm coming with him," said Prince Dysart quickly. "After all, I'm the one who found him. I rescued him."

"I've sat on his windowsill and looked in at him a thousand times," Heriot told them once again, but he was telling himself, too.

"Put him on my horse," Lord Glass told Dysart, and

Dysart bent, cupping his hands so Heriot could put his foot on the small platform of locked fingers and hoist himself high into a saddle so grand that in a curious way it seemed to Heriot he had lifted himself into a safe room with invisible walls.

"I'll take him on," Lord Glass said. "Prince Dysart, you've been a friend to him, so walk with us."

Heriot felt himself hunching forward, longing to lie along the horse's neck. And as they left he heard Carlyon the Hero of Hoad saying, "Perhaps he is some sort of Magician, but did you see that smile he gave us? He's a monster as well as a Magician."

By now Heriot thought he might be right.

ON BEING PROTECTED

Linnet would remember forever the way Dysart behaved when he came upon Heriot being beaten and kicked by other boys. They had been walking together, arguing and joking, speculating about the possibilities of peace—a peace that would last. They had been arguing in a curious, lighthearted way, laughing at each other's arguments, and it had seemed to Linnet that their voices were weaving a pattern of thought in the air around them as they danced along through a little forest of ideas.

And then, within seconds it seemed, Dysart forgot her completely. He had leaped in to save the strange beggar boy as if the boy were a friend of his. And the beggar sat up, bleeding, bewildered, and staring, covering one of his eyes as if seeing Dysart with both eyes was too much for him. Afterward, though she followed them and even asked questions, it was as if she had ceased to exist. Linnet was taken aback to find how deeply this sudden exclusion hurt her feelings and how angry she was with Dysart, who was apparently able to forget her so easily. When, later that night, back in her parents' tent, Linnet was told that she and her mother were to go home to Hagen in three days' time, she was delighted.

"I've had enough of this place," she said, but her mother, who was brushing her own hair, did not look up or smile an agreement.

"Your father thinks it is too dangerous for us," she said. "They say there's an outbreak of sickness among the camp followers." Her voice was calm . . . too calm for Linnet, who wanted her mother to rejoice. She wanted her mother to make their return even more real by flinging her arms wide and singing, "Home to Hagen!"

So she flung out her own arms and spun around joyously, dancing on her mother's behalf as well as her own. She saw her skirts spinning too—a wheel of colors.

"Isn't it wonderful?" she cried.

"Of course," her mother answered from behind her veiling hair, and Linnet came to a sudden stop.

"Don't you want to go home?" she persisted, made suddenly uneasy by her mother's curious calm.

"Of course," repeated her mother, sounding like her own cool echo.

"I'm tired of all this," Linnet went on, not wanting to explain that somehow the third Prince, the mad one, had become a friend and, being a friend, had also been able to hurt her feelings by suddenly ignoring her. "I want to be home again. Will Father be coming with us?"

"Soon . . . soon," said her mother, her words sounding like the beginning of a sad song.

"It's all starting again tomorrow," Dysart told Linnet when they met that afternoon. "Carlyon's back again. And so's Lord Glass. They're close to working it all out in ways that suit everyone. That's a victory for my father. And then we'll have a party and we'll all go home."

"I'm going home now!" Linnet told Dysart triumphantly, and this time his expression did change. He looked at her with a dismay that made her feel like a significant person once more, but for some reason, the fact he had this absent-minded power in her life annoyed her.

"What? Now? Back to the ice and snow where nothing ever happens?" he asked half-jeeringly, and Linnet had her revenge by agreeing joyously.

"It's beautiful up there," she cried. "It's the land of white hares and eagles. I'm Queen of the Sky in Hagen." Then she was suddenly alarmed to find herself sharing a secret game she'd played with her father ever since she was a little child. But Dysart had paused, his odd-colored eyes still fixed on her face.

"Queen of the Sky?"

"In Hagen we're close to the sky," Linnet said. "I can almost touch it. Someday I will."

"You'll never grow tall enough," he declared.

"I'm catching up, though," said Linnet, and this was true.

In the late afternoon, still bickering, they walked out on the plain with members of both courts to witness a riding display by the gypsyish Orts, who, having been part of Tent City, selling horses to those who had lost horses in the great battle, were now about to take the road again. Their wagons, painted canvas stretched across hoops of willow, were making ready to travel down through County Doro and onward into the heart of Hoad. Linnet stared, as she always stared at the Orts, half-enchanted by this display of an ancient but unknown history passing by.

The King, his Lords, the Hero and his campaigners, and the Dannorad Hosts were seated on platforms spread with furs. Betony Hoad and Talgesi sat side by side, while the King's Dragons made a place for Luce to stand beside Carlyon of Doro. And there, sitting on the edge of the noble crowd, was the boy Dysart had rescued only the day before, with Dr. Feo standing over him. Linnet saw Dysart staring at the boy.

"Who is he?" she asked, annoyed once again by Dysart's sudden concentration on this stranger. The boy had been washed and tidied up and dressed in warm clothes. His many braids of black hair had been concentrated into a single long, thick braid of black that hung like a rope over his shoulder. Seeing them there together, he smiled and lifted his hand, palm outward. Linnet thought there was something in his smile that shouldn't be there. He was smiling at Dysart as if they were close friends . . . had known each other for many years.

"Nobody knows," Dysart said a little complacently. "Mind you, they're guessing away." She was immediately sure there was something he wasn't telling her . . . something secretly thrilling. She made up her mind not to gratify him by asking any more questions. But then he said, lowering his voice, "I told you. He's the one, the one who's been spying on me all these years. And I can feel him recognizing me." Linnet was about to ask questions after all, but her mother's maid nudged her into silence.

There was a ceremony in which the captured banners of the Host were given back to the Dannorad Dukes . . . a sign of the Hoadish King's determination that there should be goodwill and peace between Hoad and the Dannorad. And then the riding began.

Linnet had wanted to stand with her father and mother, but once again she found herself standing off to one side with other children and their nurses and attendants, set between her maid Lila and Dysart, with Dysart's watchdog Crespin a step behind them. At first it was entertaining, and they all applauded the elegant tricks of the horses with true pleasure, but then Linnet couldn't help boasting sideways to Dysart—boasting, yet again, of Hagen, of its pure skies and strange stunted forests, and of Warning, the volcano her family displayed on their banners.

"But it's only one little county of Hoad," Dysart said at last, in a lofty voice, boasting back at her, grinning as he did so because he knew it would annoy her.

"It isn't," Linnet argued. "It's high above Hoad and the Dannorad. . . ." She sketched its height with her arms. "It's the country of the air."

"You are the air," Dysart seemed to say, and she was about to smile, thinking he was agreeing that she was the Queen of the Sky, when she realized that what he'd really said was, "You are the heir." She nodded proudly. Someday Hagen would all be hers. It was hers now, intricately hers, hers in everything but name.

"But what if your father has a son?" Dysart asked unexpectedly.

Linnet knew she would be displaced by a son, but she couldn't believe her father would really allow Hagen to be taken away from her.

"I'd still be the heir," she told Dysart. "I was born first, and my father wouldn't love anyone more than me."

"Crespin says your father has fallen in love with a Dannorad girl," Dysart muttered, pointing secretly. "That one there!" Linnet looked in the direction in which he was pointing and saw a group of Dannorad women watching the riders. At the front of the group stood a girl with long braids that fell almost to her knees. She was half-veiled in the Dannorad fashion, but she looked as if she might be very young and very pretty under her layers of silk gauze. Linnet thought of her father's unexpected remoteness and her mother's sad voice saying, "Soon! Soon!" She was taken over by a dark astonishment that turned almost at once to fear, swelling rapidly into fury.

"What do you know about fathers? You haven't really got one," she hissed as cruelly as she could. "Your father is too grand to be father to anyone—especially anyone *mad*." And she glanced scornfully across at the distant golden image of the King, sitting in the great chair, his arms folded in front of him. The honey-colored fur that lined his helmet shone like a circle of light around his forehead; the spiked helmet made him look as if a rod of gold was thrust down through his skull and neck to merge with his straight spine. The clothes were so grand that the face between collar and helmet hardly mattered at all.

"I told you that," Dysart said, looking serenely toward the mountains. As he did so, the sun, settling into the west beyond them, came out from behind a bank of cloud, so that within seconds not only the sky but the mountains and the plain—the very ground under their feet—were dyed with a wild light.

Far out on the plain the Ortish horsemen had gathered for their final stampede. A cry set the horses galloping. The whole horde thundered toward them, the ground trembling under the impact of hoofs.

Dysart suddenly turned to her.

"But I don't need a father," he cried. "I'm protected. I always have been. I can feel the protection. It's around me now. It's never been as close as this. Watch me!"

And then, without waiting for a reply, he leaped away from them all, sliding away from Crespin, who exclaimed desperately as he grabbed for him. But Dysart had broken free—he was running out onto the plain toward the oncoming horses. He cartwheeled twice, then ran again. Almost no one saw him to begin with, except Crespin, Lila, and Linnet. Linnet, impressed by a crazy exultation in his running, was almost tempted to follow him just to show him she could be free and crazy too, but Lila caught her arm, moaning and exclaiming under her breath, while Crespin gasped and groaned and swore, as he set off running in a desperate but lumbering fashion. He had no chance of catching the mad Prince. Looking around wildly, hoping for some sort of rescue, Linnet saw the King and the Hero leaping to their feet and, vaguely, saw the strange boy raising his right arm high, as if he were giving a command.

Springing into the path of the oncoming horses, bright in his crimson clothes, Dysart looked as if he were on fire. Determined rather than graceful, he came to a sliding stop and flung his arms wide as if he might fly up over the stampede. Even those riders and horses who saw him weren't able to halt their furious pace—they rode him down, and he vanished under their hoofs.

The noise was astonishing. Some of the Ortish riders, either failing to see him or too caught up in the power of their charge to change their mood, raised their clenched fists, saluting the King. Then they swept on by and were gone. The grass was crushed flat. Yet there was Dysart, standing as straight as ever, his arm still flung up high, turning toward Linnet, smiling back as if he was dedicating a clever trick to her. Linnet stared at Dysart, then, still staring around wildly, saw the strange boy collapsing. Dr. Feo was bending over him—he was being watched over. She looked back at Dysart, wild, triumphant, and standing tall, while beyond him the horses seethed and reared and neighed, touched by some huge alarm.

Now there was something new to be talked about. There was astonishment beyond reason . . . an assertion of the power of Hoad. And the next day a wild rumor began to circulate. The King's Magician, the strange Izachel, had vanished. There was no longer a man of mystery to stand at the King's elbow to tell who was being devious, who was lying, who was planning alternative possibilities to those the King preferred. Izachel had gone.

But by then the King's Peace was mostly worked out between Hoad and the Dannorad. The King had been formidable, yet generous in a way no victor in history had ever been. With or without his Magician to tell tales on other men at the table, his agreements and treaties would be signed and the Peace of Hoad would become more than a dream. And, the rumors ran, he already had a new Magician, a strange child of power. The land of Hoad might have taken away one blessing from its King, but, so the whisper went, it had delivered another.

Linnet didn't get a chance to speak to Dysart again on the edge of the battlefield, yet on her way back to Hagen, and over the next five years, she thought about him every day, remembering him, tiny but untrodden and triumphant, making it seem, for the moment, that he was the true center of that great plain set in the ring of mountains, able to hug the sunset, the charging horses, Linnet of Hagen, and time itself, every wild moment of it, along with everything around him, to his heart.

INTO DIAMOND

Diamond! thought Heriot, looking out at the world but keeping his horse's ears in his line of vision. He was grateful that, in this world where everything else was too dissolving to be guessed about, he could still recognize a horse and still feel himself to be a confident rider. *I'm being taken to Diamond. I'm being treated with glory.* He laughed, shaking his head.

The horses ahead seemed to be moving up into the air, then sinking away. The King's procession had been winding up a hill—one of a line of hills—and now it had begun winding down again. Heriot and Dysart, following the flow, came in turn to the hilltop and were able to look down on the other side.

There, where a broad river met the sea, on a delta made up of little islands, was the confusion of a great port, and behind the port a city contained by a straggling outer wall and two inner walls, one inside the other. It was a city of guildhalls, libraries, arching galleries, markets, houses, and streets whose intersections were celebrated with conduits, fountains, and statues. From the hilltop Heriot felt as if the city already knew him and had leaped forward to take him over. His first sight of Diamond was like a soft explosion somewhere inside his head, but by now he knew his head was untrustworthy. The city was too big to be looked at properly, even from the hilltop. There was one shape, however, that stood above all others, seeming to stare directly yet blankly back at him.

At the city's heart, set on a long island in the river, a huge irregular shape pointed to the sky, sprawling sideways even as it stretched upward—a castle with four towers. And just beyond those towers on the far side of the river lay yet another great block of stone, a building so dark it seemed at first to be a deep shadow cast by one of the towers. Remembering the stories of his brother, Wish, and Nesbit, Heriot was suddenly sure he was looking at Guard-on-the-Rock, the King's home, and its black companion, the huge prison known as Hoad's Pleasure, humped and poised like a monster, blind and crouching, about to spring out on the world. The biggest tower, the one standing at the head of the island, looking out to sea, was the oldest—older than history itself.

When the men of Hoad first sailed up to the mouth of the Bramber River, they found an empty country . . . or so their particular story declared, since they didn't count the Travelers or the tribes and families, like Heriot's own, as a real population. Yet that old tower, the Tower of the Lion (like the Tarbas ruins and the broken aqueduct) had been standing there to greet them, proving that well before the days of the first Hoadish King there had been a powerful people in the land . . . people who had vanished, leaving empty shells behind.

The tower just behind it must be the Tower of the Swan, the tower of the old Queen and her women. That third tower, built of dark stone, would be the Tower of the Crow. After that Heriot had no idea. Impressed without wanting to be impressed, Heriot followed Dysart down the hill toward the first of the city gates, riding into early afternoon.

Passing through a grubby outer settlement, they came at last to the first wide gate, set between squat towers from which they were watched but not challenged. They moved on through the gate into a street so crowded it seemed that even the procession of a powerful King must be halted. But people hurried to stand back, bowing their heads as the King rode toward them, and then, as his horse moved on, they began shouting and waving, somehow becoming part of his victorious progress. Everyone in these streets seemed to have blond or brown hair, blue or gray eyes. Everyone appeared to belong to a different race from Heriot's own.

"This is the Third Ring of Diamond," Dysart called across to him.

"I knew it must be," Heriot replied, not wanting to seem too much of an ignorant peasant.

One marketplace, crowded with stalls, then another, and a few streets farther on, a third. The markets were not hugely busy, for most business was concluded in the morning. Nevertheless Heriot was confounded. People shouted up at him and he received an unwelcome shock, for though the crowd was genial he could barely understand a word they were saying. There were so many voices and so many accents all struggling against one another.

The idea that he was dreaming, that at any moment he would wake up at home or under the tree by the road, nudged Heriot continually. He knew his clothes and his long hair must make him stand out, riding as he was in the company of Lords and Princes, and the thought of being looked at by so many strangers became increasingly alarming. He glanced sideways at Dysart, smiling and waving, responding to something in that shouting welcome that Heriot just could not recognize. But, after all, this was Dysart's city. This was Dysart's home. All the same, after a little while, Heriot felt the city reaching greedily toward him, embracing him. *Mine!* The city of Diamond was telling him, in a voice both passionless and possessive, *Now you are mine!* Then it fell away to cleave and divide before him, unrolling its tangle of streets, and then, having declared its power over him, seeming to lose interest in his progress.

It was the names and mottoes on the wagons and carts that most distracted Heriot. It seemed as if the city was constantly sending messages into the world. LOVE ME; I'M YOURS, said one. DEATH OR GLORY, said another. BEWARE THE DEMONS OF THE NIGHT! warned a third. Quick, painted words flew by, often before he had a chance to catch them, so he gave up trying with something like relief.

On they went, then on again, past taverns, past crowds of people waiting by a bakehouse for their bread and roasts to be given back to them, past open drains, past stalls that sold little sausages and pies, reminding Heriot that he was ravenously hungry. On one street corner men, setting dogs to fight, suddenly straightened, stared, and cheered. Other men and boys, furiously kicking a stuffed leather ball, leaped back as the first guards advanced before they, too, began waving and cheering.

The procession of the returning King came toward the second wall of the city, an inner wall, yet almost as well defended as the outer one. They passed through huge gates into the Second Ring of Diamond, emerging into wider spaces and rather emptier streets . . . streets where banks and business halls pushed ahead of ranks of houses. There was a crowd here, too—but a different crowd, a better-dressed crowd, less jostling and noisy. Many were on horseback. All the same they, too, gave way before the guards, flung up their arms, and cheered, just as the poorer people of the Third Ring had done, for the King's victory belonged to everyone. The King raised his right hand in a calm, remote fashion; Prince Luce and Prince Dysart waved back with pleasure; but Betony Hoad, the oldest Prince and the King's heir, barely acknowledged the applause. Sometimes Heriot, looking over his horse's ears, could see Betony Hoad inclining his head as if agreeing with some secret proposition . . . some unvoiced argument. But he didn't wave, and Heriot, who could only see his back, knew his smiles would be tight and frosty. Luce, the second Prince, flung his arms wide, and Heriot knew he would be smiling widely. Betony Hoad didn't want to be part of this occasion, even though it was a celebration of Hoad, and Hoad was part of his name. Luce was rejoicing in the glory of it all, making himself part of the glory, and Heriot suddenly knew that in his own mind Luce *was* the glory. It was certainly what he wanted to be.

And then at last they came to a third wall—the innermost wall, its stone cloaked in ivy—and there before them, filling the whole view, were the towers of Guard-on-the-Rock, rising above its own gardens, orchards, and lawns, looking over them remotely, as if they did not exist.

"Home!" said Dysart. "My home, anyway. Yours, too, from now on."

"Not mine," said Heriot. "Not ever!" And then he added, "But it looks a good enough stopping-off place."

Dysart laughed. "Yours, too," he repeated with emphasis. "Wait and see!"

Heriot heard the clang of the great gates closing behind him.

PART TWO

THE RAT OF DIAMOND

A MAN OF **DIAMOND**

After a few scrambling days, Heriot was transformed. When he was led past mirrors, he looked sideways and didn't recognize his passing image, though it wore his face and hair. It was made grand by new clothes—by black and gold, velvet and silk. Silver glasses sat on his nose, correcting his uneven sight; threads of gold were plaited into the single braid he preferred these days.

Within a few days he found himself seated at the right hand of the King, with the expectation that he would read the minds of those men bowing below him, something that was often easy to do, for even their most secret thoughts seemed to reject their own secrecy and leap toward Heriot, as if he (and only he) could give them the recognition they most desired. The thinkers of those secret thoughts didn't always speak the language of Hoad and needed translators, but for the most part, Heriot had no trouble reading them, for thoughts expressed themselves in a language beyond all others, often at variance with the words coming so swiftly out of the more formal and controlled mouths. Some councilor from the Dannorad would assure the King of friendship and cooperation. *But I am a trick,* the statement would say, flying into Heriot's head. *I am more than a trick. I am a lie.* Then he would look up and meet the eyes of the liar, who would regularly hasten to adjust what he had just said, trying to change it into some half truth, laughing a little nervously. *Of course it's not as simple as that, Your Majesty. We have nothing but good intentions toward Hoad, but of course we do have aims of our own that must be acknowledged. . . .* and so on and so on. Often Heriot would meet the eyes of some messenger and see them filled with hatred, would feel mad cats of hostility striking in at him, claws unsheathed, but he quickly learned to protect himself.

All the same, to himself he was no longer a complete self. Part of him was being endlessly devoured by the city. His days belonged to the King, as he sat performing his strange function at the King's elbow, reading treacheries and envies out of the court around him, just as the King's vanished Magician, Izachel, had once done.

He also found himself able to arrange strange illusions and astonishing entertainments for the royal court, and the King was pleased with him. Lord Glass praised him. And then, of course, there was Prince Dysart. Linked as they were by the memory of those early dream days when he had sat on the wide windowsill of Guard-on-the-Rock, staring into the Prince's bedroom, saying, "Know me! I know you!" . . . linked also by the curious moment when, to his own astonishment, he had somehow dissolved the Prince under the hooves of galloping horses and then reassembled him, though he was still unsure how he had done that.

They had a strange friendship. Heriot needed Dysart as a sort of brother in Guard-on-the-Rock . . . as a family. And Dysart needed Heriot if he was ever to grow beyond being the mad Prince.

Dysart's behavior was now calm and rational, but his madness was still remembered. It had been strange beyond any other sort of strangeness, and had become one of the stories that wound through all the Rings of Diamond and out into the world beyond. Dysart now had Heriot as a friend, and underlying that friendship was the memory of their shared childhood dreams . . . of Dysart looking out of his bedroom window and locking gazes with Heriot, sitting on the window ledge looking in. Heriot knew he was valued—more than valued. Where Dysart was concerned, he had become a necessity.

When he wasn't sitting beside the King, he went with Dysart and other noble boys to a series of studies—accounts of the bewildering history of Hoad, of its victories, its defeats, its adjustments and readjustments. Once the ruler had been a single King, but then Cassio, the Hero of the time, had become so revered, so loved by the people, it became necessary to give him equal honor with the King. Since then Heroes had ruled over their small island kingdom; and the Hero sat, like a glorious twin, beside the King on all grand occasions and whenever the policies of Hoad were being formed. But there was one great difference between King and Hero, for Heroes were not allowed to marry or have children, in case the children of the Hero should try wrenching the Kingdom of Hoad from the children of the King.

"It works," Dysart told Heriot.

"It mightn't work forever," Heriot said. "What if the Hero wants to marry and have a family? That's what most men want to do."

"The Heroes want to be the equals of the Kings," Dysart replied. "The power to rule Hoad, that's what they want to share. Betony Hoad will be King one day, so Luce practices to be the Hero. He wants to be equal in power to Betony when the time comes. Mind you, my father wants him to marry, so I suppose he will."

"And you—what do you want to be?" Heriot asked innocently enough, but immediately he was flooded with the knowledge that Dysart, too, yearned to be King—that Dysart longed for the throne far more than Betony Hoad, who wanted something for himself far beyond being either King or Hero. On occasions when the court assembled for some festival or other, and Heriot slid briefly into mind after mind, touching them all and persuading them into sharing the magical illusions he created for the King's entertainment, all glorifying Hoad, he could feel Betony Hoad watching him with an envy so intense he shrank from him. For Betony wanted something beyond simple humanity. He wanted to command the sun.

The work Heriot did had a sort of mysterious triumph about it, and yet, as time went by, he felt increasingly sure that, whatever his powers might be intended for, they were not intended to winkle out the secrets of diplomacy from heads that could not defend themselves, nor to invent entertainments for the glory of the King. Yet that was exactly what he had been brought there to do. Even his good and growing friendship with Prince Dysart was touched by the curious knowledge that someday Dysart would want to make use of him in an undefined way. And, as he obediently followed orders, he felt not only Dysart watching him with secret expectations, but also the outside city constantly peering in at him, guessing about him as it tried to shape him to its own needs. At times he felt himself becoming a toy of the city—a powerful toy, but still a toy, his strange powers reduced to mere functions of the court, when, he was certain, they had some other vast purpose he could not define. Day after day . . . day after day . . . time went by.

* * *

Heriot woke.

Five years. That was his first thought. He had been Hoad's Magician for five years. And this morning, as on so many other mornings, he woke feeling that the source of his strange powers—that wild, disconnected part of himself he often thought of as an occupant—was being somehow misused. It was not intended simply to serve Kings. Somehow he was being blocked from being the complete self he was intended to be—he was being reduced to a series of freakish functions. "Where's the rest of me?" he asked the plain walls of his room, a room that had never, in all the five years he had slept in it, seemed to be really his. It contained him obediently, but he didn't live in it. Though he asked his questions aloud over and over again, it never had any answers for him . . . not even an echo.

Five years. He had been in Diamond for five years and during that time had seen very little of his family.

Hey, you! he said to himself, moving to his single window and staring out into the city. *This place is eating you. You're not a full person anymore . . . you're nothing but a magical machine, being cranked on and on by the King and Lord Glass.* The words ran like a hunting pack through Heriot's head, carrying a suggestion with them . . . more than a suggestion . . . a commandment. *Take charge of the city out there. Be free of the King and Lord Glass. Be independent of Dysart, even if he is your friend. Remake yourself. Remake yourself today.* This command welled up in him, and was accompanied by yet another inner order. *Celebrate your five years. You're seventeen. You're grown up. Be free.*

His suddenly dominating wish was to be out in Diamond, wandering in the city without a Prince on his right hand or a Lord on his left. He put on the silver-rimmed glasses they'd given him to wear and stared out across the castle bridges and into its retreating gardens and orchards. Five years good! Five years—the same five years—frightened, sometimes for himself . . . often *of* himself. It was partly being frightened by what might happen next or by what he might become that kept him good. But this morning his dream had nudged him. Time for a change.

Five years, the city declared incessantly, as he walked over the bridge linking the inner island dominated by the towers of Guard-on-the-Rock and its dark shadow, Hoad's Pleasure, toward the First Ring gardens and promenades.

To get into the gardens he had to walk through an alley of cages—the King's Zoo—past a lion and a lioness, whose cage gave onto a spacious run, past a long pen with a leopard. All this was ordinary enough, perhaps, but then the cages changed. The wire nets held small gardens and sheds that looked like cottages.

Standing in her garden, watching him go by, was the two-faced woman, a woman watching the world with a face that was ordinary enough, even pleasant. But if she turned around, she had another face on the back of her head, a fierce little face, rolling its eyes and continually dribbling and grimacing. Dysart declared she was happy in the zoo; her life in the city had been a wretched one, and Heriot thought this was probably true. She seemed to give off a sort of relief he picked up as he passed by.

But this wasn't true of the man in the next cage, a very tall, dark man, tattooed all over . . . the illustrated man. Every inch of his skin was covered with tiny pictures linked by curious designs. He was both man and map. This man gave off fury and despair, as a fire gives off heat and light. Every so often Heriot would stop beside this cage and stare in at the man, amazed to find how the tattoos created some sort of barrier between the man displaying them and anyone looking in at him. The cage seemed to contain . . . not a man but a moving design, and no matter what feeling flowed out between the bars to merge with Heriot's own moods, it seemed impossible to see the actual man everyone knew must be lurking behind those patterns and pictures. The lines and images cut into his skin somehow turned sight back on itself. There seemed to be no looking past them.

"Five years!" Heriot kept muttering to himself, echoing the city's announcement. "Which means it's just a bit over five years since I took off for Cassio's Island and met their

Hero." Half-unconsciously he touched his side, tracing the old scar under his silk shirt and smiling a curious smile alive not only with self-mockery but with menace as well.

He strode along, anticipating with pleasure the solitude of the orchard, planning to locate that richer self that seemed to be waiting to embrace him somewhere out among the apple trees, only to find a moment later that the orchard wasn't as deserted as he had supposed it would be.

Through an arch of green in the dense hedge that divided the orchard from the neighboring orchards, he saw Betony Hoad's companion, Talgesi, standing quite stiff and still, almost as if he was on guard, though Heriot knew there was nothing there worth guarding. A moment later and he was looking into a square, sunken garden, clasped around on all sides with low hedges, empty of flower beds but with a graceful fountain rising out of a pool where water lilies sometimes bloomed.

Knowing at once that Talgesi was very unhappy, Heriot turned away, hesitated, stopped, spun around, and then walked back again.

"You're not feeling so good, perhaps," he said tentatively. "Can I help in any way?" The other did not reply, but someone spoke from beyond him.

"Magician, is that you?" said the voice of Prince Betony Hoad. "It must be. No one else I know has an accent like that. Come here."

Heriot grimaced but stepped, obediently, all the way down into the sunken garden, becoming yet again a function of Diamond.

Prince Betony Hoad sat beside the fountain with a little

crumbled bread in a silver dish, feeding the fish. He studied Heriot for a moment in his deceptively gentle fashion, and then spoke dreamily. "Unbraid your hair!"

"It's very long these days, Lord Prince," Heriot said apologetically. "And there's a bit of a breeze. It'll blow everywhere."

"But why make yourself fantastic and then hide your fantasy?" asked Betony Hoad. "Just do as I say. Don't argue."

Heriot, watched by both men, reluctantly unplaited his hair from a braid as thick as a rope.

"What a thunderstorm," Betony Hoad said appreciatively. "Now you look rather more exceptional. I heard you speak a moment ago to Talgesi. How long have you worked for me, Talgesi?"

"Twenty years," Talgesi replied in a colorless voice. "Since we were both learning to walk, Lord Prince," he added, almost whispering.

"Talgesi and I are saying good-bye," Betony Hoad explained. "I am to be married. My future wife's father, the King of Camp Hyot, has decided his daughter is old enough to bear the rigors of a royal marriage, and my father has decided that a program of stringent virtue might enable his heir to act as a man and husband and even father in due course—so good-bye, Talgesi." The sun shone on the Prince's smooth face, revealing fine lines about his eyes. "I don't care, you know," he added. "Talgesi was nothing when we first met, and he is almost nothing now. For myself, I'm prepared to marry." Betony Hoad closed his eyes. Then he opened them again and looked at Talgesi. "He's so unhappy, I don't think he'll live long."

"People can find new friends," Heriot said, looking at Talgesi. "Even people who're only halfway lucky."

"There's a difficulty there." Betony Hoad now gave Heriot a glance of satirical reproof. "I wouldn't fancy being part of a succession . . . even to be the first of a few would be most distasteful to me. I just don't know how we can resolve it. If he were a man of honor, he'd kill himself, but he seems to be dithering."

"Dear life!" exclaimed Heriot. "Would you do that, if it was you?"

"But I'm not honorable," Betony Hoad replied. "I don't have to be. I'm noble. And of course I don't want him ever being happy without me." He looked sternly at Talgesi, then turned back to Heriot again. "And so you've been in Guard-on-the-Rock five years today, Magician?"

Heriot's amazement must have showed.

"Oh, I very well remember riding back from the battle-field and the great welcome as we came in." Betony Hoad got to his feet and took Heriot's arm. "Walk with me down the path until it divides." It was an order, not a suggestion. "It's only a few steps away. Then I will wind my way back over the Bridge of the Lion, to meet the Lords from Camp Hyot who are here to negotiate my wedding plans. And you will doubtless take a few deep breaths, then go to your studies with Dysart and other noble boys, where I understand you distinguish yourself admirably. Mind you, I must say I think you could try harder to eliminate that unfortunate accent."

He stepped forward, pulling Heriot with him.

"Talgesi, do try and make up your mind," he added,

speaking severely over his shoulder. "I don't wish to have to take matters into my own hands."

"Lord Prince," Heriot declared, "what you are suggesting is wicked!"

"Oh, I do hope so," said Betony Hoad. "That young man is only a dull machine unless he suffers. So it's five years for you? You've been very quiet . . . a little boring, really. But here we are. I go my way and you go yours—if you have a way, that is. Good-bye, Magician—and run hard, won't you?"

"Likely I've got a bit to run from and a bit to run after, Lord Prince," Heriot said, emphasizing his slow speech very slightly.

"Likely you have," said Betony Hoad, and, grimacing and turning away, he walked off along a broad, paved path toward the King's Zoo and the Bridge of the Lion.

Heriot watched him go, then thought a little about the day ahead of him. The King wouldn't need him today. There were always those studies, of course. Yet suppose it really was time for rebellion? As he thought this, there was a spasm in the air, an agitation that resolved into something like a rapid muttering in his ear. Once again the stones of Guard-on-the-Rock had begun instructing him. *Be free! Be free!*

Replaiting his hair into that single braid as he walked, Heriot moved out from under the trees and onto a wide path that followed the green curve of the towering, ivy-covered wall toward the gates between the First and Second Rings of Diamond. There were guards at the gates, but Heriot knew the passwords. No one questioned him as he moved into the Second Ring.

It was like coming into another world. Early as it was, there were people up and about, setting up their stalls, trading, and tallying.

In one of the Second Ring marketplaces among relatively elegant stalls, between a man mending broken china pottery with his own mixture of egg and lime, and another concerned with spices, stretched a busy counter piled with vegetables and baskets of gooseberries, raspberries, and oranges. Heriot, stopping to buy an orange, suddenly had the strange feeling he had seen a face he somehow recognized. Or perhaps it was a face his occupant wanted him to know. He turned slowly, sure he must not seem too urgent.

There beside him at the stall was a child thief, a boy of about twelve, practicing his art. Heriot stared. *I know that boy,* he was thinking. *But how can I know him?* The child stared into the air while lifting with incredible speed and skill orange after orange from a row of baskets, slipping them into the front of a baggy shirt. *Who is he?* thought Heriot, searching his memory, but that particular face, though familiar, was nowhere to be found . . . and yet the certainty that he knew the boy strengthened.

The boy caught his eye, hesitated, and then smiled, a smile of such vitality and shared fellowship that Heriot, though he had paid for his own orange, was instantly won over. The child's face was thin and bruised, but the smile was entirely joyous. Even as Heriot marveled, there came a shout from behind the baskets of fruit. The smile vanished. The boy spun around, weaving desperately out into the scrambling crowd without waiting to see if, in fact, the cry had been directed at him. A moment later one of the Second Ring wardens pushed past Heriot in pursuit, and Heriot, worked on by that mysterious sympathy, first put out his foot to trip the warden, and then began to run too, though there was absolutely no necessity for him to get involved in someone else's wild adventure.

REFUSING TO BEND

Hagen was barren but always beautiful, a county of long winters and short, brilliant summers, of winds, lakes, and stunted forests. In the northeast, the volcano Warning, its plume of smoke perpetually streaming, reared up between fans of rock where nothing would grow except pale medallions of lichen or small, tough shrubs. Yet, in the spring, whole slopes could be transformed overnight by a sudden flowering of silken poppies, delicate as tissue but tough enough to survive the harsh winds. They survived because they knew how to bend. But the volcano, rather than the flower, was Linnet's chosen sign—an unyielding cone with fire at its heart. All the same, bending of some sort became unexpectedly necessary.

Until the expedition to the edge of the battlefield, Linnet had always had her mother's full attention, but suddenly all that warm concentration shifted and focused passionately on someone else . . . a child forming inside her. She acted as if she were trying to create a son through concentration . . . by some perfect act of will. She performed ancient rituals and even invented spells, anxious not to miss out on any right magic, no matter how accidental, that might allow her to bear the Master the male heir he had always longed for. Her love for Linnet was still there, but it became more and more distracted.

Meanwhile traders, selling precious glass and woolen cloth and buying hides, furs, and fire opals, brought stories from Diamond . . . stories of Luce, who had left the city to fight under the command of Carlyon the Hero on fretful borders in County Doro; of Betony Hoad's perpetual arguments with his father; or even stories of Dysart, the younger Prince, the lesser one—the unexpected one.

And suddenly it seemed, according to the gossip, as if Dysart himself had nothing better to do with his life than to fling it away. One morning he had been seen leaping and scrambling along the walls of Guard-on-the-Rock, dancing on edges hundreds of feet above the river. Cornered, at last, by the King's guards, he had listened to Dr. Feo's appeals, laughed, and then flung himself, arms wide, into space, plunging eagerly toward death. But, incredibly, the river caught him, cradled him safely, and swept him on to a wharf in the mazy, active port beyond the castle. There he had hauled himself out, still laughing and apparently joyous, to sit on stone steps, dripping and drying in the sun. But this was, perhaps, his last mad adventure. From then on, stories suggested, he had quieted down. Gossip also suggested he had become a friend of that weird, magical boy who had replaced the vanished Izachel at the King's court and become the Magician of Hoad. There was no way secrets could be kept from the King when his new Magician was sitting at his elbow, and the magical displays at the King's banquets spread overwhelming enchantment over everyone who saw them in the King's Hall.

These stories of Guard-on-the-Rock, a castle she had never seen, distracted Linnet, particularly when her own home was filled with the sense of hard, cold waiting. The baby was born at last, and it was indeed a boy, but he died and Linnet's mother died with him.

Linnet imagined that from now on she and her father would stand back to back, facing outward against both the Dannorad and Hoad, protecting Hagen and each other, too. But her father was negotiating a new marriage before the end of the year, and his second wife, the daughter of a Dannorad Duke, was the same shy girl Dysart had once pointed out to her.

Linnet refused to bend. No matter how her father threatened, Linnet would not sit sewing at her stepmother's elbow or listen meekly as the newcomer gave instructions in a soft but determined voice to the stewards of the castle (*My castle!* Linnet would be thinking. *Mine, not yours!*). Shouting and swearing aloud, she would break away, run down stair after stair to the stable, saddle her horse, and ride out across the tilted plains of the plateau, yelling at the sky, consumed by thrilling rage, until she was hidden by forests where the prevailing winds bent all growing things to the north, so that whole hillsides seemed to be paying some sort of deference to Hoad. Even with everything pointing the one way, it was still possible to get lost in the forests of Hagen. Paths were soon stippled out by layers of tiny, round leaves or by a deep cross-hatching of needles. Among the trees lay hundreds of small lakes gouged out by retreating glaciers, milky, blue-green eyes staring steadily upward or, depending on the season, dreaming under lids of ice.

Linnet crouched, shivering and looking deeply into these eyes, waiting for a revelation that never came, until cold drove her home to her father's rages and, sometimes, to a beating. But by then, disobedience seemed the only way to get his full attention. She was glad he found her difficult, and yelled back, reminding him that Hoad was not happy with a Dannorad marriage, particularly as there had been times over the last two hundred years when Hagen had struggled under false masters—all Dannorad men.

And now, from time to time, alone in her room, Linnet studied herself in the glass, willing her freckles to fade or fall off, leaving her skin pale and pure, or wishing her hair might fall in golden waves rather than standing out around her face like a rusty bush. But her freckles and her hair persisted. It was her treacherous body that began changing. "Don't change," she commanded her reflection. "You changed before I did," her reflection reminded her. "You're the first traitor."

Standing in front of the polished glass, Linnet remembered Luce with his first and last unwilling smile; she remembered Carlyon of Doro, and then, abruptly and deliberately, she made herself think of Dysart. He leaped up obediently in her head every time she called him, arms outspread, offering to embrace the galloping horses, yet smiling sideways at her. Something inside her tightened, then melted, and that strange, thrilling spasm dismayed yet fascinated her. She invoked him over and over again . . .

turning and smiling . . . turning and smiling . . . a puppet of her will. Was he drawing power from his new friend, turning himself from a mad Prince to a clever one? Was he so obsessed with the Magician that he had forgotten her? Then she would shrug. It was all such a long time ago—years ago now, five years. She was seventeen . . . well, almost seventeen. And she was the heir to Hagen.

But then one day, after yet another fight, her father looked at her mildly, speaking in a voice that was almost loving again.

"Linnet, my dear girl, life is too difficult for us all. You need a new father, one who can do the right things for you."

"You're the only father I can ever have," she said, far more frightened by his suddenly kind voice than she had ever been by his angry one.

Her father's reply was not a true one. It was a ceremonial formula.

"The King is father to the children of Hoad. I'm sending you to Diamond. It's time for you to go. You're too rough, Linnet. Too wild! But in Diamond you'll be one of the ladies who attend the old Queen . . . you'll make friends . . . have the best tutors . . . you'll have more chances to read there than you have here."

"You'll learn to be a lady," said Shuba, Linnet's stepmother, sewing in a corner. The Master glanced over at her, and Linnet suddenly understood that certain kinds of love could make every previous love irrelevant. She understood something else, too.

"Is it because you've married into the Dannorad?"

she blurted out. "Are you sending me there to make the King feel safer about you and her? I'll be like a hostage, won't I?"

Her father looked away, frowning. "There's no point in arguing," he said. "You've made life impossible for us all. You know you have." Then he added, "Shuba is going to have a baby, and I don't want her troubled."

"Hagen is *mine*," Linnet whispered. Her words could not have been heard on the other side of the room, but the Master read her expression.

"I do want to have a son, yes!" he exclaimed. "I want my land to have a true Master. Is that so terrible? As for you, dear girl, I want to protect you. Women are destroyed by ruling!" He looked into her eyes. "We're going to Diamond, and that's my final word."

THROUGH A HOLE IN THE WALL

I F THE WOLF IS NOT BEHIND YOU, HE IS BESIDE YOU. Heriot read these words, painted carelessly on a blank wall, as he ran, twisting wildly through the crowds of the Second Ring—crowds who largely ignored him. The street boy Heriot was chasing turned as he ran, clenched his fist, and shook it once in a gesture of triumph. His sharp features broke into that brilliant smile, and there among the indifferent, jostling crowd, he suddenly danced—danced a few steps with astonishing grace and elegance.

"Well, what about that, then," Heriot said rather blankly, continuing to stare at that familiar—that impossibly familiar—face, marked on its skin and around its eyes with the infections prevalent in the Third Ring. "Hey! Who are you? What's your name?"

"No name," the boy replied, shaking his filthy hair, which was, under the dirt, the color of honey and butter melted together. "No name, no history."

"Come on, you've got a name," Heriot said. "Don't get clever with me. I could read you like a book if I wanted to."

He was astounded to hear himself adding this, like one child boasting to another.

"Some can read," the boy agreed, looking interested. "Not me. Do you have one?

"One what?" Heriot asked. "Oh, a name. Yes, I've got a name. Heriot." His occupant moved in him, unexpectedly insisting that the gift of their shared name was only half of what was needed.

This is the one, the occupant was saying. *This is the one.* Over and over again. Heriot shook his head, trying to shift things into an understandable order.

"What's your name?" he insisted.

"I'm called Rat, mostly," the child admitted, "but my name's Cayley, which is my first name littled down. Before that it was grand and noble, all that, but it's nothing but a stump now, shrunk to nothing. Just do this, do that, bring this, carry that, stand up for me, lie down for me. Give me! Get me!" His voice sounded hoarse, as if one of the city coughs had him in its grip. He laughed softly to himself, though nothing in his rapid babble sounded funny to Heriot. The boy looked desperately pale, as if he were the victim of some shocking illness, yet for all that, he gave off such exuberance that there was no feeling of death in him. Around his neck was wound and rewound a man's sash, once beautiful, now shredding away, its embroidered butterflies unraveling in threads of blue and scarlet and gold.

"Where's your home?" Heriot asked, knowing as he asked that it was a stupid question. He was rewarded with the wild smile once more.

"Home? Me? Everywhere! Nowhere!" said Cayley, and laughed again. "No home for me, only hidey-holes!"

"Where do you hide, then?" Heriot asked, determined to pin the boy down.

"Wherever I tumble," Cayley said. "I flatten out and no one sees me. It's all city land, 'n't it, and me"—he flung his arms wide—"rats *are* the city, right? I know all the ways in and the ways out. I know its hidey-holes more than most. This city wants me dead, but me—burn it all up! I stay alive." He started to trot away, looked back, and jerked his head. "Come on."

Heriot moved after him. It was impossible to be sure of the age of such a wolfish child, so battered, so desperately thin, but Heriot guessed he might be twelve or thirteen. His teeth were astonishingly good for a Third Ring child, which added to his predatory appearance; the irises of his weeping eyes were deep blue, set around in scarlet inflammation.

"You going into the First Ring?" Cayley asked.

"I am," Heriot said.

"I'll come with you," the boy announced. "You're strange, and I fancy strange company. And you feel like a sort of good luck. And me—I need good luck. Always I need it. Over and over again! If I don't get it free, I have to steal it."

"They won't let you through the gates . . . not unless you know the passwords," Heriot said.

"Passwords!" exclaimed the boy derisively. "Likely *you* have to know passwords. But me, I don't need those. I've got my cleverness. All ways open up to me."

Heriot smiled, moving on. The boy came too, not so

much walking beside him as dancing around him, singing a little under his breath. The stolen oranges bounced like impossible breasts under his dirty shirt.

An evening bird sang somewhere. Just for a moment it was almost, thought Heriot, as if he were back in the country again. The gates between the Second and First Rings came into sight . . . a distant barrier at the end of the road they were on, but Cayley grabbed Heriot's arm.

"This way," he cried. "Sideways! I know where to go."

Heriot hesitated, then turned sideways and followed obediently, increasingly fascinated by this dancing, smiling ruin of a child. Walking through the Second Ring, he felt unconsciously sure he could glide into any of the heads bobbing past him on those crowded streets. He had always been unconsciously sure he could invade their thoughts and dreams any time he wanted. But he could feel the boy Cayley was somehow defended against his powers, and, paradoxically, this tempted him to try an invasion. He half tried, and came up against a barrier of a kind he had never encountered. Until then every mind he had tested had opened to him to some extent. Every head had its secrets, and though Heriot shrank from intruding on secrets, he knew they were there. But this child presented him with blank obstruction.

By now they were up against a section of the city wall that divided the First Ring from the Second. *He'll have to stop now,* thought Heriot, yet the boy slid in under the ivy that grew over this part of the wall, just as if he were slipping behind a familiar curtain. Heriot hesitated, then felt his way in after him.

At first he could see nothing in the dark green dusk but twisting stems and the undersides of crowding leaves. Then, as he became used to what dim light there was, he made out a dark oblong, put out a hand to touch it, and found he was touching nothing but space.

"I'll never get through," he said, speaking to the vanishing head and shoulders of Cayley.

"Try," said Cayley, his voice coming back in a muffled command. "Breathe in! Pull yourself down into yourself."

Heriot tried, angling his wide shoulders. He breathed in. Pushing himself, half-sideways, into this narrow slot, he inched his way forward, stopped to gasp, then wriggled on yet again. Slowly, slowly he groped his way into yet another curtain of ivy; dived down under it, twisting as he went; and broke out into the evening, only to find himself once more rolling on the grass in one of the sprawling outposts of the orchard he had left hours earlier, with the towers of Guard-on-the-Rock looking down at him through the branches of apple trees.

Heriot scrambled to his feet.

"This way!" said Cayley. "Slink along!" So they slunk through trees, which were reaching out to the breeze and beginning an illusory dance of their own. The trunks seemed to change places, curving their branching arms toward the sky. Cayley, trotting a little ahead, was so flecked with evening light he sometimes seemed to break up and vanish into the dappling of the very last sunlight and advancing shade, flashing in and out of existence.

Suddenly the mazes of this arboreal dance fell apart,

revealing nothing more sinister than an old gardener's cottage, falling into disrepair, three rooms of plaster bricks, packed earth, and stone built up around a timber frame, grass growing tall against walls that had once been white. Heriot had sometimes seen it there during his wandering in the orchard, but he had never really thought about it as a place that might be lived in.

"I sleep out here sometimes," Cayley said. "I'm the rat of the city out there, but then, as well, I'm the King's neighbor. Hello, Mr. Your Majesty!" He waved at the Tower of the Lion, visible through the leaves and branches of apple trees.

Then, bending down by the door at the back, he struggled to remove two blocks of plaster and compressed soil, and wriggled through the space, turning to fit them back in behind him. A moment later the front door opened grudgingly.

"I bolt it up, see," Cayley said as proudly as any Lord showing off a new estate. "Mine these days." Heriot entered a dim, dusty little room lit by whatever daylight seeped through the sheets of oiled linen stretched over the windows and through a hole in the roof. As he looked around him, thinking of his own room in Guard-on-the-Rock, he felt an idea forming.

I was happy here, said his occupant. *I will be–I am–I was . . . happy here.* But Heriot already knew it had no recognizable sense of past or future. He leaned his back against the wall and slid slowly down to sit on the floor, resting his elbows on his knees and his chin in his palms. He could live here himself. He could belong to the King, yet have solitary, stolen times among the apple trees, times when the history of Guard-on-the-Rock and its Lords, Princes, and Kings wasn't a necessary part of the air he breathed. Perhaps he could find his way back to being a total self, rather than a mere aspect of the King's power. He watched Cayley take a long-stemmed pipe from a ledge, then take a flint from beside it and strike it against some stone half-buried in the floor beneath them.

"It's been a strange day so far," he told Cayley.

"Aren't they always?" Cayley said resignedly. "Every one of them!"

"You live by stealing?" Heriot asked.

"Stealing and finding," Cayley agreed. "My stomach—it's glad of anything it can get. No questions. And what it gets, it holds on to. Well, mostly it does. It gets all sorts," he added, in case Heriot was unclear on this point. "I've et what they put out for dogs. I've even et rat stew, which is not too bad, all in all. Hard on the rats, though."

Heriot laughed, not so much at the story, which he felt was partly invented to entertain, but at the way Cayley was watching him, reading his expression intently, trying to match something in himself to whatever he read there. Down below the torn, elliptical voice of the street child, he thought he detected a faint echo of his own voice and of Radley's.

"Are you from the country?" he asked idly. Cayley looked at him warily.

"What if?" he asked. "Back a bit, perhaps. 'N't there now, am I? Not never again. Borned there, die here."

"How long have you been in Diamond?" Heriot persisted.

Cayley shook his head. "I told you before—no history." He stretched himself. "Just always now! Now, now, now, over and over again."

"What's in the pipe?" Heriot asked.

"Happy smoke," Cayley said. "I know where to gather it," he added. It wasn't just because of the happy smoke, however, that Heriot was finding himself immediately tempted by this small, dark space and the wolfish child smiling at him. Living here, he suddenly felt, he might even become a family man again, and some sort of family life would tie him back to the farm that he missed every day of his city life.

"You take a risk showing me this place," he said, and was startled when Cayley burst into laughter, spilling the oranges from the front of his shirt.

"I mostly guess right," he said. "Dead if I didn't." He pulled a particularly threatening knife out of a leather sheath at his belt and began to peel the oranges.

"I'd better get back," Heriot said, nodding in the direction of the castle. "I've been gone a long time, and they'll come looking. I'd take you with me, but they wouldn't let me keep you. Suppose I come back whenever I can, bringing some food and money?"

"Happy smoke talking!" said Cayley scornfully. "You've breathed it in. They don't let you out alone, 'n't you the Magician of Hoad?"

"Too true," Heriot agreed. "But my five years good are up. Maybe from now on, five years shifty. I'm out alone now, aren't I?" He found himself adopting the pattern of

Cayley's speech as if it were a private language spontaneously invented. It was partly his occupant talking, as it had never spoken through him before. He took what coins he had left out of his pocket. "Housekeeping!" he said, passing the money over, laughing as he did so. "But I'll have to go. Better to go and show myself, rather than be hunted out."

"No one hunts me," Cayley said through a mouthful of orange. "Or everyone does," he added rather more clearly. "No one and everyone—they're like the same thing to me."

"They only want my head." Heriot shrugged. "The thing is, there's only one of it, and I need it too."

Cayley laughed his strange, breathless laugh once more. "Too much of me, too little of you," he said.

A few minutes later Heriot left the shed, and the private feast of oranges that was taking place inside, and began walking home through the orchard.

Suddenly he heard someone shouting at him. He turned, recognizing the voice. Dysart came charging toward him though the early evening twilight.

"Where have you been?" Dysart was shouting.

"Walking! Walking in the orchard," Heriot replied. "I wanted silence. And your city owes me a bit of time."

In the next moment Dysart was beside him, glaring at him and shaking his shoulder. "The city doesn't owe you anything," he cried. "It's a question of Diamond telling you to do what Diamond needs. You're not just a Magician, you're the Magician of Hoad. Hoad! You don't belong to yourself . . . you belong to the King."

Heriot was startled by Dysart's fury. As he gaped in

astonishment, Dysart suddenly struck him on the side of the head. The blow wasn't hard, but once delivered, it took them both aback.

Dysart's grip on Heriot's shoulder relaxed. His hand fell away. "Oh damn!" he cried impatiently. "I didn't mean . . . I'm sorry, but . . ."

"Why?" asked Heriot, wrinkling his face with disbelief as he tenderly stroked his ear.

"Because . . . ," Dysart said, his voice milder now. "Because you'd vanished away, and I was frightened you'd somehow truly gone. And you're my good fortune. Don't you know that by now? The good fortune of a third son."

At that moment, as if Dysart's words had somehow given birth to a possible new perception, Heriot found he suddenly knew something—knew it in an irrational, almost visionary way. Dysart was a true friend, yet he was revealing a certain vulnerability—a certain need—and a particular possibility now buzzed out of the orchard air and lodged resolutely within Heriot.

Within a moment he decided to bargain over something.

"There's a little old garden shed behind me," he said, pointing with his thumb back over his shoulder. "I'd like to live there sometimes. Sleep there, perhaps, out among the trees. Because being among trees might make more of a Magician of me. More of a friend, too—we'd both enjoy that, wouldn't we? Not just 'enjoy,'" he added hastily. "We'd benefit."

Dysart looked taken aback. "You might!" he said. "But I wouldn't."

"Listen! It would work out for both of us if I became an even more powerful Magician," Heriot told him. "We could look out for each other. And anyhow, things are going to change for you soon," he added, reconnecting to the distraction of a moment ago. "Linnet of Hagen's on her way here. Linnet! Her father's bringing her. Won't that make Guard-on-the-Rock a different place for you?"

A RAGGED SHADOW

After his day of rebellion, Heriot settled down with a different and unexpectedly comfortable feeling about the shapes and routines of the city. The city was still there, of course, still spying on him, looking down on him from all angles, peering over his shoulder as he wrote or read, but he no longer felt like a mechanical device, ticking over within it. Now he knew that, given a chance, he could escape. And he had a new acquaintance out there . . . a boy who suddenly seemed like his own ragged shadow, struggling with words yet able to talk joyously. Not a possession of Hoad but a true part of the city, able to come and go freely. Heriot felt liberated at the thought of the boy Cayley's strange freedom, conferred by neglect, freedom that the whole clockwork of Diamond could not control, for the boy wasn't confined by any necessity except staying alive, laughing as he did so.

This secret internal image of escape and of an intermittent friendship made his routines in Guard-on-the-Rock things he was able do from day to day, no longer feeling that he had been reduced to a mere movable device. Even when he sat at the King's elbow, some part of him was out in the city, stealing oranges, dancing down streets, and passing effortlessly through stone walls.

To his surprise, Lord Glass obligingly gave orders for the old shed to be restored, so that he could use it as an orchard retreat. Heriot had won himself a place where he could enjoy a little solitude. So the season grew restful and mellow around him for a while, and though he knew it couldn't last—for no season, neither sun or storm, lasts forever—he was happy to enjoy it while he could.

A month went by with Heriot doing exactly what Guard-on-the-Rock instructed him to do—moving from under the double gaze of the King and Lord Glass to the study room and the penetrating stare of Dr. Feo, and then off over the bridge to his shed in the long orchard. Though Diamond was no longer pressing in on him, he could still feel it watching in its inexorable way, but he no longer cared.

He was the Magician of Hoad, and that was that. Nothing he could do about it. Apparently, it was what he had been born to be. Every now and then he reached beyond the city walls, out into County Glass, to touch his family and feel them farming and thriving, often smiling when no one else could see anything to smile at.

And now, like a bright, broken thread stitching through his thoughts, ran the street boy, Cayley, the rat of the city, coming and going through the hidden hole in the first wall. Sometimes Heriot's brief, stolen orchard hours coincided with Cayley's own furtive ventures under the ivy and into the First Ring. Then they would sit together in the old shed, talking about nothing much . . . simply joking, gossiping about the day, perhaps, and its casual happenings or about the city beyond the wall. *The time will come,* Heriot found himself thinking in an absentminded way. *I'll know every grain of dust. I'll walk out into the Second Ring and then the Third Ring—walk into forbidden realms—and I'll take Diamond over. But then I'll walk out of it, and beyond it, carrying it all folded up in a corner of my mind. In the meantime I'll just work on, winking at it from time to time, and it can wink back at me, sending me its secret messages.*

The daytime city swung down into darkness, and Heriot, often set free from the demands of royal duty and royal friendship, released to be a true nighttime man, came running though the orchard to his shed. He ran without hesitation, for at night he could see by something other than light.

Although he had just left Lord Glass with the King and his tight circle of trusted men, he half feared finding Lord Glass waiting for him in the garden shed, inquiring with an ironic and coercive civility whether or not he was giving his best attention to the King's business. The shed door wasn't locked, for Heriot had nothing worth protecting. He slid gratefully and easily into darkness, pulling that door closed behind him. Yet, as he did so, an even darker figure rose from the one chair behind the table.

"It's me," said a shadow among the shadows.

"I'll light a lamp, said Heriot. "Where have you been?" he asked over his shoulder.

"Round and about," Cayley answered, croaking a little. "I had this friend put down with the coughing sickness.

Couldn't just leave him to cough and die alone, could I? I'd to be nurse, even doctor to him. But . . . well, he's gone, poor bastard, dead now. Then I 'n't too good myself."

"I've not seen you in ages," Heriot said, still busy with his lamp. "I thought you might be dead as well.

"I 'n't to go yet," Cayley said huskily. "I've something to do first. Something I must do. But I'm wore down a bit." There was an extreme thinness about his voice, a flattening of its previous buoyancy. Heriot turned, suddenly alarmed, and saw for the first time just what was sitting in the chair behind his table.

The boy was reduced to nothing but a witch's doll made of sticks and bird bones, his blue eyes abnormally large, sunken back into a face where the cheekbones seemed sharp enough to cut through skin that was cracked in places with open sores. His lips showed patches of infection at the corners, and his filthy blond hair hung lanky around a face that already seemed inhabited by death.

"I 'n't catching," Cayley said quickly. "Well, not so very. But people notice me, and stealing's hard enough without being noticed. And no one wants me working for them . . . not looking like this. And I 'n't eaten so much lately—not that I'm hungry, but, well, you know." He smelled dreadful in the warm room. It crossed Heriot's mind that he might already be dead and decaying but was too obstinate to acknowledge the fact. The rags he wore were peeling away like a disgusting skin and probably filled with vermin. All the same, he smiled his transforming smile, which now seemed to illuminate his worn face with a ghastly light, showing the skull close under the skin.

"No need to do any worrying," Cayley added, seeing Heriot's expression. "I'll get by for a bit now, if I get to sleep."

In the main part of the shed, which had become pantry, kitchen, and washhouse all in one, Heriot had a round wooden tub pushed under a bench. On the edge of his fire, burned down to embers, were two ponderous iron kettles filled with water. He blew up the fire, piled on logs, and managed to produce sufficient warm water to wash his orphan of the savage night.

"There," he said, standing the tub before the fire. "You clean yourself and I'll get you something to eat. Dear life, do you call this a shirt?"

"The one that had it before me . . . he called it that," mumbled Cayley. "Anyhow, I'm not going all naked. That means trouble to someone like me," he declared unexpectedly, and Heriot shook his head.

"You don't have to be scared of me," he said. "I don't fancy you. I'm not a man who goes after boys. You know that."

"Going naked in front of other men—that takes practice," Cayley exclaimed, clutching his rags around him. "Maybe I don't fancy being seen. I have to have myself to myself. It's all I've got. Anyhow, there's no point in washing and then putting my clothes on again. Dirty within two seconds."

"I'll lend you something of mine," Heriot said. "You don't look as if you worry too much whether things fit or not."

He had already noticed the scars on the boy's throat, but

now his attention was arrested by a pattern of blue lines just below the scars, springing into intermittent prominence in the firelight, and he exclaimed in astonishment. "You're illustrated. You've got a picture on you."

"I'm a book," the boy said, "I'm to be read there, but not farther down. No words! No pictures, even."

He was tattooed with a picture of a singing bird on its nest, and the nest was shaped like a heart hung with blossoms. Beneath the picture were the words "Love and Courage."

"My mother, she paid money to have that cut into me," Cayley said with tired scorn. "Good money paid over. I starve, maybe, and all the time that bird sings on me, 'Love and Courage. Love and Courage.' I think it might be a fool, that bird. I'll try courage, but I'm not never going to love. Courage is enough for me."

Heriot didn't want to be distracted by this babble. "Forget all that," he cried. "Here's a towel. Wash yourself. I'll turn my back if you don't want to be looked at."

Cayley still fingered his tattoo. "If I die, I'll die real," he mumbled.

"Wash a bit," Heriot insisted. "Then if you die, you'll die clean."

He took a bucket and a dipper and went out to his rainwater barrel to fill it. Then, edging in to stand at what was now his kitchen bench, he cut bread in thick slices and, having no butter, put slabs of farm cheese straight onto it. He could hear Cayley splashing around behind him.

"I've been off a bit," Cayley muttered monotonously. "Otherwise I'd make do. All that happens to me, well, I get up, face up, and mostly make do. But this time round, it wasn't so easy. It was my little brother that was taken first, not me. I saw that. Back a bit I saw him taken . . . saw his blood run! I cried back then. A long time ago, that was. I never forget. Never forget that crying. But I don't cry now. These days I'm as dry as stone."

Heriot listened to this sinister prattle. "I'm not," he said. "I cry easily. I've never grown out of it."

"Once!" Cayley said, exclaiming with a strange emphasis. "I used to once. Never again. My brother dying back then, that was like a—well, it was like a sort of question. And me, I'm to be the answer. What I do finishes *his* story. Or that's how it feels."

Heriot turned back toward Cayley with bread and cheese, then turned again to get a pot of milk, stooping to stand it on the hearth. Cayley stepped out of the tub and stood, shivering and scarred, wrapped in Heriot's towel.

"Have you washed your hair?" asked Heriot, though he could see Cayley had neglected to do this. "Bend over and I'll help you. We'll get some of the dirt out and then maybe wash it again tomorrow when I've got more warm water. You look as if you might be full of lice. Fleas, too."

"I do have some of them little creepers on me," Cayley admitted. "I'm a world, and they're my citizens. But these days . . . all starve . . . them as well as me." He kneeled down and bent over the tub he had been standing in a moment earlier with the weary obedience of a blind man being instructed, step by step, up a long stair.

"What's happened to you?" Heriot cried out in sudden consternation. "Your shoulders!"

"That's just lawful punishment," Cayley replied indifferently. "What's left of it, that is. I was caught and hit a good many times when I was just catching on to my power, sometimes on my shoulders and mostly on my back. See, it's five strokes right off, to learn you better. Worse if you're fetched up before the warden. Sometimes it's hanging, but I 'n't been stretched yet. The rod's not so bad. Some captains, they know it's a hard life for us that's out there. They hit, but they could hit harder, and anyhow, hit like that you need to get away . . . you learn to be quick. And those marks, they're what's left over. I don't get caught these days. Still, you can work out why I don't want anyone looking at my skin. I don't want anyone reading what's been beaten into me."

Heriot washed the dirty hair with an infusion supposed to kill lice, one he constantly used himself. "I'll have to cut it off," he said at last. "This isn't hair. It's nothing but a mat."

"Not to mind!" Cayley comforted him. "I give up being pretty. Use my knife, it's sharp—sharpening's free."

Heriot cropped the fair hair closely if unevenly. "You'll feel better now," he said. "You smell better already." He threw the mat of hair onto the fire and watched it flare and writhe in the flames, before draping another towel across the inscribed shoulders. The smell of that dirty hair burning filled the shed.

Cayley stood, hitching the towels around him with one hand and holding the dark soap in the other. He sniffed at the soap with interest. "I 'n't think of smelling," he said, grinning briefly. "Live with it, you likely don't notice. Or care."

Heriot was still distracted by those marks of beating, old stripes crossing very old ones, now all wrapped in under towels. "You're like a wall that's been written on," he said.

"In the Third Ring they write on the walls," Cayley said, "and they write, 'Rid the world of a rascal. Die!' Or that's what they tell me, them that can read. But I'm not obliging. Anyhow, I can't read my own back."

"And what's written here?" asked Heriot lightly, as he traced the line of a scar just above the edge of the towel, the scar running from under Cayley's ear across his throat. As he touched it, remembering the ragged sash with the unraveling butterflies that had concealed it on their first meeting, he felt something wild flare up in him, something he suppressed with shame and astonishment and more disturbance than he allowed his face to show.

"That!" said Cayley scornfully. "Once my mother thought to kill me. She thought it was an act of mercy. She started thinking that love and courage and all that would never be enough. She thought she was doing me a kindness, setting me free from it all. But she didn't cut deep enough. Her hand turned cowardly. Maybe she didn't really want to." He looked up at Heriot. "Everything heals that can. You learn that at my school."

Heriot went to search for something for Cayley to wear and the boy's voice followed him, though he spoke more to himself than Heriot. "There's those that die but take no notice. Don't they just get up and go on walking. Likely I'm a bit of a ghost by now." His voice wavered, as the voice of a ghost might be supposed to do.

"Somewhere back a bit you were certainly lucky," Heriot said, coming back with a shirt of his own.

"I don't know." Cayley sighed. "It's doom, 'n't it, and I was doomed to live on."

"I wouldn't be too sure of that," said Heriot. "Put on the shirt and I'll find you a blanket." He was sure he had a blanket somewhere. After a little searching he found it, and turned to find Cayley now draped in the shirt, which came down to his knees, the towel dipping farther down beneath it. Covered, Cayley slumped onto a stool by the fire to eat the bread and cheese Heriot had prepared for him, though with nothing like the unashamed greed he had shown whenever they had wandered in the Second Ring together. Then he leaned forward and was violently sick into the wood bucket on the edge of the hearth.

Heriot exclaimed with irritation. "I should have thought!" he said. "You should have started off slowly with milk and eaten just a little."

"I'm sorry, mister. My stomach 'n't clever, not even hungry. But it hates to miss out on any lucky chance. That's habit."

Heriot laughed at him as he carried out both bucket and bowl.

"I'll do the same for you one day," Cayley persisted. "Tidy up after you, clean up after you, smiling too, that's a promise."

"A promise from a man with luck—that's worth something," Heriot said gently. He came back and searched a shelf until he found a pot of honey. "There's some milk left. I'll put this honey through it. You just sit back, don't move, don't talk."

"I talk always. First I didn't, now I do," Cayley said obscurely. "Words have got power over us, you and me both. It confuses them."

"Confuses who?" Heriot asked, busily stirring milk.

"Death, doom, that lot," said Cayley. "Off they go, fingers jammed in their ears."

"Don't be silly," Heriot told Cayley. "If you're trying to hide from doom, don't talk aloud all the time."

"Think so?" asked Cayley skeptically. He drank some of the sweetened milk, after which Heriot wrapped him in a fur rug.

"You look better already," he said, but Cayley shook his head.

"Not better, just tidier," he said. He let Heriot put him to bed and feed him the last of the milk and honey from a spoon.

"Sleep!" suggested Heriot.

Cayley looked at him, exhausted but not sleepy, twitching with restlessness. "I can't sleep," he complained. "Close my eyes, maybe, but nothing else."

"I thought you weren't a man to be afraid," Heriot said severely.

"It's not fear," Cayley answered. His hoarse voice was little more than an indignant sigh. "I just don't want to go off when I'm asleep. If it comes at me, I want to see it coming. I want to face it . . . laugh at it, tell it I just don't care."

"You'll wake up again," Heriot said, all the more impatiently because he wasn't entirely sure this was true. "Here, look at me!"

Cayley obediently turned his eyes toward Heriot, who almost casually let his occupant lead him toward a mind that at first shocked, then chilled him, as it had done from the beginning.

There was none of the usual confusion of memories, no tangle of personality, no scattered threads of old dreams, none of the assaulting legion of needs and desires sweeping out from the point affected by Heriot's entry. Once again, Heriot was in a hugely defended place, a blank place of imprisonment, doors closed, memories measured and hidden. Cayley's mind admitted no past and no future, living only in a narrow present. Though Heriot could read Lords and Princes, diplomats and messengers, though he could find his way through dark and unknown landscapes, there was no way he could read this boy from the streets of Diamond.

Cloud and Tree, the King's Assassins, had impressed Heriot as men lacking the warm variety and untidiness of other people, purposely tying themselves to a single function, but Cayley was more single than any Assassin, certainly more so than the King of Hoad, distracted with symbolic guilt and concern for his children, more touched by love than he was ever prepared to admit.

Now Cayley's singleness took charge of Heriot and turned him, aligning him along the axis of a compulsion. He found himself looking along the blade of a sword so sharp its edges seemed to dissolve into the air. And suddenly it was a blade no longer but a silver road, a causeway that led straight without any deviation into a dark mass on the very edge of sight. Cayley was aimed along that particular causeway and into that anonymous darkness as surely as if he was an arrow in a bow, though he was both archer and arrow, the actor and the act itself.

So intense was this image that Heriot struggled to break away. He had sometimes speculated that he might get lost in a complicated and tangled mind, but he had never imagined anything like this simplicity, where there were no landmarks, only a field of insatiable intention, meaningless to any outsider. Nevertheless he instructed his occupant, and his occupant spoke to Cayley, commanding sleep. Sleep took over immediately. The relaxing of the field around the despotic image allowed Heriot to break free, and a moment later he was back in his own mind, in his own body, in his cottage, a shaken and successful Magician standing over a sleeping child, ravished by illness, compelled by commitment to some secret dream of doom, statements of punishment inscribed on his skin like lines of merciless poetry.

PART THREE

CHOOSING THE CAGE

CELEBRATING A WEDDING

And at last spring came again, after which the city moved, with self-conscious majesty, into early summer. Heriot turned eighteen. (*Growing up. Growing out. Growing in,* he thought.) And at last it was that particular time the city had been anticipating . . . the time of huge festivity . . . the time of Betony Hoad's wedding. Heriot knew some great act of magic was expected of him and tried out various things in his mind, though he had no doubt he would be able to astonish people with imposed illusions. He did an inner rehearsing, strangely becoming the roses thrown and falling through the air, flower petals scattered, spreading out into the allegories acted at the gate in each wall. All the same he refused to go beyond the garden walls to join the crowds, whose spirits were high with the excitement of the febrile celebration the city had engendered within itself.

"The Hero is riding into Hoad for the wedding of Betony," Heriot muttered to Cayley. "Are you sure you don't want to see him ride into Diamond?"

"Not me," Cayley said with a strange derision in his voice. "He's got enough to watch him. He doesn't need me."

"Why not?" Heriot asked, as the afternoon burst apart yet again with cheering voices.

Two months of food and care had changed ruined Cayley back to what he had been when Heriot first knew him, a tall, tough boy, thin but broad across the shoulders, strong enough to throw off the infection that had wrestled so furiously with him. He entertained Heriot with black cheerfulness and with his scorn for the images by which Diamond sought to control its people.

Working in the garden between his royal duties, Heriot talked half to himself, half to his companion, while Cayley, not so much an incalculable visitor these days as a constant attendant who despised gardening, would stare at his face, watching his lips move, following or even anticipating his words, his own lips silently framing them, so that he was repeating these conversations a fraction of a second behind Heriot.

Cayley had begun speaking with exaggerated care and, unexpectedly, produced out of distant memory perhaps, words and expressions that came to him from the folktales of Hoad, for Heriot gathered Cayley's mother had been a great storyteller and, once upon a time, Cayley had sat cuddled on his mother's knee, in between her moments of despair and madness, listening to tales of love and death.

"It would be a good afternoon for collecting," Cayley now said rather wistfully. He meant stealing. "I used to collect a lot on busy days. I hate to lose a skill."

"Think how you're gaining one," Heriot replied, distracting him from past glories by reminding him of present ones. "These days they're trying to make a warrior of you, aren't they, even though you're only about thirteen? You work out with Voicey Landis when I'm not around. Who'd have thought it, six months back?"

"That Voicey, he's a master," Cayley declared, his face brightening with anticipation. "But I'm to be better. In the end, that is. There's others he teaches that's noble or born to it, but I'm best of all."

"I'm astonished he took you in," Heriot said. "You looked more like a victim than a victor when I brought you along."

"He fancies a fighter first above everything," Cayley replied. "There's bigger than me, prettier, nobler and all that, but Voicey, he *knows* me, he *roars* for me." Cayley was speaking familiarly of the old Warden of Arms, Voicey Landis, who worked in the castle arena, conducting the war games, the fencing, archery, wrestling—the fossilized remains of noble aggression brought to the level of a sport for everyone except Luce, and now Cayley, to whom it represented something more serious.

Heriot cocked his head at the cheering, now so close it was almost as if the sound turned trees, gardens, and walls glassy, and he could look through them all, to see Carlyon riding by on his black horse, stirred by a wind that seemed to be blowing out of the past.

"You worried that you've got to be magic tomorrow?" Cayley asked.

"No, I know what I can do," Heriot answered, "but I don't feel anything much for it. I could often be magical out of lightheartedness, but lightheartedness can't be commanded. It's wonderful in its own way, this royal wedding, but not enjoyable. It's heavy and stiff as if someone had made a clockwork horse of gold and silver and set it all over with jewels. It glitters, but it won't gallop. It just walks on stiffly to an ending that mightn't be happy."

"Happy?" Cayley spoke the word as if it was one of uncertain meaning. "You think the Prince mightn't fuck the Princess? He always does in fairy tales."

"Do you have to put it like that?" Heriot said irritably.

"It's the right word for it," Cayley answered blankly. "Everyone knows. He's to make a boy to follow after him. So what other way is there?"

Heriot was silent. In this case at least, he could think of no word that Cayley might use equally well to define the fact, hung around as it was with the fantasies of entertainment and ritual in the city beyond.

"They talk about it over in the arena," Cayley went on, "but how would they know if he did it or not? It doesn't show, does it, not on the outside."

"I'm not interested in all that," Heriot said, not entirely truthfully. "It's Prince Betony's private business."

The shouting outside the garden walls retreated. The Hero was passing through the Amphitheater of the Lion, perhaps crossing the bridge and entering the castle. Relieved of the possibility of a chance encounter, Heriot straightened up and stretched himself.

"Let's be off," he said to Cayley. "Let's go all the way down to the sea." They left by a northern gate and skirted the Amphitheater of the Lion, crowded with people who had collected to see the Hero greet the King.

Only yesterday Heriot, a step behind the King and the Princes, had stood there watching the entry of Princess Quaeda into the city arena, carried in a litter held by Lords of her own land and Lords of Hoad, Prince Luce among them. Trumpets had been blown, white doves released; the steps by which she descended into the public streets had been covered with flowers, all of which she acknowledged while being escorted—pretty, painted, and enameled after the Camp Hyot fashion—through a crowd of strangers. Assaulted by music and acclamation, the last part of this strange journey was made across tapestries laid under the feet of her bearers as she was carried to meet the King and his eldest son, neither of them less polished or artificial than she.

The King glittered in a dragon skin of gold and diamond, not natural but supernatural, as if he might, in a startled moment, put out wings and soar off after the trumpet notes of his own annunciation, a phoenix among the wheeling doves. His aura of difference surrounded him, so that he wasn't dwarfed by the wide arena, its tiered seats dappled with the faces of the ebullient men and women of Hoad. He somehow filled it with a feverish brilliance that seemed to flow directly out from him and his absurd crown.

In that moment Heriot, himself a specialized instrument of reception, felt a multitude of other minds open to take in the image of the King, gaining some personal direction from the crown. For the first time he came to believe the King was not simply the possessor of Diamond but was possessed by it, an act of imagination thrown up by the city's need. But did the King imagine the city, or the city the King? Was Hoad's image of himself so strong that he managed to project it into every other mind in Diamond?

And what of Betony Hoad, successfully transformed into a Prince of dreams? Was he his own dream, or the projection of an ancient fairy tale, shining through and focused by the prismatic surfaces of the books of Diamond?

In one of the deepest channels of the port, moving between flowery islands, chains, wreaths, and garlands flung into the sea to welcome her, guarded by men with dragon masks in front of their helmets, the ship that had brought the Princess to Hoad rocked sinuously, its brilliant banners rippling in the wind.

"Rich man's washing," Cayley said, untouched by the beauty of the silk stroked by sensuous air. Beyond lay channels filled with ships from Camp Hyot and the Islands, even one from Cassio's Island with the Hero's device on its bow, though the Hero himself had ridden into Diamond . . . had started off, of course, by riding down the Hero's Causeway, Heriot thought, perhaps watched by Radley and Wish, their wives and children, from up on the hill.

★★★

The next day Betony Hoad and Princess Quaeda were married in the crowded Amphitheater of the Lion, in the presence of the King and the Hero and various noble visitors from the Dannorad and Camp Hyot as well as the Lords of Hoad. The Magician of Hoad stood among them as a sign of Hoad's power.

And in the evening, at the banquet, Heriot was called

on to present an amazing entertainment. The hall was lighted with pinewood torches and lamps shaped like doves. Smoke collected up under its arched roof, clouding the geometry of interesting curves. The painted designs and cornices older than either city or hall, hanging between the lamps, included stone roses of so dark a red they looked black, set among circles of laurel leaves and pictures of men and women hunting and picnicking in the forest rides. The tables were set out in the form of a letter E and covered with fine linen and damask.

Hoad, dressed in gold, sat like a hieroglyph of power at the head of his table. Dysart waited on his father, Luce on the Hero, the man he hoped one day to kill with honor. Behind Hoad's chair, beside Dysart, stood the Assassin Cloud in pure white, his head glittering with its swarm of bright pins, and behind Carlyon, a purposely dark balance perhaps, was a hooded figure in black, his face impossible to see. Between the Hero and the King sat Betony Hoad and the Princess Quaeda, she looking very young, even childish, in a way she had not during her procession through Hoad. Heriot felt suddenly anxious for her, this girl delivered into Betony Hoad's life like a well-wrapped present, though the Prince, at this moment, looked particularly charming, and happier and kinder than Heriot had ever seen him.

Over the past five years Heriot had met with Lord Glass in many moods—cheerful, ironical, sometimes even angry— but he had never seen him as troubled as he appeared to be on this occasion, an occasion that seemed to Heriot to be both brilliant and successful.

"I do hope my dear . . . ," Lord Glass said in a mechanical imitation of his usual birdlike voice, "I do hope you have it in your power to perform something quite, quite incredible. You promised me forests and fairy tales, and I require nothing less. . . ."

"Look at me closely," said Heriot, but Lord Glass didn't hear him.

"I needn't hesitate to tell you," he murmured, "that Carlyon has been very difficult. Oh, very inexorable. Only the most unremitting diplomacy has saved us from a clash of personalities and a rehashing of old incidents and insults, quite out of keeping with the season of rejoicing we hope to celebrate tonight. He is too intelligent for me to think he's simply being tactless. I cannot speak highly enough of the efforts of my Camp Hyot counterpart farther down the table, who has appeared on some occasions to have been quite deaf. We have been most fortunate that he has more in common with Hoad, the same sympathies and ambitions, than you might think possible." Lord Glass stopped speaking to sip his wine.

"The thing is," said Heriot, "once Carlyon thought being Hero would be enough for him. But by now it isn't. Maybe he wants to be King of Hoad, too. Wants to be both." He spoke in an absentminded way but felt Lord Glass looking at him intently. Servants were passing around the table with jugs of rose water and napkins. Heriot was momentarily entranced by a jug of rock crystal, with a rim and lip and handle of engraved gold.

Let me through . . . , the occupant was saying within him. *Make a guest of me.*

Soon! Heriot promised, speaking back into his own head. *We'll share ourselves soon.*

"Well, we all have our theories," Lord Glass said at last. "But I do hope that you won't let us down. I just know Carlyon is planning something. There is a certain entertained restraint about his provocation, as if he was distracting us with one effect while secretly preparing another. I feel it might be demonstrated here tonight. This is a grand occasion, and—"

"We will now have the Dance of the Clown," announced the steward of the hall, and out came dancers, one of whom, the clown, was dressed as a parody of the Assassin Cloud, with a red mop-head wig sewn over with glass beads.

"In festivity we try to deflect what we fear," Lord Glass said, turning and looking at last into Heriot's eyes. His expression slowly changed as the dance proceeded, and he divined Heriot's other, inner face imposing its alterations on familiar flesh and bone.

"There is another Magician in this room," Heriot said very quietly. "What are you playing at, Lord Glass? You'd better tell me."

Lord Glass frowned, silently shook his head, then slowly looked across the dancers to the Hero and the dark figure behind his chair.

Heriot nodded. "He's strong. He recognized me when I came in, though he didn't see me and I don't think he's put a face to me quite yet, but it won't be long. He's so public there, standing behind the Hero. Something's intended."

Lord Glass said nothing.

"You know him, then?" Heriot asked. "Or do you think there's no face in the hood?"

"I think there is a face," said Lord Glass, "and that if it is revealed, I'll recognize it, but to find there was no face might be preferable."

Heriot watched the acrobatic clown weaving through the dance, nervously mocking the King's Assassins. Carlyon looked over at Heriot with a suddenly arrested expression. Heriot didn't know that the top half of his face was entirely hidden by a little explosion of light reflecting from his glasses, but he stared out of the disruptive glare and the shadow of his womanish hair with an expression so inimical that the Hero, if he had been able to read it, might have looked more cautious.

A moment later the dance ended, and Carlyon rose to his feet and addressed Hoad, praising the hospitality, the food, the wine, and the entertainment, in a warm, embracing voice. Nevertheless, as he spoke, he also seemed to be mocking the very things he was praising, with a secret derision. "I, too, shall honor Prince Betony Hoad and his bride with an entertainment," he said. "I am not without facilities. You have many entertainers, and I have brought only one, but though he is a single man, he has a strange gift. He can appear to be many."

In spite of these troubling words, however, it was still Heriot that Lord Glass studied in the light of the dove-shaped lamp that trembled above them, hoping, it seemed, that Heriot might explain just what the Hero had in mind.

"We will receive your entertainment with delight,"

Hoad was saying to Carlyon. The Hero raised his hand, the hooded figure stepped forward, and the lights went out. Suddenly the air seemed to tremble, not with any sort of joy or celebration, but with a curious savagery. A murmur arose from the crowded tables . . . a wave of apprehension filled the room. A dark possibility was making itself felt.

"Oh, dear." Lord Glass sighed. "It's doom!"

"It's Izachel, then?" Heriot asked. A face swam out of the darkness, bearded with a straggly beard, gray around the lips. The eyes were so black the pupil was swallowed up in them, which made them seem undirected. They moved constantly, pacing like caged animals anxious to escape the confines of a head that no longer suited them. If they stood still for a moment, those eyes became so round they seemed completely circular, the white showing all around the dark iris. Stillness seemed to confront them with an unbearable view.

Heriot had seen this face before, years ago on the edge of the battlefield. And he had other, more curious memories. "What did you do to him?" he hissed to Lord Glass. "What's happened to him?"

"It would seem we mourned him too soon," Lord Glass replied. "I haven't talked about him, I must confess. I didn't want to depress you." The face began to withdraw into the blackness. "We all believed he must be dead, but apparently he simply crawled away and changed masters. What is that sound?"

Light quickened. Incredibly the tables seemed to have become as remote from one another as branches in a mountain range, the spaces between them expanding to contain a rough, stony land, a plain set with distant forests. Out of those forests came the horses, heavily harnessed, even armored, bringing the light with them. Out from among the rocks rose men armed with bows and arrows, and along the top of the nearest ridge, barely visible in the gloom that bordered Izachel's magical stage, came even more riders. Voices cried from afar. The cries were faint but clear, coming out of the past at the Magician's bidding. Made thin and sinuous by the weight of time, they had to struggle to reach listening ears. Then battle was joined, and the merciful faintness of the sound of it was more than compensated for by the visible clash of men and horses. At first the figures seemed flat and simple, but then, taking breath from the tide of memory that began to surge around them, they swelled out with approximate life. Men of Diamond and the Dannorad clashed violently, and the air was filled with those threadlike but nonetheless terrible cries, for unlike the suspended figures on the wall of the study room, these men fell pierced through, chopped down, hacking one another with a graceless skill.

Confronted with spouting, twitching, screaming men, Heriot's stomach twitched with its own violence, wanting to volunteer its own comment on the spectacle the Hero was providing, but he was not sick, for almost at once, he noted a new fact with considerable interest. The moment any man began to die, he assumed a new, different kind of reality. The fighting men were approximately real, but at odd moments they might blur or sag, one eye might swell up and burst, one ear might grow larger than its partner, or a hand might detach itself, not because of any blow but according to some whim of its own, and go floating across the field like a disembodied emblem.

Izachel couldn't entirely control such a complex creation, and details were subject to strange variations. But the moment a man began to die, his reality became intense, beautifully held for the duration of this ending, every detail displayed with loving skill. Bloody bubbles swelled out of nostrils, eyes turned up until only bloodshot whites showed, fingers clutched and scrabbled convulsively while bodies demonstrated hysterical angles among the stones. Death was so vivid and painful it could not be turned away, and all were bound to witness the true horror of the hundreds of terminations that inevitably marked Hoad's success in the battle. The armies fought, irrationally disintegrating, while the true entertainment offered, there under the feet of the illusory horses, was the galvanic extremities of death in battle. Men of the three kingdoms lay crushed and oozing among the stones, or twitched in grass that was not grass but a dim green mist the Magician had not been interested in resolving into its constituent blades and seed heads.

After the first shock Heriot was interested in seeing what another Magician might do, and must have been the only person in the room not directly considering the effect that this recreation of an old battle might have on a touchy company, some of whom had fought and lost friends in such battles . . . battles still well within the living memory. The time of the friendship was a brief season; enmity was a glorious tradition.

At last Hoad triumphed. The men from the Dannorad

were either dead or fled, and one of the warriors turned to the company, showing the vivid face of young Carlyon, bloody and exultant, the age, perhaps, of Luce, who was standing entranced behind the older Carlyon's chair. But then the visionary Carlyon faded, and they were left in darkness with the violated dead before them, beginning to pass into shocking and accelerated decay under the Magician's power.

"Alas, for our past!" the living Carlyon now said, his leisurely voice coming from somewhere beyond the borders of the battlefield. "Let us all hope, on behalf of the happy bride and groom, for future tranquility." And his words were accompanied by a soft, voiceless laugh, trembling with breathless pleasure.

"Dear life, he's got to be fed with blood, that poor old Izachel," Heriot muttered, more to himself than Lord Glass, as darkness became absolute.

There was a moment of stillness, then an angry scraping. Chairs were pushed back and visiting men were on their feet, shouting and hissing with outrage. Hoad and Carlyon were being reminded of other reciprocal atrocities and defeats, of old grievances and broken promises of safe-conduct. Then, as if to accommodate any answer Hoad might have to give, silence fell, and into the new silence Heriot laughed as his occupant came pouring out of the space in his head, interpenetrating his bones and overflowing out into the darkness. *I'm giving myself over*, he promised it. *You can be free to play a bit.*

At the sound of his laughter, the stillness that had seeped into the room extended itself. Heriot fastened on the silence, taking it industriously away from King, from Hero, from angry Lords alike. Then, exaggerating his country voice, he spoke into the air of the banqueting hall, making his drawling accent a message to the Hero.

"I am the Magician of Hoad," he declared, restoring the scene in the center of the room. The dead men lay in the grass, each blade of which now became discernable while Izachel struggled vainly to hold down the concealing dark. Speaking steadily, if rather absentmindedly, Heriot used his sense of Izachel's struggle to locate him precisely. The Hero's Magician was tired and shocked by the huge power Heriot was suddenly revealing. Fight as he would, Izachel could not regain any control over the dream he had set loose in the King's Hall.

SETTING THE FOREST FREE

I am the farmer, the uniter, the twist in the air . . . ,"
Heriot said, improvising and inventing such phrases
as he thought would be enigmatic and healing to the
consternation and anger boiling in the shadows around
him. "I am the resolution of Hoad, both the child and the
brother of Draevo who records births, deaths, and unexpected meetings."

He felt Carlyon twitch unexpectedly at the mention of
Draevo, twitch like a fish caught on a line. He felt Izachel
fighting on, trying to regain some power over the minds of
the company, but Heriot, having the advantage of surprise,
of variety, and of sheer power, filled the watchers easily, letting his occupant free to flow through him and out into the
world, touching them all, gathering them up like threads
he would shortly weave into some new tapestry. Everyone
in the room—the King and his sons, the guests from the
Dannorad and Camp Hyot—all began to dream Heriot's
dream, Izachel and Carlyon, however unwillingly, among
them.

"There is no last word," said Heriot. Slowly the blood that had crept over the stones became a grassy stain, the twisted bodies relaxed, then gently mossed over as if a green blush was creeping through and through them. Their stiffening grimaces relaxed, their expressions were dazed and gentle, a slow vegetable vision reanimating their dead minds. Heriot's memory of connection with the inner life of apple trees in winter, spring, and early summer became part of his spell. Slowly, slowly the dead men rose up again, arboreal men turning faces as mild as a green spring up to the sky. A Dannorad man held out his arms, becoming a living tree, supporting flowering vines, his wounded side putting out crimson flowers, the chains that hung like a shifting metal curtain from the sides and back of his helmet transformed into leaves and tendrils.

"The mystery of the changes of Hoad," Heriot said, entranced himself by the images moving through him in answer to his occupant's call. "They enter upon a pure vocation, take in air once more, offer out brightness to the world." The faces, restful and at ease, became part of the mosaic of the bark. "Their green children grow around them," said Heriot, and up from the grass and stones came little saplings, each one completely true, for he had been there and he knew the nature of trees.

There were no words in the language of Hoad for the layers of cells or the busy inner life of the tree, but he could make others feel, as he felt, that each tree was not only a changing object but also a process of spirit. At that moment he could make each blade of grass live, each leaf, each root hair reveal itself as both one and many. The outrage of guests and hosts alike began to surrender as they were invaded by that verdant tide, remorseless but tender, too, turning them always toward the source of light, which, in that dark room, was nothing other than Heriot himself.

"Our tears have made it all grow green again," Heriot suggested, and tears obediently slid down under the silver rims of his glasses, down his cheek as, for the first time in his life, he allowed himself to fade away and his occupant to inhabit without any restraint that carefully maintained fortress they shared . . . the fortress of his head.

Trees so tall their tops were now lost in distance, smooth trunks brocaded with tiny luminous mosses, shed tears of gold that ran down the bark and then fell, burning harmlessly, into the perpetual twilight under their branches, while the forest retreated without visible end. The space between the tables, between the people sitting at them, grew vast beyond understanding. Each man and woman in the hall was alone with the trees. A wind composed of light and the breath of dragons beat through the company, rustling carefully assembled clothes and tangling hair, and there in the dimness Heriot began to shine, the broad planes of cheek and forehead remaining dark, the lines from nose to mouth and the creases of his eyelids etched on the night with fine lines of fire, each hair a thread of silver, lifting with reluctant grace when the wind blew. He appeared to be not so much contained by the air as embroidered on it.

"They have become the quiet heart of the world," he said, and though the words were his own and were gentle, the voice that uttered them was filled with unappeasable longing. A moony shine burst through him, as if he had become nothing more than a human skin, while everything within him dissolved into light. And now he felt an echoing awe and kindness, a new resolution taking form in the hall around him.

"Our brothers have blended and become the heart of the first silence and the last silence. They have gone beyond us. The old treacheries are gray dust, and only dust bothers to remember them."

He moved away from the table as he spoke, leaving the whole company, including Izachel, his prisoners, caught in his transformation so that they themselves were transformed like the fabulous dead into a woven vision of peace and gentle resolution. But unexpectedly he felt his arm seized and, turning, found Dysart beside him, trying to hold him back. Something in Dysart—some secret necessity, some element of friendship perhaps, was enabling him to fight against Heriot's spell.

"Let me go!" Heriot cried. His everyday self was coming back to him, but his occupant was still dominant, raging with the energy of its release. "Let me go! I'm not safe."

"Don't . . . ," began Dysart. "Don't go! Forget anything you ever promised me and just . . ."And then his expression changed, as the occupant surged through Heriot to overwhelm him. "Don't . . . go!" Dysart mumbled. "Be nothing but a friend, not a promise." He was crumpling as he spoke.

"I'm not safe!" Heriot cried again. His voice seemed to come from some distant and barely connected place within him. All the same he could hear his warning echo in the outside world.

But it was too late. Dysart fell onto his knees, then tumbled sideways. Heriot stared down at him, certain that anything he might try to do could only make things worse. Wildly he turned and made for the door.

The door opened before him. Unchallenged by the guards, all caught up in the same vision just as their masters were, he paused in the doorway and spoke into the mind of Hoad the King.

"Lord King, move now. The vision will begin to fade, and me—I am already fading. Share grief. Share the mystery. Move on into reconciliation and joy. Speak before the Hero moves. And Dysart's fallen. Look after him!" At the same time as he sent these inner orders to the King, Heriot touched Izachel into deep sleep and felt Hoad begin to rise, still half dreaming, preparing to follow his instructions.

At once he began to break his connections, releasing the audience, sure that he was leaving Hoad strengthened and able to correct any damage the Hero's invocation of that violent past might have done. And if Carlyon should try to challenge the new mood, Heriot knew he would not succeed.

But Heriot himself was in an intolerable condition. Kindled by his own force, he thought he might burst into incandescence through attempting to control that raging occupant, who was still burning through him, feeding on him as flames might feed on a living tree. Trying to give himself some necessary pattern to work with, he began to run out through the main doors, across the courtyard beyond, then along a familiar path toward the castle gardens. A summer wind came to meet him, leaping up like a welcoming dog, rubbing itself against him, pushing his heavy hair aside, while his forest continued to swarm out of him, endlessly reproducing, until it seemed impossible he could run himself free of it. Heriot shouted as he ran, or thought he did. He felt the cry go out of him, but couldn't hear it in the outside air and didn't know which part of him was doing the crying.

Yet, at last, the forest faded into real night and he came to recognize himself . . . just Heriot running, though, even as he ran and remembered himself, he thought he also stood still, a rock outside time, a brother to Draevo, the rock on the hills overlooking the farm. Diamond, with its restless opinions and maneuverings, fell away from him like tattered leaves in a black autumn, and history flowed under him like a river of dust.

"What am I? *What am I?*" he shouted, shaking his head, for his triumph was also a kind of despair. Ordinary humanity seemed to have deserted him. "I'm a freak of freaks!" he mumbled.

A moment later and he was surrounded by the general celebration that was briefly transforming the castle gardens . . . by peddlers selling ribbon, bells, gingerbread, dolls, sweets, and pretty laces, by jugglers and tumblers, and by men dancing an ancient dance. People ate and drank and kissed; a group of twenty men dressed in different colors walked past on beautifully painted stilts; thieves stole; gifts were bought and exchanged. On this occasion the boundaries between the First and Second Rings dissolved. Their various celebrations flowed into one another.

Heriot stood on the fringe of the unfamiliar crowd, watching them as if they were a series of narrative pictures. A hand touched his arm. It was Cayley.

"I saw you running," he said. "A mad ghost, you!"

"I am," Heriot replied, shuddering and talking not only to Cayley but also out into the fantastic city as it surged around him. "I was so keen to put it over the Hero, I nearly turned all Diamond over to the forest of night. If I was braver I'd die now on the world's behalf."

"'N't so easy to die," said Cayley, smiling. "You can't just do it for wanting. You've got to know how. I told you that."

Heriot said nothing. "Anyhow, you stopped it, didn't you?" Cayley went on. "Whatever it was, it's you here now, not any forest of the night."

Heriot, twisting his finger in his hair, began to smile in turn. "Listen!" he said in a cracking, unfamiliar voice. "I'm going to put myself where I ought to be. Come with me. You could be useful."

ENTERTAINING VISITORS

Morning had taken over the King's garden, but it made way for a distinguished company wandering among the flowers and trees. Dressed in crimson velvet, their hair frizzled into still haloes, the King's dwarfs rode their big dogs through the zoo, ahead of the noble visitors. A young girl walked beside them playing a pipe. The Dannorad Lords, Luce, Dysart, the Camp Hyot nobles, the King with his Assassin Cloud, and Carlyon with Izachel at his elbow all strolled behind the dwarfs, who were flickering like prismatic butterflies. It was a very still, hot day, summer like an unseen dog panting in the air around them.

The lions, still upset by the lights and fireworks of the night before, paced up and down their arena, complaining loudly. The woman with two faces laughed, then slowly turned, drawing aside her hair to reveal her other shrunken countenance grimacing like a very new baby.

"Poor soul," said one Dannorad Lord, grimacing himself. "Lord King, to speak honestly, I wonder at this, I really do."

"It is a head with two faces," said the King. "A warning sent to Hoad, an instruction to balance itself between King and Hero, or one will lose its power and shrivel, to blink and sigh behind the other. And this poor creature lived a hard life until she came here, where a woman is paid to care for her, even to love her. In the world outside the bars, no one would pay to have her loved."

They walked on, past the place where brilliant fish with filmy tails came up to the surface of the water, hoping to be fed, then past a gray pool from which a crocodile grinned at them, his collar glittering in the sun.

"There can't be many treasures better guarded, Lord King," said Carlyon. Hoad met his unrepentant and derisive stare, sighed, and looked away as if confronted by a wearing prospect.

"Hero of Hoad," said one of the Camp Hyot men, as if he had been puzzling over a question for a long time and had finally brought himself to mention it. "I confess I for one was rather confused by last night's entertainment. At first it seemed we were insulted, later glorified, and finally, all of us, rebuked for any bitter memories we might have. It was a strange way to celebrate a wedding."

"I was the only one rebuked," Carlyon said without rancor.

"Your own Magician placed a very distressing tableau before us," the Lord persisted, "which was alarming enough, but the compliment that followed was stranger still. Was such annihilating flattery intended to test our courage? Those trees revealed to us as the apotheosis of lost friends, as that weeping forest, made it seem as if the room had filled with spirits from the beginning of the world. I couldn't help feeling a spirit had been invoked, that we were somehow being entertained with the wrong part of our minds."

"I must admit," said Carlyon lazily, "I felt for the young Prince and Princess. To be married must be frightening enough, although that's one act of heroism from which the Hero is exempt. It would surely take the most dedicated love to successfully shut a bedroom door on such a spectacle."

"Your new Magician is not very old," said one of the Dannorad men to the King.

"He is eighteen," the King replied. "Lord Glass is our expert in the condition of Heriot Tarbas. You must ask your questions of him."

"He was born among the Gethin ruins," said Carlyon, perhaps maliciously, and the two Lords of the Dannorad stared briefly at each other, before moving on to peer at another barred enclosure.

"This is the cage of the illustrated giant," said the King, "but he is in his house." The chain lay stretched across the enclosure from the block of iron used to anchor the giant. The gardener Nidd rang the bell, the chain moved, and abruptly Heriot, the Magician of Hoad, appeared in the doorway of the illustrated man's enclosure, staring out at them without his glasses, then slanting himself across the door frame.

"I'm not quite as decorated as your last pet, Lord King," he said, "but I speak more freely. I can recite the rhymed histories of Hoad, list the Heroes who have submitted to the demon, and tell stories of Horun and Hoel, Cassio and both Martel Hoads, father and son." Self-conscious as it was, there was a defiant sincerity in his voice. Beyond the bars there was a cautious silence.

"Magician," said the King at last, "what are you doing there? Where is my illustrated man?"

"Gone, Lord King. I turned him loose," Heriot replied. "I gave him a cloak and a guide through the city . . . over to him after that. But you've lost nothing—under his illustrations, he was nothing but a man, I promise you. Safer for everyone if he goes free and I'm the one kept behind bars."

The King turned to his companions. "My Magician is young and dramatic," he said with apologetic tolerance. "He does not always enjoy the peculiarity that makes him so interesting. I shall leave him until common sense and boredom force him to leave the cage."

Heriot, rather taken aback by this easy acceptance of what he had intended as a challenge, saw that others of the group stared at him with expressions ranging from open fear to distaste and an aloof curiosity. They had all felt his occupant storm out through him into that darkened banqueting hall and seen his face outlined in light, a star, cool enough on its surface and showing, through its cracks and apertures, that it was coldly lit from within. The King, apparently on the point of moving on, turned back.

"Magician," he said. "You must know my younger son, the Prince Dysart, is still lying in a faint as the result of your enchantments. He is something of a friend of yours. Are you happy to leave him like that?"

"Dysart!" Heriot exclaimed, suddenly disconcerted. There was silence on both side of the bars. "Good for him to rest," Heriot said at last, though there was doubt in his voice. "Your city has twisted both of us. We have to take whatever shape it tells us. Maybe it's Diamond, not me, that is telling him to sleep."

"Well," Carlyon said to Heriot. "At least I think you are in the right place."

Heriot promptly thrust his hand under his arm, as if he had felt a sudden pain in his side. When he took it out, his fingers were bloodstained. "Old blood," he said. "A little more than five years old. But I'd hate to tempt a Hero into a further display of heroism. Lucky for me there are these bars between us." He met Carlyon's eyes at last. "I still think a lot about that first time we met." He held out his hand, palm upward, dreadfully stained. "And the bars go both ways. They not only keep the monster in. They keep the Hero out."

"Then we both see them as appropriate," Carlyon said lightly.

"Magician, you presume!" warned Hoad, but without anger.

"I hope to be nothing more than a parrot and say back to the world what it says to me." Heriot's voice became hesitant again. "But I nearly became a true basilisk last night. Don't be misled, Lord King; at last you've got a real beast in this cage."

"So much for the Magician of Hoad," the King said in a tranquil voice. "Let us move on and see the white foxes."

Heriot was left standing at the bars of his cage. After

a moment he went in and lay down on the straw mattress and woolen blankets. The iron collar around his leg was incredibly uncomfortable, though there was an anklet of fleece that fitted under it. He was puzzled at his own mood, which was neither one of despair or moral fortitude, but of a totally unexpected shame, as if he had been caught in some act of petulant self-indulgence.

There was a slight sound, felt rather than heard, and Cayley was with him. "They 'n't noticed the lock's undone," he said, using his old Third Ring voice, as if this was the voice Heriot would remember. "So you can come out now. It's no way homely here."

Heriot shook his head. "I'm not safe in the world."

"Don't tell them, then no one will know," Cayley advised. "I'm not safe either, but no one guesses that about me."

"I'm warning the world, trying to save it, maybe," Heriot said, and Cayley made a sound of irritation.

"It's one of those thoughtful games, but I don't play them," he said. "Wasted on me. I'm common sense, and you're nothing but poetry in this mood. Not dancing poetry neither—nothing but rubbish."

"Still," said Heriot, laughing and feeling comforted for no reason he could understand. "Suppose it was you?"

"I'd let the world go hang, and save myself," Cayley said frankly. "No question!"

They sat together in a companionable silence, but as the evening advanced, Heriot was to have notable visitors. He heard someone coming hesitantly through the orchard toward his cage. "Quickly! Hide in the hay," he told Cayley. "If they find you with me, they might take you away."

As Cayley obediently pulled hay over himself, the soft but determined footsteps came closer. For that night Linnet had not returned to the Hagen house in the First Ring. She had told her father she had been summoned by the old Queen, which wasn't true, although she visited friends in the Tower of the Swan and watched as the light of the setting sun blazed, then faded on the stone walls of the opposite tower, where she supposed Dysart must still be lying in trancelike sleep.

As darkness crept over Guard-on-the-Rock she excused herself, saying her father's servants would be waiting for her, and wandered through the mazed castle, past a library, past the door to the room where Lord Glass assessed petitions to the King, across the Bridge of the Swan, and came, at last, into the garden and then the orchards. Beyond the trees, a faint filtering of silver light hinted at an approaching moonrise.

But Linnet turned away from the moonshine. Walking into shifting blackness, guiding herself by the sounds of caged animals crying in the night ahead of her, she moved hesitantly forward, trying to remember the trees and corners from a garden walk earlier in the day, and, at last, began moving steadily onward, turning only once to look back at the castle . . . the Tower of the Lion, not so much a tall rectangle eclipsing the stars as a hollow place, into which she might fly if she had the right wings—fly and be changed forever.

At the other end of the castle the Hero's Tower blazed defiantly, lamps in every window. Linnet looked longest at the Tower of the Crow, but could see no light in Dysart's room. She turned away and walked on, imagining the ghost she had been told about, that familiar—the disconnected, prophetic, damaged part of Heriot—patiently sitting on Dysart's windowsill, herding him first this way, then that, for its own purposes. She thought of Dysart's madness and the ruffling papers, the whirlwinds of twigs and dust that had once accompanied him, like the pets of childhood, giving him the edge of incoherence that had isolated him. Dysart's wish to own the Magician had been nothing more than a reflection of the Magician's determination to own Dysart, because, somewhere along the line, he would need him.

There was a guard by the cage door. Linnet was quite prepared to march up to him and order him to stand to one side, but as she watched, he moved of his own accord, marching off around the line of cages and out of sight, so that she had time to run the last few yards, open the gate of the last in the line of cages, and scramble toward the shelter at the back. The door was so low Linnet had to stoop to slide through it, but then she immediately felt space around her and over her and stood up cautiously in the dense night.

"I know you're in there!" she hissed. Somewhere she heard a flint strike, and a flame leaped up. Heriot was leaning back against a large pile of hay, his face lighted from below by a little candle in a pottery holder. Shadows shifted rapidly across his skin. Linnet caught the gleam of his teeth as he directed a feral smile in her direction.

"What do you want?" he asked. "I mean, you're not here just to be nice to me, are you?"

"How could you do this to Dysart?" Linnet whispered,

surprised to find herself whispering, surprised, too, to hear how savage she sounded.

Heriot stared at her, biting his lower lip. "You've never liked me that much, have you?" he asked her curiously. "Why not? I've never done you any harm."

"Dysart!" Linnet insisted. "I'm here to talk about Dysart."

"Him?" Heriot said. "All right. Talk away." She could see him shrug as he spoke. "It's funny, really. I've always fancied you."

"Dysart saved your life that first time we met," Linnet hissed. "Those boys might have killed you."

"He did save my life," agreed Heriot. "Is that what you came to tell me?"

"I want him safe and happy," said Linnet stubbornly. "That's all."

"That's all?" Heriot exclaimed incredulously. "You think safe and happy is easy?" His voice suddenly tipped toward fury. "When I saw Izachel, I remembered! I remembered too much."

Linnet closed her eyes, in case her courage would somehow leak out and run down her cheeks like tears.

"And it wasn't ordinary memory. It was recognizing a voice I hadn't ever really heard before. Listen!"

She heard his breath now as he panted a little in the shadows.

"Do you know what my first memory is? My very first? It was feeling someone pushing a hook through my head, ear to ear, and I grew up with that hook being pushed into me, sometimes several times a day . . . all the way from here to here." He slapped first one side of his head and then the other. "And when I hung from that hook, I'd bleed . . . bleed at my nose and out of the corners of my eyes, even though the hook wasn't what you'd call real. But it did something real to me, didn't it? I spent hours of my childhood sleeping off the pain."

In spite of everything, Linnet was affected by the horror of his story. She waited, and at last he spoke again, sounding rather more resigned. "I thought it was just something that had gone wrong with me. Some people are born to have fits, and that's just nature. But when I saw Izachel I recognized the hook. He'd felt me out there in the country, being what I was, and he'd tried to feed on me, using the power he hooked away from me as his own. That was his particular talent. And the King of Hoad, and Lord Glass, too, without knowing it, had been pushing him into my head, day and night, night and day, until I somehow learned the trick of holding them off. Which I did. At least my rag did . . . the bit that had been ripped out of me by Izachel. That torn-away bit hid in me for years. Mind you, it came out when it was ready, and it's still there, off to one side, flapping away. Sometimes we get together, but only as—like—like twins. I should be one single thing, but I'm not. I'm two forces in the one body."

"Dysart didn't have anything to do with that hook," Linnet declared, sure of what she was saying.

"I know. He's got a kind heart," Heriot said. "Come to that, I think I must have put a hook of my own into him. I promised him a kingdom, didn't I? Not that I actually remember promising anything." He sighed, screwing up his face and half turning away from her, shifting the hay as if he might burrow into it. When he spoke again it was as if he were explaining something to himself. "The part of me they really want is that restless part that twists the world. None of them want me to move on to . . . to become what I'm truly supposed to become. And I'm a stranger to that part of myself. I know it's there . . . but I don't know what *it* knows, even if it's still me . . . even if it's me that's doing the knowing. There are two people inside my head . . . the farmer and that other one, both signaling to each other, waving from hill to hill, and then having to guess what the signals mean.

"When I saw Izachel the other night, the magic man and the farmer ran together, and I became a single man—the completed one I should be—just for a little. Then Dysart grabbed my arm and gave me back his promise, and"—Heriot gave his familiar shrug—"I must have tumbled in two again."

Linnet wasn't interested in Heriot's puzzling.

"Stop thinking about yourself all the time," she cried impatiently. "I'm here about Dysart."

"I want to stop thinking about myself," Heriot declared, frowning and staring into the dark air. "But you can't, when Kings and Princes are watching you, ordering you to do what they tell you to do, offering a sort of glory, asking for kingdoms and hooking you out of yourself. You have to wonder what you really are. Why did Lord Glass come looking for me? Why was I stolen away from my family where I was happy and driven into Diamond? I have a family—a brother, a sister, a mother, cousins. I've got a great-great-aunt. I had to leave them all behind me."

"I don't know anything about that," said Linnet impatiently.

"But if it had all happened to you, you'd start thinking about yourself, right?" said Heriot quietly.

Linnet sighed with weariness and exasperation. They stared at each other across the candle flame. Somehow Heriot had grown easier. He pushed the hay well back from the candle, then, smiling, he slid his pack of cards from his pocket and began shuffling them idly, watching the stiff images eclipse one another on the face of the pack. Suddenly he seemed at home in this cage, almost contented as he leaned easily against the rigid back wall.

"So what was it you wanted, exactly?" he asked her. "You want to say something about Dysart. What is it?"

Something new had come into the glance he directed at her. His smile was unexpectedly familiar. Confronted with that knowing smile, she suddenly found it difficult to talk about Dysart.

"There's no need for you to put yourself into a cage," she said crossly.

"There's every need," said Heriot. "I'm a good monster. Aren't I?" he added, leaning forward a little. His eyes, looking at her across the cards, widened briefly and alarmingly.

"Nobody thinks you're a monster," Linnet declared.

"Everyone does, deep down," said Heriot, "and so do you."

"You can walk out of this cage at any time you want to," she said. "It's just a game to you." All the same, she thought that Heriot might quickly become crazy enough to insist his game was a reality, and spend the rest of his life in a cage with an open door.

She passed her hand to and fro across the candle flame, making a series of little eclipses. "They say the Hero told a strange story this morning," she said at last. "He told the council he once tried to kill you."

"Oh, that," said Heriot, rubbing his ribs. "Ages back. One good thing about my life, it's never been boring." He looked at her directly. "Did he say why? Everyone thinks I know everything, but I don't. I've always wanted to know. Carlyon was as sweet as pie to me one moment back then, hiding me from Lord Glass and Cloud. And then, suddenly, he pulled a knife on me."

"He says he was thinking treason," Linnet explained. "He says you read his thoughts."

Heriot sighed. "He was unhappy," he said at last. "Dark with misery. Is it treachery to be unhappy in Hoad? Then they should hang *me*. You too."

"He said it was treason," Linnet repeated. "He said he acted on impulse."

"Some impulse . . . ," Heriot muttered, looking back at his cards. "Yes, he tried to kill me, but I saved myself. Then, later, I ran off, trying to hide, and after a few adventures here and there, I wound up in Diamond."

"Why didn't you tell them?" Linnet asked. "The King might have been on your side."

Heriot laughed unexpectedly and held his cards out at arm's length.

"Let Dysart go!" Linnet said, both commanding and begging at the same time.

"What do you mean, let him go? I haven't got him."

"He's lying on his bed in the Tower of the Crow," she cried. "He can't see or hear. He can't move."

Heriot looked at her incredulously. "You think I've put him under a spell?"

"Haven't you?" she asked.

"No." The familiar and somehow disturbing expression was creeping across his face again. "He touched me, back when I wasn't safe, but—" Heriot hesitated. "Well, if he's lying there," he said at last, "perhaps it's because deep down he doesn't want to wake."

"Can't you do something for him?" she persisted. "Bring his true life back to him?"

"Yes, if I knew where he kept his true life," Heriot said scornfully. "But he doesn't know himself, does he? His true life shifts around in him."

He looked down at his cards, then up again, very slowly this time, up at Linnet once more, staring at her with an expression she could only describe as mischievous.

"Look at me!" he commanded. Light oozed out of him like sweat, and she saw his face clearly for the first time, looking out of its tangled hair, colorless and wild in this light, eyes like pits. He held a card toward her.

"Now look here!" he commanded. "Look hard!"

Linnet frowned at the picture.

"Dies heart!" said Heriot, his voice distant, and from just beyond the card, he looked to Linnet like a smiling demon. "Dice Heart! Dysart!"

Suddenly Linnet found she was kneeling, peering into the card almost as if it were a fortune-teller's mirror. Time had been stolen from her life. She could feel the discontinuity, knew something had happened, but had no idea what it might have been. She had been given an instruction. It was there in her head, her feelings and intentions aligning themselves around it, but she had no idea what it was.

"What have you done?" she cried, shivering.

Heriot replied with a question. "What does it feel like?"

"A break," said Linnet, forcing herself to speak with all the detachment she could muster. She wasn't going to gratify him by showing fear. "As if I'd gone out of existence for two minutes and then flashed back on again, the same but different."

"That's what I feel like from time to time," Heriot said, sounding surprised and suddenly companionable. "The same but different." Then he leaned forward, his dark eyes openly alight with the mischief she had glimpsed earlier, and touched her lightly but somehow powerfully on her right cheek. "On your way!" he said, still smiling.

Linnet mistrusted that smile. "What did you do?" she asked, rising, vaguely aware of a slow warmth spreading through her, a curious spasm of excitement in the pit of her stomach. Why was she getting to her feet and moving to the door? Nothing had been accomplished. Dysart was not saved.

"Good-bye!" Heriot said, lying back and shutting his eyes. "And do call again soon."

"What did you do to me?" she asked once more, looking back over her shoulder.

"It's a riddle," Heriot said. "You lot and your kingdoms!" he added, turning his back on Linnet, pulling his knees up, bending his head down, curling himself up and laughing in his own darkness. "You'll find out! Dysart! Yes! Meanwhile I'll get some sleep."

His gentle laughter terrified Linnet. She scrambled away from him out of the unlocked cage and into the garden through which she had felt her way so blindly only an hour earlier. The familiar stars had curved a little across the sky, but the garden seemed to be springing up around her in lines of light, things flaring into existence as she passed them, then dying back into darkness as she left them behind. Yet this flaring was not a flaring of light. Time was illuminating the gardens. Somehow she was perceiving the world by the smoldering residues of its past.

She turned toward the Swan Tower but found herself brought to a standstill as if she'd lost her way, though she knew exactly where she was. Then, slowly, she turned to look sideways toward the Tower of the Crow. Light came from a torch burning over the doorway, and there, by a little brazier beside the door, she could see a group of men talking in low voices, glancing upward from time to time, no doubt gossiping about Betony's wedding, Heriot and Dysart, and all that had happened around them. If there had been only one guard she might have walked up and demanded admittance, but it didn't seem possible to show herself to a whole crowd and walk past them into the Prince's tower.

Linnet looked up to the very top of the tower. *That's where I should be,* she thought to herself.

The tower rose into the night, dwarfing the patch of light at its own doorway, and then, as she frowned to herself, measuring its height, ascending hyphens of dim light, one above the other, seemed to ooze toward her from its blank surface. She was reminded of notes on a page of music, recording a rising scale. It took her a moment to realize what a freak of starlight was showing her. There before her, seen more clearly than ever before, was an ancient exterior flight of steps, similar to those that wound around the Tower of the Swan, but even more worn and crumbling.

Unseen by the men at the door, Linnet crossed the Bridge of the Crow, slipped along a thin path to trees and bushes at the base of the tower, then twisted herself, as silently as possible, through leaves and twigs until, at last, she laid her hand on the wall of the tower, felt the deep chill of the blocks of stone, and there, under her palm, very faintly, the actual curve of the tower's side. She even imagined it might be breathing.

Sliding sideways, she searched for what, in due course, she found . . . a first step. Finding it so easily filled her with such excitement and determination that she had no room for ordinary fear. She was terrified at her own plan, and yet it was an exalted terror . . . a terror that was also a necessity . . . a terror she could somehow enjoy.

She felt above the first step and found another one and then another, but they were unclimbable, or so she thought at first. But then her blind hand, circling up and around, discovered, almost as if it had known just what was there to be found, a short crescent of steel set in the stone, a hand-hold. After only a second of hesitation, Linnet put her foot on the first step of the crumbling stair, locked the fingers of one hand around the steel bar, then felt for the one that must surely be above it. She began to climb, rising high into the airy night.

Her first steps were desperate ones. *I can't do this,* she thought wildly, but doing it nevertheless. *I really can't do this.* Experimentally she faced the stone, then flattened herself against it, finding herself almost spread-eagled, arms stretching desperately from handhold to handhold. Feeling sideways with her foot, she stepped again, trusting her weight to the next stone, and then to other stones, some of which accommodated only her toes and the ball of her foot, and left her heel treading air. *I can't do this, but I'm doing it. I'm on my way.* She breathed in the dust and grit of the weathering stone . . . felt the very substance of Guard-on-the-Rock filling her lungs as she hung in darkness. More than once she stepped on the hem of her own cluttering dress. Once a step wobbled like a loose tooth in the face of the tower, and she tilted backward. *Falling!* she thought, growing sick with fear as one of her shoes tumbled away into the night. But the air around her grew somehow hard and unrelenting; she found an impossible purchase in it, and pulled herself forward again. As she did, she felt a tenuous but determined presence collecting itself around her, and knew at last exactly what Dysart had meant when he had talked, years ago, about someone being there to catch him.

After this, she climbed carefully yet with increasing

confidence, believing she was protected too. She had no fear that gossiping men at the main door of the tower might hear something scrabbling overhead and look up to see her struggling upward in the dark. Though she hated the emptiness at her back and the way in which night gaped over her, eager to take her into itself, she closed her eyes and came to feel she was climbing not just the side of the tower but across the face of the night itself. A little later she had the odd feeling the castle was sinking beneath her, rather than that she was rising up its side. The steps led her past Luce's windows, which were dark, for Luce was in the rooms at the base of the Tower of the Hero, singing battle songs with his campaigner friends and watching Carlyon with an altered expression, more openly predatory than ever before. Increasingly the rim toward which Linnet struggled—the rim she knew to be Dysart's windowsill—appeared to be gilded in starlight.

Though it had been invisible from the ground, she could now see the room was faintly lighted. Step up and step up again. She was able to look in, her eyes just a little above the plain edge of the window, and see Dysart lying on his bed. Two men were looking down at him, one of them Dr. Feo. As she watched, they straightened the covers of wool and fur over Dysart and left the room, as if someone had called them away. Candles burned in tall holders on either side of Dysart, who looked as if he had been laid out for burial.

At last Linnet's groping fingers found a ridged edge. She hauled herself up onto a windowsill wide enough for her to sit high above the city and catch her breath. Then she swung her quivering legs sideways and thumped forward into a space that was unexpectedly familiar territory, for it was almost a twin to her own space at the top of the Tower of the Swan. Her fingers and leg muscles immediately cramped, so that the first minutes after her climb were spent struggling with pain and trying not to cry out, though a few protesting groans forced their way through her clenched teeth.

But even as she fought to stretch her muscles into obedience, she was warmed by a great blush of triumph. She was there . . . safely there. Her leg muscles grew loose. Her fingers, knotted like a bundle of twigs by the cramp, became their lively, separate selves again. Linnet stood, stretched, walked around, trying to stamp a continuous trembling out of her knees and ankles, then moved to a square opening, which gave onto an inner stair that corkscrewed into darkness, down through the heart of the tower. The darkness was not complete. Light was seeping from somewhere below her. She turned her back on it and tiptoed toward Dysart's bed. *I mustn't hesitate,* she thought. *I'm protected,* she reminded herself.

She looked down on Dysart. He lay on his side, flanked by candles, his eyes closed, his whole face sealed like the face of a dead man.

"Dysart!" she said. "Dysart!" She touched his face, and then, when he did not wake, she looked, with puzzled wonder, around the room in which he had spent so much of his life.

It was a small, round room. His bed took up most of the available space. At the foot of his bed was the desk. In the wall beside his desk was the window through which she had climbed, crossing the very windowsill where once some vagrant, disconnected part of Heriot had sat, watching over Dysart's childhood, and both threatening and luring him . . . setting up the moment it would need his friendship, courage, and authority.

And here she was, standing in Dysart's room and looking down at him, while, somewhere in time, she felt she was still on that plain watching him vanish under the hooves of charging horses. Somewhere beyond the castle the Magician of Hoad was curled in his cage, and it seemed to Linnet that his head was not so much a head that took up space, but space itself . . . a curious space into which the real world spiraled like water through a hole, emerging altered in some way, because, as the world went through him, the Magician watched it spinning, and the power of his watching changed everything.

Looking down once more, she saw that Dysart's eyes were suddenly open, and he was staring at her, wide awake and asking her a silent question. And, as their eyes met, she felt once again the wave of heat, and the disturbance Heriot's touch on her cheek had transferred to her. Dysart slowly sat up, without taking his eyes from her. Linnet moved a step toward him, touched his cheek as Heriot had touched hers, then, bending like some tall flower gently pushed by a wind no one else could feel, she kissed him.

Dysart put his arms around her and pulled her against him so tightly it was as if he were trying to catch, between their very bodies, all their misunderstandings and ambitions, all the illusions that had kept them apart. It was as though he was determined to crush all distractions out of existence. In silence they kissed and kissed and kissed again.

"In the old story," Dysart murmured at last, "everyone woke when the lovers kissed."

"In this story everyone sleeps," Linnet answered. "Everyone except us."

"I've always been mad, but I didn't know that I was a fool as well—not until now. Linnet, I love you."

"And I love you," she replied, "and I'm the fool. I'm promised to Luce. I'm signed and sealed."

"Luce doesn't want marriage. He wants to be Hero," said Dysart, "and the Hero doesn't marry. You're free." Speaking from the confines of his narrow bed, he made it sound simple. "We tell them . . . declare ourselves . . . and then we hold to it. Hold to each other and forget Hagen!"

"Forget Hoad!" she replied, laughing.

He didn't argue. He nodded. Then he put his arms around her again. She was cocooned in the heavy folds of her dress, cold from the outside air. She pulled away from him, her back to the candle and her face in shadow, whereas his was lighted. Sliding her hand from his shoulder, she tucked it behind his head and drew his face toward hers, and they kissed yet again.

"We've signed now," she said, then sighed and leaned against him like someone yielding up a heavy burden to a fellow traveler who was somehow fresher and better able to carry it for a while.

"So you'll marry me!" he said, in the reflective voice he used when committing something to memory.

"But are you allowed to marry twice over? You're already married to your city," Linnet said, surprised to hear a little melancholy along with mockery in her own voice.

"Oh, that!" Dysart replied, debating. "Well, my father gave up his first marriage . . . gave up love, that is . . . to take on Diamond. I'll divorce Diamond and take on love. If we do things backward, we just might unknot the past."

Far out, many leagues beyond what anyone in Diamond could see, far out in distant Hagen, the volcano sighed out dark smoke, unseen in the greater darkness, while the calm eyes of the glacial lakes looked through the mountain forests toward the stars. But Dysart and Linnet didn't think of brothers, Magicians, Hoad, or Hagen. They clung together, kissing in the room at the top of the tower, with the fidgety castle below them, the restless city and the land of Hoad around them, and windy darkness encompassing the world.

★★★

In a room of Guard-on-the-Rock, Betony sat leaning forward, elbows on his knees, smiling a little and talking intently with his doll-like bride. In the Tower of the Hero, Carlyon looked across the room, looked past a cluster of wildly gossiping friends, and lifted his glass ironically to Luce's predatory gaze, something he had learned, over many years, to recognize in his own. Behind him, Izachel sat listlessly, looking like the shell of a man, his center burned away.

And out in the night, not particularly comfortable on his straw bed, though he was used to straw, Heriot listened to Cayley breathing loudly beside him, worked on by such exhaustion he suddenly felt guilty, sure he had used the child's offered energy and time unfairly. Then he felt a movement outside, heard the gate scrape and clink. Quickly he tossed more hay across sleeping Cayley, turning as light swung around his darkened room and fell on his mattress. He flung his arm over his eyes, for it seemed unreasonably bright.

"You are distinctly favored, Magician," a voice behind the light said with a sigh. "It is the man visiting you, not the King. He seldom appears, this man, but he has come out at midnight to speak to you."

"Lord King!" Heriot said, and was silent.

"I have Cloud with me," the King said. "But only by way of simple company. Magician, as I understand it from Lord Glass, who has sought to be your advocate, you have chained yourself up because you feel you have transformed yourself into a monster, and you wish to exemplify this state in the most ironical fashion."

"Since I was relieving you of one prodigy, Lord King, I thought I might as well offer you another in his place," Heriot replied.

"What makes you prodigious?" asked the King, and Heriot was silent for a while.

Then he said, in the slow voice of someone unraveling a mystery, "After that first vision, back when I was a boy, no one behaved the same to me, and since then, I suppose, I've been trying to get back to what I used to be . . . contented with my true place in the world, contented and complete. . . ."

"You're asking for paradise," the King replied. "Take

it from me, life thrusts us on, and there is no true going back."

"But I had it once," Heriot cried. "I was *there*. Everything around me was my meaning."

"If *you* hadn't changed, something else would have," Hoad replied. The candlelight shone up into his eyes. "I'm sure you know that in the beginning I didn't want to be King, nor did I expect to be. But the moment came, and immediately I began imagining myself as a man who might do good. I was tempted by power—the power of remaking the kingdom by the conceit of kingship—and so I embraced the possibility. And now I cannot imagine myself as anything but King, struggling to achieve peace. A lot of people support me, though there's still a number that don't." He sighed and looked into the shadowed air over Heriot's head. "You could support my ambitions. You could help me, even though such dreams have their dangers." He sighed again. "Those of us who think, either grow discontented with our setting in the world or make the world so uneasy around us so that it strives to work us out of its flesh, as if we were festering thorns. And then we must live ever after like parasites trying to eat our way back in."

"I'm nothing true here," Heriot said. "Just a magical function living in the city's gut."

"What would you rather be?" asked the King. He was dressed in gray, the color of his sighs. All his color lay in the glance he now turned on Heriot. And, in considering this question, Heriot was brought to admit to himself again that, by now, he didn't want to surrender his magical nature and return to what he once had been. He groaned at the contradiction and shook his head helplessly.

"You are not singular in any tendency you might have to be monstrous," said the King. "We can all be monstrous, and balancing a complicated nature is the most wearing of all responsibilities. Think of that." Heriot was silent. "For the rest, as King, I am interested in you only as a Magician and in the function a Magician might have in Hoad."

A moment later he was gone into the night. Heriot stared after him, their conversation turning over in his head. After a while he put that seething head down on his arms, which were folded across his knees. He fell into a tense, cramped sleep, only to wake in the first dark gray light of dawn, with Cayley leaning heavily against him, then waking too, as if he sensed that Heriot was awake, blinking and swearing with astonishment.

"So, are you going to stay here, then?" Cayley said in a resigned voice.

"It's hard to explain," Heriot said, sliding his fingers down between the iron fetter around his ankle and the protesting skin beneath.

"It doesn't make sense to make things rougher than they need to be," Cayley said simply. "But it's a fairy tale, 'n't it? You think you've grown too strange to be born. Maybe, says the rest of the world, but we're all strange, this way and that. But *me*—I'm a bit stranger than most, you mutter on, mutter on. That's why, 'n't it?"

Heriot grinned unwillingly. "That's more or less why," he agreed. "But already the idea of it is something different from what it was when it came to me last night."

"I used to hear fairy tales and that," Cayley said. "My

mother told them, over and over. And if you tell them over and over like that, they get to be true, don't they?"

Heriot looked straight ahead, smoothing his tangled hair.

"See, another man wouldn't do what you're doing," said Cayley. "Another man would lie low and get what he could get. But you leap around, thumping your chest and saying, 'Look at me! I'm a monster!' and that's a fairy-tale thing to do."

"I've used that word too much. It's suddenly gone all cozy on me," mumbled Heriot. "If I'm a monster, I'm a cozy monster."

The morning light grew, not lighter but bluer. Cayley put his mouth against Heriot's ear. "You're not a monster, but I am," he said in a very quiet voice. "I'm not as old as you, but I'm a long way ahead of you in being one."

Heriot felt the hair prickle on his neck at the dark, breathy tone. He tried to smile, but his smile refused to be completed.

"You stay in here, you let me go loose," Cayley went on. "You might save the city from yourself, but you leave it open to me. It's had its turn with me, that city out there. Soon I'm going to have my turn with the city, unless you come out to watch over me. Listen!"

Heriot listened. He could tell that in the following moments of silence Cayley was struggling to break down something of that terrible, guarded blankness he carried within him.

"Once my mother tried to cut my throat. I've told you that. She did it out of a sort of mad sadness about things.

Not that it worked, but I still carry the mark of her sadness. And then there was the man I call my stepdadda. He lay there drunk, and his boy, my little half brother, was coughing and dying under a blanket. I come out from under the bed. Twice . . ." He held up two fingers. "Twice I put the point of the knife I had back then against my stepdadda's eye—wrinkled his eyelid up with it. See, the rest of him, it was full of bones. . . . I couldn't be sure I would get past them back then. No point in just hurting him for nothing, was there? An eye—that's a sure way in, 'n't it?"

Heriot shrugged. "We often think terrible things and don't do them."

"What do you think I am?" Cayley said derisively. "I'd have done it. Sometimes now, well, I could cry at having let the chance go by. But I couldn't be sure I'd get away with it. That stopped me. They'd have stretched me, and I wouldn't stretch for him. See, I got to thinking I might be allowed just one"—he bent one of his fingers down—"and my stepdadda wasn't the right one. Not the one I wanted. Not the one I've been practicing to have!"

Heriot turned his head very slowly. Cayley wasn't looking at him but out into the growing light, a dreamy expression on his patched face as if he were remembering some wonderful honeyed flavor, still tasting its ghost on his lips.

"Things were looking up for me out there," he said regretfully, turning to Heriot. "Eating and sleeping and that, working out with Voicey Landis. But now? Shall I live in the straw with you? Steal a chain to match? I can be all sorts of company. You say it and I'll *be* it."

There was a silence.

"You're a clever little bastard, aren't you?" Heriot murmured at last. "You've been brought up so badly I can't resist looking after you. So undo the lock on this chain and we'll go home."

"Is that right?" Cayley said, busily drawing a long pin from the thick hem of his shirt. There was a blob of sealing wax on its end.

"Don't you know it!" Heriot exclaimed, as his companion began to work on the lock that Heriot himself had closed on his own ankle the night before.

"I know this," Cayley said indistinctly. "You like playing just as if you were a little one. All this—it's nothing but a game, and I can't be bothered with the rules."

"It's not simple," Heriot said. "Once I watched children playing a game in the Third Ring—they were practicing for love. They tied it down with names and running and kissing, chasing, and catching and screaming. . . ."

"There's a lot of screaming to it sometimes," Cayley agreed, working at the lock.

"Listen. A child from one line would try to fetch away another from the other line back onto his own side. 'The boy'—no—'the *burning* boy shall fetch'—or was it 'catch'?—'the girl and he shall be her lover.' Do you know that game?"

"I've already said I don't play," Cayley pointed out.

"I play," Heriot said. "I'm playing all the time—acting Magician, acting monster, acting man, to see which feels right. It's what you call a metaphorical life. . . ."

"I wouldn't call it that, just playing, playing, playing," Cayley put in.

"Perhaps I'm a bit like those children," Heriot said,

"acting out future choices so I'll get a bit of practice before they come upon me. I thought it might be right to live in this cage, but maybe everyone else is right and I'm wrong. One thing's certain, *you* need looking after, you threat to the world."

"So do you," Cayley said. "Need looking after, I mean."

"But it hurt my feelings that Dysart couldn't look at me directly," Heriot complained. "I mean, he grabbed me, but he was careful to look past me."

"He was scared." Cayley twisted his face, still concentrating on feeling his way into the lock with the pin. "But I always look direct, you'll never scare me." The lock clicked, and the anklet fell open with a ringing sound. "See, I'm ruined for beauty and all that, but suppose you was to drop down right this moment into a pool of blood or turn into a devil with looking-glass eyes. I'd still look straight at you. 'That's him, that's my man. Hey you! Stop fooling around!' I'd say."

"A devil with looking-glass eyes." Heriot was momentarily diverted. He laughed with sudden ease. "Now there's a thought."

"I made it up," cried Cayley with a shout of triumphant laughter. "All the time I'm learning your words, catching your ideas, stealing thoughts. Pity to lose a skill."

"Watch out—words can be an illness," Heriot said, but without bitterness. He stood up, then cautiously moved his ankle from side to side.

"They won't sicken me," boasted Cayley. "I've nearly died of thoughts already—always other people's, not my own. You don't sicken twice."

"What are you talking about?" Heriot asked with weary amusement as they came out of the cage together, leaving its door swinging open behind them.

"Your sickness," said Cayley, dancing a little, like a dog pleased at the prospect of a walk. "It's got a name, 'n't it? Im-ag-in-ation!" He pronounced the one word as if it were four.

The morning was already laced with the voices of birds. The two-faced woman, the dwarfs, all slept. The lions paced backward and forward.

"It's so beautiful," said Heriot, looking around him with astonishment. "Cayley, it's so beautiful. All over again!"

The garden was filling with a mysterious and tender light, each tree, each leaf, each blade of grass displaying itself against a color between gray and silver. Ill at ease with the rest of humanity, Heriot found there was a space in the morning into which he fitted exactly. "Supposing the simple act of asking, 'Am I human?' *makes* you human?" he said, coming to a stop.

"Supposing," said Cayley.

"And who hasn't got a beast in them anyway?" Heriot asked again.

"Supposing . . . just supposing," Cayley agreed, nodding.

"I've tried being good," Heriot said, "being clever, too . . . but there isn't a final answer. I'm wonderful compared to Carlyon, for instance, better off, too. His cage might be a whole island wide, but there's no one to unlock *his* collar. He's the great freak of Hoad, displayed."

"Maybe he sits and asks, 'What am I?'" Cayley suggested. "It's easy to ask."

"I think he did ask once, and didn't like the answer," Heriot replied. "I don't think he's asked properly since." The gate to the zoo was a little ajar.

"That royal old fox," Cayley said half-admiringly. "It's like a little message, saying, 'I know you'll go,' 'n't it?"

They crossed into the First Ring, watched by the guards at the gate. High above them, over in the Tower of the Lion, a window shone palely, picked out by the light in the east. They moved on farther; the light deepened and suddenly became miraculous. Heriot found himself weeping, for he thought the morning was extending an irrevocable welcome back into the world of natural men, even though he was bringing his occupant with him, unruly but not outlawed.

"I'm a true man after all," he said to the air and to Cayley.

"You can do better than just being a true man," said Cayley, dancing around him.

"I value it," Heriot exclaimed. "You will too, one day."

Cayley's dancing stopped. "I won't ever live to be one," he said seriously. "I'm more opposite to all that than you guess."

"We might both live forever," Heriot suggested. "I'm becoming immortal, walking in this light. I've got a lot of questions unanswered, but I'll stay still for a little, not fretting and not asking them."

He looked up into the sky, which was beginning to color, its blush deepening from moment to moment, as if his stare had set love and blood free to contend across the clear skin of the air. Heriot couldn't think of a more adequate response than falling on his knees and staring ahead of him, his face rapt and still.

"It's so beautiful," he repeated. "If only I could just dissolve into it." The morning grew, if anything, more intense. But then he shook himself. "Here!" he exclaimed. "I'm getting lost. Hug me back. I want someone to touch me."

"I'm not good at it," Cayley said, but obediently knelt and, putting his thin arms around Heriot, hugged him energetically.

"Good enough!" Heriot told him. "Rough but real." He looked up at the trees, their top twigs burning furiously with the approach of day, quite unable to see Cayley's face, which was taking on an indescribable expression, tender, triumphant yet menacing, the expression of a demon, not of the night but of the bright morning.

TRUE KINGDOMS

You're all I ever really wanted. You're my true kingdom," Dysart said to Linnet. "The city was only a sign of you." At the moment it seemed completely true. "Back there in the dream, I just cut the world out. I didn't want to know anything, because there was nothing worth knowing anymore. I wasn't even curious. I didn't want to know what was going to happen next. I didn't understand."

"Understand what?" Linnet asked.

"You're my true kingdom," Dysart told her.

"It was always meant to be," Linnet said. Her happy voice came to Dysart from his own shadow, which lay across her. "But we had to be tested." He couldn't tell that, as Linnet spoke, she was testing every part of her memory and awareness, fearful of detecting some secret contamination of her own will by the will of the Magician of Hoad. She couldn't bear the thought that she and Dysart had achieved each other only because Heriot had somehow slipped desire under their skins. But there was nothing there that was not her own. Heriot might have hovered around her as she risked her life and climbed the wall by its disintegrating steps, but her declaration of love was hers alone.

Outside she could detect the first alteration of light. It was still dark, but it was a transparent darkness. Morning was on the way. "My father will be looking for me," she said with a sigh. "There are terrible fights ahead of us. He wants to be the one who chooses my husband."

"Let's stroll out of here. Let's walk like civilized sentries around the rim of the castle," Dysart suggested. "Just once round the walls. Then you can go back and fight with your father, and I'll go and argue with mine. Don't straighten the bed! Don't touch a thing. I'll come back, see the mark of your head on my pillow, and I'll know it was all true."

Linnet stood up, feeling so light and free without her clothes, she was reluctant to dress again. But the night had become part of a time that was attainable only through memory. Day was bearing down on her. She slipped a linen chemise over a silk one. Dysart buttoned a crumpled shirt, and they dressed, putting on the world along with yesterday's grubby clothes. "Your father . . . ," began Dysart. "Linnet, you must think hard about what it really means . . . being in love with me."

"I would always have fought for you if I'd known you were going to be fighting beside me," Linnet declared.

She meant it. She *meant* it.

They walked down the winding stair toward a guttering torch, paling in that first morning light, and then out under an arched doorway onto the battlements. Far below them the Bramber flowed; far beyond them the three Rings of the city stretched toward the first rising hills of County Glass. Nothing in that outer world had changed, yet Linnet had never felt as consciously free as she felt now, as easy, as pure within herself. The Hero's Tower still blazed with light, but, as morning advanced, as edges and curves began to shine, and hints of depth and distance crept back into the world, these lights too were losing their power. The sound of voices singing came toward them intermittently. High in the Tower of the Lion, the King's window shone faintly. Perhaps the sleepless King of Hoad was celebrating his son's strange wedding with yet another night of careful work.

Watching the morning and strolling along the battlements beside Linnet, Dysart felt he was made of paper and ink, made out of stories, and not all of them his own. *Stories never sleep*, he thought. *They tell themselves over and over again.* Beneath him, in the tunneled walls, the campaigners were changing the guard. Celebration fires still smoked in distant city squares. They walked in silence, and the dissolving midnight beast, which had consumed Dysart when he was a dreaming child, grew hazy and doubtful. Inwardly he laughed at it, and drove it away.

At last they paused and leaned together in one of the embrasures, looking out into the King's garden. Neither of them thought of the Magician, who had declared himself a monster and shut himself in the cage.

There was a step behind them. They turned together, looking away from the garden and the sea into the more resolute light staining the sky beyond Hoad's Pleasure.

Betony was standing behind them, holding a goblet and a bottle of wine in his pale hands, his face more naked than Linnet had ever seen it. His expression altered at once, as it always did when anyone looked into his eyes. Nevertheless Linnet had fleetingly glimpsed something in Betony—a terrible injury, old and mortal—before he had the chance to conceal it once more.

"I see you have been celebrating my wedding," Betony said. He stared at them. "Rather too well!" he added.

"Someone has to," Dysart said.

Betony sighed and took his place beside them, facing the morning and turning his back on the bulk of the sprawling city.

"Oh, I've celebrated in my own way," he said. "I was able to talk to her—my wife, that is. We can't stand the thought of each other. We've agreed not to contaminate ourselves. And we do understand each other . . . we've even become friends of a sort. Willing conspirators, anyway! My father can whistle and wait for the miraculous child, heir to both kingdoms. It just won't happen. I don't mind taking life out of the world, but I'll never feed it back in. I may be cruel, but I'm not as cruel as all that."

He looked sideways at them.

"You seem to have celebrated my wedding in a particularly personal way," he went on.

Without turning, Linnet could tell he was smiling.

"Linnet and I have promised to marry each other!" Dysart

said abruptly, anxious to hear what the idea sounded like in the outside world. Once spoken, it became both more and less than a private ecstasy . . . it became a policy.

"Oh, of course you have," said Betony. "And I do think you should!"

Dysart and Linnet both looked at him suspiciously.

"You might even get away with it," he said, smiling his wincing smile at their doubt, "now that Carlyon's shown a little of his hand . . . well, of his heart, really! Have you told your father?" he asked, turning to look at Linnet. "Or have you had other things on your mind?"

"The King didn't seem to be worried by anything Carlyon had to say," Linnet answered casually. She hadn't given Carlyon or his visions of death and decay a thought.

"Oh, don't be naive," replied Betony scornfully. "Our father has never trusted Carlyon as Hero . . . he's always wanted to hold Luce in reserve. Otherwise Luce would have been married, probably to you, well before this. And he'll never forgive Carlyon for that trick last night, for turning Izachel loose at my wonderful wedding feast. So someday he just might give Luce the chance to do what Luce already longs to do. To do more than admire Carlyon . . . to kill him and *become* him. A sort of devouring! That cuts out marriage for Luce. And the Master wouldn't mind you marrying Dysart, would he, if Dysart was a second eligible son, rather than a third." He shook his head. "It's almost too neat a chance. Don't trust it." He sounded neither sympathetic nor hostile . . . simply curious in a slightly drunken and weary fashion. "Or perhaps you'll live happily ever after," he went on, smiling gently, "in Hagen." It was hard to understand how a voice so empty of expression could, nevertheless, express profound derision.

"I could learn to do that," Dysart said defiantly, but as he spoke, his thought twisted in his head. "If I could have Linnet and Diamond, too . . ."

We could live in Hagen, Linnet thought, like Betony's echo, then pushed the thought away. Dysart must never know how quickly she had imagined him among the mountains and forests of her home, how she had already stood him on the edge of a plateau from which one could look out over the whole land of Hoad.

"Because," Betony went on serenely, "since I'm forced to be King, I must warn you I plan to be King, childless or not. Actually, I can hardly wait. So no secret hopes of something beyond Hagen. I shall become King out of spite." The gentle flow of his voice suddenly sounded particularly sinister.

"Besides, Dysart, you'd never be a true King. You'd be like our father. You'd try to do good; you'd try to be kind; you'd try to be human, and that would bleed the sense out of our sort of kingship. And, over and above any question of your inadequacy, I do so want my father to have the fulfillment of seeing me become what he's forced me to become."

"You want to be King out of revenge!" exclaimed Dysart.

"It's a good reason," said Betony mildly. "I'll be different from my father in essence, because I'll never be taken in by my own story."

Glancing back at him, Linnet suddenly caught a vagrant reflection of light from a wet streak on his cheek. Betony was weeping. As she watched, he touched the tear away with his right forefinger.

"Rare wine!" he said, looking at her. Then he licked his fingertip.

Linnet leaned more deeply into the embrasure, staring down into the garden. Far below she could now make out an archery lawn. Something flashed out from the trees, a wheel spinning across the grass and chamomile. A strange child was cartwheeling through the King's retreat, seeming barely to touch the ground. Betony and Dysart, backs to the garden, didn't notice the somersaulting figure.

"I really loved my father when I was very small," Betony said, still holding his glass goblet high in the air, narrowing his eyes as he looked at the world through it. "I have no depth, as you know. I'm fascinated by surfaces, and back in the beginning his surface seemed so wonderful, I thought he must glitter all the way through. And then, as I got older, I began to think there might be blackness, a perpetual bitter howling, and that was fascinating too. . . . Since he didn't love me, I thought perhaps he hated me, and I enjoyed the drama of being hated. But when I realized he was nothing but a gray, dull struggler, who'd given up his own life for an inferior one—a royal donkey with a capacity for taking detailed care of things—when I realized I'd been born to be nothing more than a marker in his dreary labor, then I knew I'd never forgive him."

"From what I can make out," Dysart said cautiously,

"people have been happier since he's been King."

"But *I'm* not happier," Betony said. "I was born with a longing for extremity, and none of this is anything like enough. The crown, the ritual, the castle . . . all nothing but tinsel!"

"Well, perhaps you *can't* be happy," Dysart suggested, rather brutally. "Maybe that's one gift you don't have."

Down in the garden a second figure was strolling onto the archery lawn. Heriot, whose last words to Linnet had been a promise that he would never leave his cage, was walking between the trees. She stared down at him, frowning and transfixed, while Betony watched Dysart with a suddenly inimical stare.

"You are completely wrong!" Betony said. "I *know* about happiness. I can feel happiness beating off you this very moment, and how do I recognize it? Because I *have* been happy, on rare occasions. I want happiness very badly."

But Linnet, watching Heriot Tarbas and wondering what on earth could have brought the Magician out of the cage, wasn't thinking of Betony's happiness. Something had happened to change the Magician's mind. And, even from this distance, calling on sharp memory rather than sharp sight, she now recognized the cartwheeling boy as the one who often followed him. Strange rumors circulated about them, but Lord Glass had never tried to cut the boy out of Heriot's life. She looked at Dysart, who was leaning against the wall beside his brother. As if her gaze were a touch, he now turned his odd-colored eyes toward her, and then, together, they looked out over Diamond.

"Funny!" said Dysart. "I've never felt so close to the city

out there before. It's as if giving it all away has mixed me into it more than ever."

Betony understood as well. "You!" said Betony. "You'll never give Diamond away. Linnet, be warned! He'll break every other promise but that one."

Dysart treated Betony as if he were a whisper as impersonal, as errant and senseless, as wind or rain. He simply laughed, and shook his head. Though he answered Betony, it was Linnet he was really talking to.

"You're only jealous," he told Betony, before saying what was real to him at that moment. "Anyway, I'm a Magician in my own way. I'll fold Diamond up and carry it always, tucked into a little press in my head. Then, whenever I need to, I'll take it out . . . shake it free . . . I'll have it all." And, as Dysart spoke, Linnet believed he really might be able to contain the whole city: that the castle at its heart, the river like a flowing question mark, the three Rings, the merchants, markets, Magicians, mottoes, libraries, laundries, lines of washing, the jewelers, the poems on walls, and the gongfermors carrying buckets of excrement to dump in the poorer part of town, even the King and the Hero, would all be Dysart's forever. He might even be able to share it with her, if ever she wanted it. And suddenly it seemed as if all the shifting entities of the city had really been standing still, and it had always been Linnet, the heiress of Hagen, and Dysart, the third son, who had moved and changed, dancing among all the confusing others.

"Dice heart!" Dysart said suddenly, but whether he said it to Linnet or Betony or to the morning no one could tell. "No one will ever be able to take it away from me. I'll gamble on that."

He took Linnet by the hand, without noticing the Magician in the garden below, and turned her to face the east and the confidently rising sun.

PART FOUR

GONE

CHALLENGING THE HERO

Time!" said Heriot. "It doesn't give up, does it? Hard to think of myself as being twenty-five years old."

"One moment little, the next big," said Cayley in his husky, damaged voice. "Me, that is, not you. You've always been big."

"Neither of us has ever been as big as we are now," Heriot said. "Are you off to fight somewhere? Fight! Fight! Fight! That's all you think of."

"I'm working out with Voicey Landis," Cayley said. "I'm his favorite, and it's not just being big and strong. I'm—what's that word? I'm agile. That means *quick*," he added, proud of a new word. "The ones that are even stronger than me, they dive in to strike me. Down comes the sword, but—hey—I'm already over there, and spinning in from the side." He mimed a graceful movement. "I'm strong enough, but quickness, that's my skill. And I work at it more than most."

"I know," said Heriot. "When I ask you to tidy our shed, you always say you've got to practice."

"Oh, that!" said Cayley. "Well, *you* don't tidy. You just

crouch by the King, telling him who means well and who doesn't."

"That's my work," Heriot said. "That, and spreading a bit of fantasy around when the King has noble guests." But as he spoke, his expression became remote. Over and over again, with every new day, the old questions still worked through him. The world around him seemed to thrill with intention, but he somehow knew he wasn't being what he was intended to be.

"Do you tell him about Betony Hoad?" asked Cayley.

"I don't have to," Heriot said. "Anyone can read the Prince. The King can. Lord Glass can. Betony Hoad wants to be marvelous beyond anyone else—even when he's King it won't be enough for him. He'd like to be a Magician, too, but being a Magician is something you're born to, like me." He sighed. "Be noble! Be strong! Whatever! Being a Magician isn't something you can win."

"Then off you go, and get on with the work you were born to, and I'll get to mine," said Cayley. "If I don't see you tomorrow, I'll see you the next day."

Heriot walked through the orchard, across one echoing courtyard, then another, then up a short flight of stairs, choosing to enter the castle through the kitchens, where the cooks and butlers, the butchers, cleaners, and other people who lavished care and attention on the halls and chambers of the castle greeted him with a certain caution, but with friendship, too. He was the Magician of Hoad, but he understood their work. There had even been occasions when he had joined them, scrubbing platters and benches, listening to the castle gossip and gossiping in return.

Moments like this gave him a homely feeling. But today he simply grinned and waved and walked on, climbed other, grander stairs, and came into a lobby whose stone walls were softened by tapestries. Suddenly he found himself confronted by Dysart.

"You're late," said Dysart. "The Lords of the Islands are here already."

"They're early," said Heriot. "And I hope they don't talk too much. I'm tired of their conversation."

"It's all useful to me," Dysart said. "Linnet and I get together to exchange notes."

"You two!" Heriot said. "Why don't you just marry and settle down?"

"It's her father," Dysart said. "He wants her to marry Luce, because he thinks Betony and his wife won't have children, and one day there might be the chance for Linnet to be Queen of Hoad. But Luce won't agree to marry because . . ." His voice faded. He looked around almost as if he thought the walls might turn treacherous.

"Because Luce thinks that he will challenge Carlyon and become Hero," said Heriot. "And though the Hero mustn't marry, he can probably have any woman he chooses."

Dysart looked up and down the hall through which they were now striding. When he spoke it was almost in a whisper. "Things like that are meant to be muttered out in your orchard, not shouted between these walls. Someone might listen to the echoes. So let's talk about these Lords from the Islands. My father doesn't trust them. The Islands are restless, though what they would do if they broke away from Hoad I don't know. Go back to fishing, I suppose."

For the rest of the morning Heriot sat at the King's elbow, listening to requests for money and attention registered by the Lords who made up the Council of Ten. The King lay back in his throne, which held him in an embrace of gold and crimson, becoming not simply a place for him to sit, but a frame for him. On his right hand Betony yawned, worrying his thumbnail in between yawns. On his left sat Luce, staring at Carlyon. When at last the Island Lords retreated, bowing and smiling, the King turned, not toward his son, but toward Heriot. Heriot recognized the summons in the King's glance. He took a deep breath and stepped forward.

"Well, Magician! Were they speaking the truth?"

Heriot moved restlessly, hating this question, which was one he had to answer over and over again.

"Mostly they spoke the truth, Your Majesty. I'm not perfect in the way I read minds, but—"

"You tell us that every day," the King said. "Forget your shortcomings. Use your skills to give what impressions you can."

"There was a lot they didn't tell," said Heriot. He hesitated. "They've had a noble from the Dannorad staying on Cresca with Lord Summel, and they talked about their old relationship, I think, but I can't be sure. And the image of Lord Summel was moving in all their minds, like a spirit swimming in wave after wave."

Heriot heard a curious murmur of fulfilled suspicion scuttling around the room as he spoke. Lord Summel was a hero in the Islands but a declared enemy of Hoad.

"They protected themselves as well as they could,"

he added. "These days they try to train the men who sit in front of Your Majesty to present blank minds to your Magician."

"Do you think the Lords of the Islands are plotting to change their loyalty?" the King asked.

Once again Heriot hesitated. Then he sighed. "It's dancing in their minds."

"Ah!" said the King. "We will think about this." He turned away from Heriot, looking to Carlyon and murmuring to him inaudibly, while Heriot moved back to stand beside Dysart again. The King looked out into the room.

"The day's business is concluded," he announced. The Lords of his Council began to stand, but suddenly a clear voice cut into the air of the throne room.

"Your Majesty! Your Magnificence, Lord Carlyon, Hero of Hoad."

Every head in the room turned. Luce had not only risen from his chair but had stepped forward to stand in front of Carlyon. Carlyon, at once alert, looked up at him with a smile that suggested he already knew just what Luce was about to say.

The King looked at Luce and inclined his head gravely. "Speak on!" he said with curious cool formality, Heriot thought, for though it was indeed a formal occasion, the King was speaking to his son.

"The time has come," Luce announced with a formality of his own. "I put forward a challenge to Lord Carlyon. I challenge him to an encounter on Cassio's Island. I challenge him—"

But Carlyon interrupted him. "I accept the challenge

of Prince Luce," he said briskly, somehow reducing the challenge to an irritating request. "We will fight on Cassio's Island according to ancient traditions." And then he added, "Whether I win or lose, I will enjoy the occasion. Mine is a still life, and I long for the variety of action."

Luce looked taken aback by the speed of Carlyon's reply. His mouth hung open slightly as he glanced from Carlyon to his father.

Once again the King inclined his head. "A challenge has been made. A challenge has been accepted. This evening the challenge will be announced and celebrated in the Tower of the Lion."

Heriot was released. He was a free man for a few hours and made for his orchard, feeling the day reaching toward him. He would lie on his back, perhaps, looking into the sky. He might read. He might slide through that hidden gap in the wall and wander between the stalls of the Second Ring. He might, just for a little time . . .

But Cayley was suddenly beside him once more, startling him with such a sudden appearance.

"Made you jump!" he said with satisfaction.

"It's funny," Heriot said. "I can feel everyone else creeping up on me, but mostly I can't feel you."

"I've learned to shut myself in," Cayley said in his wandering but mysterious way. "Things happened to me back a bit and I had to close myself down tight. I taught myself how. It was that or dying. So! No choice! Anyhow, was it interesting sitting in there and gossiping with the King and Hero?"

"It was interesting today," Heriot said. "Luce challenged

the Hero. Well, we've known for some time he was planning to, but . . ."

And then he fell silent. Cayley might have shut himself in, but suddenly something was leaking out from him. He was angry; he was, perhaps, frightened. Heriot looked closely at him. "Why should you care?" he asked.

"Who says I do care?" Cayley replied in his usual lighthearted voice, and as he spoke Heriot could feel him closing in on himself, growing unreadable once more.

"It jumped from your mind into mine," Heriot replied. "I could feel you growing fierce at the news."

"You're not always right," said Cayley.

Heriot said nothing but knew he hadn't imagined that furious, inner alarm Cayley had betrayed. Perhaps he could have pursued it, but then he thought, *People are entitled to their secrets. It may be the Magician's job to winkle out secrets in the King's throne room, but out in the city, secrets can be secrets, hidden and unviolated.*

LUCE'S CHOICE

A month after Luce's challenge, a glowing worm of color began writhing slowly through the great Rings of Diamond, then beyond the city along the open road. The King and his entire court, together with envoys and ambassadors from the Dannorad and Camp Hyot, set out in a formal parade along a road that had been cleared and widened and decorated with colored poles and banners in anticipation of the royal progress. The King, mounted on a white horse, rode at the head of the procession. Betony Hoad and his doll-wife rode on the King's right, Luce on his left, while directly behind him came Dysart, together with the Master of Hagen and the Lords of Argo, Dante, Bay, Isman, Doro, and Glass, along with their families.

Linnet of Hagen rode beside her father. Heriot Tarbas, the Magician of Hoad, rode beside Prince Dysart, for in a curious way their friendship expressed the power of the King. Behind them came the lesser Lords with their wives and sons, attended by ranks of guards and servants, and among this lesser crowd rode the Magician's servant Cayley, the transformed rat of the city, staring around him intently, occasionally smiling his vivid smile, as if in following this road he were remembering a story he had been told as a child—a story he knew well. They were bound for Cassio's Island, where Prince and Hero were to fight. Within two days, one would be dead.

Some members of the procession talked to one another as they rode, but for the most part the riders were curiously silent, many of them tied into themselves with thoughts and speculations. The silence became part of the ceremonial progress between the city and Cassio's Island, yet somehow it was as if the thoughts of men and women sang in the air, not as words but as strange vibrations, felt but not recognized.

At last! Luce was thinking. *At last I'll become what I was born to be. And when I'm set up on Cassio's Island I'll remake the world. I'll change the rules. The Dannorad will fall into line. Camp Hyot will bow down before Hoad. Who knows? Betony doesn't want to be King. He might step down and . . . and I might even merge the King and the Hero into one man again.*

A breeze crept in from the sea and lifted the golden curls on his forehead. Dysart, staring sideways, saw them stir as if gentle but determined fingers were twisting themselves in his brother's hair. *Luce must win,* he was thinking. *He must. It's not just that I want to be King after my father. But if Luce wins, I win in every way. If Luce becomes Hero, he moves off to one side in a glory all his own, and I'll be second son. I'll inherit Linnet.* And then another voice—a vagrant from some dark and unacknowledged part of his mind—whispered slyly, *But even if Luce dies, I'll still move up a step. I'll become the second son of the King. Either way I'll win.* He recoiled in his saddle, shying away violently from this thought, which had become almost immediately an unwelcome yet indissoluble part of a profound longing.

It's not enough! Betony Hoad was thinking. *Nothing is enough. Look at this display, this charade. Look at all this posturing, this game they're playing, this pretense of true wonder. Of course death has excitement, but this will be death carefully arranged, death reduced, made tedious. I don't care who kills whom. Somewhere there are things wonderful beyond all dreaming. But where are they? Why am I shut away from them? Why do I have to waste time watching these gesturing puppets? I want to be remade. I don't want to be the mere sign of the sun. I want to be the sun itself.*

Heriot was thinking too, remembering another time. *Funny how well I remember it, seeing it's not a thing I want to remember. I struggled along this road, bleeding, thinking there was no place for me . . . there would never be a place for me. But now I have a place. I live in an orchard with a family of one. It's not my first place, but it's come to be a true place. Yet I still don't know just what it means to be a Magician. I know how I'm used in Diamond—I've been used like that for years now—but I know that's misuse of what I could be . . . what I ought to be. Somehow I'm being reduced. When I was a child, a baby, Izachel got into my head and tore me apart, and I've never worked the way I'm meant to work. Somewhere out there I have a true meaning, but I don't know what it is.* These thoughts faded away when he saw they had reached the ancient aqueduct, built and broken long before, back in the days when the first people—his own people—the Gethin and the Orts, were Hoad's only inhabitants.

That curve of water! he thought. *It's still like a question mark, asking me something, but until I know what it's asking, there's no way I can answer.*

The sound of the falling water advanced to meet the passing riders as it gushed endlessly through the ancient channel of stone, as it sighed through the air, then burst furiously toward the river far below, applauding its return home.

The procession moved on, made up of many people, yet moving like a single thing with a single life of its own.

The King turned to Betony Hoad. His movement was smooth and practiced, yet for all that there was something slightly uneasy about it. "You must enjoy this splendor," he said, and there was something awkward in his simple comment . . . an advance uncertain of how it would be received. "It's the sort of thing you take pleasure in." He was both stating something, yet asking a question.

"If I must, I must," said Betony Hoad.

Hoad raised his eyebrows. "You don't enjoy it?" he asked, more directly this time.

"It's a children's game," Betony said. "I was thinking, as you spoke, Lord Father, that I was longing for something much more—oh, *much* more—extreme than this."

"Your brother's life is in the balance," the King pointed out. "Surely that is an extremity."

"It's what he's chosen," Betony said. "I long for something beyond arrangement and choice."

"You want to be an elemental?"

Betony didn't look at his father. He laughed.

"Being King is perhaps the closest any human being can come to being an elemental," the King suggested, but Betony laughed again, shaking his head as if the words were annoying gnats singing in his ear.

The procession moved on. The King turned to Luce. "And you truly want to be the Hero?" he asked. "It's not too late to turn around and ride back to Diamond."

"It's much too late," said Luce. "It's been too late for years. When we last came this way I wasn't much more than a child. I saw Carlyon win and stand over Link—I saw him *become* the Hero of Hoad. He glowed with it all, and in a little while I'll glow like that. I'll be transformed. Carlyon may be a great warrior, but he's older, and I don't think he has the same skills he once had."

They moved on in silence.

"A King makes a poor father," the King said at last. "Of course I hope you will win. I hope for your victory more than I have hoped for anything in years."

Somewhere in Heriot's divided head, the occupant gathered in the hopes of the King, Luce, and Dysart, along with the derision of Betony Hoad, as if it were feeding itself on these drifts of human feeling, and then somehow feeding them back into Heriot himself.

Feeling tired of the intrusion of other people's conjectures and longings, Heriot spoke ahead to Dysart. "I know this place," he said. "I saw the last procession as a child from up there on the hills, looking down. Now I'm on the road looking up and seeing myself back then." He waved at the hilltop. "I can feel them all watching . . . particularly Wish."

"Don't get too mystic," Dysart warned.

"Why not? Then and now, it's the same procession," Heriot replied. "It's always the same procession, along this causeway. . . ."

His voice had changed. Dysart looked at him curiously. "What's wrong?"

Heriot didn't reply.

Remember! Remember! his occupant was asserting somewhere inside his head. Heriot remembered and spoke silently back to the occupant. *Under that arch up ahead is the gate without walls. Beside that gate I saw freshly flattened grass, its blades still rising up again. And later, up there on the hill I won back enough strength to recover. Part of me—you—had hidden and slept. And, back then, you began waking.*

The occupant answered him gleefully. *Here on the causeway I woke! We had been torn apart, torn in two. But now we're twins. We work as twins.*

Heriot nodded, continuing his inner dialogue. *And over there, off the causeway. That's where you unwound yourself and saved me from the Hero of Hoad.*

"What's wrong?" Dysart asked. That outside voice startled Heriot. "Why are you rubbing your side?"

"Just the memory of an old scratch," Heriot said. "It's left its mark on me in different ways."

"Oh, all right! Be mysterious!" Dysart said. "After all, it's part of your job, isn't it?"

And in due course they moved on under the arch, and through the gate without walls. The curving road, newly cleared to make way for a royal procession, twisted toward the heart of Cassio's Island. And suddenly there before them was one of the island's great harbors, with a city rising around it. High on a spiky hill stood a spiky castle encircled by a curious lacework of buildings and walls, streets and spires. If it didn't have the power of Guard-on-the-Rock . . . if it didn't give off the same feeling of impassioned history, this island city still had a strength of its own. And there, riding to meet them, like a curious reflection, came another procession.

Heriot heard Luce exclaiming with something like joy touched with a curious note of relief, as if he recognized his own reflection—as if he, at least, was coming home.

Carlyon, the Hero of Hoad, advanced to meet them. Heriot watched him smile politely at the King, then look past him at Luce. Then, impulsively it seemed, Carlyon rode forward, leaned sideways out of his saddle, and embraced Luce as if he were greeting a true friend . . . more than a friend, perhaps . . . as if he were embracing an earlier self.

"Welcome to my challenger," he said, and Heriot was astonished at the warmth and passion in his voice. "You might remake me."

Heriot couldn't see Luce's expression, but he imagined it might be showing some confusion. Luce didn't have the subtlety of mind to understand that a man might be the Hero, yet still remember himself as the challenger, that he might find himself overtaken both by an ancient presence he could not anticipate, and by a sudden reunion with the passions he had felt as a younger man.

Carlyon killed Link, but that wasn't all he killed, the occupant said, speaking as it sometimes chose to do, in Cayley's broken voice. And almost as if he had heard, Carlyon looked across at Heriot, who smiled back, absentmindedly stroking his side. The scar was nothing but a faint white line, but Heriot sometimes felt that pucker in his skin as an enigmatic road mapped on him. Carlyon turned away from him to greet the King with a cool formality. He sat straight in the saddle without bowing, as those on either side of him were doing, for he and the King were equals in the land of Hoad.

Carlyon's host led the procession of the King through the streets of his city—streets that were wider and lighter than the streets of Diamond, for Diamond had flung itself carelessly together over its many disordered years, while the Hero's city had been built with beauty in mind. All the same, it lacked the vitality, the savage mystery of Diamond, for Diamond's age and sprawling contradictions made it something beyond beautiful.

As they rode in, a great white space on their left suddenly opened like pale cupped hands, empty and begging to be filled, and indeed, the day after tomorrow, that pale cup's implicit request would be answered. But for now the blended processions rode past the arena and into a series of wide, linked courtyards. Men hurried forward to help them dismount, to take their bundles and lead their horses to the pastures and stables below the castle. The King's family and followers began to climb the wide staircase that zigzagged up the slopes to the castle door.

"It's easy to be dignified on a stair like this," Dysart said to Heriot. "Even for a mad Prince and a mixed-up Magician." A few moments later they came into an upper courtyard that was also a great garden. The pointed doors of the castle swung wide, and within minutes, though they were such a grand company, it had swallowed them all.

There was a night of sleeping and then a day of feasting and friendship—a formal celebration of the duality of Hoad, throughout which Luce and Carlyon sat together like brothers. And then, the following day, late in the morning, both the Hero's and the King's people filed through the open gates of that pale arena. Music played and trumpets blew traditional fanfares as the gathered company took their places. Some whispered, but on the whole the arena was filled with grave silence until, at last, a great gong spoke out, making a single metallic announcement.

Luce emerged through an arched doorway to the east, while Carlyon came out through a twin doorway to the west. They advanced and faced each other across a stretch of short green grass. Heriot could feel Luce's ambition, certainty, and exaltation like an echo of the trumpets, but the feeling that flowed from Carlyon was quite different. There was no exaltation. Carlyon gave off nothing beyond ruthless intention as old skills sprang to life within him. Both men, oiled and armed, shone like spirits. They held swords in their right hands, daggers in their left. Trumpets sounded, and once again the arena echoed with the single note of the gong. Prince and Hero closed on each other without a moment's hesitation, slashing at each other with the swords.

The Hero struck; Luce parried, laughing as he did so.

Then Luce struck, and the Hero parried. They swung and circled around each other, then closed in again. The clash of blade against blade came faintly but distinctly to the high seats where Heriot sat among the King's company.

"It's stupid," said Heriot under his breath, speaking to Cayley, who had been allowed to sit at his elbow. "It has a sort of magnificence, but it's stupid." And as he said this, he saw Betony Hoad turn a little in his seat and look at him with an expression in which surprise and recognition were mixed together.

"Just being alive—that's got its stupid side," Cayley muttered back, focused on the two figures below. "And none of us asks to be born." Then he laughed, flinging out his arm as if he too brandished a sword, but an invisible one.

The two men clashed again, striking in at each other with a series of rapid and skillful blows, then curving briefly away from each other to gasp and balance themselves before closing in to strike again. Blood leaped from Carlyon's shoulder, and a great sigh arose from the crowd. Tributaries of blood ran down from his shoulder and wound across his chest, but he seemed to ignore these thin crimson streams, leaping forward and thrusting at Luce, inflicting a small gash low in the Prince's side. Luce struck the Hero's sword away, but Carlyon moved in on him almost in the same moment. The blades slid against each other, and just for a moment the men struggled, their faces almost touching, both grinning savage grins of ferocity, not friendship. Their left hands rose. Light gleamed on the daggers, but somehow, before either of them could truly strike, they tore apart. It was Luce who had sprung back this time, trying to free himself, hoping perhaps for a better chance, but as Luce retreated, Carlyon moved in on him. Heriot was suddenly seeing, somewhere inside his head, a face he had seen before, a face twisted with a ruthless fury. He was seeing it from a distance this time—he was not the target—but it all came back to him, and he took a breath, half intending to protect Luce as he had once protected himself. Luce smashed a sword blow down at Carlyon and the whole arena gasped, but Carlyon was already whirling away, beads of blood pumping out into the air around him. Luce, committed to his savage blow, lost his balance a little, and it was Carlyon's turn to dive in. Once again the two men fought skin against skin, not clashing swords but left-arm wrestling with each other, shouting with wordless fury. Heriot thought that one or the other must drop his sword, but even as they embraced they struck at each other with their daggers, inflicting shallow cuts on shifting shoulders, but no wound so great that either gave in. Then they tore apart from each other yet again—sweating, panting, bleeding—trying to move constantly, refusing to be any sort of target.

But even before Heriot had drawn a following breath, Carlyon let out a sound—a mixture of a scream and a roar— that seemed to ring around the arena. He charged forward, then seemed to slip in the blood underfoot, for by now the blood of the Prince and the blood of the Hero had became a single stain. So Carlyon slipped, staggered, and fell to his knees. Luce moved in behind his sword, a flash of light catching on his teeth for a second, though whether he was smiling or snarling was impossible to tell.

"No! No!" Cayley hissed behind Heriot. "It's a trap. A trap!" For suddenly Carlyon was springing to his feet again. Luce leaped back, but Carlyon was in under the blow and suddenly it was Luce who was bending . . . bowing deeply before the Hero of Hoad. Carlyon pulled his sword free, but only to drive his dagger into Luce, slashing him across the belly. Now Luce dropped, first his sword, which clanged on the stones at his feet, then his dagger, which tinkled faintly. He swayed, clapping his hands over his wound, but he could not hold back the blood and twisting entrails that now burst out of him, spreading in a tangle on the flat arena stones.

"Quick! He needed to be quick," Cayley was muttering. "And it's under, not over." He had been a ball of tension beside Heriot, living every blow as if he were the one delivering it, but suddenly he relaxed as if the battle was over. "See, it's not just getting in a glorious blow," he said sideways to Heriot. "It's being able to dance away from the other glorious blow that comes at *you*. That's part of quickness. And that Prince—he's dead."

Heriot knew Luce as a handsome figure moving through the Tower of the Lion, barely glancing in his direction. Now he watched him bowing deeply over his erupting wound with something approaching grief. Carlyon lifted his sword once more. There was a huge power in his movement as he raised the sword above the staggering Luce—still bowed before him, entrails sliding between his fingers, blood spouting wildly—then brought that sword down on the back of the Prince's neck. Luce's head seemed to leap free from his body with a bright zeal, seemed to bound as if it were glad to be set free from ruined flesh, then scampered wildly across the arena floor, before slowing down and coming to a stop, staring up into the sky.

"And that's *it!*" Cayley breathed in Heriot's ear, alive with a bizarre excitement. While Heriot was horrified that anyone could be thrilled by a violent death, there was something in Cayley's response he didn't understand . . . something like relief. He turned and looked at Cayley with sudden curiosity. Around them the whole arena was erupting with a single shout, as if every person held between those pale, cupped hands of stone knew how to shout in chorus. It wasn't a shout of joy or a shout of fury, but a simple shout of recognition . . . of concession. The Hero of Hoad was being recognized yet again. It might have been Luce, transfigured, but this shout was once again for Carlyon—Carlyon remade. Within a few bloody seconds Dysart had become the second Prince of Hoad, and with Betony Hoad determined to remain childless, he would eventually be heir to the Kingdom of Hoad. Heriot glanced sideways at him and saw a strange expression struggling on his face, an expression of horror melting into something else, as Dysart looked down at his headless brother, then glanced sideways toward Linnet, who was looking back toward him, also horrified at an emerging hope, yet defiantly hopeful all the same. Feeling like an intruder, Heriot turned away from Linnet, only to find himself staring at her father, the Master of Hagen, and was suddenly aware that the Master was caught up in a dilemma so much his own he could never discuss it with anyone.

RETURNING TO DIAMOND

The failed challengers were always buried on Cassio's Island and their names inscribed on the stone walls of the Hero's house. There was calm and dignified feasting as Luce was laid out in glory, robed in silver, displayed for a day, his severed head joined to him once more, made respectable by a silver collar, his belly wound decently concealed. And then he was coffined and buried in the Hall of Challengers, embraced by stone rather than soil. Flanked by Luce's father and brothers, Carlyon presided over the traditional Feast of the Victor, at the end of which he was embraced and congratulated dryly by the King. After this, the ceremonies of the challenge were finally over. Across the leagues, Diamond inexorably commanded the King and his court once more.

So they answered the call, riding back on a cloudy day, that long, bright procession, that worm of color, winding out of the Hero's city. On the way to Cassio's Island people had talked a little and thought a lot. On the way back to Diamond the progress was more disorderly. The procession straggled at its edges; this time men and women mixed together, thinking less and talking more.

"Curiously enough, this is a good place to talk . . . here we're surrounded by people but they're all gossiping to one another, and no one is listening to us," the Master of Hagen was saying to his daughter. "Linnet—the time has truly come and gone for you to marry."

"You know I want to marry," Linnet said. "And you know *who* I want to marry. Luce is dead, but Dysart takes his place. . . ."

"No!" said her father. "There has been another death—a death among the Dannorad. Shuba's father has died. If you marry her brother, you will be an undisputed Queen. You won't have to make do with a mad Prince, waiting until the King dies, and then again for that distant day when Betony Hoad chooses to die. Linnet, I want more than safety for you. I want glory."

"You want glory for Hagen," Linnet exclaimed, so loudly her father looked anxiously left and right.

"I do admit," he said quietly, "I am tired of being the Lord of a land that exists merely as a mountainous county on the edge of Hoad. And you are my child. I love you. I want everything for you. Everything!"

"Dysart is everything to me," said Linnet, but now she spoke very quietly indeed, and even if her father guessed what she was saying, he probably couldn't hear her. "You want to use me to get everything for Hagen," she said more audibly.

"Why not?" asked her father in a low voice. "Why not? We come and go, but the land is the land."

So the procession wound on home. The horses were tired. The riders were tired. Heriot suddenly felt someone edging up beside him, and turned, half expecting Betony Hoad. But the intruder was Cayley.

"I'm moving up in the world," Cayley said, and laughed joyously.

Somewhere inside Heriot's head the occupant moved restlessly. *He means more than he's letting on,* the occupant was telling Heriot, *but I can't . . . I can't quite . . .*

"How did you get to be riding up here, mixing with the Lords?" Heriot asked, looking amused.

"Like I said! I'm moving up in the world," repeated Cayley, grinning. "No one tried to stop me."

"Luce! Luce!" sighed the wind in the tall grass on the edge of the road. "Luce is dead."

I barely knew him, Heriot said to the occupant. *But he was a living man yesterday morning. He woke up alive with his strength and skill and hope . . . and who truly mourns him?* Was that his own thought, or was it the occupant, or was it the land itself—the very land of Hoad—weeping for a lost son?

"Luce is dead," Heriot said aloud, just to see how the words sounded coming out of his own mouth.

"He didn't read it right. He hesitated," said Cayley. "Like I told you, you've got to be quick. And you've got to laugh. Laughing gives you power. You've got to dodge from out under, laugh and then strike home."

The procession moved on, wearily now, words winding around it, clashing and merging into one another. As it passed, the land sighed and stirred around it, trembling a little, perhaps under the touch of the wind, then settled again. It had seen many processions come and go. The hills shrugged the glory of Kings and Heroes into nothing, settling back into their own ancient calm.

REVELATION

Somehow the world of Diamond had changed. The hills beyond the city might ignore the shifts of Kings and Heroes, but the city had Guard-on-the-Rock as a pulse. Luce's challenge and death might have done nothing more than make certain Carlyon would remain the Hero for the foreseeable future, yet in a curious way, Heriot could feel a shift in the quality of the King's Peace. At times it seemed to him that the stone walls whispered . . . that the echoing streets muttered . . . with news of changes.

"Betony," Heriot whispered to himself, trying to work out the messages the city was trying to send him. "The King wants a reliable heir, but Betony refuses to be reliable. So the King wants to remake Betony. But how can you remake anyone so set in place? Betony Hoad is utterly himself. Not even a King can remake him." He stood up, half looking for Cayley, though he already knew the boy was off in another part of Guard-on-the-Rock, working to make himself strong so he could be powerful as well as quick. Quickness might be the skill of which he boasted, but he was determined to be as strong as possible.

Morning touched the trees, which reached out to catch the first sunlight, but it was time for Heriot to leave morning and the trees behind. He must desert his orchard and make for that gilded room of reception, its arches carved with waves and, where the arches intersected, stone faces, wild and yet still, peering down, seeming to mock the grandeur below. Sliding into the room, moving to his accepted place, Heriot smiled briefly up as if he were sharing a secret with them, then sat passively at the King's elbow, a little behind the King's great chair. Voices made declarations. The fanfares sounded like announcements repeated so often their meanings had become a line of nonsense. The King stood to receive the new ambassador from the Dannorad, and did not sit again until his guests were settled in the chairs the servants carried forward from the bright edges of the room. Then the talk began.

The King and the new ambassador discussed trade and treaties of friendship. As they negotiated, Heriot listened to the arguments and propositions, voices advancing and retreating, and felt his occupant receiving everything that was being said, while reading things that were not being said from the minds of the men who talked back and forth so carefully. At a sign from the King, he rose and moved forward to provide a closing entertainment, something he was often required to do . . . something he generally enjoyed, and something that half concealed the true reason for his presence at the King's side.

Heriot laid a sliced apple on the floor at the Dannorad

ambassador's feet, then closed his eyes. The ambassador stared down at the apple, smiling a polite smile that had a little puzzled contempt concealed within.

The pips split. Delicate shoots came out, sipping eagerly on the power Heriot was feeding into the air. Heriot opened his eyes, stared down at the pips and their odd tendrils, then moved forward two steps to pick up a tall glass from the metal table at the ambassador's elbow, stepped backward again, and cautiously trickled wine over the glowing plants, which suddenly leaped up as if he had commanded them. The shoots turned into green wood, growing and dividing. The trees that now stretched up toward the arches were not quite apple trees, though the blossoms bursting out at the tips of their branches were very like apple blossoms. Leaves brushed against the roof as twigs, still dividing, spread out like arms among the arches, and suddenly the arches themselves were transformed, covered with mottled bark while the stone faces in the corners of the room and in the curves of the arches came alive, blinking and smiling. The ambassador's own smile vanished, for he was unable to hide his astonishment, nor, a moment later, his apprehension, as the strange trees that were not quite trees closed in around him. Branches that were partly arms embraced the King and the Princes, who suddenly became spirits of the wood, gazing up and out rather as the stone faces on the arches above were gazing down. Blossoms fell and apples formed. The King sat still, smiling in his curious, unpracticed way at the ambassador, but Betony Hoad reached up to pick one of the apples and bit into it, directing his smile not at the ambassador but at Heriot, somehow challenging the Magician's power. *Do more. Transform me! Make me marvelous!* Heriot shifted his glasses farther up his nose, sighing a little while the trees shrank into themselves, sinking down into the floor, or sideways into the stone walls. The faces in the arches froze again, becoming nothing more than carved decorations. The act of magical entertainment was over, and the new ambassador relaxed, exclaimed, and applauded, unable to disguise the fact that his hands were shaking slightly. He glanced briefly at Heriot with an uneasy respect, mixed with something like animosity, before turning to the King.

"King of Wonders," he said, bowing politely before he and his companions withdrew, knowing they would be discussed, and making for the rooms where they could begin a discussion of their own, part of which would be about the power of the King of Hoad, who could sit so easily with such strange capacities at his elbow.

Back in the reception room the King sighed and slowly turned toward Heriot. "Well, Magician?" he asked. "What is your impression of our new Dannorad ambassador? And those attending him?"

Heriot replied, "He and his companions spoke honestly. . . ." He hesitated.

"But . . . ?" asked the King, seizing on this hesitation.

"There are things he hasn't been told. And he knows he hasn't been told. All I could do was to pick at their ignorance. They feel there are shifts in his own King's policies, and here in this room, where everyone knows that secrets can be read, he was glad he and his friends hadn't been told."

"I see," said the King. "Lord Glass, we may have to look further. Concealment in the Dannorad and trouble in the Islands. It is time my son took more responsibility."

There was a silence. People looked at Betony Hoad, who sat, turned away from his father, eating an apple that could not exist.

"I am not sure the Lord Prince Betony Hoad would be happy at the prospect of more responsibility," said Lord Glass. "Well, would you, my dear?" And he, too, looked at Betony Hoad.

"I daren't even guess at my own response, Lord Glass," Betony Hoad replied. "I enjoy being a mystery, even to myself."

He sounded calm, even amused, but Heriot could read a busy tumult alive in Betony Hoad. And even more intrusive was Dysart's mood of confused anger, which had nothing to do with the Dannorad men or Heriot's magical event, for three days earlier the Master of Hagen had called Linnet home. The different confusions of the two Princes came and went through him like tides drawn this way and that by some invisible, inner moon.

***

"It doesn't make sense," Dysart cried to Heriot, after the ceremony of reception was over, after the ambassador had gone. "Just as I've turned into the second son, just as I've become the heir to the heir, Hagen backs off. It's crazy."

"Something's happening," Heriot said, "but I can't tell you what it is. It has the feeling of a great gamble. A dangerous one," he added.

"Betony?" Dysart said with resignation in his voice.

"No, it's *about* Betony, but it doesn't come from him. It's coming from your father," Heriot replied. "He's working his way toward something dangerous. It's to do with the Islands, but I think he's really hoping to force something out of Betony Hoad . . . to make him become something he doesn't want to be."

"Something dangerous from my father?" Dysart cried. "My father's the most careful man alive. And he would tell me," he declared, but didn't sound entirely sure of this.

Heriot continued. "And before he left, I could feel a shift in the Master of Hagen. But I don't know what's shifting in him. I can always tell about *you* if I try, because you come halfway to meet me. You're like a partner in a dance of friendship. But Cayley—well, when I've tried reading him it's like coming up against a wall. Not a word, not a memory, not the color of a feeling. Just blankness! Something happened to him once that drove him so deep into himself that he's all protection these days. Mind you, I do know that back in the Third Ring, we recognized each other— well, recognized something in each other—though how we could possibly have recognized anything when we'd never met before I just don't know."

He hesitated, realizing that Dysart was not interested in the enigma that was Cayley. Dysart remained silent. Heriot began again.

"Anyhow, as I've told you before, some of these men who now come to the King have something of the same blankness. Not in the way Cayley has, but I can't read them the way I read the men of last year and the year before. I think it means the counties, the Islands, the Dannorad of course, are trying to send men who might have some inner protection against the Magician of Hoad. I'll tell you what, though. Your brother . . ." He fell silent.

"What about my brother?" Dysart asked sharply.

"Yes, what about his brother?" asked a new voice. Neither of them needed to turn to know who had come walking silently up behind them. He was brilliant in his purple and gold, and yet the very magnificence of his clothes seemed to be a secret jibe directed at the world.

"I was about to say that in the back of his mind your father is angry because you won't go to bed with your wife," Heriot said, defending himself by way of an immediate attack.

"I've made no secret of the fact that I will not have children," Betony Hoad replied. "I may be cruel, but I'm not totally without mercy."

"Oh, Betony!" exclaimed Dysart impatiently. "So you want to be wonderful. All right! Being a father and being King will make you wonderful."

"Ah, but not wonderful enough!" Betony replied. He looked at Heriot with something approaching the animosity he had revealed earlier—a glance of less than a second, but one that Heriot read easily.

"Good night, Princes," he said, going downstairs and then down more stairs, making for the kitchen door, the closest door to the orchard.

"Good night, Magician," said the maids, yawning as they washed the last dishes of the day. Flaring torches lit the first courtyard at the back of the castle, but Heriot knew the linked courtyards so well by now he could have walked them in the dark. He knew every ridge—every slight subsidence, knew the places where the stones caught the light of the torches bracketed into the castle wall and the places where they dipped into darkness. As he moved into the orchard at last, with all the relief of someone coming home at the end of a long day, he wondered if Cayley was likely to be there, and then rather hoped he wasn't, for he had to sit beside the King early next morning. He needed to sleep. There would be no time to talk or joke together, telling stories that seemed like pins holding the day back for a minute or two before it moved on and dissolved forever.

As he came up to the door of his shed, feeling relief at the thought of darkness and rest, darkness betrayed him. The orchard night seethed with a sudden movement, and a blow fell on his shoulder with such force that his arm froze to its very fingertips. Not just one man, three at least. An arm was drawn back—an arm with a sword. He saw the blade gleaming. In another second . . .

Protect me, he cried back into his head, where he could feel the occupant moving. But protection was already there, coming not from the occupant, but from a fourth figure that suddenly wheeled out of the shed. Heriot couldn't tell what was happening. A ringing clash and the urgent blade was deflected. Movements so quick it was as if a puppet master was flicking his fingers and making his puppets dance. Someone screamed. A second blade slashed down at him, there was a clatter of steel and the blow slid sideways, striking the wall. He was aware of another, immediate blow somewhere to his left—not directed at him this time. One of his attackers screamed and fell. Shivering movement all around him, as someone slashed at his defender, then something or someone thumped down onto the ground beside him. The sound of limbs thrashing came out of the night, and then a spasming in the orchard grass that had brushed so peacefully against him only moments before.

"That's three to me," said Cayley's voice. "Big ones too. I told you it was important to be quick on your feet."

A groaning rose from the grass under the trees.

"Why?" Heriot exclaimed furiously. "Why did they attack me?"

"You tell me," said Cayley. "You're the Magician." There was something unexpectedly distracted in his voice.

"Are you hurt?" Heriot asked with sudden anxiety, staring through the shadows at his companion. His expression changed abruptly as Cayley, just as abruptly, stepped back into even deeper darkness.

Heriot did something he almost never did outside of the King's throne room unless forced. He became a Magician for his own purposes, drawing light from the air around him, for, though it was night, there was always light to be found in darkness—starlight, the glow of lamps and torches seeping down from the tall towers of Guard-on-the-Rock or from the Ring beyond the castle, all reflecting faintly on orchard leaves and boughs. Three men lay between him and his doorway, one still alive and trying to drag himself into the shadows that disappeared as stolen light spread around them.

"Help me," mumbled the man on the ground, thinking, maybe, that his friends were still alive. But Heriot was staring incredulously at Cayley, who, caught by the suddenly intrusive light, was hastily gathering his slashed jacket around himself. But as he did so, a piece of the jacket peeled away and fell to the ground. A thin worm of blood snaked across pale skin and softly rounded curves. Cayley looked up and met Heriot's eyes.

"You're lucky to be alive," Heriot said at last. Inside he was filled with a huge confusion, as if the world was remaking itself around him.

"It was close," Cayley replied. "But it wasn't luck. Like I said, I'm quick."

There was a short silence.

"All these years . . . ," Heriot began.

"You've never caught on, though, have you?" Cayley said, that damaged voice defiant but also filled with a curious, shaken triumph. "Not to what I really am. What I've always been. A girl."

"I'll talk to you later," Heriot said after another silent moment. "Right now we'd better get the guard. And a doctor for the hurt one. No doubt he was only doing what he's been told to do by someone a lot farther up in the world."

"Or been paid to do," said Cayley, struggling with her ruined jacket. "You! You're too kind. It'll be the death of you."

They stared at each other across the groaning man.

"Are you . . . are you hurt?" Heriot asked. "I . . . I could see enough, but I couldn't see everything."

"See it now, then," said Cayley, and flung the slashed jacket wide. "I took on one, bending away from the others. Then one of them came in again, slashed twice, cut my jacket, but mostly missed me. It's only a scratch. Because

I've learned to be quick, and I'll keep on learning. No one will ever get me. Not so it counts."

They stared at each other for a moment more.

"You might have told me," Heriot said at last, in a low voice. "You didn't need to be scared of me."

"Scared of you?" Cayley laughed bitterly. "Everyone has secrets from the rest of the world. You've got your secrets and I've got mine. And this isn't my only one either."

Heriot crossed over and pulled the slashed jacket across her small breasts.

"Why didn't you tell me?" he asked for the second time.

"Help me," groaned the man at their feet.

"You're the Magician. Why didn't you guess?" she asked, half-mockingly. "You never did, not even that first evening here, when I was sick but wrapping that towel round and round myself. Mind you, I was a lot flatter back then."

"People out there have had funny things to say about our friendship," Heriot said at last, "and at times I've wondered too. Perhaps I knew, without knowing I knew."

"I've been good at being a man," Cayley said. "Back when I first came to the city with my mother, we soon caught on it was a dangerous place all over, but more dangerous for a girl than for a boy. So my mother got me boys' clothes, and I've been a boy ever since. And I don't plan to change, not until . . . well, I just don't plan to change. My voice didn't deepen up like a man's, but then, having had my throat cut about makes me speak with a mixed voice anyway. At the time it seemed bad luck having someone try to kill me back a bit, but really it was good fortune disguised."

"Well disguised," Heriot said. "Mind you, I've got a scar myself. We're a matching pair." Then, almost without realizing what he was doing, he pulled her across the space that separated them. "You're your own sort of Magician of Hoad," he said, and began kissing her.

It was a long time since he'd kissed anyone, and, as he kissed her, the kiss changed from one sort of kiss into another. He had never kissed like this before and knew he was clumsy at it, but Cayley was even clumsier.

"What's happening to us?" Heriot said at last, speaking breathlessly. "It seems like we've become something else, and all in five minutes."

"You tell me," said Cayley. "You're the one who does the changing. Me, I feel like what I've always been." However, her damaged voice was shaking. Like Heriot, she had been taken aback by sudden inner revelation.

But then, as they kissed yet again, Heriot heard the groaning coming up from his feet.

"I'd go along with it," Cayley was saying. "The kissing, I mean. Only there's this one thing I have to do. I can't just turn away from it—it's—it's what I *am* by now." But Heriot was listening in an entirely confused way.

"I'll have to get a guard," he said, looking down at the fallen men. "And a doctor. Just wait for me. Wait for me and we'll talk it all through."

"There's not much to say," said Cayley, laughing in her strange way. But as Heriot set off, loping rapidly back through the orchard, running across first one courtyard, and then another, and in once more at the kitchen door.

A VANISHING

Back again, Magician?" the maids called, but he simply lifted his hand and jogged on past them.

Climbing the stairs, searching for a guard, all Heriot could think of was Cayley. He struggled with the double image he now had of her . . . the boy . . . the girl. He wanted to kiss her again. He wanted to pull her so close to him they became fused, finally becoming what he now found himself believing he had always wanted them to become—something single and indissoluble.

He came on a guard and was trying to argue him out into the orchard, when suddenly one of the King's Well-wishers, a man called Fern, both familiar and fabulous, joined them, listened to Heriot's story and, turning to the guard, ordered him to send one of his fellows out into the orchard to look at the wounded man and perhaps to identify the others.

"Treat him kindly to begin with," Fern said. "He will have things to tell us, no doubt." He turned to Heriot. "You must come with me. The King must be told."

They strode through halls that grew livelier as they climbed, with each door guarded, and with guards at the foot and top of each stair.

"I had no clue they were waiting for me," Heriot said, talking as much to himself as he was to Fern. "I wasn't looking for anything, and that can make a difference. Sometimes the feeling comes out of nowhere, telling you someone's there . . . sometimes it doesn't. I miss out on a lot of things if I'm thinking of something else."

"I think the King might know who set it up," said Fern.

They came to the door of the old schoolroom where Dysart, Heriot, and Linnet of Hagen had once studied together. The guard standing at the door swung it open, then leaped back. Heriot followed Fern into the room.

"Welcome, Magician," said the King, sounding, for once, a little surprised. However, Heriot was more surprised than the King, for the King was sitting where Dr. Feo used to sit, Lord Glass on his left, Dysart and Betony Hoad on his right. "I'm glad to see you well," the King added, and Heriot inclined his head submissively. He felt he wasn't really there—all the best of his attention was back in his shed, touching Cayley, teaching her how to kiss, and learning to kiss himself.

There were other men sitting in the room. In a chair a little to one side, two guards standing over him, was Dr. Feo, who was looking at Heriot with an expressionless face, but simultaneously, horror, fear, and guilt were pouring out of him, invisible yet forcible, striking deeply into Heriot, who could not retreat from this new shock on a night of shocks.

He felt his face twist into an expression of incredulity.

"Why?" he shouted at Dr. Feo, and on the great map on the wall behind him the Islands suddenly shone out as if they were set there like malevolent jewels, rather than inscribed with simple paint and ink.

"I don't know what you mean," Dr. Feo began. "This is foolishness. Lord King, I swear I'm innocent of . . . of any disloyalty. I swear it. I am innocent."

"What a claim," said Betony Hoad.

Heriot ignored him. "Lord King, three men have just tried to kill me. I only just escaped, and even then I needed help. But why?" he repeated, momentarily unaware of everyone else and looking at Dr. Feo. "What have I ever done to you?"

"This is remarkably felicitous," said the King. "We were planning to call on you, so you could observe while Dr. Feo was questioned. There is a suggestion he might be involved in treachery against us."

Heriot, ignoring the King, still stared incredulously at Dr. Feo. "But none of it makes sense," he exclaimed. "Dr. Feo paid the killers and someone else paid him. . . ." He looked across at the King. "What's coming out of him is an image . . . he was paid by a man from the Islands . . . a man with ginger hair . . . well dressed, but not a Lord."

Dr. Feo's hands, firmly folded in front of him, suddenly tightened on each other. "There's no name in his thoughts," Heriot said, knowing that mentioning the absence of a name might cause that name to spring alive in some form he could read . . . and a second later it was there. "Grevalle! The man was called Grevalle."

Dr. Feo tore his hands apart, flapped them wide, then hastily cupped them side by side, dropping his face into them.

And then, it seemed, everyone began talking at once—everyone except Betony Hoad, who leaned back, smiling as if the whole scene before him had been arranged purely for his entertainment.

"Why?" Heriot asked Dr. Feo again. "Why?

"The Islands," Dysart was exclaiming. "Lord King, the Islands have been restless for months now."

"I can't believe the Island Lords are treacherous." Lord Glass turned to the King. "There is some discontent . . . there is always some discontent . . . there is discontent even in Diamond . . . discontent is part of the human condition. All the same . . ."

"It is strange to think we must fight so hard to maintain peace," the King was murmuring. "Why do we have to live with such contradictions? Peace should be of value to every one of us. Why do some resent it so bitterly?"

"The city owes me mercy," Dr. Feo was screaming, now clapping his hands together with a slow beat as if he were applauding himself.

Who's whispering? the occupant was murmuring inside Heriot's head. *What is that whisper saying?*

For, coming out of all this chaos, there was indeed a whisper, though Heriot couldn't quite make out what it was trying to tell him. He heard the sound of it . . . had the picture of lips moving . . . but the meaning of the whispered words dissolved before he could pin it down.

When, an hour later, he walked yet again into his

orchard, Dysart walked with him. The familiar trees that had become so suddenly unfamiliar, had become recognizable again, nothing more or less than apple trees.

"Something wicked is going on," Heriot said. He hesitated. "I think it might have to do with . . . to do with . . ." He shook his head. "I'm not sure of anything. There was too much going on, too quickly. There were things I couldn't untangle."

"Let's sleep it off," said Dysart. "You know it already, but I'm going to tell you anyway—I'm lucky to have you as a friend. And I hope you're lucky to have me. Since you won't come into the castle, I'm setting guards around the orchard. We don't want anyone else creeping in on you."

"I *am* lucky to have you," said Heriot. "Forget all that Magician-Prince business. Right now, we're just good friends." And spontaneously, without hesitation, they hugged each other. Then Dysart walked back toward the castle, which was the closest thing to a home he had, and Heriot went into his shed. He was exhausted, and yet for all that, he was anticipating embraces of another kind.

But the shed was empty. Heriot went from one of its two rooms to the other, then back again, yet immediately knowing that Cayley, who believed she was frightened of nothing, had found herself terrified by their kiss and had chosen to run and lose herself in Diamond. She was gone, and he understood almost at once that she wouldn't be back. What was it she had said? There's this thing I have to do first. Heriot had always recognized in his curious way that she had a dominating inner commandment driving her on. Perhaps, an hour earlier, she might have talked to him about it, as, just for a few minutes, their embraces made her vulnerable. But he had been swept away on the King's business, and while he was gone, that unreadable commandment had exerted its power over her. Cayley had vanished, just as quickly and cleanly as if she herself were a Magician and had chosen to whisk herself out of his life.

PART FIVE

THE MELTING

TO THE **ISLANDS**

Time! thought Heriot. *I was twelve when I left the farm. Two years since I lost Cayley. I've been a Diamond man for thirteen years, but it seems like the blink of an eye. I'm dissolving in time.*

But somebody spoke his name. "Magician! We first met on the edge of the battlefield, didn't we?" the King said, looking at Heriot. "That was how many years ago?" It was strange that the King's question came as an echo of Heriot's own thoughts.

There they all sat yet again, King, Princes, Lords, and a solitary Magician in that throne room, its stone walls arching up over them, picking up their voices and swinging them around its curves. Once again those sly stone faces looked down on a royal assembly, seeming to narrow their eyes as they listened. The conversations and arguments rising from the room in a mixed puzzle of words were immediately haunted by their own ghosts. "And there's no end to being a King," the King went on. Dysart was sitting on his left hand, Betony Hoad on his right. Lord Glass sat a step lower than the King and Princes. Heriot, like someone partly discarded yet still essential, sat opposite Lord Glass but almost on the same level. For Heriot, at least, there was a huge tedium about the ancient room, about the placements, both magical and monotonous, locking them into an ancient pattern.

"Perhaps I have clung too closely to my city," the King was saying. "Perhaps I have protected myself for too long. Things are changing in the wider world, and perhaps I don't change enough to keep up with them. I still want peace. Why does it suddenly seem that no one else cares?"

No one could answer this question. Dysart and Heriot exchanged glances, each reading inner confusion in the other. Looking away, Heriot saw that Betony Hoad had twisted in his grand chair, and a curious alertness had replaced the tired derision with which the Prince usually listened to his father. The King, for his part, was looking across at Lord Glass, who did not reply immediately.

"We have said before that peace is not as simple as we have imagined it would be, Lord King," Lord Glass said at last. "We believed, did we not, that it would be universally embraced. We knew we would have to work to attain it, and having attained it, I think we believed we would find ourselves living, not in a perfect world, of course, but in a state of partial grace that might last forever. But it seems contentment is elusive. There are many beyond this castle longing for the assertions of battle. It causes grief and distress, but for all that, perhaps battle is one of the necessary adventures of the world."

"No rest, then," suggested the King, smiling at him.

Lord Glass was one of the few people at whom he really smiled.

"It seems not, my dear," said Lord Glass with an unusual familiarity. "You can surround yourself with peacemakers who share your passion. But there are others who—"

"I don't believe my sons share my passion," the King said, interrupting him. "If some of our distant lands and allies have forgotten that peace is the essence of our kingdom, it seems I will have to travel there in order to remind them."

There was an arrested moment, as if the listeners were taking in an incredible announcement. Dysart was the first to break the silence. "To Hagen?" he cried, leaping to his feet, but his father, without looking at him, waved a vague hand at him, commanding him to sit.

"To the Islands," he said. "And maybe home again through the Dannorad. Though maybe not!"

"Lord King, it might be . . . risky," objected Lord Glass. His voice was not so much calm as playful, yet something was creeping into his expression that Heriot had never seen before. Try as he might, Lord Glass could not hide profound alarm. "Remember, you are the very essence of the peace of Hoad, and—"

"I'd go with good protection," said the King. "And I would leave my city well protected."

"Lord King, you'd be taking our best protection with you," Lord Glass persisted, "because *you* are the protection of the city. You would be leaving Diamond without a King, and the King is more than a man. The King is the sign of dominion, of power. . . ."

"I would leave you in charge," said the King. He turned to look at his oldest son. "And Betony Hoad is old enough to try being King in my place for a few weeks. It is time he went beyond contemplating the outer color of kingship and made some connection with its inner ferocity."

Heriot knew beyond all doubt that, while Lord Glass was filled with something approaching dismay, something entirely different was leaping up in Betony Hoad. His elbow might rest languidly on the gilded upward curl of his chair's bright arm and his chin might rest between his thumb and forefinger. All the same, somewhere inside his head, he was transfiguring. Heriot, tempted to read the Prince, straightened his glasses. *I'm not that fond of looking into another man these days,* he was thinking. *I was never that keen on it, and now it's even lost its novelty. All the same, I'm going to read Betony Hoad. I'm going to read him now. . . .*

"Magician," said the King, interrupting. "I might want you to come with me . . . but then, perhaps not. You are sometimes seen as a threat, rather than an entertainment. I will think about your place in my plans."

"If you are planning to move into debatable company," said Lord Glass, "and the climate of the Islands suggests there is considerable debate in progress, it might be good policy to have something of a threat at your elbow."

"Oh, I will be defended," the King said. "I'm not planning to go alone. We have a navy, largely unused these days. They need a project. I am planning to take a brigade with me, sufficient presence to impress the Lords of the Islands. After all, a grand escort will be expected, and it can be both my glory and my defense. And if I take my Magician too . . ."

"I don't know if I would make an adequate replacement for you without the Magician at my elbow," said Betony Hoad unexpectedly. "The journey you are talking about is a long one, and the inner business of Diamond, and of Hoad itself, will presumably need to go on while you are traveling."

"Well," said the King, "it is early days. There is time to turn it over and argue. We don't have to come to any immediate decisions." He looked at his oldest son. "Of course it will give you considerable power, perhaps more than you want. But you can think about that, and perhaps we can talk about it later."

He stood up, which was a sign that the session was over. Heriot knew Betony Hoad and Dysart were both looking at him, hoping to read something in his expression, but he refused to give any clue as to his thoughts about the vulnerability of Diamond without its King. *Two years since Cayley vanished*, he was thinking. But that was what he found himself thinking almost all the time. *There's this thing I have to do first*, she had said, and disappeared.

What am I? What's left of me? he thought incredulously. *The world is still wonderful. I can feel it around me and I can still move into it. I can be a seed, a branch, a whole tree. I can be free drops of water flung up from a breaking wave. Why am I sitting here at the King's elbow, nothing but his threat or his promise . . . his point of power?*

Then he thought he would enjoy—no "enjoy" was too casual a word—he *must* have a glass of wine, so that he could relax with the world, and let his inner loss become not his master, but one of many things flooding in on him over and over again. These days Heriot found himself drinking a lot and enjoying the immediate ease and escape wine offered him. It was like relief from pain . . . a relief from this golden room, from the castle beyond it and the city beyond the castle and, in a different way, a release from Dysart's friendship, too, shot through as it was with strange, unspoken expectations.

A BLOW FALLS

ays later, as Heriot snatched time to work in his garden, he found Diamond nudging in on him, muttering, singing, and wailing. Sometimes it came to him as a deep single voice droning on, sometimes as a chorus—manipulative voices from the First Ring . . . that controlling core of Diamond . . . as those around the King twisted and jumped and elbowed, to find places for themselves and their ambitions. Sometimes voices burst in from the Second Ring as the merchants and the dealers in trade counted their profits, struggling to become rich and make themselves powerful. And sometimes the voice of the Third Ring also burst in, dominating the other voices with a single savage scream, as if those Third Ring people, trying desperately to stay alive, had all cried out together, shrieking about their intricate struggle. Even voices from beyond the walls of the city beat in on him . . . voices not only of Hoad's living people but from its history.

The oldest stones of Hoad spoke to him strangely from its walls and from the winding mazes of its streets, crying out about lives beginning, lives ending . . . singing of times so ancient that time itself became timeless. These voices exploded in him from time to time in a demanding chorus. They seemed to require some response from him . . . some offering of self . . . but he had no idea how he should respond. Stunned, he listened to them over and over again, unable to hold the song at bay; listened transformed and transforming.

"Heriot," said a voice, and he looked up, blinking, to find Dysart standing at the end of his garden, looking at him cautiously, no longer certain which face would look up at him over the handle of the spade.

"You were in your other place, weren't you?" Dysart said, with just a little accusation in his voice. "That place you go to. That place you get lost in."

"I was totally in your place," Heriot said. "Your city took me over. It does from time to time."

"Are you drunk?" Dysart asked.

"I don't think so. Just a little lifted up," Heriot said. "What about you?"

"I think I am drunk," Dysart said. "And it's only half-way through the morning."

"Well, then," said Heriot, and he propped his spade against an apple tree, and then flopped down into a patch of sunlight. Dysart, just a little unsteadily, took a few steps, then sank down beside him. They sat there, side by side in the same shaft of warm light, both illuminated but in contrasting ways.

"It's strange the way things are turning out," Dysart said reflectively. "When Luce was killed, before I could stop it, I felt a burst of joy, and I was horrified at myself. I had seen my brother killed and felt a sort of grief, but it was a symbolic grief. When you mention *your* brother, there's passion in your voice, but Luce was just a bright shadow to me. We'd been held apart, probably because I was a mad Prince back then, I suppose, but also because of our family. We're treated as if we're devices, not people. We're the King's signs, not his sons. What was truest in that gruesome arena was that burst of guilt mixed in with joy. Because I thought Linnet would be mine—she thought so too. But it turns out her father is determined to marry her into the Dannorad, which is a sort of treachery to Hoad. She's fighting against her father . . . she tells me so in the letters she smuggles out, and I know she is, or she'd be well and truly married off by now. And here am I, sitting here with my father's Magician, confessing to guilt about that moment of joy. Isn't it all mad? Mad to be several people all at once. Prince! Man! Thinker! Feeler! And what about you? You miss your boy Cayley . . . not that he was a boy anymore; he was becoming a grown man, quick and strong."

"He saved me, no doubt about it. He took on those three men so neatly," Heriot said. "And I'm told they'd had a lot of practice at what they'd been ordered to do to me."

"They were after money," Dysart said sharply. "They thought you had money hidden in your hut."

"Dream on!" said Heriot derisively. "You know Dr. Feo sent them, either to beat me unconscious and take me somewhere or kill me outright. But I don't know why, and I don't know who stood behind Dr. Feo. Someone did. I can tell so much about a lot of secret things, but I still can't tell about that."

Dysart was silent for a moment.

"Well, you're the Magician," he said at last. "I'll have to take your word for it that you're a faulty Magician. Anyhow, how are you finding it with Betony in charge?"

Heriot looked around the orchard as if the very trees he trusted might have suddenly become treacherous . . . might be taking in his words in order to report back to some hidden authority.

"I'm finding it dangerous," he said at last. "Something's going on. I can feel the danger, but I don't know what it is. It's so mixed up. Why has your father taken off like this? Why has he left your mad brother—whose madness is entirely more serious than any madness of yours and mine—in charge? He knows Betony isn't fit—he's not to be trusted as a King should be trusted. Betony works on an entirely different plane from your father."

"I've wondered too," said Dysart slowly. "But I think it's a test for Betony. Maybe my father hopes a taste of kingship will turn out to be something of that marvelous life Betony says he longs for. And it may even be a trap. If he tries anything too impulsive, you'll be able to report to Lord Glass. The men of County Glass will be there to protect Diamond, and the King would then be able to displace Betony as heir to the throne. And . . ."

Heriot interrupted him, exclaiming incredulously. "You mean he'd have his own son executed?"

"If his son tried to cut him down, he'd be entitled to," Dysart said. "It's happened before. But I think he'd probably exile him to an island prison off the coast, and Betony would have to live out his days on his own. It might suit him. He might find that extremity he longs for in being solitary on a solitary island."

"That's not the sort of extremity he longs for," Heriot said contemptuously. "You Kings and Princes! Isn't there any sort of ordinary kindness left in any of you?"

Dysart was silent, as if he was puzzling something out. "You go on about kindness and family life," he said at last. "But what about the life of Hoad itself? There's life there and a different set of rights and wrongs. You've read the histories. You know there's always been shifting and sliding, and maneuvering, treachery and death around the throne. Everyone wants to be a King. Everyone wants to be as powerful as it's possible for an ordinary person to be. It's a longing lodged in the human brain."

"Not every brain. Your father didn't want it—well, not to begin with," Heriot argued. "He had to give up certain possibilities . . . a certain sort of happiness . . . children— children other than you and your brothers—other children who were never born."

"But he was obedient. A new sort of longing moved in on him," Dysart replied. "Now he has to make do with the children who *were* born. And he wants to be infinitely powerful on behalf of his peace. Peace is his truest child, it's melted into his dreams."

"And, deep down, you think you're the only one who'd look after the King's Peace for him, don't you?" Heriot asked.

Dysart said stoutly, "Not until after my father. If I

was King after him I'd try to look after his peace and the changes he's made. Whereas Betony would take pleasure in destroying it all, burning it up, and burning himself along with it."

"That feels about right," Heriot agreed, nodding slowly.

"You read that in him?" asked Dysart curiously.

"I get close to reading it," Heriot said. "Sometimes his moods come out to meet me, and then linger on in my head, like flavors of despair. But since Cayley disappeared, it's as if that reading part of me has stepped back."

He didn't want to talk about his occupant even to Dysart, didn't want to admit he was living through days when his occupant had retreated back into some deep crack in his head and was unwilling to reveal itself, even to him. At the same time he was astonished to find he had become so proud of his power and his difference he didn't want to acknowledge its incomprehensible diminishment. He had not only lost Cayley, he seemed to have lost something of that extra sense that might have enabled him to find her. Fleetingly he wondered if this had happened to Izachel, and if it was from that despair he had been driven to steal power from the child Heriot had once been. And, as he felt this, he also felt himself flooded by Dysart's despair over losing Linnet.

"I don't think Linnet will let her father marry her into the Dannorad," he said. "I think she'll fight against it, even if she beats herself to death in the battle."

"Maybe," said Dysart, "but are you guessing as a Magician or a peasant or a family man? Now, Linnet and I—we're not just people. We're noble, signs of Hoad and Hagen, and it's part of our tradition to be loyal to the Lord of the land and to the King. Being noble isn't the same as being free. And what if Linnet gets worn out by it all and gives in? I couldn't blame her, could I?"

★ ★ ★

Later that afternoon Heriot set out, as he had set out every day when he had had the freedom to do so, to wander into the Second Ring, hoping to pick up some echo of Cayley's wild laughter, or catch the reflection of her brilliant smile on some shining surface, hoping his occupant might dissolve into a mist of awareness, eager to seize on any clue. But these days when he went out into the city the occupant refused to blossom out. If anything, it shrank deeper into him, forcing itself into some sort of hibernation. Sometimes it seemed to Heriot that it had received a sign from the outer world and was saving itself for something. Sometimes it seemed as if he had unconsciously cut himself away from its contradictory powers. He could not tell. There was a certain freedom in his new isolation, but most of the time he felt he had been lessened, that his occupant had turned its back on him.

Heriot was to be betrayed. Returning at last to his shed in the shadowed evening, he received no warning and no protection.

Once again a blow fell, but this time Heriot fell too, toppling forward not only into the grass under the apple trees, but into a darkness stabbed every now and then with daggers of white lightning. And when he woke once again, he woke into darkness of an entirely different kind.

HANGING FROM THE WALL

At first Heriot thought he was lying on his back, hands clasped somewhere over his head. Then his aching arms spoke to him urgently, and he realized he was hanging by his wrists, unconsciously trying to brace his back against a stone wall. Scrabbling with desperate feet, he found a floor, balancing himself on his first and second toes, believing, for a moment, he might be standing. Pain shot up through his calves and into his hips. Was he standing?

Yes, he was definitely standing—or at least he was able to touch an invisible floor. He tried adjusting his arching feet, groaning at the cramps that immediately took over, knotting him into himself. Yes. But those feet had been wearing laced boots only a moment ago. Why were they bare now? Why was he was bare all over, hanging naked in the dark? He was chained to a wall, and only trying to stand. Standing, then slumping, swinging by his chained wrists.

"Magician," said a voice out of the darkness. "You're waking up."

"Lord Prince," Heriot replied automatically, a picture of Betony Hoad framing itself around that voice. "I can't see you."

"I can't see you," Betony replied. "But I can hear you groaning."

"No surprise there," Heriot replied, gasping. "I've always been a coward. Where am I?"

"You know where you are. Chained to the wall in a dungeon under Hoad's Pleasure," Betony replied. "Can you set yourself free? Be a Magician! Try!"

"I don't think I can," Heriot answered, testing himself. "It's like . . . like something in me has decided to sleep until the King comes home."

"But what King? For now I am the King. You know that," said Betony Hoad.

"Standing in for the King isn't the same as *being* the King," Heriot mumbled, hearing his own voice, faint and dreary, drifting back to him from some other space.

"I am being what my father has declared me to be," exclaimed Betony Hoad. He was invisible, but the intense triumph in his voice brought its own reality with it. Heriot was able to imagine him, blotted out by blackness, yet flinging his arms wide with a vivid intensity. "My father has left Diamond. I am King. Think that over as you hang there. And think about saving yourself if you can. I strongly advise it. You know I long for wonderful extremity, and what could be more wonderfully extreme than killing the Magician of

Hoad . . . even eating him. Digesting him and feeling his power dissolving into my blood and becoming part of me. Now, there's something for you to think about as you swing there in the dark."

An altering, oblong grayness flashed somewhere in front of Heriot. A door was opening, and a featureless shape moved through it. Almost immediately the grayness surrendered to the original blackness. The door had closed. Heriot, still half-hanging, half-standing in the dark, was blind again.

Where are you? Heriot asked, speaking inwardly to his occupant.

Here! Here! it replied, in no real voice but a voice all the same, a soft voice, blurred with sleep, yet carrying its own echoes.

Help me! Heriot groaned, twisting himself, hoping to find a point of painless rest. *Let's get out of here.*

I must save myself, the occupant said. It mumbled incomprehensibly, then said clearly, *There must be a true melting.*

Melting? Heriot exclaimed inwardly. *What do you mean?*

But there was no reply.

Very occasionally, footsteps could be heard somewhere beyond the darkness. Or was it his own heartbeat he was hearing? The door Betony had used was fitted so tightly there was no indication of its place, not the finest line to indicate its secretive shape. Heriot continually struggled to stand, but his struggles brought on agonizing cramps in his legs. If he tried to spare his legs, other pains attacked him, shooting down through his wrists and shoulders.

"What's the point of being a Magician," Heriot muttered, "if I can't save myself? What's the point?" He tried to command his occupant again, but it refused to emerge from that secret hole in his head. Suddenly he was nothing more than an ordinary man, hanging by his wrists over a stone floor. He was powerless.

At last the door was opened. Someone moved through the darkness toward him and held a jug of water to his lips. He tried to drink—his thirst raged—but the jug was snatched away and the water poured over him. Much later someone brought in food, setting it down deliberately close to him. He could smell cheese and freshly baked bread, but there was no way he could reach it. It had been put there not to feed him but to torment him. His fingers opened and shut uselessly in the air above him.

At last the door opened for a third time, rather more slowly. Betony Hoad came in, carefully carrying a small flare, a light that shone upward, painting the underside of his chin a warm gold, and spilling downward to touch the embroidery on his clothes into strange life, so that he seemed to be advancing through a small jungle of vines and butterflies. He wore the crown of Hoad, and his hair hung from beneath it like yellow threads of silk. A giant shape, tall and broad, stalked in behind him carrying a chair, which it set down carefully. Betony Hoad sat down cautiously, then settled himself comfortably back into the chair, arranging his opulent robes around him. Then he crossed one leg casually over the other, his right ankle resting on his left knee.

"Well, Magician," he said. "How are you?"

Heriot wondered for a moment if he would be able to

remember how to speak. He swallowed, cleared his throat, swallowed again, and spoke at last.

"You can see how things are, Lord Prince," he said, and his voice sounded in his own ears to be as damaged as Cayley's had been.

"It warms my heart to see you so appropriately displayed," Betony said. "Now, be a Magician! Perform some astonishing act. Save yourself, and maybe I will applaud, and save you too."

Heriot coughed. "All Hoad would rejoice to find that you have a heart, Lord Prince," he mumbled.

The dark giant . . . a jailer, perhaps . . . stepped out from behind Betony Hoad and struck Heriot a huge blow to his face. He felt his nose crack and twist, and thought he would lose consciousness. However, the blow had been well judged. He was not to be so lucky. Warm blood ran freely down into his mouth. As Heriot tasted himself in the dark, Betony Hoad clapped his hands languidly.

"I still don't know quite what my father had in mind leaving me here," he said. "I know he doesn't trust me. How could he, when I have declared myself to be untrustworthy over and over again? So did he hope I would lay myself open to criticism? Did he hope I would overstep the mark to such an extent he would be justified in chaining me to the wall, just as you are chained? It wasn't an innocent decision on his part, was it? Innocence is beyond him. Perhaps you know. Tell me!"

"But I don't know," Heriot began, croaking, then saw the guard stepping forward once more.

"Wait!" said Betony, holding up his hand, and the guard

hesitated. "Plead!" Betony said seductively. "Do plead for mercy!"

Heriot closed his eyes. "There's no point," he muttered wearily, and as he shook his head, the guard struck him again, across the knees this time. Heriot heard himself cry out as his awareness spun away from him, then spun back again. He had no idea if he had been unconscious for a few seconds or for an hour. He only knew he was swinging from the chains around his wrists, pain in his ribs . . . agony in his knees. He had been struck and struck again. His human structure of bones, joints, and muscles no longer worked in the way he automatically expected it to work.

"But I've done nothing," he cried, and heard, in his own blurred, exhausted voice, not only appeal, but a great irritation.

"It's not what you've done, it's who you are," someone said. "*What* you are!" It wasn't Betony Hoad speaking. The words came to him, loaded with memory.

Heriot tilted his battered head against the wall behind him.

"I'll leave you for now," he heard Betony Hoad say. "But I will be back again. And again. Why don't you save yourself?" His familiar face advanced out of the darkness, only inches away from Heriot's own. "We'll move on to something more intricate than a simple beating next time. Your eyes, perhaps." Saying this, smiling as he said it, he stabbed his forefinger into Heriot's right eye before he could close it. The guard spoke.

"He's seen too much already," he said. Through

the screaming agony in his eye, Heriot forced himself to listen and knew at once the name of Betony Hoad's companion.

Touching his fingers in the blood still running around Heriot's mouth, Betony Hoad studied his stained fingertips, and then, while Heriot still struggled with the pain of his violated eye, slowly licked them one by one. "Mmmm! Delicious!" he murmured. "What a vintage. You see, I want to be more than a mere king. I want you to make a Magician of me. I want to explore that particular ecstasy I can sometimes feel in you. I'm sure there must be a way to bleed the power into me. Think about it, if you want to keep on seeing the world."

But Heriot, his right eye screwed up, weeping and possibly bleeding, was now looking over Betony's shoulder with his left eye, staring wildly at the guard.

"Lord Carlyon," he croaked, talking past the Prince. "Hero of Hoad. You have such talent for attacking the helpless."

Carlyon turned, pulling the hood away from his face. "Both of the central powers of Hoad . . . King and Hero . . . have come to wait on you," he said. "We've merely patted you so far. But next time we'll flatter you with intricacy—with steel. There are no rocks here to fall on me this time, other than the stones of the walls, but they are well sealed. Besides, you seem to have lost your skill as a Magician, and without it, you have no future." Heriot said nothing, and his occupant did not stir. "I don't think our dear, departed King will be imagining a partnership between Prince Betony and the Hero, do you? But you can hang there, monster, and do more than imagine it. You can think about it . . . and remember this." Then he stepped forward, displacing Betony Hoad. What happened next Heriot was never able to remember. The blackness that suddenly enveloped him was hugely welcome.

A DAMAGED VOICE

Blackness still, but a different blackness from the one someone had fallen into in an earlier time. Someone . . . Ah! *He* was the someone who had fallen. Who was he? He was . . . he was Heriot Tarbas, the . . . the Magician . . . *the Magician of Hoad.* He had fallen . . . how long ago? Time had gone by, that was certain, but time was irrelevant. Still those cramps . . . still that agony in his eye . . . still the arrows of pain in his arms and shoulders . . .

"Heriot," said a voice, then added, speaking to itself, "well, that's rough work. Nothing delicate there."

The words were clear. The voice was a voice he knew, a voice he would remember forever . . . that voice damaged, yet with a curious, struggling music implicit in its damage.

Heriot opened his eye . . . his contrary left eye . . . the right eye seemed to be too violated to be usable. There was light in the cell once more . . . a faint, flickering light . . . a flare, but he wasn't looking directly into the light, simply staring down into a patchwork of shadows. The blackness, it seemed, had been entirely his own.

"Come on!" said the voice, speaking with impatience rather than sympathy. "We've only got a little slot of time. I've let you down a bit. Up on your feet! Move! Move!"

"I don't think I can," mumbled Heriot.

"Try!" the voice said. "Enchant yourself!"

And this time there was something in that voice that made Heriot jerk his head up and brace his feet against the floor . . . for it turned out he had feet after all.

"Here!" said the voice. "I've brought shoes . . . boots . . . for you. I'll slide them on."

Heriot felt someone handling his feet . . . felt his toes twisting yet again with cramp. But he was being shod by an unknown blacksmith. He looked downward, which he could do all too easily.

There below him, defined by the fugitive light, was a head of scarlet braids wound into a crown. Someone was kneeling at those feet, twisting with cramps . . . someone was working at one of his chains. As he stared down, Heriot felt the chain fall away from him. The cap of red braids rose. Eyes looked briefly into his own left eye. A mouth smiled. Hands rested briefly on his shoulders, then, as the eyes lifted, the hands rose too, to tinker with the lock on the chain that held his right hand above his head. "You can't have forgotten me already," said that damaged voice. "Aren't I grand these days?" she said. She leaned forward and kissed him passionately. "There now! Remember that? And not so many people get kissed by an Assassin."

Cayley had become a Wellwisher.

Set free, Heriot's right hand fell to his side . . . fell so heavily he felt the weight of it tug him down toward the floor. But Cayley was already working on the left-hand chain.

"Have you got a key?" Heriot croaked. Cayley laughed very softly.

"Not this time," she said, turning away from him, "but I've still got that old skill. Remember? I can work locks like they was my well-behaved family doing what I tell them. I don't even have to shout at them."

Now she had become nothing but a shadow once more, turning away from him and using the first flare to light a small lamp. "What you'll have to do is to lean on me to begin with," she said. "That Betony Hoad, he's tried to reorder everything, wanting to damage his father, and that Hero has helped him, but he hasn't stolen power from the Wellwishers yet. Not quite! Move your feet."

"They've forgotten how to move," Heriot said, ashamed of his immobility.

"Remind them," said Cayley sharply.

The urgency of her voice made him struggle with feet that were trying to roll limply outward. The boots felt completely foreign.

"Step!" Cayley ordered impatiently. "I know it hurts, but take no notice. It's just pain. You and me—we can be the masters of pain. We've got to use every minute we've got. Step!"

Heriot stepped. It seemed that every stiffened muscle, every inch of abused skin, his beaten knees in particular, screamed simultaneously to be left alone.

"Again! Again!" hissed Cayley. "There now, that's better. I knew you could."

Leaning on her shoulder, Heriot shuffled across the cell, turned, and stumbled back again.

"Do it by yourself," Cayley said, sliding away from him. Heriot tried to follow her instructions while Cayley bent over a narrow bag on the floor, but, pitching forward, he dropped onto his abused knees. He heard himself groaning.

"Try again. And let your hair loose," Cayley ordered, speaking to him from under her arm. Heriot stood again and took a step with more confidence, enchanted with the triumph of a single step, even if pain was his partner. He put his hand up to his head, only to find himself touching a totally unexpected stubble.

"They've cut it," he cried, suddenly furious. "They've cut my hair." For it suddenly seemed to him that, by cutting his hair, his enemies had completely severed him from Wish and Radley, from farm and family, and from what he most obstinately believed himself to be. A haircut was painless, yet it suddenly seemed to be the most ultimate violation of self.

"That Prince, that Betony-the-Toad, is probably using it as a bookmark," said Cayley. "They say he's a reading man. So keep walking!"

Curiously enough, anger at his shorn head filled Heriot with something approaching strength. He quickened his step. One knee surrendered again, but feeling its collapse coming, he shifted his weight and straightened himself, prepared now for the spears of pain that shot up and down his leg.

"Now then," said Cayley. "Bend a little." And when

Heriot did as he was told, Cayley tossed something over his stubbled head.

"Arms!" said Cayley. "Arms now! Work your arms. Hold them up." A moment later Heriot stood straight, with folds of a skirt tumbling around him.

"What's this?" he asked.

"You're dressed as one of the cleaning women," Cayley said. "Not that it works really well, you're so tall. But then they don't always look closely at cleaning women. Lean forward again." Heriot now felt something pulled forward over his head, then folded back from his eyes. "Lucky the cleaning women here wear hoods. The dress is really short on you, so bend over. Pity we can't work out some exchange. I'm tall too, and I'm strong in the shoulders, but in my line of business I could do with being even broader. When the time comes I'll have to make do, so let's practice. Let's make do now. There are two buckets outside the door . . . bit of water in one, brushes in the other. I thought they might have broken every joint in your body, but mainly what they done is break your nose, which is nothing, really."

"They promised to come back and work me over again," Heriot said.

"I'll just bet they did," Cayley replied. "But I've got in first. Now, pick up those buckets, stoop forward . . . stoop far forward . . . and let's go. That shuffle is good."

"I'm not acting. It's all I can manage," said Heriot. He picked up the buckets, stooped forward, then shuffled ahead.

"Look in front of you!" Cayley commanded, and once again Heriot did as he was told.

They came out of the cell into a long, curving gallery. A low roof twisted up over him in a shallow arch, and, even stooping, he felt his head was going to knock against it. On ahead of them, a flickering torch, set in a wall bracket, filled the gallery with a vague light.

"On! On!" hissed Cayley in that broken, urgent voice. "Walk toward the torch, and on around the bend. There's a stair going up." Heriot began to walk ahead of Cayley, the buckets swinging in his hands. "There might be a guard, though at this time of day, probably not. If there is a guard, today's password is 'Liberation.' Whisper it as if you were afraid of the guard. Once you're up the stair, you turn to the right and wind around another bend. There'll be another stair upward with two guards. The password for them is 'Eminence.' Can you remember that, or have they shaken your brains to bits? Walk on quickly! Get ahead of me."

The hall was lined with doors fitting so snugly it was difficult to distinguish them from the walls in which they were set. Once Heriot thought he heard a sound coming from behind one of them and hesitated.

"Walk on!" hissed the voice behind him.

It was just as Cayley had thought it might be. There was no guard at the first stair, but two men stood at the second, looking like unreliable shadows in the light of yet another flickering torch behind them.

"Well, here's a true Lady of Diamond," said one of them as Heriot climbed the stairs. "And what's the word today, sweetheart?"

"Eminence!" croaked Heriot.

"Clever as well as beautiful," said the other guard. "What have you got in your buckets?"

"Move her on!" That was Cayley now, coming up to the foot of the stair and speaking impatiently. "Get her out of my way."

Heriot suddenly found himself pushed forward and sideways.

"Eminence," he heard Cayley say in the soft voice of a Wellwisher. And within the next moment she was striding ahead of him. Heriot shuffled after her as quickly as he could.

A door in the right-hand wall showed itself. Once again it was guarded, but there seemed to be no password needed. Cayley strode on through. The guards stood back for her, and Heriot followed, expecting a challenge, but none came. Step after step he struggled on, bracing himself against threatening collapse, following Cayley. Suddenly he knew where he was and where she was leading him. They were moving toward the door from Hoad's Pleasure to the Third Ring of Diamond. A bridge between the prison and the city curved in front of them. The first light of a new day advanced to meet them. Only a few steps more—a few steps more—and . . .

Once again the guards rapidly made way for Cayley.

"I haven't seen you before," one of them said to Heriot, who bobbed so that the buckets clanked against the ground, trying to angle himself so that his face was shadowed under the hood.

"Let her go!" said the other. "They're always getting new cleaning women in Hoad's Pleasure. After all, there's always blood on the floor that needs mopping, even in times of peace, isn't there? And probably a bit more these days, what with that Betony Hoad being such a sensitive King."

Heriot's shuffling footsteps set curious hollow echoes running ahead of him as he limped across the bridge. Then he was safely over it and making, in his agonized fashion, for the narrowest and darkest of the streets that fanned away from Hoad's Pleasure.

"No!" said Cayley, almost at his shoulder now. She must have stepped aside and waited for him to catch up with her. "Follow me!"

"Can I stand straight now?" Heriot asked, though he wasn't sure he would be able to stand straight ever again.

"Just walk on," Cayley muttered, striding on ahead of him. "Not far to go."

And now she was leading him along a street that seemed vaguely familiar, then turning left into yet another street. Heriot felt Diamond advancing to meet him, enfolding him once more in its ancient embrace.

"Right," said Cayley, speaking out of the shadows. "You can let those buckets fall, and stretch up if you can." Heriot unlocked his fingers, heard the buckets crash at his feet then roll away. He tried straightening himself.

"I didn't think it would be so easy, getting out of the tower and over the bridge," he said.

"It isn't easy," Cayley said. "But you had me to unlock your door and tell you the passwords. And when a Well-wisher walks by, that's the one people look at, even the guards. And, though things are shifty at present, what with the King out at sea and his son playing games, it has been peace for a long time, hasn't it? Things relax. The hard part was getting up the first stair, and we danced through that. Turn right along here."

Heriot stumbled after her, swayed, fell against a wall, straightened himself, and stumbled on again, taking tiny steps, performing a painful dance. He understood there were closed doors on either side of them . . . humble doors . . . and sometimes dimly lit windows that seemed to blink as he limped slowly by. He got the impression from the smells of food in the air that he must be walking along a street that served the kitchens of the grand houses of the Third Ring. And then, suddenly, he was aware of someone coming down the street toward them.

"Cayley!" he whispered, hearing panic in his voice.

"Quiet!" she whispered back. "No worries! It's friends come to meet us."

They were suddenly surrounded.

"Is he all right?" someone asked.

"Nothing that won't heal, given time," Cayley said. "He's done amazingly well, considering what's been done to him. Let's move on quickly."

"We're ready," said another voice. "No one will wonder if we leave early. No one wonders about us. Not really!"

"Follow me," said Cayley to Heriot. "I know the way. Better to go through the wall rather than past a guardhouse."

Heriot simply obeyed her, stumbling across streets and squares into a little park, down rough steps, where he fell, only to be hoisted up again. Early morning was staining the sky over the Second Ring. His damaged knee collapsed under him and he fell yet again, but the others crowded in around him, pulling him back onto his feet and pushing him forward.

"Bring him here," Heriot heard someone ordering. It was an accent he hadn't heard for a long time, but it was a voice from a distant past—a voice he vaguely remembered. How long ago? Who? "Nearly there!" Cayley was saying, distracting his wandering memory. "Only a few steps more. Can you see to step up?"

"It's a bit of a challenge," said Heriot, suddenly confident, stepping up with his good leg and then stepping up again. His companions closed in around him and hoisted him forward into a hooded wagon. Somewhere he could hear horses shifting in their harnesses.

"Move on!" said Cayley impatiently from somewhere behind him.

"Welcome home!" said that vaguely familiar voice. "You make a considerable woman, don't you? Lie down in the bunk there and I'll do what I can to clean you up."

The voice belonged to Azelma, the Travelers' wise woman. Heriot was being taken in by the Travelers, and as he sighed with relief, closing his struggling right eye, swollen and weeping, he did indeed feel almost at home.

"THERE'S THIS THING THAT MUST BE DONE FIRST"

The Travelers traveled, and the land of Hoad opened to receive them. In the beginning they moved along wide, winding roads across gentle hills. Heriot, lying closed in Azelma's wagon, felt that wagon slowly tilting up, then dipping down, up then down, and it seemed to him, as he lay in a dream of both pain and relief, that he was feeling the whole land of Hoad breathing, huge breaths deeper and slower than his own, yet somehow in tune with them. He even felt that Hoad might be breathing for him, or that he could be doing what the Magicians were supposed to do—that he might be breathing for the land itself. And he felt, once again, his occupant stirring cautiously in his head.

At one stage the van came to rest. They had been stopped by soldiers of Hoad, who questioned the Travelers, and then began searching the vans.

"They'll be in here in a minute," Azelma said, sounding anxious for the first time. "We'll try hiding you, but . . ."

"I might be able to hide myself," said Heriot, and began

thinking himself out of existence, relieved to find himself becoming something of a Magician once more, and, simultaneously, feeling relief at the prospect of becoming nothing. One of the soldiers came in, hesitating briefly at the door. The occupant shifted and touched the soldier's mind, altering his perception. He went out again.

"No one in there," Heriot heard him calling.

"A good trick, that," said Azelma, sounding impressed.

"I'm healing a bit," Heriot replied. "I'm getting myself back again."

"But you lost yourself, back there," Azelma said. "I felt it. Just for a moment you thought yourself out of the world."

"Everyone needs a break from existence," Heriot answered lightly, and then added, "I didn't really think myself out of the world. What I really did was shift things in that man's mind. Yours, too. You could both see me, but you didn't know what you were seeing."

Why did you desert me back there? he was silently asking his occupant. *Why did you let Betony bring me down so far?*

The melting, it said faintly. *We must save our strength for the melting!*

What melting? Closing his eyes, Heriot sent this question back into his own head, but there was no answer.

★★★

After two days had gone by, Azelma and Cayley helped him out to the front of the van, and he was able to sit there for an hour or so, his injured leg stretched in front of him, and watch the world unwinding around him—watching mainly from his left eye, though his right was slowly recovering.

The Travelers went though a series of small woods, then entered a great forest. The stillness of that forest seemed to impose silence upon them all. Even the Traveler children grew quiet, and they moved on, following a road that was clear but softened by leaves, so that, for a while, they were enclosed by an inexplicable tranquility. Taking it all in, dreaming in that silence, Heriot felt himself somehow drifting, but with a profoundly purposeful drift. He was coming together again. Riding out from under the forest branches was like breaking out of enchantment. Voices rose again; someone somewhere laughed; children began shouting and arguing once more. They camped and slept, then woke and took to the road again, now following the course of a river for a few leagues before it spread out, growing wide and shallow, when they crossed it at a stony ford and came into farmlands, which meant Heriot had to go back inside the wagon once more in case he was seen and commented on, which might mean some rumor winding its way back to Diamond. After all, the Travelers were still traveling in Hoad.

At first this journey seemed timeless. . . . Heriot, more than willing to surrender to the farms and forest and river he saw around him, didn't care where they were going . . . but little by little curiosity came alive in him.

"How long have we been going?" he asked.

"Only a week," said Azelma. "Lie still!"

"I'm feeling better," Heriot said.

"Lie still," Cayley told him sternly. Her broken voice was amused, yet just a little ominous, too. "I've owed you all these years. Now you owe me. You do what I tell you."

"We're well out of Diamond," Azelma said. "They've checked us, so they're letting us go on. All the same . . ."

"All the same . . . ," echoed Cayley.

After a moment Heriot began, gingerly, to feel his face.

"And stop that," Cayley told him. "I'll let you know everything you need to know. Like, you've got a smashed nose. You'll never be pretty again."

"Forget being pretty! It hurts to laugh," Heriot said restlessly. "That's the worst of it."

"Then I'll tell you nothing but sad stories," Cayley promised him.

It seemed to Heriot that, despite the fact he was still racked with various pains, despite being dominated by a huge and puzzling weakness that seemed, in a curious way, to go all the way back to that strange seizure he had experienced as a boy out on the causeway, he was somehow more at rest with himself than he had been for years. He was beyond Diamond . . . free of the King's Zoo . . . free of the haunting mazes of the city . . . even free of his strange friendship with Dysart, all things that had become part of him but that had also, somehow, further divided his divided self. He wasn't tempted to ask the Travelers in what direction they were traveling. He wasn't tempted to ask for any map of Hoad they might have. He thought that, anyway, they probably had no maps except for one single map that was part of every Traveler mind, every Traveler dream, every Traveler movement, as they slid silently across the land, following tracks they had followed for hundreds of years. And, as he healed, Heriot found himself invaded by a curious lightness, which he thought he recognized.

"It's happiness," he said aloud, and looked with astonishment at Cayley, hunched in beside the bunk in which he lay. She looked back at him curiously. "I'm not just interested. I'm happy—truly happy!" he exclaimed incredulously.

"Good on you," she said. "Now me—I don't know if I've ever been that . . . well, not since I was learning to walk . . . I was happy back then, I think. But at times I do feel relief. Ease. A sort of sunny ease! I feel it now. For a while. It won't last, but I'll enjoy it while I can."

"Why won't it last?" Heriot asked curiously.

"I've told you. There's this thing I have to do," she replied. "Just the one thing, but it's like a commandment coming out of me . . . out of my heart. Out of my head. It was laid on me back when I was a child, and by now it's worked right into me, so it's in every heartbeat. I even breathe it in from the air. I'll never be completed until that thing's over and done. And don't you try reading it out of me. I'll tell you when the time comes."

"I've never been able to read you," Heriot said. "And I'm not even sure if I'm a true Magician anymore. I hung there in chains and I couldn't help myself."

And mumbling this, Heriot fell asleep yet again. Cayley sat there, staring at him with an expression of puzzlement and desire.

"Free!" Heriot muttered in his sleep. "Free of it all!"

MELTING

Out in the far reaches of County Doro, Heriot began walking again, striding along beside the Traveler wagons with Cayley . . . only for a short time the first day, but more the next, and then more again. As he walked his way back into himself he felt his occupant coming increasingly alive, after its apparent hibernation, stretching itself out through him as it had never done before. Some part of him was responding to this by stretching along with it, by ranging out and briefly inhabiting blades of grass, stones of the road. *I am nothing and everything,* the occupant was saying. *I am a pinpoint in you, yet I am altogether you. I am nowhere and I am everywhere. We have survived so far.*

"I'm almost what I am meant to be," he said to Cayley.

"What's that, then?" asked Cayley.

A crossover place, thought Heriot, struggling with an answer. *Everything out there sustains the Magician, and the Magician builds himself back into the world and sustains the world.*

"I don't know," he said aloud. "There aren't words for it. Back when I was a baby, the Magician Izachel felt a possibility in me. He had power, but he was greedy for more. And he wanted to use that possibility in some way that was a wrong way. I've told you how he fed on me, and part of me went into hiding. It even hid from me—hid from my thinking, understanding, everyday self, though I finally recognized it was there after something happened to me out on the Hero's Causeway. From then on it's been alive in my head. I've called that torn-away part my occupant, and I've been able to call on it when I need to make a Magician of myself. But being a true Magician isn't just doing astonishing things to take Kings and Lords by surprise. It's working its way toward an understanding that's beyond understanding. It's becoming a true part of the world's strangeness."

"You've always been strange," said Cayley.

"Right now, walking along these roads, I'm dissolving into everything along my edges," said Heriot. "Everything except you." He took her by the shoulder. She turned toward him, and they kissed.

"What is it?" Heriot asked. "Why do you defend yourself from me? What is that iron secret you have to protect?"

"I could dissolve into you," Cayley replied. "Those flowers and grasses you say you link into—I think you take them over, but likewise you give them freedom in a funny way. And sometimes I feel you could do that for me." They kissed again. "You could dissolve me, and being that dissolved creature, I would be completed too. But it's like I've told you. I can't ever be free until I've done what I was made to do."

"And what *is* that?" Heriot asked yet again.

"Oh, I'm not telling you," Cayley replied. "You'd only get that old-woman look on your face. Even a broken nose can't change *that* expression. What governs me—well—it's an old promise, that's what it is, a promise I made to the world a long time back. And a promise is a promise."

The Travelers were following a road that twisted between trees and then more trees.

"These trees!" Heriot said. "They all mean the same as one another, and yet each tree means something different from all the rest."

"Oh, very clever," said Cayley derisively. "Very magic-mystical!"

"We've both got secrets we can't tell," said Heriot. "I'd have to invent a language to really tell you mine." He came to an abrupt standstill. "What's that? There, through the trees."

"It's some old woodcutter's hut, I'd say," said Cayley. "Ask Azelma."

And Heriot took this advice.

"There used to be a town close by," Azelma told him. "But back in the times of the wars people left . . . made for Diamond, I think. We'll be into the village soon."

And indeed, within another fifteen minutes, they were trailing through a deserted village . . . tumbledown houses and stalls . . . the remains of walls and fences. Heriot came to a standstill, staring around him with a curious enchantment.

"We usually stop off here," Azelma told him. She

looked at him with a knowing smile. "I can tell you'll like it here."

"I like it already," Heriot said. "Do you stay here for long?"

Azelma laughed. "We're the Travelers. We don't stop anywhere unless we have something to sell. And there's no one here to buy what we have to offer. We'll be moving on tomorrow."

"You might," Cayley said, watching Heriot's expression. "But perhaps we won't. I think this man might have found a stopping-off place now he's not bleeding, blinking, and limping. Funny really, that just when he gets the chance to be a real traveler, he wants to give up traveling."

"It's in me to like still places," Heriot said. "And I like this one. It's my orchard hut all over again."

"You can stay here," Azelma said skeptically. "But can you *live* here?"

"We can for a while at least," Heriot said. "There's fruit on those trees in between the houses, and my friend here is probably a good hunter."

"I can outrun rabbits," Cayley said. "That's my skill . . . to be quicker than the quickest. And the quick often survive when the strong tumble over. At least I've built a lot of hopes around that idea, and one of the hopes is that I'm right."

"I'll find us a good cottage to live in," Heriot said. "With a roof and all four walls. I'll collect wood for a fire and be a good family man."

Cayley smiled the brilliant smile that had first caught his attention—that smile that seemed to celebrate life so joyously.

"A family! Great! I've never had one of those," she said.

★ ★ ★

So the next day the Travelers moved on, leaving Cayley and Heriot in the empty village. There they stood, side by side, watching the wagons jolt off along the road and out of sight. They turned to face each other. Cayley laughed just a little breathlessly.

"You look ruthless," she said. "Have you caught it from me like some sort of sickness?"

"No!" said Heriot. "This particular ruthlessness is all my own. I don't think I invented it, but it's not yours, and it doesn't belong to the King or the Hero. It's older than both of them, and right now it's all mine."

They embraced.

"Something fierce," Cayley said indistinctly. "But me—I can be as fierce as you. I'm the Wellwisher, the warrior."

"But I'm a Magician," Heriot said. "And I'm putting you under a spell."

"Only if I choose," Cayley replied, putting her hands behind his head. "And anyway, if it's a spell, who's casting it? It might be me."

As they kissed it seemed to Heriot that deep in its fortress inside his head, the occupant came sharply alive. Almost as one person, he and Cayley swayed and then collapsed together, gently, into the grass.

Melting, his occupant was crying as it tumbled with him. *Free at last. Now!* But he hardly paid it any notice.

"Now," he mumbled. "Remake me, Cayley!"

"Talk! Talk!" said Cayley, taking his ears in her hands

and shaking his head. "Leave words behind, can't you?"

"Remake me," he repeated. "And fair's fair, I'll remake you."

They kissed again. And Cayley was right. Their final embraces were beyond all the words that Heriot had ever learned or carried with him over the years. *Melting!* cried the occupant, and Heriot melted as he had never melted before.

PART **SIX**

THE CHALLENGE

SAVING DYSART

Sometimes it seemed to Linnet that she was strong enough to resist her father's intentions until the end of time. She had stood against him for years, believing herself to be married to Dysart in every true way, despite her father telling her, over and over again, that she would grow out of this particular illusion.

"You wanted me to marry Luce," she cried. "You wanted me to marry him because he was second in line to the throne of Hoad. But now Dysart has taken his place, and it is Dysart I love."

"Love!" said her father derisively. "What do you mean by that? And anyway . . . anyway . . ."

He paused. Linnet had noticed this expression of uncertainty on his face several times over the last few weeks.

"What's going on?" she cried. "I know something's going on and you won't tell me. Is it because the King has gone out to the Islands?"

And, as she shouted this at her father, she immediately knew that whatever was causing her father's doubt was indeed something to do with the King's strange departure, and she was suddenly filled with fear for Dysart.

"He seems to have left his city, his whole country, so undefended," her father muttered. "I want to know why. And the couriers who came this morning tell me that now the Magician of Hoad has disappeared."

For some reason this news sharpened Linnet's own anxieties, though, once again, she was anxious not for Heriot but for Dysart. The couriers who had brought this news to her father had also brought her letters from Dysart, who seemed to feel that Heriot, anxious to be free from Betony Hoad as ruler, had chosen to vanish for a while. *But when it's all over he'll be back again*, Dysart had written confidently.

Even as she argued with her father, Linnet could feel Dysart's letter, somehow alive with his particular writing, tucked into the waistband of her petticoats, scratching against her skin. It was almost as if the words were dissolving through the skin and into her blood. And once in her blood they were being pumped through her heart over and over again.

"I've had enough!" said her father abruptly. "I have always favored the Dannorad. Hoad has history: Diamond is powerful and it has always been a temptation, but it has lately become incomprehensible. Let's stand back from something so unreliable. Let's knit ourselves into the Dannorad. I know it's not your first choice, but . . ." He hesitated.

"You know it is not my choice at all," Linnet answered calmly. Dysart's hidden letter was like an urgent caress. Her body became a country in its own right, insisting on its own private ambitions.

"My dear," said her father. "My dear girl . . . you must understand. It is given to *men* to rule, to make decisions on behalf of their daughters . . . their women. Men must take on the weight of responsibility. It is a heavy weight . . . a torment at times. I wouldn't want you to suffer because I failed to decide. I know I have delayed making a choice for you because of your attachment to Prince Dysart, but it seems to me that his situation is . . . unstable."

"What do you mean?" cried Linnet, for she felt there was a sly meaning in what her father was saying—something dark beyond his words.

"Let's say that I have had some indication that Betony Hoad has an agenda of his own . . . not necessarily a wise one. His father has left him to rule, and his ruling may take some personal direction. And by the time the King comes back, it may be too late to change that direction."

It was then that Linnet knew her father was aware of some treacherous intention unfolding all those leagues away in Diamond. It was then she knew she must run away, for Dysart must be warned, and she was the only one who could be trusted to warn him. As her father talked on, using his most reasonable voice, Linnet was pulling up a map of Hoad in her mind . . . remembering the main roads and towns, though she knew she would have to avoid these. Her journey must be an indirect one . . . determined but furtive. She must pass through the land like an urgent shadow. So Linnet began a calculation, frightened and yet exhilarated by the adventure she was contemplating. One horse . . . she would have to take only the one horse, and it would need to carry food and water as well as a rider. Time! It would take days to reach Diamond, so she would need money, and she would also need to be armed. But, as these thoughts ran through her mind, slowly turning from disjointed speculations into actual plans, she bowed her head submissively, apparently receiving her father's arguments as a dutiful daughter should.

"After all, Prince Alain has waited very patiently for you to make up your mind," her father was saying.

"He's waited for you to make up *your* mind," Linnet said, trying to keep the sarcasm in her voice as mild as possible. "And he hasn't exactly gone without women, has he?"

"That is a Lord's privilege," said her father quickly. "It doesn't mean anything. Linnet, just think! If Hagen and the Dannorad unite, we have the prospect of becoming a country in our own right. We won't have to be a subsidiary in the conglomeration of Hoad. You may—somewhere along the line you may indeed—attain the glory of being a Queen of a new country—Hagen remade. If you were rash enough to marry Dysart, you might never advance so far. Betony Hoad is a young man, even if he replaces his father—even if Dysart becomes the direct heir. . . ." His voice trailed away. Linnet thought he had closed his argument, but suddenly he spoke again. "I think Betony Hoad might betray his father, but I don't think Dysart would. So if Betony Hoad made a move . . . if he chose to exile the King, I feel Dysart's life might be . . . modified."

Linnet stared at him directly. "You think Betony might kill Dysart?" she asked, sounding nothing more than mildly curious, though the tempest building inside her was becoming increasingly furious.

"At the very least I think Dysart might spend many years in Hoad's Pleasure," her father said. "I think Betony Hoad may like to be completely certain of his position."

It occurred to Linnet that her father was not speculating. He had been encouraged to guess at something . . . and was guessing with a strong element of confidence. The courier who had brought her letters from Dysart had also brought letters for her father, and letters for those officials of Diamond who lived in Hagen representing the King. After all, Linnet thought, being in Hagen was something of exile for these men. If Betony Hoad established a cause, Diamond men, half-exiled on the edges of Hoad, might be drawn back in to support him. As she thought about all this, her sudden, secret plan was continuing to work itself out in the back of her mind.

I mustn't do things too quickly. I must plan, she was thinking. *And I'll need a strong horse. . . . My father's horse might be the best. My father will try guessing which way I've taken, so I'll travel by a mixed road . . . spin off through the villages of the Vincey estate, then into the forest. . . .*

She smiled smoothly at her father, as wild thoughts chased themselves through her head, and after a moment, he smiled back with relief, as if they had come to an understanding and all their troubles were over.

"Good girl," he said. "You know you are my treasure, and I want happiness for you . . . happiness for you and power for Hagen. We are privileged people, but we have to serve our counties as well as ourselves."

Or I might make for Lancewood, Linnet was thinking. *It would mean a longer journey, but it might be safer. Would I need another horse?*

In three days the couriers would return, perhaps with more letters from Prince Betony Hoad to her father. Linnet went to her room.

"I'm not feeling sleepy," she said to her maid, a young woman she suspected of reporting to her stepmother. "You can leave me for a while. I won't need to change my clothes just yet. I'm planning to read.

Solitude was wonderful. She sat down then, lifted her skirts, slipped Dysart's letter from the waistband of her petticoats, and read, noticing the small sputter of ink, as if Dysart had pressed too hard on the paper.

Linnet, I just don't believe in Betony. And I long to be properly united with the land. There's only one thing I want as much, and you know what that is. And now I've lost my Magician. I hope he's simply run away for a while, because I think he'd be very wise to keep clear of Betony Hoad. I wish I knew for sure just where he has gone. Sometimes Heriot's very existence seemed to mock Betony Hoad, saying, "Here I am! And I am a Magician. You are only a Prince. You can tell men what to do and punish them if they don't do it, but I can make the seasons dance and the sun rise." It's the sort of thing that would infuriate my brother.

Linnet found her own pen and paper and began to write rather desperately.

Dysart, my dear, my dearest dear! Be careful.
Something in the way my father has been talking
makes me think he knows you are in danger from
Betony Hoad. I can't be sure. And you say Heriot has
already disappeared. So be careful! Be careful! I don't
want you disappearing too. And there are things I am
planning that I cannot write down, because there's no
certainty this letter will reach you unread by someone
else. Dysart, life is wicked, but the wickedness of
it makes it adventurous, too, and I am planning
adventure.

THE ONE MAN

Cayley woke, lying naked under her coat—the coat of the Wellwisher—the braid of her dyed hair twining out, a scarlet serpent among the wild grass. As she opened her eyes Heriot, sitting beside her, turned and looked at her. They stared at each other for a moment . . . a moment in which it seemed their two glances twisted into each other and which became an invisible tether tying them together.

"Good morning!" said Heriot.

"You look like a different man," Cayley said, smiling and drowsy, but also a little puzzled. "You really do."

"That's because I am," Heriot replied. "Do you want breakfast?"

Cayley continued to stare at him. "What's happened to you?" she asked at last. "I mean, it's not just morning, is it?"

"I might find it difficult to tell you," said Heriot. "I know what's happened, but words are not enough. What about you?"

"Almost free," she said. "Except there's that one thing set down in me. I've told you. That one thing . . ."

"I know," Heriot said. "I felt it fall away for a moment back there, and then I felt it building itself back into you again. But it's been true transformation for me. Remember I told you about what happened to me when I was a child . . . Izachel swooping in on me, feeding on that sleeping power in me and tearing me in two. I grew up to be myself and my own occupant as well . . . two of us in the one head."

Cayley nodded.

"Well, during the night," Heriot went on, "during the fire and explosion of us making true love—I felt that occupant move toward me. It took a strange energy to move across the gap, but you and me—we created that energy, and my occupant couldn't resist. And as you and I melted into each other, there was this other melting inside me. Old injuries healed. I've become what I should have been from the beginning."

He was telling her, but he couldn't really describe the overwhelming moment when he not only felt himself becoming part of her, but also felt his own completion. The division within him had not been able to withstand the simultaneous assertion and surrender of self. He had been transformed.

"You restored me," he said.

They kissed, but gently now.

"That's my story," he said. "Tell me yours."

Cayley gave him an unusual look, somehow unsure and humble. "I can't tell it yet," she said. "I want this mood to last for a bit, before that old stuff takes over. Which it's bound to do, it's my first direction."

"Well then, let's have breakfast," Heriot said. "Let's have a day or two of rest. Then, maybe, we can start all over again."

LOSING A WAY

Riding out, alone and lonely through a wild land, Linnet suddenly felt she had made a great mistake. It had been disconcertingly easy, and once on the road, in the beginning at least, there had been a huge exhilaration in cantering off through the early morning with an old moon in the east, fading from bright silver to blue, half-bracketing the new day. She was off and away . . . off to warn Dysart about his strange brother. She was becoming a heroine of the heart.

I'm free, she had found herself thinking. *I'm out in the world. I'm not just a lady of Hagen, I'm a true adventurer.*

She came to a familiar crossroads and turned left.

They'll look for me down the central road, she told herself, and then farther down the road she had chosen, she reached yet another crossroads, where she turned north, making for Diamond. But after that things became rather more complicated. She stopped, dismounted, sat down by the roadside, and unrolled her map.

That way, she thought, tapping the paper with her

forefinger, and then felt doubtful. Was the road she had taken actually marked on that map, flapping in front of her as if it were desperate to escape her and fly off on its own? Traveling the central road she would have had some idea of how time and distance should correspond—she had traveled along it several times and its geography was familiar, but this wasn't true of the road on which she now found herself. She had expected to ride through villages, those minute names on the map, but the roads she traced with urgent fingers seemed to unravel under her touch, breaking down into a maze of lines—tangled threads—dwindling to dotted tracks going nowhere. Linnet knew she was lost.

"But I'll find myself again," she said aloud, reassuring herself. "I knew it wouldn't be easy once I left the main roads."

The day wore on. Though she was used to riding, she found she was beginning to ache and decided to camp in a small glade.

From the beginning, Linnet had known it would take days to arrive in Diamond. She had known she would need to sleep on the ground and had brought a folded blanket. What she was not prepared for was just how uncomfortable it was. At first, since she was very tired, she slept easily enough. Later she woke in the dark, her right hip and shoulder hurting, the earth below her seeming determined to reject her. It was some relief to turn onto her back for a while, but all too soon her back began to ache. Hours went by, as she commanded herself to sleep, only to find herself incapable of carrying out her own commands. Twisting right and left, desperate to find a comfortable position, she comforted herself. *It's part of the adventure. Be brave! Be strong!* And then, at last, morning began to stain the sky with its first light, and she was off and away, glad to be on her horse again, glad to recognize the pattern of the map stretching out on the land in front of her.

However, she hadn't gone very far before the stiffness of the night she had just struggled through began to reassert itself. Linnet set her teeth. "We're not going back," she told the horse. "Look ahead! There's a road." It was a road and more than a road. She was trotting down the hill into a village.

At first Linnet felt relief, but almost at once this pleasure faded. For the first time she found herself wondering what she must look like, disheveled and tired, a woman riding, unattended, out of nowhere. People in the village came out to stare at her, mostly with curiosity but sometimes with something approaching fear, as if she were a tangled witch dashing in on them. And some of the men in particular studied her with curious, blank expressions she found hard to define.

She spoke to the people, asking if she could buy food, holding out a few silver coins, and found to her astonishment that, though they certainly spoke the same language, she could barely understand them, and that, judging from their frowning faces, they could barely understand her. Then one man sidled forward, staring at her intently.

"Food," he said. "She needs food. Bring her some bread and cheese. Could you do with beer as well?"

His question was asked rather insolently, and several of the villagers laughed.

"Where are you off to, little miss?" asked a second man, smiling up at her in a sickly fashion she couldn't help mistrusting.

"I'm riding to Diamond," Linnet said.

"Riding to Diamond? Just fancy, all that way. And you're right off the track," the second man said. "You should have turned back *there*." He sketched unintelligible lines in the air as he spoke.

Someone brought bread and cheese along with a bag of apples, and Linnet packed the food into her saddlebag, before passing over a silver piece. She could immediately feel people's attention focus on her money, felt their eyes flick from the hand that had received the payment, then back to her face, and then to her saddlebag.

"Thank you," she said. "I'm grateful."

"It's good you're rich," said one of the men. "That'll help you on your journey. Now if I were you, little miss, I'd make off along that path there and ride on . . . up and over until you come to the wood. You can go around the wood or—"

"She should go through it," said the second man. "It's quicker."

"Would you like us to ride with you, little miss?" asked the first man. "We know the paths round here well."

Linnet would have loved a guide, but the two men frightened her. She couldn't explain why, for their questions and comments had been reasonable enough. Perhaps it was because they were both looking her up and down with a curious calculation, not quite a threat but certainly not friendship. She scrambled onto her horse, irritated to find herself suddenly clumsy at doing something she knew very well how to do, and though she had longed for the certainty the villagers might give her as far as her road was concerned, she left the village behind her with enormous relief.

At first she rode through open farmland, but as she moved on, up and over the slopes of a small hill, the hedges gave way and she found herself on a rolling heath . . . bushes, straggling trees, and coarse grasses seemed to stretch endlessly ahead of her. A teasing wind blew as she took the bread and cheese from her saddlebag, for by now she was starving. While she ate greedily, her horse walked on up and over a rise. The heath stretched ahead of her for what seemed to be leagues, but in the distance she could make out a smudge against the horizon . . . trees. The men in the village had mentioned a wood. And the road ahead was striped with the tracks of cart wheels, bracketed with the prints of horses, coming and going. This was sustaining in a way. It meant other people must use this road regularly. But for all that . . . "Where am I?" Linnet asked herself over and over again, wondering just how tired her horse might be. Sure that this well-used road must finally link up with the central road from Hagen to Diamond, she persisted, trying to recapture that first feeling of adventure. What had the men back there said? She could go around the wood or through it. . . . *I'll worry about that when I come to it,* Linnet thought. Slowly the forest advanced out of the distance, vanishing as the road sank down between the hillocks, reappearing as she was lifted by a wave in the land only to sink again as she rode patiently on.

★ ★ ★

It was coming to the end of the day, and a faint, warm breeze was blowing, toying with the grasses and the bushes on either side of the road. Because of the quietness, she suddenly became aware that she was being followed. At first the beat of those pursuing horses came to her more as a vibration. Coming to a standstill, to drink a little water and to rest her horse, she began to feel a rhythm coming up out of the ground and into her very bones—the rhythm of a chase. Linnet was immediately sure the two village men who had watched so keenly as she took the silver coin from her saddlebag were after her. No doubt they'd gone out into some field beyond the village to get their own horses, and now they were tracking her down.

Linnet had a good lead on them, but her own horse was weary. Forced into a canter, it responded valiantly, but the riders behind were overtaking her. The vibration coming up out of the ground became a sound, the distant beat of hooves, and looking over her shoulder, she could see them on the top of one of the hillocks she had ridden over only a little earlier, momentarily standing out against a darkening sky, before vanishing into a dip in the land.

Despair seemed to gallop at her heels, but at the same time the forest ahead of her offered hope. If she could reach it before her pursuers reached her, if she could ride in among the trees, she could lose herself in shadows and silence. Filled with desperation, she struck her horse again and again. It stumbled as it tried to gallop, but it did not fall.

"Go!" she screamed at it. "Go! Go!"

Small trees seemed to spring up, their leaves waving in the wind like green fingers wildly beckoning. A narrow path spun sideward into the wood, and she veered aside from the main track to follow it. In minutes she was in a different world . . . moving into a darker space, and moving with much less certainty, for the forest path was not only darker but thinner . . . indefinable in patches.

As she struggled on, Linnet heard her pursuers enter the wood. They had slowed too, but for all that they were still catching up with her. There would not be time to hide properly, there could be no escape. She was about to lose her money, her horse and possibly her life.

Something slid backward and forward on the ground ahead . . . not an animal, not a forest breeze, but a shifting light. She looked right . . . looked left, and saw something leaping and flickering ahead of her. A fire. Someone had built a fire in the forest.

"Hey, little miss!" shouted a voice from behind. "Entertain us and we might let you go."

Linnet's horse stumbled again. She came to a decision. Listening to her pursuers, so close behind, she dismounted and slid sideways, making for the firelight, knowing as she did that it might be a treacherous beacon. But once off the track, a girl might hide where a horse could not. At the same time she was quickly aware, as she struggled through fern, fallen branches, and leaves, that she was making enough noise for the pursuers to know exactly where she was going. Her one advantage was that she was now taking a path no horse could easily follow, and they might be content with taking her horse and leaving her to the mercy of the trees and the intensifying twilight.

But those voices still sounded behind her, speaking urgently to each other. Even the moments of silence seemed shot through with tremors of action. Then she heard a more definite sound—a resumed but altered chase. The men behind her must have dismounted just as she had done, must have paused, perhaps, to tether their own horses, and were now after her once more.

"Wait till we get you, bitch!" a voice yelled almost exultantly, a violent voice she was sure belonged to the one she thought of as the first man.

A moment later Linnet burst into a totally unexpected space among the trees. She could hardly believe it. She was running along a street . . . an overgrown street but a street for all that . . . lined with empty cottages . . . all doors broken, all windows dark, though that light off to one side, that firelight, painted empty windowsills and tilting doors with an uneasy orange glow. She had stumbled into another village—a village where, surely, nobody lived. But there was a fire.

Astonishment brought on hesitation, in spite of the crashing so close behind her now. Hesitation betrayed her. A hand grabbed her arm.

"Got you!" shouted the first man.

Linnet swung around on him, beating at his face as well as she could. Some of her blows must have gone home, because he yelled with indignant pain. The other man caught her flailing arms and twisted them up behind her back.

"Be good now, little miss," he hissed in her ear. She felt his breath on her cheek. "Be good and we just might let you live."

"Let her go," said another entirely unexpected voice, a curious voice, rough and husky but with an undertone of music for all that. And it was somehow familiar. She had heard that voice before.

"Yes, do let her go," said yet another voice, certainly a man's voice this time.

"She belongs to us," shouted the first of the village men. "We got her first."

But then, suddenly, he did release her, so suddenly that she crashed forward to sprawl onto the ground. Twisting around, she scrambled to her feet and then heard herself exclaiming in amazement. For there beside her was one of the King's Wellwishers, and behind him rose the shape of a very tall man, a giant, almost blotted out by shadow. All the same Linnet had recognized in the few words he had spoken the trace of a country accent he had never quite shed.

"Heriot Tarbas!" she gasped.

"Linnet of Hagen?" he said, sounding every bit as astonished.

"Linnet of Hagen?" the first villager echoed incredulously. There was more than incredulity in his voice. He was suddenly alarmed—more than alarmed—at finding himself confronted by a giant, a Wellwisher, and a noble lady.

"Go!" said the second man decisively, and both men rapidly peeled into the forest.

As they crashed away, Heriot stepped forward to steady Linnet and brush the leaves from her hair and shoulders.

"Are you hurt?" he asked, but she ignored his question, crying out one of her own.

"What are you doing here?"

"More to the point, what are *you* doing here?" he answered.

"My horse!" Linnet cried. "It won't have gone far, but . . ."

"I'll get it," said the Wellwisher, and vanished into the shadows.

"What are you doing here?" Linnet repeated, peering at Heriot's firelit face. Then she said, half whispering, "You've changed. What's happened to you?"

"You first," said Heriot.

"I think Betony Hoad is plotting treachery," she exclaimed. "I think my father might know something about his plans. I think, perhaps, Betony might have promised to turn Hagen loose to join the Dannorad. And I think Betony Hoad plans something against Dysart. I'm only guessing, but I'm afraid." Her voice died away.

Heriot was silent for a moment. "I think those might all be good guesses," he said at last. "I think Betony might want to destroy Hoad, and maybe even himself along with it. It would be a grand way for him to go, bringing all Hoad exploding around him . . . punishing it for not being astonishing enough. Well, if that's his plan, we might have to interfere."

Later they sat around the fire, Magician, Assassin, and Lady of Hagen, their horses fed and tethered in a sheltered space between two tumbledown cottages.

"What *has* happened to you? Linnet asked again, for

now she could clearly see that Heriot's face had been altered. His nose was bent out of shape, and his long hair was gone. The ghost of his old beauty was still there, in a damaged way, and he gave off a strange power just as the fire was giving off heat.

"I spent some time in Hoad's Pleasure," he told her.

"You? How could they keep you there?" Linnet asked incredulously. "You're the Magician of Hoad."

"I've always been a faulty Magician," Heriot replied. "They took me by surprise. And then the magical part of me hid somewhere deep inside, while Carlyon paid me some attention."

"Carlyon? The Hero?" Linnet exclaimed, watching a strangely intent, wry expression forming on Heriot's firelit face.

"He's never been a hero to me," Heriot replied. "And he's no true hero to himself these days. Carlyon may have some deep plan to become King in due course, and some of the counties might jump at the chance to join him. There are men out there, nostalgic for the old days and the adventure of war."

Linnet looked over at the silent Wellwisher, stretched out on the other side of the fire. He looked extremely familiar, but she couldn't work out why.

"What shall we do?" she asked.

"Oh, no doubt about it," Heriot said with a sigh. "We make for Diamond, hoping we're not too late. Mind you, I think it would be a different thing for Betony to smash up the King's Magician than it would be to kill his own little brother. Even Betony might hesitate over that. After all, some of the counties might move against him, reminding him he isn't King yet . . . just standing in for his father. On the other hand, if he has a valuable hostage or two they might keep their distance until the King returns."

"If he's taken Prince Dysart, he'll have taken others as well," said the Wellwisher. "But the Wellwishers will stand apart from him. They belong to the King . . . not to his Princes, not even to his heir."

"Except for you," Heriot said. "And you belong to me."

"I never forget it," the Wellwisher replied.

The glance they exchanged was brief, but a strange thing happened. Linnet was suddenly flooded with recognition.

"You!" she exclaimed. "You're that boy who used to run at Heriot's heels."

"Right," said the Wellwisher. "But that was back then."

"And . . . and you're not a boy," she cried incredulously. "You're not a man. You're . . ."

She couldn't describe to herself just what had happened. It wasn't just the shape of the Wellwisher's face, though that was part of it. That damaged, husky voice could have belonged to either man or woman. Yet suddenly, looking into the blue eyes that looked calmly back at her, and taking in Heriot's expression as he looked over at the Wellwisher, she knew she was right.

"You've turned into a woman!" she exclaimed.

"It's what I've always been," cried the Wellwisher, laughing, "but I made a good boy for a while back there, didn't I?"

"I'm such a Magician," Heriot said. "I've enchanted her. I can't take total credit, mind you. She was born female."

"Living my sort of life as a child, it was always better

to be a boy and then a man," Cayley explained. "I worked at it. And I can take on any man, mind you, any man in Diamond. The Wellwishers know that, or they would never have taken me in."

"And you . . ." Linnet looked from Heriot to Cayley and back again.

"Never mind that," Heriot said, smiling. "You're right, though, and if we get through the next bit, we'll make good gossip. The thing for us to do now is to get back to Diamond . . . to make sure Dysart's all right and to help him if he isn't. We zigzagged along old Traveler tracks getting here, but how long will it take if we go straight along the main roads?"

"Five or six days, perhaps," said Cayley. "We'll have to go steadily."

"Well, let's do it," Heriot said.

"That Betony Hoad will be glad to have you back in his clutches," Cayley said. "He's already broken your nose. Of course you'll have me beside you this time round, and that'll make a difference."

"There's more to it than that," Heriot said. "I'm remade in more ways than one. Prince or not—King or not—he won't be able to touch me."

And suddenly Cayley and Linnet found themselves staring across the flame of the fire, not at a man but at a different sort of flame, a blue burning fire. A new heat beat out on them, and with that heat came words.

"I am the one man . . . the one fire . . . a single thing at last, fused into myself at last. I am entirely . . . I am totally . . . the Magician of Hoad."

A TURNING KEY

The room in which Dysart sat, the room in which he had been imprisoned for the last few days, was not a cell, but it was certainly a prison. The bed was comfortable. A bowl of fruit sat on the little table, and above the little table and that bowl of fruit, there was even a shelf of books. But there were no windows, and the door was locked.

Dysart, the royal reader, refused to read. He found reading was quite beyond him. Slumping and sighing in his chair, he found himself wondering, over and over again, just what Betony had in mind for him . . . wondering what had happened to Heriot, the Magician of Hoad . . . and dreaming about Linnet, grateful that she was safe in Hagen.

The dragging stillness that had engulfed him was broken by a grating sound, a sound that seemed to have hidden secrets. The outside bolt of his door was shifting. A key was turning in the great lock. Then the door opened.

Dysart straightened abruptly . . . glimpsed a guard in

the space beyond the door. However, the man who now loomed over him was no guard but Carlyon, the Hero of Hoad. He was being rescued. Leaping to his feet, Dysart felt his face suddenly shining and creasing into a wide smile, a great noisy sigh of relief bursting out of him.

"Lord Carlyon, I'm glad to see you. Hurrah for the Hero!"

A moment later he was regretting his childish cry of relief. Ignoring him, Carlyon made a sign, and the door was closed. The key grated and clicked in the lock, and only then did Carlyon raise his hand in an approximate greeting, avoiding Dysart's gaze. He pulled the chair away from the table and sat down. Dysart sank onto the edge of his bed, feeling his own expression changing yet again, as he tried to hide the dismay that now came rushing in on him, finally becoming blank and impassive. It seemed that, after all, the Hero of Hoad was not there to set him free.

"Greetings, Lord Prince," Carlyon said at last, mild irony sounding in his voice.

"You're with my brother," Dysart declared abruptly.

Carlyon nodded slowly. "To some extent," he agreed. "The Lord Prince Betony Hoad came up with a proposition that appealed to me. But it isn't as simple as that."

Dysart knew he was supposed, at this stage, to ask about that hovering proposition, but he chose silence, swinging around, thumping back on his bed, and staring up at the ceiling. He felt Carlyon glancing over at him, but Dysart refused to look back.

"I think your father hoped your brother would betray himself in some way," Carlyon said at last. "But I think he underestimated just how extreme that betrayal would be."

"Well, it seems he did," Dysart said. "Because you—"

Carlyon interrupted him, speaking impatiently now. "Listen to me! Your brother is a madman. He longs to step outside the cage of human limitation. He wants to be more than King. I'm not that ambitious, but I certainly want to be a King rather than a Hero . . . a Hero stuck out there on a little island, living alongside a King whose peace leaves me with no function."

"You want to replace my father?" asked Dysart. "I don't see him going along with that. He's given up too much to be what he is, and he's not going to surrender kingship easily."

"I don't want to replace your father," Carlyon cried. "It's been said before, but I'll say it again. Your father has set up a time of peace. He has dedicated his kingship to a time without war . . . a time of negotiation, and he has succeeded to a considerable extent."

"And it's done well for Hoad, hasn't it?" Dysart exclaimed. "The trade between Hoad and the Dannorad has brought prosperity to both. Young men have the prospect of growing into middle age—"

He was interrupted once again.

"But what about *me*?" Carlyon yelled, releasing a sound so unexpected that Dysart jumped with shock, and the little room seemed to shake with mad echoes. "I'm a true man of Hoad," shouted Carlyon, "and I struggle to live out there on that wretched rock, ruler of what they choose to call an island kingdom. But it's a dog of a place, a tamed dog chained to the mainland. Sometimes I come into Diamond and stand at the King's right hand so I can be displayed, but I have no function in a time of peace. I'm not allowed to marry in case I have a son who would grow up to challenge the sons of the King. Oh, I have women. I'm certainly not the pure virgin the Hero is traditionally supposed to be, feeding all his energy into heroism, but believe me, I make certain I don't have any embarrassing children."

Dysart had speculated about this chilling possibility in a long-ago conversation with Heriot. He had been nonchalant about it back then, but suddenly unexpected horror welled out of him, stiffening the line between nose and mouth, twisting the corners of his mouth down, and forcing his eyes to close, in case Carlyon took offense at anything he might read there. But Carlyon had already seen something of Dysart's shock.

"Do you think I like what I am forced to do?" he cried, smashing his fist sideways against the wall. The blow must have hurt him considerably more than it hurt the stone, but he gave no sign of pain. "Do you think I like impaling a pregnant woman or a newly born child? I want to move beyond such necessities. I want to be a twin King to your father. I want some life other than the damned empty peace of Cassio's Island. If I am not allowed the thrill of war, I want a wife. And Betony Hoad would be happy to entertain me with one or the other. Or both!"

A long silence fell. Dysart didn't know what to say. The structure of his world was going through further disintegration. "Why are you telling me this?" he asked at last.

"I want to tell someone the truth," Carlyon said. "But there's something more. I've watched you over the years, just as I watched your brothers. One of you tried to replace me. We know about that. And Betony Hoad wants to be as close as he can to being a god. He wanted to take on the power of the Magician, but the Magician has escaped and lost himself in Hoad, or so Betony tells me, and I think he is telling the truth. He may have the Magician tucked away somewhere, or it may even be that the Magician is dead. I certainly wouldn't put it past that brother of yours to have had Heriot Tarbas killed and cooked and served up as a meal in the hope of digesting him . . . absorbing the nature of a Magician. But what I want is what I think *you* want. I want you to be King of Diamond and to declare that the Hero can be a man, not a symbol, who can marry and own estates on the mainland and be chief among the Lords of Hoad."

So much had been said. Dysart felt his thoughts twisting madly. "My father is still alive, and my brother is still the heir to the throne," he mumbled.

"I think your father wants a reason to replace your brother," Carlyon said. "He is determined to wring a possible King out of Betony Hoad if he can, or, failing that, he wants a reason to replace him. He has seriously underestimated your brother's desperation. At this moment you are a hostage, and so are several others who are your father's men. Lord Glass, for example, is imprisoned in rather less attractive circumstances than these. I think Betony Hoad would have had him killed, and I certainly think he would have enjoyed killing you . . . but at this stage hostages have a value, and he is enjoying his power. He can't afford to alienate me. Most here in Diamond are deeply confused about where their duty lies. They are loyal to the King, but your brother is very much the *sign* of the King. They are puzzled by the forces I brought with me. But after all, I am also a sign of the King."

Dysart felt rather than saw Carlyon shrug. He lay on his bed, obstinately staring up at the sloping stone ceiling. "Does my brother know you are talking to me?" he asked at last.

"I didn't see anyone as I came up here, but I expect there were those who saw me. However, your brother wants my cooperation. Your father and his troop are on the way back from the Islands, and Prince Betony Hoad has sent a ship to meet them, and maybe to explain that he has taken you, along with Lord Glass and others, as hostages. Your brother and I want to negotiate for change in Hoad, and we think this is a way of getting your father to agree."

"My father might set you free from the restrictions of being a Hero in a time of peace," Dysart said, "but I don't see how he can make Betony Hoad into a Magician, or any sort of god. Or even a King! Three Kings, counting you, might be too many even for Hoad."

"There are many possibilities. Your father might enjoy embracing a hermit's life out in the Islands," Carlyon said easily. "And if you were your brother's immediate heir, who knows? The Master of Hagen might change his mind about marrying his daughter into the Dannorad. And accidents can happen, even to men like Betony Hoad. You might become King rather sooner than seems likely at present. There are so many possibilities. Help me, and I might be able to help you."

Dysart stared back at the Hero and saw for the first time that Carlyon was becoming much older than he had been. The huge complications of finding his own longings so entangled with those treacherous possibilities Carlyon was suggesting somehow reduced Dysart to a man without any power of judgment. "It's all too much," he said wearily, shaking his head on its thin pillow. "I don't know what to do."

Carlyon stood. "All you have to do is think about it," he said. "Weigh one thing against another." He moved to the door and turned the key in the lock, but didn't open it immediately. Instead he turned back, looking down at Dysart. "Just don't spend too long thinking," he added, smiling. Then he vanished into the space beyond the door, and Dysart heard bolts being slotted carefully home again.

What sort of life is it? thought Dysart. "What sort of life is it?" he muttered. "What sort of life is it?" he suddenly screamed at the stone walls. "What's happening to me? I'm Prince, yet I'm a prisoner. I'm a Prince of Hoad, and Hoad is so much more than Diamond and Guard-on-the-Rock. It stretches out in all directions, and yet, right now, Diamond seems to be all that matters. And Linnet! What's happening to Linnet out there in the wilds of Hagen . . . treacherous Hagen?"

But the walls merely turned his tormented questions back on him, until Dysart turned too—turned on his narrow bed and tried to bury his face in the thin pillow.

★★★

Two days later the King came home. Light caught the sails on the horizon, briefly at first and then more confidently.

"We'll arrange a decorative reception," Betony said to Carlyon, watching this approach from one of the balconies of Guard-on-the-Rock. "Of course my dear father will be expecting me, but he might be surprised to see you."

"Not for long," Carlyon said briefly. "He knows I am discontented with my heroic function and how empty I find it now that I am older. But I suspect the trap was laid for you and not for me."

"Was it a trap?" Betony asked, smiling first at Carlyon and then at the wizard Izachel standing at his shoulder, also staring at the horizon, and gesturing in the air above his head.

"Oh, I have no doubt your father wanted to precipitate some crisis . . . something that would justify him in clarifying the succession. I think he was hoping we would do what we have done—define ourselves in some significant fashion. But I don't think he expected anything like this level of extremity. I don't think he anticipated that I might ride into Diamond bringing all the authority of the Hero with me."

"Well, if he wanted to precipitate a crisis, he has succeeded," said Betony in his most cordial voice. "We are Prince and Hero together. And"—he glanced at Izachel— "Magician, too."

"There's nothing there we can make use of in Izachel," Carlyon said rather bitterly. "Heriot Tarbas saw to that at the time of your wedding. Any trickster down in the city markets could outdo him these days. He's nothing but a ruin."

THE KING RETURNS

In the beginning the ships were little more than flickers along the horizon. The wind was hounding them onward, and their sails winked in reflected sunlight. As they moved toward the long wharves at the mouth of the Bramber, a crowd edged out to watch them come in—a crowd made up of Lords and their small courts, men and women of Diamond, and lines of soldiers, the Hero's own men interspersed among the men of Hoad. They ranked themselves, bringing order out of their confusion, with the men of Diamond looking sideways at the forces of Cassio's Island, then stepping away from them as if they might contaminate one another.

Out at sea the advancing ships peeled away, swinging right and left, making way so the vessel with the glittering royal sign on its sail would be the first to dock. As it did so the musicians moved forward, coming into their own. The air rang with songs of welcome—both stately and joyous, songs that contrasted strangely with the mood of uncertainty surrounding the singers. A carpeted gangplank was carried forward in a ceremonious way and laid between the ship and the garlanded wharf. The King of Hoad, crowned and resplendent in blue and gold, appeared on the deck, then crossed from sea to land.

A cry went up, welcoming him, but once again it was curiously restrained, as if those who cheered the King were uncertain about what would happen next, unsure if a welcome was appropriate, as if they thought the wrong judgment might bring incalculable retribution tumbling down on them. The King responded, facing his city and holding his arms wide in a formal embrace. For a moment he stood there, looking from Carlyon to Betony Hoad. Then music made yet another announcement, and, as if commanded even though he was the King, he moved forward once more, to place his hands on Betony Hoad's shoulders and stare into his eyes.

"Dear son!" he said, but he said it in an entirely blank voice, entirely free of either dislike or love. Then he looked past Betony Hoad, studying the face behind him. "I would have expected Lord Glass to be attending you," he said.

"Now, there's a warm welcome," Betony Hoad replied, as they bent toward each other, the King's worn cheek touching the cool cheek of his son.

"And Lord Carlyon. I certainly did not expect to find you here on the wharf," the King went on, holding out his hand to the Hero, who clasped it warmly. "What a pleasure!"

"I couldn't hold back from being here to welcome you," Carlyon replied, smiling. "Diamond is not Diamond without a King."

The King's eyes were running over the guards and soldiers lined up behind them. "You have come well escorted," he said at last.

"Very well escorted," Carlyon said. "These are only a few of the men I have brought with me. Prince Betony Hoad has been most hospitable."

"I have rather fallen in love with the kingly function," Betony Hoad said, and as he spoke he saw a sudden change of expression in his father's face.

"Where is Lord Glass?" the King asked. "Where is Dysart?" There was something approaching emotion in his voice at last. He looked at Izachel, standing behind Carlyon. "Where is my Magician?" Betony Hoad glanced sideways at Carlyon.

"Lord Glass and Dysart are both very healthy," he said. "And well protected. But we can't discuss all that has happened while you have been traveling, not standing here in this irritating breeze. Let us advance grandly and allow Guard-on-the-Rock to take us in."

★ ★ ★

And in due course they stood, just the three of them, in the King's golden room in Guard-on-the-Rock, where the carved faces smiled slyly down from the high stone arches. The King peered briefly up at them with a moment of something approaching ease. They, at least, were giving him a welcome he recognized, something he could rely on. Then, his face hardening once more, he turned to his son and the Hero, gesturing at the chairs before the throne. But Betony Hoad and Carlyon were both already seated, staring at him with the confidence of men who know they are in charge of the world.

"Well, have you enjoyed your time ruling Diamond?" the King asked Betony Hoad.

"Not particularly," Betony replied. "But I have enjoyed undermining the arid tradition we represent. I have indeed felt like a man remaking the world, and I thank you, dear Father, for giving me the chance."

"The world is not readily remade . . . not against its will," the King said.

"But it longs to be remade," Betony replied.

"And it *must* be remade," Carlyon continued. "It is unnatural for any world to stand still. Lord King, I want the Hero to be more than an empty symbol banished to Cassio's Island, only coming into Diamond to be waved like an old banner. Lord King, I want to be part of the active life of this city. I want to be your true twin . . . a true King . . . ruling beside you."

"It is not possible," the King replied. "You must know that. I am the King, first, last, and only."

"First but not last," Carlyon said. "My soldiers are spread throughout Diamond. And Prince Betony Hoad and I have your youngest son, along with Lord Glass and some of your loyal followers, in our power. We would hate to do them harm, but . . ."

"I wouldn't in the least mind doing them harm," Betony put in. "I long for some extreme entertainment, and watching experts harm Lord Glass would certainly have its pleasures."

"Your men may be spread through the city," the King said, ignoring his son and looking directly at Carlyon. "But

I have men of my own. You may even have the support of some of the Lords, but I know I have the support of others. And in any time of rebellion, I don't think Betony Hoad would make a warrior King."

"But I would," said Carlyon. "I may be older and less skillful, for times of peace don't encourage my particular talents. I am rather out of form, but I am still the Hero of Hoad. It is my chosen vocation. Lord King, are you prepared for battle? Are you, the man who forced peace on this city—a city molded by *conflict*, a city whose very *foundation* is war—are you really prepared to give up your dream of an artificially peaceful world and allow a more natural one to flourish?"

"After all, dear Father," said Betony Hoad, "you knew when you went away that things would be changed. You hoped they would. You challenged Fate but failed to imagine that Carlyon and I would join against you. Even you have your limitations."

"What do you want for yourself, Betony?" the King asked. He didn't sound as if he was prepared to consider any proposal; he merely sounded curious. "Lord Carlyon has made his position clear."

"I don't know what I want," Betony said. "But if you were to step back and allow me to become King in your place, I might have a chance to define my own ambitions. Our suggestion is that you go into voluntary exile on Cassio's Island, which is an easy place to guard. And then Carlyon and I will rule as twin Kings in Diamond. He will be free to marry, and one imagines he would not have too much trouble fathering a dynasty. And me . . . I would try to become something beyond a King. I might even become a Magician. There must be a way one can learn." He looked at Izachel as he spoke.

"Where is Heriot Tarbas?" asked the King suddenly.

A silence fell . . . just for a moment neither Carlyon or Betony had anything to say.

"He has chosen to leave Diamond," Carlyon said at last, speaking rapidly, trying to suggest the moment of silence had been irrelevant. "He has deserted you."

But there was something of a light in the King's eye. "You've lost him," he said.

"Not before I put my mark on him," Carlyon said. "I think he decided the city was becoming rather too fierce for him. I think he decided to retreat. After all, he is a Magician, and they're notable for trickery, not courage."

A KEY TURNS AGAIN

Looking through the narrow slot of a window, Dysart could just see the ships coming into the port below. He imagined his father disembarking and being received by Prince and Hero, imagined him finding out that Diamond was no longer his own.

They're going to kill me, thought Dysart. *They're keeping me so they can negotiate with my father. All these years and they still don't know him. He lives by history . . . by signs. If it's a choice between his peace and his son, he'll find it easier to live without me.* Turning away from the window, he didn't so much pace around his small space as *wander* around it, pausing to touch the walls every now and then, as if, with a bit of luck, he might find a vulnerable spot, and the stone might crumble at his touch. "If I ever became King I'd watch out for the trap of the Hero," he whispered to the wall, stroking it as tenderly as if it were the skin of the woman he loved. "But then you'd set other traps for me, wouldn't you?" he asked, half believing the stones under his fingertips were in touch with every other stone in Diamond. "Wouldn't you?"

Then he asked, "What time of day is it? I know I've slept, but for how long? My father's out there somewhere. Is he worrying about me? Betony Hoad, Luce, me . . . we've never been much more than chess pieces in a game he was forced to play, and the game's taken him over. Now he's a chess piece himself. What sort of man was he before he became King? I don't know. No one knows. Well, Lord Glass, perhaps."

Then he thought of Linnet. And for the first time in his last hour of distracted thinking, Dysart felt he became fully himself. He stared down at his hands (*my hands*, he thought), flexed his fingers ("*my* fingers," he muttered out loud), and was immediately pierced with an intense sadness and a certainty of doom . . . a feeling so fierce he had to sit on the stiff wooden chair, propping his elbows on his knees and his head in his hands. "I can't betray my father. Of course, if my father was to go along with Carlyon's wishes . . ." Alien forms of hope kept thrusting up through his thoughts, even when he was trying so hard to face implacable facts. . . .

There was a sound behind him. Someone was unbolting his door. Dysart didn't turn when he heard that faint hush of the door opening, not wanting to gratify Betony and Carlyon by showing either expectation or hope . . . not wanting to betray the least interest in what was going on.

"Dysart," said a voice. He swung around furiously, made violent by astonishment, but even as his chair tottered beneath him, before he had properly faced the door, he smelled wild grass and pine needles and found himself embraced and kissed . . . found himself kissing back.

"You're alive. Alive!" she cried. "I came to warn you. Oh, Dysart . . ."

"Linnet!" he mumbled, but he was already looking across her trembling shoulder, to the shape of a familiar giant looming in his doorway . . . Heriot.

Heriot came into the tiny room almost shyly, followed by a Wellwisher. And though Heriot was definitely the man Dysart had known for so many years, yet he was that man transformed. His hair was cut short, his glasses were gone, and just as he used to do when he was a boy, he clapped his hand briefly over one eye in order to focus properly on Dysart. His clothes were rough and unraveling, so he was as shaggy as a bear in the King's Zoo. But there was another, greater change. An unfamiliar power seemed to be spilling out from him, filling the room, almost as if he were giving off heat or light.

"*She's* your true rescuer," Heriot said, pointing at Linnet. "She set off riding through all the way from Hagen—"

Linnet interrupted him. "It was my father," she declared in a voice half sob, half sigh. "He longs to make Hagen powerful, and it makes him . . . unreliable. And I had to choose. . . ."

"There's a lot to say," Heriot put in, "but right now we need to act and use our time well. The city is filled with the Hero's men . . . but I think there are just as many of the King's, all uncertain about what's going on and what to do if it comes to a battle for Diamond. There are the men who normally guard the city, all waiting to be illuminated . . . waiting to be led . . . waiting to be told what to do. Your father just came sailing in with his troop earlier today, but so far he has issued no instruction."

"Why have they let this happen?" cried Dysart furiously. "Their duty is to protect Diamond—and me, for that matter."

Heriot put his finger across his lips. "Quietly!" he said warningly. "The Hero is the twin to the King, and Betony, who was left in his father's place, welcomed him. Attack the King's son and you might be cutting into the King himself. Attack the Hero, and once again you're attacking the King's other self. It's a finely poised dilemma, and we both know Carlyon wants to escape from the prison that being a Hero has become for him. He wants to be an active King like your father, a married King. He wants to have children."

The Wellwisher laughed. Dysart couldn't remember ever having heard a Wellwisher laugh, and he looked in some astonishment at the figure behind Heriot. He frowned with puzzlement that deepened into incredulity.

"Is that your boy Cayley?" he cried.

"And he isn't a boy anymore!" said Linnet.

"I am what I am," Cayley said quickly, in that familiar damaged voice, "And right now I'm not boy or girl! I am a Wellwisher, but not the King's Wellwisher. I belong with the Magician, just like always."

"Move on!" said Heriot, looking at Dysart. "Your father hesitates to command his own men, because he knows you and Lord Glass and others are hostages. We've already set Lord Glass free, and by now he's in the Tower of the Swan, as safe as is possible. Defended, anyway. We'll stroll over there now. And then—why, then we might drop in on Lord

Carlyon and Betony Hoad and point out that yet another adjustment has taken place. They've pushed things around over the last few days. Now it's our turn."

"But what about Betony?" asked Dysart. "Perhaps he has guards and supporters all the way through Guard-on-the-Rock."

"I don't think he has many supporters, but I'll deal with Betony," Heriot said. "Can't you tell? I'm more than I was. I'm most of the way toward being what I was meant to be in the first place."

Dysart stared at him, perplexed, half smiling, half frowning.

"I can tell you've changed," he agreed at last. "What's happened to you?"

"I've become a true Magician," Heriot said. "I'm the one man now."

"A Magician with a broken nose," commented Dysart, grinning a little hesitantly.

"That? Well, I can still sniff out trouble. And anyhow, that's between me and the Hero," said Heriot, grinning too. "I'll probably remind him of it in due course. But come on now!"

"Heriot, there'll be guards everywhere," Dysart said. "I think . . ."

"Yes," Heriot agreed. "But Cayley and me, we walked here past them, didn't we? Because I have the power to change what they think they're seeing. So I'll wrap us around in dreams, and we'll walk by like the servants of Guard-on-the-Rock or attendants to Lady Linnet. Dysart, just tell yourself you are in charge now, because Cayley will talk to the King's Wellwishers, reminding them that their first and only connection is to your father, and as for you—never forget that the straggling old friend at your elbow is the Magician of Hoad."

QUICKER THAN QUICK

The golden throne room had changed. A second grand chair had been set up beside the King's throne, and Carlyon the Hero now sat beside Betony Hoad, looking so much taller, so much more powerful than the slighter Prince. Izachel, dark as a shadow, hovered behind Carlyon, and it wasn't difficult for those who had known him before to understand that he was a shell of what he had once been . . . a mere decoration. Once he had radiated force, but now, even though his face was invisible, his hunched shoulders along with his long, frail fingers revealed weakness rather than power. The King, displaced, sat in the subject's chair in front of his son, and the Hero, who leaned forward, was speaking forcefully and eagerly.

"You see," Carlyon was saying, "you are without allies here in Diamond."

"I knew there were many possible dangers when I left my son in charge," the King replied. "But for some reason I did not anticipate such a degree of treachery from you,

Carlyon. I knew that Betony longed for some impossible glory, and I thought that perhaps, if he took over the role of the King for a while, that the throne, the crown might—"

"How could you begin to think the crown or the throne would ever be enough for any man of imagination?" Betony cried passionately. "We live in a world that spins around a central mystery. And all we can do is dance and fight, gesticulate and parade ourselves like puppets stuck out on the edge of things, while up there the stars—" He broke off, shaking his head. "We play like stupid *children*," he cried despairingly. "We're always congratulating ourselves on our own glory and never admitting that, even at our grandest, we're nowhere near the heart of true wonder. Even grains of dirt have more true glory than we do."

Not only the King, but Carlyon himself, now stared at him uneasily.

"We must do what we can within our limitations," the King said at last. "Do you fancy you could ever break out of your human condition to become a star?"

"Or a grain of dirt, for that matter," Carlyon added.

Betony turned his head to one side, sneering at the long images of earlier Kings, stitched into tapestry and hanging on the wall. He twisted a little to look back at Izachel.

"He's nothing but a scarecrow these days, but perhaps he could still edge me toward transformation," he said, not, however, as if he thought there was any possibility of this. "In the meantime, you could step back from the throne, and I could play the game of Kings for a little longer. Carlyon would be my brother King, set free from all the rules that have reduced him. We could arrange a wife and probably a war or two for him. He'd be able to ride in true glory once more."

As he spoke, there was a curious change in the room. Its very light seemed to change . . . to darken a little . . . to take on a different quality as it stroked the gilded surfaces of the thrones, or sank into rich fabrics. Betony wasn't looking at the figures in the tapestries or the carved faces above him, but Carlyon must have caught some movement out of the corner of his eye, and turned to stare at the wall, only to find the figures of the Kings, sewn into cloth, had all turned their stitched heads to look back at him.

"Maybe we could even arrange rebellion out in the counties," Betony was saying, and then he broke off, for the altering light was not to be ignored. "What's happening?" he cried to his father. "Don't think you can—"

He was interrupted. The door of the throne room sprang open and Carlyon leaped to his feet, like a man preparing to face an enemy. Betony Hoad's face froze, then he, too, rose, though rather more slowly. The door was swinging wide, and Heriot Tarbas, the Magician of Hoad, came into the room. He edged in quite gently, nodded to Betony Hoad and Carlyon, and then stood to one side, making way for Prince Dysart and Linnet of Hagen, who, both disheveled, both alert, crowded in close behind him.

"Well," said Heriot, smiling and speaking into the silence at last. "Here we all are. How nice."

Carlyon, his face twisting with fury, leaped toward him, clutching at his sword, only to find he couldn't draw it from its sheath. And as he struggled furiously with his recalcitrant blade, he became somehow locked in on himself. He couldn't release the hilt and found himself staggering around in a ridiculous circle.

"Lord Carlyon," Heriot said. "I know you can hear me, and I'll tell you this. Move back to that throne you were occupying and sit quietly there, because I won't let you take a step toward me or anyone else. So give up the struggle."

"And what about me?" asked Betony Hoad. His voice trembled a little, but it was still mocking. "Do you promise to freeze me, too?"

Heriot watched Carlyon settling back into his throne, watched his cramped fingers unlocking from the hilt of the sword.

"You!" he said, not looking directly at Betony Hoad. "I've thought about you. I've got a plan for you. I promise you'll love it."

The King spoke. "My son may be a traitor," he said, "but he is still a Prince of Hoad. I don't want him to come to harm."

"Oh, I'm not going to hurt him," Heriot said. "I am going to fulfill him. I can't make a Magician of him, and I wouldn't even if I could. But I can make a work of art out of him. I can make him king of his own dreams. Now, that really is kingship."

Betony's expression was altering. His confident voice was changing. "What are you offering me?"

"I'm not going to offer it," Heriot said. "I'm going to impose it. But it won't hurt."

Carlyon hitched himself around to stare up at the black shape behind his chair. "Do something!" he commanded. "Now! Now!" But as he cried out there was a strangely fluid roar in the air. Briefly a huge image of the broken aqueduct, asking its eternal question by thrusting its curving stream of water into the air, dominated the golden room. And then things changed again. Dysart moved convulsively from Heriot to Betony, who now lay entirely collapsed in his chair.

The King sprang to his feet. "Magician, if you have harmed my son . . . ," he began.

"He's not dead," Heriot said. "Be grateful, Lord King. He's nothing but asleep . . . a special sleep in which he can examine and fulfill the extremity of his own dream, and you—well, you are released from a trap. After all, if you want a Magician, you've got to put up with his magic."

Carlyon had turned desperately to shake Betony Hoad, and shake him again.

"He is dead," he yelled. "You've killed him."

"He's asleep," said Heriot. "Don't bang his head now."

Carlyon released Betony Hoad, who flopped back into his chair. Everyone stared at him, and in the profound silence that followed the only sound that could be heard was the sound of Betony's even and relaxed breathing.

"He'll sleep and dream for a long time," Heriot said at last. "He'll make a land for himself, a land of the glories and nightmares he's longed for but a land of exaltation, too. And then we'll see, because one day he might want to wake as a transformed and fulfilled man."

At this moment there was a familiar sound. The doors of the reception room were opening yet again, and a cluster of figures with whitened faces and scarlet braids flowed into the room. Only the last in the line presented a bare face to the world.

"Lord King," said the first of the Wellwishers. "We rejoice at your return."

The King stood. He inclined his head. "I am glad to see you," he said. "As you may know, these have been troubled times."

"And *I* am the trouble," Carlyon announced, his voice filled with confidence and scorn. "But remember, according to the tradition of the land the Hero is the King's equal. My acts are as legitimate as yours, Lord King."

The Wellwisher with the naked face moved forward.

"Lord Carlyon, equal of the King, Hero who is anxious to father other Heroes," the Wellwisher said, speaking in a curious, damaged voice. "Look at me very carefully."

Carlyon frowned, staring at the naked face. "You're the boy who used to follow Heriot Tarbas," he said at last. "You've moved up in the world."

"I'm more than that," said Cayley. "I'm a forbidden quantity. It was forbidden that I should ever be conceived. It was forbidden that I should ever have been born, but here I am, and damn everything that's tried to stop me. Because me, I was born in Senlac. Remember Senlac and the brave way you saved it? I've been told about it, but more than that, I actually *remember* Senlac, so that's you and me both. I was born there nine months after you left it the first time. And, being a child of Senlac, I am challenging you—the one who destroyed it. I am challenging you to a confrontation in the Arena on Cassio's Island."

Carlyon's expression was changing. He was looking

more and more incredulous, like a man confronted by an impossibility. Then his first incredulity was replaced by an expression totally alien to the Heroes of Hoad. Suddenly Carlyon was terrified. "Who are you?" he now asked, whispering as if he had been confronted by a horror.

Cayley smiled. "Look at me closely. Your reflection, perhaps, though twisted a bit, and mixed in with another face you might remember from a long time ago. But forget looking. Did you hear me? I challenge you as Hero."

Carlyon continued to stare at her as if they were the only two people in the room. "I refuse the challenge," he said at last, speaking thickly. "How can I possibly accept a challenge from you, of all people? A girl! A young girl!"

"Yes, but how can you turn it down? You! A man! An old man!" asked Cayley. She moved forward to stand over him. She struck him on one cheek and then on the other. "Some Hero!" she said. "And some act of heroism that was, back by the gate of Cassio's Island all those years back. Remember?" She struck him again. "Shall I tell them all?"

"Did I ever hurt you?" Carlyon yelled.

Cayley laughed. "Through what you did to others you damaged me forever," she cried. "And then the world—that city out there—hurt me over and over again, toughening me up. But you're supposed to be better than the ordinary world, aren't you? I challenge you."

Carlyon turned to Izachel. "Magician . . . ," he began, but Izachel suddenly crumpled sideways, collapsing into a pile of blackness at the foot of the King's grand throne.

"There's a Magician finding his limitations," Heriot said.

Now Carlyon moved suddenly. Leaping up, he tried once more to draw his sword. Once again it remained obstinately sheathed.

"I'm strong," Cayley said, as if she were reassuring him. "I've practiced being strong. And maybe being strong is in the family. And I'm not only strong. I'm quick, too. Quick beyond quick!"

Carlyon stepped back, as angry with himself for his brief loss of control as much as he was with Cayley. They looked into each other's eyes, but Carlyon looked away first. When he spoke again, his voice was flat and expressionless. "I accept your challenge," he said. "If the King," he added, his voice touched now with savagery, "if the King of Hoad allows it."

"Of course I do," said the King. "To accept challenges is part of the function of the Hero. To witness and celebrate them is part of the function of the King."

IN THE ARENA

And so, in due course, that bright procession wound along the road and across the Causeway to Cassio's Island. Once again Heriot found himself looking around that arena, at its space and its white walls—those pale hands cupped to catch blood. Once again he saw those curving seats ascending like stairs as the men and women of Hoad and Cassio's Island took their places . . . the Lords of the counties and their wives and children . . . the merchants and bankers from the Second Ring, whole households from Diamond, along with soldiers from the Hero's City and Diamond, too. Above the crenellated rim of the arena the sky was blue, pure, cloudless, and remote, rather as if the day was somehow holding itself off at a distance, preparing itself as a witness while standing back from the challenge and from a conclusion that must end inevitably in blood and death.

Dysart took his new place as heir to the throne to the right of the King's chair, but on his left sat Linnet, attended by young women and girls from all the counties of Hoad.

Heriot stood behind Dysart at first, but then Dysart had another chair carried in so that Heriot could sit, looking over his shoulder, and they could easily talk. There was so much they had talked about already over the last incredible weeks, and each discussion made the recent furious and violent happenings more manageable. Little by little those happenings were being classified and filed as history.

"Congratulations! You're fulfilling your dream," Heriot murmured to Dysart, smiling rather mischievously.

"But are you fulfilling yours?" Dysart murmured back.

"Who said I had any dreams?" asked Heriot.

"I'm guessing," said Dysart dryly. "Mind you, if the worst looks as if it's coming to the worst you'll be able to intervene, won't you? Freeze the Hero's arm? Melt his sword?"

Heriot stared out into the arena.

"It won't work like that," he replied at last. "This is the climax of a nightmare that is in her very bones. She has to live through this part of the dream in order to be set free of it. And she has to do it all herself. If I intervene, I'll ruin it all for her."

"But why?" Linnet said, leaning across Dysart.

"Revenge for an old injury," said Heriot lightly. "Things she once saw. Something that happened to her as a child, and it's twisted itself through and through her. But she's never really told me."

"She's tall and strong," Dysart said restlessly, "but not as tall and strong as the Hero, even though Carlyon isn't a young man anymore. It's not too late to—"

"It's always been too late. And these moments are so much a part of her they have to be lived through so they can be over and done with."

The trumpets sounded. The great ridged gates on one side of the arena opened, and the Hero of Hoad advanced with men on either side of him, one carrying a shield and one a sword. The trumpets sounded again. Doors on the opposite side of the arena opened, and Cayley came through alone. She had no shield, and her own sword swung at her side. She was dressed in close-fitting clothes that seemed to be made of links of silver. Trumpets sounded yet again, and once again Heriot saw the King of Hoad, attended by Lord Glass and an elaborately dressed marshal, ride into the arena.

The marshal edged his horse beside the King's. They sat side by side for a minute as the King spoke to both the Hero and his challenger, speaking, Heriot knew, in the language of the past, giving both combatants the blessing of Hoad. Then the King wheeled, retreating in a leisurely fashion. At the watchtower by the main gate he dismounted, climbed the stair, and seated himself, staring across the arena at the challengers. The marshal didn't speak until the King raised his long hand, giving permission for a declaration. Then the marshal's voice boomed out into the arena. All the same, Dysart doubted whether those in the topmost benches would be able to make out what he was saying. The words, set free, rang clearly around the lower forms, but as they flew higher they seemed to fade and become eternal elements of the arena air.

"Aligning ourselves with the great history of Hoad," the marshal was once more declaring, "following the tradition of King and Hero, we gather here in the arena of Cassio's Island to witness the fulfillment of a challenge issued to the Hero. Lord Carlyon has accepted the challenge of Cayley

Silence. They meet in the presence of the Hero's twin—his double in power, the King of Hoad—to fight to the death. This is no common confrontation. We citizens of Hoad are assembled here to witness a sacrifice . . . a sacrifice that will be absorbed by our land, feeding into its hidden power. We are here to immerse ourselves in the limitless mystery of our beloved country. We are here to observe the enigma of Hoad, the rebirth of the Hero—the birth of one Hero burning upward from the death of another."

The marshal stepped back, retreating to stand under the watchtower by the gate. Cayley and Carlyon faced each other. Overhead the sun was inching down a little, and Cayley shone like a woman of silver.

Then, at last, the great gong sounded, and before its first echoes had died away Carlyon had leaped into combat. His sword rose and fell ferociously, but Cayley was already spinning away from the blow. Carlyon turned, parried, struck again, but once again she was gone, diving in with her own sword, not to deliver any fatal blow but to cut at his left arm. Amazingly it seemed (for the battle was hardly begun), Carlyon began to bleed. However, he was quick in his own way and was already diving in to strike at her again. She caught his sword on her sword, which sagged under the sheer strength of his blow, as Carlyon whipped out of range, swinging himself away so that, once again, drops of his blood spun away through the air. It suddenly seemed to Heriot that he would never remember Carlyon without remembering those tiny scarlet splashes in the air around him. Cayley began shouting at him. Many people in the arena could hear what that wounded voice was saying.

"You killed them all," she shouted. "You killed every man, woman, and child in Senlac, just to get me and my brother." Carlyon was in at her again, but Cayley had anticipated his next blow. She was already dancing out of reach, then standing briefly back, pointing her sword and laughing at him. "Some Hero!" she cried, as she dived in at him. But Carlyon defended himself almost casually as she struck in under his guard, dashing her blade aside. And suddenly they were truly fighting—striking and defending, striking and defending—the Hero's blows falling more heavily, Cayley spinning in and out of reach. People in the arena leaned forward, gasping as it seemed some blow must smack home. There was yet another engagement of blades that slid along each other in a steely dance.

"See! I've got *your* skill!" she yelled. "You passed it on to the wrong one." It seemed their two faces were only inches apart. And now Cayley said something to the Hero. What she said this time was inaudible, but even from the King's watchtower, even from the stands where Heriot, Dysart, and Linnet sat side by side, even from the benches that rose above up around them, anyone could see something had altered and was continuing to alter. Carlyon leaped back, staring at her incredulously. Cayley stood still, smiling over at him. Then he thrust in at her, but thrust rather incoherently this time. His sword rose, slashing at her again and, quickly, once again. Again and, quickly, once again, she swung out beyond it only to slide in and farther in, though she was moving, of necessity, too quickly to make any truly aimed blow herself. All she could do was defend herself and mime a few distracting blows.

But Carlyon was being betrayed by his own wild impetus—less skilled and more incoherent than his usual judged movements. He stumbled and fell, then sprawled helplessly at Cayley's feet. Her sword was immediately at his throat, and he braced himself, not even daring to strike back at her.

But Cayley paused and looked over at the King, then at Heriot. She smiled. She began to laugh. She laughed aloud into the air of the arena—laughed at the sprawling Hero of Hoad. It was possibly the only time laughter had been heard in that white shell.

"I could kill him," she yelled. "But I can't be bothered." She shook her head, then lifted her sword and half turned away, still laughing. "Some Hero!" she shouted. Heriot knew she also was laughing at herself and at her own deep ambition, just as much as she was laughing at the sprawling Hero. She was choosing to close the encounter with ridicule.

Carlyon rolled out and away, before swooping clumsily to his feet once more. His face was twisted with fury. It was as if her laughter had inflicted an injury more profound than anything he had ever suffered—a wound that must be paid for or it would immediately become mortal.

The crowd yelled. Cayley turned. The long blow it seemed Carlyon was about to make was feigned, and, as Cayley altered her course, he slipped in yet again, to engage at close quarters. Seeing what was about to happen, Cayley shifted her flow but could not entirely avoid the blow that fell on her left wrist, severing her left hand. A cry went up all around the arena. Carlyon now flung his arms wide in triumph, so confident now he didn't even step back, flinging his sword for a final blow. But Cayley spun yet again, first away and then in toward him, so that they were almost touching. Within a second she had swung her handless arm in an arc across Carlyon's face so that her leaping blood filled his eyes. Carlyon staggered to the left, flinging up his own left arm in a wild effort to put distance between them and to wipe his eyes clear, but as he did this, Cayley, thrusting that handless arm up into his face, also delivered a blow with the sword she still clasped in her right hand. In! Straight into him almost to the hilt. In and then down. Carlyon staggered away from her and dropped his sword, clapping his hands to his stomach in a curious echo of the way Luce had once done. Cayley jumped back, dropping her sword in order to grasp her own wrist.

Suddenly the crowd was standing and shouting. Suddenly there were people bearing down on the combatants, as Carlyon slowly toppled forward. He was kneeling now, kneeling before Cayley, who hesitated, then squatted down in front of him, still trying to suppress the flow of her blood. Her lips moved. She was saying something to Carlyon as he toppled sideways and lay there, twitching and convulsing.

"What on earth could she be saying?" Linnet exclaimed, staring down into the arena with horror.

"Something like, 'Good-bye Daddy!'" Heriot said. "Civil of her, really. He was never much of a father."

CAYLEY'S STORY

And in due course they wound their way back to Diamond once more. They took their places yet again in the throne room of Guard-on-the-Rock. Yet again the King took his traditional place, restoring himself to his throne. But now it was Dysart sitting beside him in the smaller throne that had always been Betony's place . . . new heir to Diamond . . . heir to all that lay beyond Diamond . . . heir, at last, to Hoad. The chair seemed to open generously, just as if it had been waiting eagerly to embrace him, but though he had dreamed of sitting in that chair for so long, Dysart didn't look altogether at home. Heriot moved like a battered shadow to sit behind the King's throne, the true Magician of Hoad . . . the only one. The Lords of the counties were assembled, the Master of Hagen among them, Linnet beside him, smiling just a little ironically at Dysart, looking over at Heriot and then back around the golden room as if she were seeing it for the first time. Guards stood at the doors, but though they were alert men, they also had a certain ease, as if some battle had been won and they were able to relax even as they kept their traditional watch over the King.

The trumpets sounded yet again. A cushioned chair was wheeled into the room and placed in front of the throne. Cayley, the street rat of Diamond, looked back out of the chair at the King. Her injured arm, bound and rebound, was strapped across her chest, and two court doctors stood beside her. She was as pale as milk, but her eyes were wide and sharp.

"It seems we celebrate a new Hero," the King said.

"Not me," Cayley replied, and there was a startled—an uneasy—ripple, not so much of voices as of movement in the great room.

The King looked at her severely. "You are too modest," he said. "There is a first time for everything in a history like ours. I, at least, am prepared to consider a female Hero."

"No more Heroes," said Cayley. "At least not Heroes in that named way. It's not just Carlyon I wanted to kill, but that old idea, because it all but smashed me back when I was a child. See, Lord King, I've got this story to tell, and the Magician has been teaching me to speak proper—properly, that is," she added, sending a mocking look at Heriot, standing in his usual place behind the King's throne. This time the ripple was not simply a movement, but a sound as well, for people not only shifted but whispered to one another.

"I was born in Senlac," Cayley said, almost as if that would make her entire story clear. She closed her eyes.

The King looked anxiously at her pale face. "Lady

Cayley," he said. "Would you like to rest before you release your story?"

Cayley's eyes opened. "That's a good word. 'Release' is good," she said. "Now that story's got a sort of end I want to turn it out into the world. It's my tale, and I want to tell it now. Lord Carlyon came to Senlac, and he met my mother. Well, no doubt they fell in love, but she was one of those polite, careful ones, and so they married—well, she wouldn't do it with him unless they were married—and they lived there a little while, being happy and all that, until Lord Carlyon grew tired of Senlac. Off he went, off and away, cutting back to Diamond. He was very young in those days, but there were still wars and he was called on. He did well over the next two years, didn't he? You know more about that than I do. And suddenly he knew he might challenge Link and actually become the Hero. But you see, he was secretly married, and the Hero mustn't marry, must he? That's the ancient rule. And suppose he won his way to be Hero and was able to move into all that glory—a seat beside the King and an island all his own, all that grandeur—and then it turned out, after all, that he was married?

"But then he thought of an answer. He'd lived in Senlac, and he knew Senlac was one of those mixed towns, only partly loyal to Hoad. Just at the right moment there was a bit of trouble there, and he rode in with his men and killed nearly everyone in the place, destroying all the records, too. If ever anyone did mention he might have been married, there would be no proof. He did away with the lot, but not my mother, who was the one he wanted most. She wasn't there at the time. And what he didn't know was that he'd left her expecting a child—children. There was me and my brother. We were twins. And we both looked like our father . . . particularly my brother. She was so happy about that."

She fell silent, closing her eyes.

"Lord Carlyon came back to Diamond to live a Hero's life before he became Hero," said another voice. It was Heriot speaking. "Before he came to the arena and killed Link in front of you all. How you people need your sacrifices."

"Birth, love, and death," the King said. "They underlie all human life."

Cayley had closed her eyes; now she opened them and smiled at Heriot. "See!" she said. "The King says so, which makes it true. So over there, on Cassio's Island, was Lord Carlyon, my dear daddy, Hero of Hoad. And over in the ruins of Senlac there was my mother and her children, not knowing what had happened. Not knowing who had made it happen. She was one of those simple people, my mother, and she walked backward and forward through those ruins, weeping and waiting, weeping and waiting. And we waited with her, my brother and I, that is. I can just remember it, in broken bits. I wasn't so old—three years, maybe just four. Anyhow, Carlyon didn't come. She waited longer. Still no sign. And at last she packed up a few things and made for Cassio's Island. She thought the Hero would take one look at her and at his dear children—particularly his son—and then he would take us in and treasure us, even if we were *secret* treasures.

"It wasn't an easy journey, all that way, walking, begging, and then limping and straggling on again. But we got there at last and walked—well, straggled, like I say—out along that causeway. On and on. My mother lost her nerve a bit as she came onto Cassio's Island. I think she suddenly worried that *two* unexpected children might be a bit too much, even for a Hero. There's a limit to heroism, isn't there? I didn't have the glory of being a son, so she pushed me in the grass by the side of the path, telling me to hide until she came back, and took my brother into the city, because having a son is impressive to a man, isn't it?"

Heriot closed his eyes, remembering . . . remembering all those years ago, when he had strolled up to the place where the gate without a wall was making its strange declaration. He remembered the flattened grass and the curious horror that had overcome him. And then he remembered walking back toward the haven of his own farm and the wave of alteration that had swept over him, reaching into his head and twisting whatever it found there.

"She found him all right," Cayley was saying, "your great Hero. And he half welcomed her, and walked with her and my brother too—promising this and that, stopping to kiss her every now and then—back to the gate that's there, just where the causeway runs onto Cassio's Island. And there and then he killed my brother, my twin, and slashed his face away. I looked out from my hiding place. I saw him do it. I heard him tell her to get out and never come back again. He might have been a Hero, but he was in a panic, because what he had just won might be taken away from him. He told her that even if she did claim he'd married her there was no proof anymore, and no one would believe her. You don't remember that much when you're only three years old, but I remember my brother's blood, and some of the words as well, like they was burned into me. He told her that if she ever came back to Cassio's Island he'd kill her, too. He thought he'd killed his only child. He didn't know he had another hidden there in the long grass by the gate, watching everything."

She paused, closing her eyes.

Heriot cut in. "I was close by right after all this happened. That causeway—it's close to my family farm. I somehow took on all the horror and grief when the boy was killed, and it was so powerful it shifted me in some way . . . shifted me toward being the Magician, I suppose, though at the time it was nothing but terrifying. And later I stood on a hilltop, watching the woman carrying her bleeding boy back down the causeway, with a second child trailing at her heels."

Cayley's eyes sprang open. "You? That was you up there on the hilltop? I remember looking up and . . ." She burst out laughing. "We've been tied together all these years?" She looked back at the King. "My mother didn't carry my brother much farther. He was too heavy. She did what she could, but in the end we covered him with leaves and grass and left him to rot away. And we walked on to Diamond, and then our troubles really began. Different troubles, that is. But I won't tell you all that now.

"After a bit my mother died, and I lived on the street, pretending to be a boy and practicing to be strong, until that Magician there noticed me, and somehow recognized something in me, and made me his helper . . . his wild boy. That's a huge story, hours of telling in it. The thing is, as I grew into understanding who the Hero was, and what the idea of Hero was, I become determined to wipe him away . . . not only the man himself, but the whole idea of the Hero. I dreamed of the arena, but I'd have done it some other way . . . some cheating way . . . if I had had to. To be a finished person, it seemed I had to even things out.

"So, like I said, I worked to become strong, and more than strong. I worked to be *quick!* Spun! Danced! Because in times of peace a Hero slows up, doesn't he? And grows older. That's partly what he was afraid of . . . my father. Losing himself, drifting back into nothing. And as for me—well, that story I've just told, that story has been my cage almost all my life. And its beginning—the once-upon-a-time of it—was looking out from the side of the road and seeing my father, the Hero of Hoad, cut my twin brother's throat."

She looked up at the man on the throne. "Your Hero— he's what? He was nothing but dirt . . . made that way by the history of the idea of him . . . and now he's dead too, and I'm not going to become Hero in his place. There'll be lots of brave men in Hoad, no doubt, but maybe they'll be brave on behalf of your peace . . . maybe they won't secretly long to be that golden man riding into war and adored afterward. Maybe they won't have to kill their children to be part of your world. Maybe you won't have to be careful of them, like you had to be careful of my father. Maybe you can cut through that causeway and Cassio's Island will float away out to sea."

She had finished her story. Silence rose up like a mystery into the room around them.

"Maybe," said the King at last. "Those who live will see."

PART SEVEN

INTO THE WORLD

HAPPY, BUT NOT AN ENDING

That night Dysart did a marvelous thing. He could have climbed by inside passages and stairs through the Tower of the Swan, but instead he climbed up the outside wall of Guard-on-the-Rock, up and up again, on and on again, edging his toes and fingers into crevices in the stones. The whole city dropped away beneath him, and though he dared not look back over his shoulder, he could feel it out there, set out like some sort of a game below him . . . and after all, that's what it was . . . a great game. At last he scrambled over Linnet's little balcony. Her balcony door wasn't locked, and just as she had once slid into his room, he slid into hers, half expecting to find her asleep.

But Linnet was sitting in her chair, reading by candlelight. He said her name, and she looked up at him without apparent surprise.

"Were you expecting me?" he asked.

"I think I must have been," she replied. "Though I didn't know I was until now."

She stood up, moved toward him. He flung his arms around her, only to find himself strongly held too.

"Happy ending," he said a little hoarsely.

"Happy," she said, "but not an ending. You're the direct heir to Hoad now, aren't you? And my father—"

"Don't tell me! He's fallen into line," Dysart exclaimed. "Is that what we're doing, being together now? Falling into line?"

"He was so angry with me when we met again," Linnet explained. "And yet he couldn't hide that he was excited, too. What with that baby Shuba had a while back being a girl, I think he felt he was being edged out of all the possibilities of glory, so he loved the thought that I would someday be Queen of Hoad. In spite of everything, it's so much more than being Queen of the Dannorad."

"Nothing's certain," said Dysart. "All the same . . ." He felt her breasts pressing against him. "Linnet, let's get married very quickly. Really, we're married already. But let's get married again. Now!"

Linnet gently stood back from him. She dabbed her finger toward the door.

"Casilla's just through there," she whispered. "She's been told to watch over me. We'll have to wait and do the grand, parading thing before we do the grandest thing of all, even though we've secretly done it once already. For us there's what we do as you and me, and what we do on behalf of our kingdoms."

Dysart sighed, then smiled, stepping back a little.

"Well, the grand, parading thing might be fun," he said. "And in the end it *will* be just you and me together again.

It's been a long time, though, hasn't it, fighting our way through."

"You were the mad Prince," she said. "I remember the battlefield. I remember you running out in front of the horses. But you're free of him now, aren't you, free of Heriot? You don't need him in the way you thought you did. He might be Magician of Hoad, but someday you'll be King, and he'll have to stand behind your throne."

"He won't worry about that," Dysart said. "After all, we're friends beyond all that King-and-Magician business."

"Do you think he'll marry that wild girl—that Cayley?" Linnet asked, her voice becoming more uncertain as she spoke, for somehow the idea of marriage seemed irrelevant where Cayley and Heriot were concerned.

"Those two? Oh, I'd say they were well and truly married," Dysart replied dryly.

But Linnet, smiling, then frowning, then smiling again, wasn't really thinking of Heriot.

"It's all been so strange," she said. "Like some story straggling out this way, then unraveling in another. I find myself thinking about Betony Hoad and wondering . . ."

"I think Heriot was right. In a way, all there was for Betony was to dream," Dysart said. "Waking life could never offer him anything that would be enough for him. He had the chance to be King, but the Magician's very existence was always some sort of challenge to him—the constant reminder that there was someone much more wonderful than he could ever be in waking life. So he lies asleep in a room in the Tower of the Lion, and no one can wake him. Heriot says he might awaken some day, but when he does, he'll be beyond any King and Hero dreams."

But Linnet didn't want to hear about Betony Hoad, sleeping his strange enchanted sleep in the top room of the Tower of the Lion. "Do you think we'll be happy?" she asked, though she thought she knew the answer with certainty. She just wanted to hear Dysart say it aloud.

"Happy?" Dysart looked at her as if she had asked him a nonsense question. "Of course we will. And even when we are married, just for the fun of it, I'll climb the castle wall out there and come in at your window. Darling Linnet, we'll be happier than any other King and Queen of Hoad have ever been. But now I am going."

"Back down the castle wall," Linnet said. "Do be careful!"

"Well, I will be careful," Dysart said. "But by now I know some of the handholds and footholds. And anyhow, that power to climb was a gift in the first place . . . a gift to both of us. I don't think it will ever be taken away."

And he climbed down again, sure of himself, but being careful all the same.

Back in his own room, filled with the mystery and excitement and astonishment of the day he had just lived through, he knew he would never sleep, and walked through the halls of Guard-on-the-Rock, silent now, yet never quite deserted, to the room that had once been Heriot's before the shed in the orchard took him over. The door was open—these days there was no one to close it—and the room was empty, but there, on the desk in the corner of the room, were sheets of yellow paper . . . a letter. Filled with sudden apprehension, Dysart snatched it up. He read.

★ ★ ★

Dysart, I know you will come looking for me. I know you will come here, out of nostalgia, really, since I haven't lived in this room for a long time. But my shed in the orchard hasn't been the room we have shared. It's been mine and only mine. Anyhow, enough of that. Tonight you won't be able to sleep—none of us will be able to sleep much tonight. We have to stay awake, and work ourselves into what we are, in our various ways.

This is just to tell you that I am going off and away for a while. I don't think there will be any need for a Magician of Hoad any more than there will be a need for a Hero. You will marry Linnet, and for many years your father's peace will go unchallenged. Not forever, of course. Nothing lasts forever. But as for me, I need to wander a bit, and though I am completed at last, I need to complete the completion. I need to find out just what it truly means to be a Magician of Hoad. I am an unknown country to myself, but I know by now that being the Magician doesn't mean standing at the King's elbow reading his enemies or providing entertainments on grand occasions.

It's taken so much struggle to find out what I am intended to be. One thing it does mean is becoming a true part of Hoad, melting out into its trees and grasses, flowing with its waters, aging, perhaps, in its stones. I think when the Magicians have been able to do this, the country has been strengthened in some remarkable way.

Trees have always haunted me, haven't they? Perhaps when the Magician springs to life in some tree, flowing with its sap, the tree understands in some peculiar way just what it means to be a tree, tied into the soil of the land. Maybe the very stones understand, in their strange, resilient way, what it means to be a stone, and that understanding, even if it is not a human understanding but a curious unspoken awareness (down below thought, down below feeling, so deep down that it can't be recognized) binds the land into itself.

Dysart, you are my friend . . . always will be. I sat, immersed in our mutual dreams, on your windowsill—_our_ windowsill—so that when I needed saving you were able to save me. And in a way, since then, when you have needed saving, I have saved you.

So be a friend and watch over that Cayley for a while . . . until her arm is healed, anyway. After that, I think she might set out to find me. Just at present, she has yet another secret she thinks is entirely her own. But being what I am, I can't help knowing. The voice of that secret comes to me, claiming me, like a secret of a growing seed—an unfolding leaf—like another secret of the earth itself.

Anyhow! You! Keep on loving your Linnet in that magical way. I know it seems at the moment that love is easy, but it's got its challenges, too. Make sure you do what I tell you.

This isn't good-bye. Sometime when you least expect it you'll look up and I'll be there, and we'll sit down and gossip—talk about what it was like when we were boys, before you became King, and I became whatever it is I'm going to become. We'll joke with each other— maybe weep a little too as we remember the hard times. But now I must get out and away to become what the Magician of Hoad is meant to be—a secret essence, a connection of the land, which, when I fuse with it, will use my understanding to understand itself and become even more wonderful than it is now.

Heriot

BECOMING THE **TRUE MAGICIAN**

So Heriot wandered out into the world, leaving the towers of Guard-on-the-Rock behind. He strolled through the Third Ring, his back to the Bramber and the great castle embraced by its flowing waters. Strolling on in a leisurely yet determined way, he stared with a new curiosity at the great houses and gardens that were so familiar by now but that also seemed as if, given the right command, they might be able to renew themselves.

Leaving them behind, he came out into the Second Ring and felt himself touched with an edged energy, almost like a fury burning up within him. It was not his own fury, but the fury of people wheeling and dealing, arguing, planning, clashing, resolving. He strode on, staring around him almost as if he were a visitor who had never seen the city before. Something like wonder crept into his expression as he slipped between the tall buildings and out into the open spaces of the seething markets, for maybe true life was being lived here. It was impossible to be sure.

As he went by, people stopped talking midsentence and

looked around, apparently bewildered for a moment, as if some alien thought had intruded into them, blotting out their own thoughts. But then, as Heriot . . . that distortion in the world's unconscious view of itself . . . moved on, the moment of puzzling possession moved on with him, and the people shrugged, and laughed. "A ghost walked over my grave," they told one another, as they went on talking, choosing to shrug off that moment of incoherence that had come out of nowhere. So Heriot wandered on, moving unchallenged through the gate between the Second and the First Ring, and all the time it seemed to him that Cayley, the wild and damaged child, the central sign of the city, was dancing beside him, laughing and talking, carrying in her very center the image of the man who had killed her twin . . . who would certainly have killed her if he had known she had been born, if he had known she was hidden there in the long grass . . . that Hero who was her father.

But the very moods and determinations that had enabled Lord Carlyon to become the Hero had enabled his daughter to sleep in gutters and steal from stalls, to dance, making up songs and chants to dance to, treating each blow the city aimed at her like a thrust from a possible striking sword. The Hero had passed on his power and skill to his girl child. The Third Ring, her ruthless tutor, had taken her in, imposing challenges of starvation and death, and she had laughed, being quick—quick—dodging from under its slashing blows.

Heriot thought of her scarred throat and damaged voice and wondered how he—how anyone—could ever have taken her for a boy. But they had. He had himself. He had believed in her because she had become, in so many ways, what she had commanded herself to become. And he had also believed in her because, as a boy wandering on the causeway, he had been struck down by the power of a trauma—a trauma that was still in the process of forming her. Heriot knew it had somehow formed him, too.

So he walked on beyond the city, reaching out to inhabit advancing trees, birds, plants, and miraculous dust—dust so wonderful, each grain holding a whole universe—trekking on and on over days and nights, circling around towns and villages, and finally crossing a wild heath until he found himself in a forest he knew.

Pushing along a winding track through the trees, taking in every branch, every twig, every changing leaf, he found himself, yet again, in that deserted village in the wild wood. Once he was there he slept . . . not because he was unduly tired, but because in sleep he was able to dream his way back through his past life, correct the distortions Diamond had imposed on it, able to sink at last into the true mystery of existing like a true Magician—to soak outward into the vast spaces beyond the moon, to soak inward, down and down, into huge spaces at the heart of wood and stone, the space within his own heart and head, spaces that were not simply emptiness, not simply the absence of anything else, but an essential part of the structure of the world.

For weeks he lived a very simple life—eating fruit and watercress, catching fish from time to time, wandering to the nearest village to buy bread and cheese, dreaming himself in and out of it all.

★ ★ ★

And then one day he felt an intrusion and opened his eyes to find Cayley standing over him.

She still wore her hair in Wellwisher braids, and was rather more richly dressed than he had ever seen before, but there was an entirely new feeling about her . . . a sort of huge ease, as if she, too, had been released at last from some ruthless oppression.

"I found you," she said. "No hiding from me."

"I wasn't hiding," he answered, then added, "well, maybe from Diamond. But I knew you'd find me whenever you wanted to."

She made a gesture, sweeping the folds of her cloak, left and right. One of her hands was covered in a black velvet glove. As he watched, she drew it off and held out toward him a hand beautifully shaped, molded of silver and set with small jewels.

"That's a work of art," said Heriot admiringly.

"It's what we both are," she said. "Both of us. Works of art."

"I knew you'd come. I was always in touch with you there, and then I could feel you, coming closer and closer. Do you remember how to kiss?" inquired Heriot.

★ ★ ★

Later he asked after Dysart and Linnet.

"Them?" said Cayley. "They're so happy, they give off happiness like candles give off light. And the thing is, the King's still there, but somehow he's sharing what he is with Dysart. Betony sleeps on . . . dreams on . . . smiling in wonder at his own dreams . . . but Dysart and the King, they talk it all over together—policies for Diamond, plans for Hoad, peace for everyone. That game! Oh, they're so pleased with themselves."

"We should call in on them," Heriot said. "Though maybe not for a while. I think we should go wandering . . . wander through all the counties of Hoad and tie them together, reinforce the land, and ourselves at the same time."

Cayley was silent for a while. "It sounds wonderful," she said at last. "Your idea of wandering, I mean. If I had to choose over the next year I'd choose to wander and see it all. Being free, that is. Free of Diamond. But mostly free of myself . . . free of what I've been. You know, suddenly, as I was fighting Carlyon and he lay there in front of me, all I could do was laugh . . . laugh at him, but mainly laugh at myself, too, because I'd been ridden for so long by the vision of dealing that final blow. I turned away from him. I felt suddenly free from the charge of it all, and I was going to let him go free too, poor fool. I laughed a bit. But he couldn't stand that, could he? Being laughed at, I mean. And I've inherited a bit of his pride. I'd like to be set free of myself."

"I don't suppose we're ever totally free of ourselves," Heriot said. "But let's try. Let's set out together. If you *can* travel, that is."

Cayley smiled almost shyly down into the leaves and grasses. "You know already, don't you?" she said. "I was planning to surprise you, but no surprising a Magician, I suppose. Do you know if it's a boy or a girl?"

"I can't help knowing. It calls out to me, wanting attention. "Hey, you!" it says. "I'm on my way. Do you want me to tell you who I am?""

"Not a word! Let it surprise one of us," Cayley said. "I never dreamed of this for myself, so it's a surprise already, but I like to think there are still amazements ahead. So let's walk on!"

★ ★ ★

One fine day, as the sun rose, tranquil but implacable, four different lives—remarkably different lives—began working their way away from one another. They had been such mixed lives it would have seemed impossible that the people living those lives would ever manage to live either together or apart, but a noble girl and a Prince were being drawn together, embraced by a city, commonplace in many ways, yet always mysterious. A Magician and a wild girl set off, walking through a forest with the sun behind them, feeling the endless growth around them, the bursting of seeds, the impulses of nesting birds, feeling the way the world worked, dissolving, always dissolving, yet locking itself together over and over again. On they went, both finding some part of themselves, not only in each other but waiting for them in the world out there. Magician and warrior, they were about to be completed in ways they had never totally anticipated.

A story has to end somewhere. This story ends here.

MARGARET MAHY

has lived in New Zealand her entire life. A former children's librarian, she decided to become a full-time writer in 1980. Ranging from picture books to YA novels, the books she writes vary as much as the characters in her stories. She won the British Library Association's Carnegie Medal for *The Haunting* and *The Changeover: A Supernatural Romance*. Her other books include *Alchemy* and *Maddigan's Fantasia*. An author whose books have received many accolades and praise around the world, Mahy was awarded the Order of New Zealand, the highest honor a citizen of that country can receive, and in 2006 she won the Hans Christian Andersen Award, given to a living author whose works have made a lasting contribution to children's literature.

DISCARD

Shepherd Middle School
Ottawa, Illinois 61350

500364   12/09